THE
HONEST
SPY

THE
HONEST
SPY

Translated by Steve Anderson

ANDREAS KOLLENDER

Previously published as *Kolbe* by Pendragon Verlag in Germany in 2015. Translated from German by Steve Anderson. First published in English by AmazonCrossing in 2017.

Published by AmazonCrossing, Seattle

www.apub.com

Amazon, the Amazon logo, and AmazonCrossing are trademarks of Amazon.com, Inc., or its affiliates.

ISBN-13: 9781542045001
ISBN-10: 1542045002

Cover design by David Drummond

Printed in the United States of America

For Heidi

"You realize that you might be willing to accept any risks and it doesn't matter what the outcome is."

—*Edward Snowden*

PROLOGUE

HIT ME IN THE HEART

Berlin, 1944

"They should hold hands," Marlene said. "That would be nice."

She was sitting with Fritz in the kitchen, the last of the coals crackling in the oven, the yellowish glow of the lamp reflecting in the glass of the cabinet. On the table lay a stack of top-secret files from Hitler's Foreign Office, which Fritz had smuggled home. Dull red stripes marked the cardboard covers, along with Reich eagles bearing swastikas printed in black, the various department stamps overlapping. He and Marlene would transcribe the most significant information onto thin paper, and tomorrow Fritz would take the files back to his office at the ministry and deliver them to the burn barrels as ordered.

Marlene drew up a little sketch. "Take a look," she said.

"Like someone's watching us from above," Fritz said.

Marlene's two stick figures were sitting at opposite corners of a table. One of her figures had a hint of breasts. The figures each had paper and held a pencil in their right hand so that they could interlace the fingers of their left hands as they wrote.

"Nice," Fritz said. "Let's do it that way."

He moved his globe off the table and onto the sideboard, then they lifted the table and carried it into the middle of the kitchen. They pushed the chairs over just as Marlene had drawn them, sat down, reached out their left hands, and formed a tiny mountain range of fingers.

They wrote together for a while. "Keep going?" Fritz asked, and Marlene nodded. They kept writing until Fritz went to make a pot of tea, warming his hands over the steam. He let a spoonful of sugar trickle into Marlene's cup, stirred it, and set her cup down for her. He wrapped his arms around her from behind and whispered for a kiss. Marlene turned her head, her neck muscles flexing, and Fritz saw the blue in her eyes.

She tapped on Heinrich Himmler's signature. "Bastard," she said. She touched the signatures of von Ribbentrop, Kaltenbrunner, and Göring. "Let's keep going for another half hour."

"You're quite fired up about getting this done, aren't you?"

"I am," Marlene said. "We're going to finish them off."

"Sometimes I still regret it—telling you what I'm doing."

Marlene smiled, shaking her head. "My beloved spy," she said, "and adulterer, and liquor thief."

She stood and turned to him. As they put their arms around each other, Fritz caught sight of their silhouettes in the glass of the kitchen cabinet, Marlene's taller than his.

"My Marlene," he said. "You're so beautiful."

She kissed him with her lips all puckered. Fritz still didn't know why she did that sometimes—kissing him like a schoolgirl who'd never kissed anyone before.

Someone banged at the front door.

An electric shock seemed to shoot through them, severing their embrace. Marlene knocked over her cup. Tea ran over the stolen secret documents and blurred a Himmler signature.

A hoarse voice roared, "Herr Kolbe! Herr Kolbe!"

The door shook from the banging. The sound of the hard raps echoed down the hallway.

"Herr Kolbe!"

Marlene placed her hand on his. He savored her grip, one final grasp. Her eyes glistened. Fritz kissed her, staggered into the bedroom, ripped his jacket off the coat hook, and pulled the revolver from a pocket. He went back, positioned himself in the middle of the kitchen, and aimed down the hall at the front door.

They've got us now, he thought.

Sweat ran down his armpits to his ribs. How many people had they sent? Gestapo? SS? They'd kick in the door any second and storm into his apartment with their noise and shouting.

"Fritz . . ." Marlene stood nearby but sounded far away, as if she were in the next room. God, he loved that face so much—her straight nose, that broad jaw.

"Please, Fritz."

They banged on the door three more times. Again they called his name. Marlene unbuttoned her dark-blue blouse and pulled it open a bit. The skin of her breast shimmered in the white-wine glow of the lamp. He turned the revolver on her. His muscles weakened, the revolver weighing a ton now, dragging his arm down.

"Here," Marlene said. She placed a hand on her heart.

"Herr Kolbe! Open up! Right this second!"

He turned to the door, holding the gun with both hands. The hall seemed to grow shorter and shorter, the door practically touching the revolver barrel.

"It was right," he said. "What we did."

He felt Marlene's body behind his. She put her arms around him, turned him to face her, and pressed his hand with the gun to her breast. When she felt for the trigger, he pushed her shoulders back against the wobbly kitchen cabinet.

3

"You want to live," he said. "You said you did."

He grabbed the files off the table and unlatched the oven door. A blast of heat shot out at him, painting the floorboards red-orange. He threw the tea-soaked pages into the blaze. Flames licked at swastikas, curled the edges of the pages, and devoured it all. In his haste he'd dropped a couple of pages onto the floor and he stuffed these in, burning the side of his hand, little hairs sizzling. He kicked the door shut, the oven sucking back in the orange and the heat.

Marlene was begging him to do it. This shouldn't happen when two people loved one another—one of them having to beg. What would these men do with her if he left her alive? What would they do to her body? Fritz aimed the revolver at Marlene's breast and felt the trigger against his finger. Again his resolve left him.

Another bang on the door, just one.

"You don't know anything about this, Marlene. You know nothing . . ."

He wanted to disappear. He wanted to dissolve into thin air, with Marlene.

"Play the good Nazi woman for them. Nothing will happen to you."

Fritz could hear her heart, her beating red heart. The tortured look on her face brought back a torrent of memories: alleyways in Bern; his daughter, Katrin, in Africa; Hitler; maps of the Wolf's Lair; a forest cottage; voices; smuggled secret files; his heart pounding; corpses . . . The memories spun so fast that he couldn't think clearly.

"You need to live," he said, and for some reason his voice sounded clear and strong. Doubt flashed in her eyes—and a sliver of hope.

"Herr Kolbe!"

Fritz turned to the door. "Marlene, send my daughter all my love. Tell Katrin what I did. Tell her what you did."

He looked back. Marlene had bowed her head, her chestnut hair hanging in her face. His knees weakened, and he had to lean against the framed map of the world that hung on his wall. Marlene pulled open a drawer, the silverware clanking. Her jittery hands drew out two knives, the blades flashing. It was so crazy and senseless that he should be proud of her even now.

"I love you so much," Fritz said. Then he moved toward the door, holding the revolver out in front of him. *I betrayed you, you Nazi pigs!* He bumped into a stack of books on the floor. The tower of pages collapsed with a dull thud. He was close to the door now and could feel the murderers' presence out in the hallway. He stared down at the books. *Someone must tell Katrin what we have done. My daughter. For God's sake, someone has to tell her our story.*

He felt Marlene's eyes on his back.

1

THE HIDEOUT

Somewhere in Switzerland, a few years after the end of World War II

When he attempts to write down all that happened, he begins with a name. Marlene. His tongue moves around his mouth when he utters the word. Marlene. *Mar-lay-nah.*

It's the same in every draft he writes. He didn't even know her in 1939, when he returned to the hell that was Germany back then. That was years before he heard her voice for the first time. He can still remember clearly the day he heard her clear and joyful laughter as it passed through a closed door in the Berlin Foreign Office. At that point in the story, he was already facing much danger. He had wanted to keep Marlene out of all of it. He wasn't able to.

I had only gotten her involved much later, he writes, *because it had to be, it had to.* She is where this story begins. Lies, swastikas, betrayal, pretending, death, and love. He is scared of the grand words—love and war, decency in barbaric times. He heard enough grand words during his time in Hitler's Foreign Office. He still struggles with this. It was a time of war, a time of love. He'd tried to be a good person. And where had that gotten him?

He looks out at the green valley from the window set deep in one of the cabin's wooden walls. It doesn't matter which slope the cabin stands on or which stream snakes through the valley meadows below in a rush of silvery lead—no one needs to know any of that.

He goes into the kitchen and fills a cup with coffee from a thermos. He adds fresh milk and a spoonful of sugar, and stirs while gazing out the window at the valley downhill from here. A gravel road runs along the river and continues over a small bridge with planks that clunk as a car crosses it. He often watches that road from the kitchen window, and has done so ever since he began hiding out in this cabin. He can't be sure they still won't come to silence him.

The car driving up today is supposed to bring a journalist. Fritz's friend and confidant Eugen Sacher has been speaking with the man for months and reports back to Fritz about it. This man is supposed to be reliable and has been researching what happened for some time. "You can trust him, Fritz," Eugen told him. "He wants the same thing as you—justice. Finally."

"There's far more to it than that," Fritz said.

After hesitating a moment, Eugen tried to bring up the dark patches in Fritz's story, but Fritz, evasive as always, congratulated Eugen on his new suit and said he looked as stylish as ever.

Eugen Sacher is the only person who knows things about Fritz that Fritz would rather keep to himself. For so long he's wondered, *What must finally come out, and what do I keep to myself?* Doesn't everyone ask such questions? He's becoming insecure, thin-skinned. Yet giving in to his fate is the last thing he'd do. When a person gives in they might as well call it quits. Whole streets in the new Berlin have been named after men and women who'd acted as he had. Yet hardly anyone knows who he is. No one does, really. He was given the codename *Kappa* and was more secret than secret, a mere whisper in the hallways of the White

House over four thousand miles away in Washington, DC. President Roosevelt knew about him.

Fritz goes outside. A broad strip of well-trod earth encircles the cabin. He sits on the bench in front of the kitchen window, looks to the road, and lights up a cigarette. He got used to smoking during the war, yet he doesn't smoke a lot, just enjoys it at times. Marlene smoked. He'd always loved how she held a wineglass and a cigarette between the fingers of the same hand. He'd then ask her to open one more button of her blouse, and sometimes she did—her long fingers finding that little button, her thumb tugging on it while her index finger kept it in place, until the button parted from its hole. Fritz would place a hand on her cheek and behold her. She wouldn't always do it, though.

If he doesn't like this newspaperman, he told Eugen, he'll send him away at once. Did the man really swear not to reveal Fritz's whereabouts? And is he not just some psychiatrist in disguise? His friend pulled that one before.

"No, no, he knows how to treat his sources," Eugen replied.

"Others claimed that too," Fritz told him.

In the distance, where the road comes in from the left and runs between two slopes, he sees something flash, catching sunlight and then discarding it. The car approaches at a steady speed, travels over the bridge, and halts at the fork where one road leads to the cabin. The driver's door opens and someone climbs out and looks around. It could be that he's staring up at the cabin, though it's hard to tell. Fritz doesn't move. He feels the wooden beams against his back. The figure bends down next to the passenger door—there's someone else in the car. This was not agreed upon.

Fritz could simply shoulder his already packed rucksack, lock up the cabin, and disappear into the mountains, where he knew every cow path, every cave, every bolt-hole shrouded by tree roots. Whoever was coming would try shaking the door, maybe circle around the cabin, peer into windows with a hand to their eyes, then just drive off again.

The car reverses a bit, takes the turnoff, and drives on up the road. It disappears behind a green hilltop and then comes around it, heading toward the cabin. Fritz hears the engine and the pebbles crunching under the tires. The car halts at the cabin's rotting and hardly adequate fence. A man of medium height, wearing a hat, climbs out and leans an arm on the open driver's door.

"Fritz Kolbe? Are you Fritz Kolbe?"

"Who wants to know?"

Fritz hates rudeness, but he has to protect himself.

"Eugen Sacher told me about you. I'm Martin Wegner." He names the newspaper he works for. A well-known paper. "I will make sure your reputation is restored, Herr Kolbe. You are a great man."

"Sure you will. Who's in the car with you?"

"A photographer. A woman."

"Send her away. And she shouldn't try taking any photos. With all due respect."

"I guarantee she'll only take photos if you allow it. I give you my word of honor."

Fritz can't see the woman through the reflections on the windshield, yet thinks he notices a head moving. Wegner bends down and talks into the car.

A woman with brown hair tied back climbs out. She's wearing a khaki blouse, olive-green trousers, and sturdy footwear. A person he could go hiking with. Smart of her to leave the camera in the car.

"Veronika Hügel," she says. "I'm sorry you didn't know I was coming. Herr Sacher said he was going to keep you updated about everything. Maybe he forgot?"

Unlike Wegner, she doesn't stay by the car. She pushes open the slanting gate, comes right up to Fritz, and shakes his hand. Her grip is firm and she keeps her hand in his.

"That goddamn Eugen," he swears. "Nothing against you, Frau Hügel."

"The man is a true friend, Herr Kolbe," Veronika Hügel says. "Also, it's Fräulein, not Frau."

Fritz notices that Wegner is looking at the woman's back. His mind always records things like that. In the corridors of the Foreign Office, he used to gaze at Marlene's tall back, draped ever so gently with the fabric of her clothing. Should he ask these young journalists inside? Should he let them cross the threshold of his story? If he does, he knows there's no turning back. Yet he can't bear remaining silent like this. He squints at the sun, feeling its warmth on his cheeks, and slaps at his thighs.

"You like coffee?" he asks. "Two young guests, here in my modest abode. Well, come on in. Consider yourselves welcome."

He leads the way into the cabin, which greets them with an arid aroma that is both summery and woodsy.

"Huh," Veronika says. "This cabin's nearly all white on the inside. Pretty neat."

"Whitewashed, not painted," Fritz says. "It's better for the wood. My apartment in Berlin that we shared was always blacked out during the war. Darkness can be nice for a love affair, but it does wear on a person."

"So when you smuggled Nazi documents to Bern that first time," Wegner asks, "did it surprise you to find windows in Switzerland were blacked out as well?"

"You're well prepared, young man."

"Always, Herr Kolbe. With clear and solid facts."

"Ah yes, the facts. How would you like your coffee?"

"Black with sugar," Veronika says. "Wegner takes milk and sugar."

Fritz pours the coffee. "Factually, this is black coffee, right, Herr Wegner? Now, watch"—he lets sugar flow into the cup from a spoon—"as I add sugar to it. So what does your objective eye see now? Black coffee."

Wegner doesn't respond. Veronika stirs her coffee, then drags the spoon along the edge of her cup. Perhaps what he said was a little too

11

dramatic, Fritz thinks, a little too simplistic. But, in the end, is his story not a simple one?

"I baked an apple pie," he says.

In the kitchen he pulls the pie from the oven, sets it on the table, and opens a drawer. Inside, next to the knives and forks, sits the revolver. Fritz touches the metal and feels the textured grip, and the memories roll over him, tumbling together like rocks rolling from a cliff. All the desolation and all the exuberance he'd felt rebound from one remembered incident to the next; sometimes two or three memories crash together before bouncing off again, leaving him with a strange feeling of weightlessness. He pushes the revolver to the side, picks up a knife, and cuts big slices of pie, the apple chunks soft and sweet smelling. He sets the plates of food on a tray and carries it into the main room.

Veronika and Wegner have taken seats at the table. The sun is shining through the windows onto the bookshelves and the painted tile stove. Wegner lays paper, pens, and pencils on the table. Fritz puts down the tray and lines up the pens and pencils in the center of the stack of paper. Wegner grins.

"Always the civil servant, eh, Herr Kolbe?"

Fritz has to laugh at himself. "I don't know. Perhaps. I should've been Foreign Minister! An ambassador, or at least a consul. It's true. In the new Germany? Me, I . . . ah, to hell with it."

The coffee, the pie, the chatting—Fritz realizes he's evading again. He feels his usual urge to stare out the window, to separate his recollections from his current surroundings. Doing so wouldn't be hard. Veronika and Wegner would put up with it for perhaps an hour or so and then leave, thinking, *This man is ready for the insane asylum.* Perhaps he's already insane; he's really not sure. Whatever he is, he's not one to give up a fight.

As they eat the pie Fritz lets the young folks tell him the latest from the city. He watches as they prepare for the interview, sliding their plates gently to the side, Wegner picking up a pencil, Veronika forming a square with thumb and index finger and taking imaginary shots of the cabin—and of Fritz.

"So, by 1943," Wegner says, "you'd already managed to—"

"Hold on!"

Fritz gets up, grabs the bowling-ball-size globe off a bookshelf, and sets it on the table.

"That sure has seen better times," Veronika says.

Running his fingers over the resinous glue scars, Fritz spins the globe toward the south.

"Cape Town, South Africa," he says. "That's where this begins. We have to start there."

"I'm not sure we have that much time, Herr Kolbe. We actually wanted to begin in 1943, the first time you traveled to Bern."

Fritz stares at Wegner and taps on South Africa. His finger can find every country he's been to without a glance at the encrusted globe.

"Cape Town, 1939," he says. "Do you know how incredibly blue the sky gets over Africa?"

He clears the plates off the table. The sun shines on the globe, halving it into day and night.

"In 1935," Fritz says, "the order came to raise the swastika flag in the courtyard of the Cape Town consulate. This was one part of a Nazi decree demanding that all German foreign missions start dealing with the Jewish Question. Such madness hadn't begun gradually. It had hit like a bombshell with the Enabling Act in 1933. Once that law passed there was no holding back. That was when the delusions of grandeur started. The hysterics. The idiocy."

Fritz feels his trusty old colossal rage overtaking him. He could throw the plates against the wall, pound on the table, scream. He makes a conscious effort not to lose control.

"We don't have to talk about Hitler, the Holocaust, or the war yet," Wegner says.

"This is about you, Herr Kolbe," Veronika says. "You called for us, more or less, by way of Herr Sacher."

"There must have been some incident that made you take action," Wegner says.

"Relating to the Nazis? No. I hated them from the start. Deeply."

"From that far away?" Veronika asks.

"From Africa," Fritz affirms.

"But you returned," Wegner says. "You went back—to Hitler's Germany."

Fritz lights up a cigarette. "I did, yes. I was naïve. My superior was as well. He was the one who wanted me to; I went back for his sake. Was it a mistake? Perhaps. But if I hadn't . . ."

"American intelligence would have never gotten a source like you," Veronika finishes for him.

Fritz likes that she said that. She's eyeing him through her finger lens. He smiles, turns his face to the left, then the right, and Veronika says, "Click, click."

"I wouldn't have become a spy. And I wouldn't have met Marlene."

"We should discuss the ramifications of that," Wegner says.

Fritz reaches out, lowers Veronika's finger lens to the table, and keeps his powerful hand pressed over her fingers. She puts up with it for a few seconds, then pulls her hand away. Wegner holds his pen ready. Fritz hesitates, feeling himself getting agitated. It's all too much.

"Herr Kolbe, this is what you wanted," Veronika says. Her hair is roughly the same color as Marlene's, chestnut with strands of copper red.

"The way it feels to me now, I don't know. It's as if Marlene were standing right there next to me in the courtyard of the Cape Town consulate when that goddamn Nazi flag came down in '39, because war had broken out. As if she were there with me when I had to leave my young daughter behind."

His young guests glance at each other, Veronika raising her brow like a person hearing things she already knows.

Fritz drifts through space and time back to Cape Town: there under the sun where his shadow self first began. If he had known what he would end up doing, had known all that would happen because of it, would he have gone back to Germany? He's not sure. On the table, the globe casts an egg-like shadow over the journalist's blank snow-white pages.

2

"I Will Come Back"

Cape Town, South Africa, fall 1939

Fritz's daughter was sitting on the sofa when he arrived home that hot and humid afternoon. The screen door clacked in the doorframe behind him, dimming the sunlight in the room. He had telephoned the maid, Ida, and sputtered that he was coming home. He needed to be with Katrin now.

Katrin watched him, her fair face framed with that raven hair that always reminded him of oil paint freshly brushed onto a canvas. Fritz could barely manage to meet his daughter's gaze. He set his briefcase on top of the bureau, poured himself a whisky until the glass was heavy and honey colored, then sat down with her. The ceiling fan stirred the air, and bougainvillea branches tapped at the window whenever a breeze from the ocean whooshed down the streets and over the yard. Fritz placed an arm around his daughter's slight shoulders.

"What is it, Papa?"

He didn't know how to say it. At the German consulate the staff had gathered around the radios in various groups, their backs bent forward for listening, champagne glasses ready in their hands as they waited for the news to be announced. Fritz, appalled, had closed up his office and for the first time in his life left the consulate before the workday was done. He saw no one and said good-bye to no one. He walked out the door with his head lowered, smack-dab into the sunlight, down the steps, and into the throngs on the bright city streets.

"Papa?"

Fritz didn't want to turn on the radio but he did it anyway. Sounds rasped across the ether like a coarse file over hard wood. He turned the knob and here came the voices from faraway Germany. His hand trembled, shaking his glass. He looked into Katrin's bright-blue eyes. She was already fourteen, and yet he still went into her room every evening to see that she was tucked in, placing a kiss on her cheek and whispering that there was no one he loved more. What should he tell her now?

"You're acting a little strange, Papa."

He still didn't know what to say—he only knew that everything in their world was about to change, absolutely all of it. Katrin had to be kept far away from what was about to happen.

Blaring through the bars of the radio's brown grille came the latest on the Greater German Reich and its Führer, Adolf Hitler. The announcer sounded intoxicated by the great event: *"Adolf Hitler, our Führer, will soon speak to the German nation on this very broadcast."* Fritz went into the kitchen and poured Katrin a lemonade, the bottle knocking against the glass—the last time his hands had trembled like this was when his wife died, years ago. Katrin had been just a baby that he'd held to his chest, one hand cupped around the back of her head.

He brought her the lemonade, the glass glowing a rich yellow in the intense sunlight.

"Can't you just tell me what's going on? Papa? I'm right here."

"It's coming on now," he said. He pointed at the radio as if the device were some wild animal about to pounce. Hundreds of people could be heard cheering, the transmission hissing as if the airwaves could not abide what was about to come. But it came. And though he had known it would, the words still pounded him like a hammer heavy enough to destroy planets. He couldn't believe this was happening.

"As of five forty-five this morning, we are returning fire!"

Hitler's rolling *r*'s. Fritz could imagine his plump nose, the silly mustache, those fists of anger the man couldn't give one speech without. Fritz felt his face turning to stone.

"Papa, what does *returning fire* mean?"

He pulled his daughter close to him, wishing he could keep his arms wrapped around her until this world was no longer able to harm her.

"War, my dear. We're going to war. The worst possible thing. The stupidest thing humans can do. War, Katrin. For God's sake."

"So why do it?"

He turned off the radio. He didn't need to hear any more of this idiocy, didn't need to subject himself to the crowd's hysterical cheering.

"Why go to war, Papa?"

"A hunger for power, fanaticism, megalomania. Endless stupidity. I don't know what to tell you."

"Then we won't ever go back to such a place."

Fritz gave a despairing laugh. He placed his arms around Katrin, and her hand found his shoulder. The girl was so skinny it nearly broke his heart to even hug her.

"Exactly, Katrin. We will not be going there. My old friends Aunt Hiltrud and Uncle Werner live in South-West Africa. I know of a few opportunities there, all part of the job. It won't be easy but we'll make do, we will make it somehow. And now"—he grasped Katrin's hand—"let's go take a walk by the sea. Because a walk by the sea, my dear, can never hurt."

"Your walks are always so long."

"Perhaps we'll see a few penguins."

"But let's not go so far, okay?"

"We'll turn around whenever you say."

The next day the consulate telephones shrilled incessantly, and urgent footsteps echoed down the corridors. Many of the staff had put on their swastika armbands. As fast as he could, Fritz processed departure requests and applications for German citizens who came in to give up their citizenship, contacting the embassies of countries he guessed would remain neutral.

One thing had become clear to him after the Nazis' catastrophic policies of the last few years: this was not going to end with Germany's shameful invasion of Poland. Hitler had already annexed Austria and taken Czechoslovakia, so his latest attack would have to bring grave consequences. Fritz felt like he was being dragged into events that never should have been allowed to transpire. Throughout the day he kept running his fingers through his thin hair or clutching at his forehead. At moments he had to breathe in deeply and compose himself just so he wouldn't vomit. He heard people cheering out in the corridors. They saw themselves as players in a series of grand events. He wanted to smack them on both sides of their heads.

Normally he met with his superior, Consul Biermann, twice daily, but today Fritz managed to find the consul in his office only as evening neared. The old man was standing at the window, dressed as always in a three-piece suit, his bowtie knotted securely.

"It's madness, Herr Kolbe," Biermann said. "They've all gone mad."

"Plenty of people feel otherwise, Herr Consul. What will you do?"

"That depends on what happens in the coming days. Watching and doing nothing is always a poor choice, though."

Biermann sat at his desk, straightened his glasses, and started going over consulate plans with Fritz. "All done with reservations," the consul said of his orders. Biermann had often said he could hardly imagine what would become of Germany if life in that splendid city of Berlin was ever reduced to what it has now become: home to thousands upon thousands of waving Nazi flags, its parliamentary system abolished by the Führer.

"He is the one who can take everything away," he said of Hitler. "The one who decides everything. The rest of us have no individual responsibility anymore; we only follow along dutifully."

"Many people like it that way," Fritz said. "I don't."

"You are a good man. The best staffer I ever had. I truly do need you, Herr Kolbe. All is not lost, not yet."

"That's what I think too, Herr Consul."

On the way back to his office, Fritz passed the small office of young Heinz Müller. Müller was responsible for the mail and radio and telegraph traffic and encoding. His pale suit hung off his scrawny frame. Fritz had always liked the boy for his reserved nature. Now he paused and asked Müller if everything was all right. Müller asked him in and closed the door. He tidied a stack of loose papers on his desk and tapped on the top page. His hands were slender like a girl's.

"I'm afraid, Herr Kolbe," he admitted. "But please, don't tell anyone else that."

"Me, I've had it up to here with being afraid," Fritz said, pointing to his head.

"What do you think will happen?"

"I don't know." Fritz was still keeping his dread and hatred of Hitler to himself. Even here in Cape Town, so far from Berlin, it had been a long time since he could say what he wanted.

Fritz felt as if he were buried under heavy stone. The heat he usually liked so much now felt intolerably oppressive, the ring of the telephone made him angry, and the Hitler salutes in the corridors—along with the gloating of many staffers—made his stomach hurt as if he'd swallowed a live crab.

On the following afternoon, September 3—two days after the attack on the poor Poles—Biermann summoned him to his office. Fritz found him there holding a cream-colored sheet of letterhead.

"The Declaration of War from the British and French," Biermann said.

Fritz closed his eyes. The giant *no* within him was welling up so fast he thought he might burst.

"It'll be a massacre," he said.

"The gentlemen in Berlin didn't figure on this move," Biermann muttered. "Everyone back there is quite horrified, especially because of the British—though surely not Foreign Minister von Ribbentrop, an Anglophobe," he added. Biermann told Fritz he felt nauseous just hearing the name von Ribbentrop. It used to be that types like von Ribbentrop had no chance in the Foreign Office. The Office, according to Biermann, had always been the home of great diplomacy.

"We can do little from here, Herr Kolbe," he said.

Fritz didn't know exactly what Biermann meant by this, but the consul's words solidified his decision not to return to Germany under any circumstances.

"Churchill is a strong-willed man," Fritz said.

Biermann, who'd met Churchill once, agreed and called him an impressive figure. He looked at the letterhead, folded it down the middle, and stuffed it into an inside pocket of his jacket. "A historic document," he said.

"Proof of the abyss, Herr Consul."

Biermann adjusted his bowtie and positioned himself at the window. "Included in all these senseless directives now coming over the teleprinter are several intended to remind us here at this post that the Negro is generally inferior to the German race." The consul tapped his fingers on the window frame. "How's your daughter dealing with all of this?"

"Do not ask. Your wife?"

Biermann shook his head.

As Fritz left the consul's office, he glanced back for one more look at the man. In the sunlit window Biermann was like a statue, a flinty relic from an age long past.

21

Back in his own office, Fritz shut the door, set the telephone handset next to the phone's base, and drew the curtains. Laying his suit jacket aside, he pulled his tie off over his head, took several deep breaths, and cocked his arms back. First he shielded his face with his fists, then he swung: leading with his left, throwing right hooks, then jabs. Dancing around his imaginary opponent he kept on swinging and ducking, then he stopped and, shifting his weight, swung again, holding off for a moment before picturing himself landing one hit and then another. After a few minutes his shoulders and chest were wet with sweat. He kept on boxing, hammering on his dimwitted, flag-waving opponent, laying him out on the floor. Fritz boxed until he could barely lift his arms, until they gave way and his knees went weak.

At his sink, behind a Chinese dividing screen he'd had a colleague bring back from Peking, he splashed water onto his face and stared into the mirror. His blue eyes looked severe, his brow puckered with lines, and his cheeks shone like polished wood. He didn't like his face when it looked like this. A hand towel draped around his shoulders, he sat at his desk, gave the globe a spin, and looked at his two photos in their golden frames.

The first one was a portrait of his deceased wife, Katrin's mother, taken long ago now. Next to it was a photo of Katrin, who'd gotten her black hair from her mother. God, was that girl pretty! And so curious about the world—her ears perked up whenever he recited tales from the old travelogues he loved to read to her. He was the one she'd come to when she had her first period. Fritz had coughed and said he needed a whisky; Katrin had mumbled back that his response wasn't exactly helping. Despite feeling helpless, he'd told her that her becoming a real woman was pretty amazing, and that without its happening there couldn't be any children . . . He'd stopped when he'd noticed the way she was eyeing him. She only had to say "Papa"—that long *a* on the end extended in admonishment—and he stopped and stared at his feet. As if all that wasn't enough, she'd then asked him when she would finally get breasts. He'd said, "Er" and "Uh," not really sure where to go with that conversation or even where to start. He'd begun to tell her that her mother had had rather small breasts and that they were actually quite pretty, but Katrin had cut him off and suggested that maybe it was better not to discuss it.

So what now? He pressed the frame to his forehead, feeling himself begin to sweat, verging on tears. He swore and hammered the desktop with his fist. *Germany.* Beethoven, Schiller, Schubert, Kleist. The Baltic Sea coast with its seaside resorts of Binz and Sellin; the Alpine region of Allgäu; Hamburg and Berlin, that brilliant shining city of Berlin. His friend Walter Braunwein and Walter's wife, Käthe, had been sending him postcards from Berlin for years—Fritz had asked them to send cards instead of letters so that he could get a look at the capital. He could see the avenue Kurfürstendamm full of cars, buses, and well-dressed pedestrians; the cafés on Friedrichstrasse full of people and glittering glasses; that friendly doorman at the Hotel Adlon. As he looked at the postcards, he could practically hear the kids squealing at Wannsee Lake, its water spiked with the triangles of little sailboats. Beginning in 1936 the motifs had begun to change, with the addition of swastikas flying from buildings and uniformed men appearing among the individuals in the pictures.

Another photo on his desk showed Walter and Fritz together with two black men on a safari in South-West Africa. *Those were the good old days.* The sun reflected off the faces of the four in the photo, finding plenty of room to shine on Fritz's high forehead. Walter was leaning toward Fritz a little and appeared to be saying something to him, while the two hunting guides laughed into the camera.

At one point during the safari, Fritz had trained his sight on an antelope with coal-black eyes but hadn't fired. Walter had asked him what was wrong. Fritz lowered his rifle, placed a hand on his shoulder, and told him that Katrin had made him promise not to shoot.

"Why go on a safari then?" Walter asked.

"It's just as lovely without shooting," Fritz replied.

Walter had watched the antelope dash onward through the savanna, leaping wildly at first before proceeding all lissome and spindly legged. After a few seconds, the glittering sunshine and fine dust swallowed it whole.

Walter, his old friend. He lived back there, in Germany, and worked in the Foreign Office.

A year before, Walter, Käthe, and their son, Horst, had come to Cape Town for a visit. They'd ridden along the coastal highway in Fritz's Horch cabriolet from the consulate, Käthe in the back between Horst and Katrin. She and Katrin kept pressing their hats to their heads to avoid losing them in the breeze. Katrin was laughing the whole time, and Fritz kept turning to watch her until Walter warned him to keep his eyes on the road.

During their picnic Fritz tried to talk to Walter about Germany, but Walter wouldn't engage him. Later, back home, Fritz tried him again at dinner. Walter pressed his lips together and avoided his stare. Käthe told Fritz he should just let it go. It had been a while since Fritz took a good look at Käthe. She was pretty. At times the corners of her mouth twitched, and whenever Fritz started talking politics she threw Walter a threatening glance.

The next day they drove north of the city, into the green valleys between Table Mountain, Lion's Head, and Devil's Peak. Katrin and Horst leaned their backs against Käthe and hung their bare legs out of the car. Fritz would have liked to just keep on driving like this, on into the center of the African continent, following the explorers' routes through deserts and jungles, and then prolong their hearty idleness back in Cape Town with evening strolls along the sea. Yet he could tell that something wasn't quite right between them. Fritz didn't want their time together to be spoiled by differences of opinion or arguments; he saw his friends too seldom for that. In Cape Town he had plenty of acquaintances—his shoemaker, the flower lady in New Market, several waiters in the cafés in Darling and Adderley—but no actual friends.

Walter did at least answer his question about von Ribbentrop. "A pompous ass. If you end up back in Germany and run into him at the Office, don't forget the *von.* The man puts utmost value in that *von* before his name. Most important thing you need to know."

Horst, ash-blond and even taller than the last time Fritz saw him, reminded Fritz that he'd promised to take him fishing.

"Very well then," Fritz had said, and found gear for him and Horst to cast from the surf: heavy rods and good weights for sending the lures far out over the waves. Around midday the boy got hungry and devoured the sack lunch Ida had made them. Afterward, they sat in the warm sand and talked about sports. Fritz asked Horst how he liked Germany nowadays.

"Oh, I don't know, Uncle Fritz. A lot has changed," Horst said, adding, "You know we haven't even caught one fish?" Fritz said they should keep at it then. "But with you it's just as fun not catching anything," Horst said.

Fritz laughed. "We'll get one eventually," he said.

On the evening of their final day, Fritz went strolling with Walter along the sea, their shadows long and the sand gray in the dwindling light. It was the first time during this visit that Fritz had been alone with his friend. Walter was a head taller than Fritz. For a high-level Foreign Office official, he looked oddly unkempt. The part in his brown hair was tousled, as if heavy winds blew over him wherever he went.

For a moment, Fritz sensed that old trust they had shared, and he again asked how things were in Germany. Walter buried his hands in his trouser pockets, looked out over the sea, and shrugged. Many men ended up talking more when their wives weren't around. Walter, Fritz knew, was a different person when Käthe was sitting next to him in all her beauty. So Fritz tried again, just one word: "Germany?"

"To be honest, Fritz, I'm really not sure. I still can't comprehend it. It's like people are drunk on it. It is impressive, in its way."

"Drunk on it? Damn, Walter. Will there be war?"

"He won't go that far."

"What about the Jews?"

Walter rubbed his forehead and let out a deep sigh. They continued along the beach. Fritz could sense his friend's desolation, his indecision. Walter looked to the city's lights, then to the now-dark ocean rushing onto the sand. A feeling of immense powerlessness washed over Fritz.

Walter said he could see that Fritz liked it in Cape Town, that it truly was beautiful. "But it's got nothing over Ireland. Living there's the way to go, Fritz. In better times, especially."

Fritz laughed. "You and your Ireland," he said. "Someday, someone will understand whatever's between you."

Walter looked out at the water again. "Let's go swimming, old buddy," he said. As they undressed, the wind cooled their skin and heightened their awareness of being present in their bodies. They ran toward the waves and screamed like little boys when the cold water broke over them. They planted their feet to withstand the waves, then threw themselves headlong into the sea when the sand slipped out from beneath their feet.

"We'll make it through all right!" Walter shouted.

"Of course we will," Fritz responded with water in his mouth. They fell into a favorite old challenge: first one to make it to the buoy. They crawled through the waves, eyeing each other's faces as they swam, each one trying to slash through the water faster than the other. They slapped at the buoy's metal shell right at the same time, Fritz panting out that he had got there a second faster, Walter protesting the claim.

"Did so . . ."

"No, you didn't . . ."

"I did . . ."

"Nope. How about a tie?" Walter proposed. Fritz said they could both agree on that. Walter's wet shoulders glowed white in the emerging moonlight. He looked happy.

The Braunweins departed the next day.

In the evenings Fritz would come home from the consulate to find Katrin sitting on the sofa with her legs pulled up to her chest. Ida was often in the room with her, trying to play with her or bringing her books to read, but Katrin only stared at the wall where Fritz had hung a map of the world.

"What is it this time?" Ida asked him now. He didn't know, he said. But he could guess, and he felt as if he were in an insulated cell where he could hear nothing but the pumping of his own blood.

"I'm not leaving you," he told Katrin.

"Promise me?"

"Yes, dear. I could never leave you on your own. That just won't happen."

She jumped into his arms, and he squeezed her little body as hard as he could. There was no more wonderful feeling in the whole world.

"A bunch of Boers insulted me on the street," Ida told him. "I was scared, Herr Kolbe. One of them was wearing a swastika armband."

"What else did they do to you?"

"Nothing, Herr Kolbe. With all due respect, do you know what I wish? I wish that South Africa would declare war on your Germany too."

"It's no longer my Germany, Ida." Fritz let Katrin down.

"Would it mean more war?" Katrin asked.

Ida ran fingers through her hair. "Come now, honeybun," she said. "None of that has anything to do with you or your Papa."

"That remains to be seen," Fritz said.

◆ ◆ ◆

On September 6, three days after the British and French declared war, a delegation of two uniformed and two civilian-clothed men marched down the corridor of the consulate toward Biermann's office. Fritz watched as one of the men shoved open the door to Biermann's office without knocking.

"Herr Consul!"

Then the door was slammed shut from the inside.

"What's that all about?" asked young Heinz Müller. He'd been wearing a swastika armband on his scrawny arm for a couple of days now.

"What do you think? Use your brain once in a while, for God's sake."

Müller stammered something unintelligible. Fritz apologized—he hadn't meant it to come out the way it sounded.

The four men left Biermann's office after only a few minutes. They strode down the corridor to the front door, a rectangle sparkling with light. One of the uniformed men had his hands balled into fists.

Fritz watched the men go, the sunlight swallowing them up. He walked into Biermann's office gently. He might as well have been stepping over shards of glass.

The old consul sat leaning to one side. He was sweating. Fritz had never seen him disoriented before. The world was breaking apart, more and more, piece by piece.

"We're both persona non grata now, Kolbe. South Africa has declared war on Germany. We must close down the consulate." Biermann pulled himself up from his chair. "We have to go back." He went to stand at the window and pointed to Table Mountain, its crown flat as if sliced off. "A strange hill, that. I liked Cape Town very much. So did my wife. You and your daughter liked it here too, didn't you?"

The use of the past tense annoyed Fritz and made him anxious. "I still like it," he said. "Katrin and I like to take the trolley buses up and down Darling Street or Adderley, past the parks and all the shops with their awnings, then on down to the sea. We love the sun. They have plenty of that here." He walked over and stood next to the old man. "I'm not going back to Germany, Herr Consul."

Biermann straightened up military-style and pointed his index finger at Fritz. It was a gesture Fritz wouldn't have thought him capable of.

"Now you listen to me. My grandfather was a diplomat, my father likewise. I have influential friends. My word means something. I will go face what's happening in Germany. And I guarantee you," he said, balling up his fist, "I can do far more than you might think. I have contacts around the world. I know Molotov personally and others. I will do something, I will try to save what can still be saved. And I can. I can do it, you understand? But how do you think all that will look in Berlin if my closest colleague, my own vice-consul, goes sneaking away? If he lets himself be interned in Africa or ducks out in the South-West? You'll be undermining my reputation. You'll weaken my influence. You know very well how the men now calling the shots back there will react if my best man stays behind in Africa. You can't do it, Herr Kolbe. It's irresponsible."

"My daughter, she . . ." Fritz's love for her sapped his voice.

"You must leave Katrin here. You can't take her with you. Not there."

Fritz's heart seized up. He turned away and stared at the floorboards.

"She will understand, Herr Kolbe."

"She's fourteen. I promised never to leave her."

"She cannot go to Germany."

"No. Not ever."

"But *you*, Herr Kolbe? You must. If you are not there by my side when we return, then I'm powerless. Then it's all over."

Biermann opened a cabinet in his desk, pulled out a bottle of cognac and two brandy glasses, and poured them drinks. He let the liquid swirl in the glasses, a time-honored ritual never to be abandoned, not even now. It stirred Fritz, this tiny moment with its hint of fading fortunes. Inside him everything tightened up; his thoughts grew dim and muffled.

Biermann ended the conversation by inviting Fritz to join him for dinner, and after he left the consul's office, Fritz prepared the consulate for closing. He made phone calls and gave instructions, without really hearing anyone. He didn't bother with the radio messages from Germany.

He spent the evening as if in a trance under the gaze and gentle words of Biermann and his wife, Therese. In the end, he knew one thing only: the two of them had persuaded him to return to Germany. On this night, amidst the aromas of braised vegetables and roasting meat, with a pleasant breeze coming through the window, he recalled for the first time in years the words his father had told him to take with him on his life's journey: *Do what is right and have no fear.*

As he stood out on the balcony, clutching the railing, Biermann's wife came and stood next to him. She steadied herself on her cane and lit up a cigarette.

"You'll certainly see her again, Herr Kolbe. We won't let these philistines call the shots. Trust in my husband. Between you and me? He's quite the old warhorse in his way. His word carries weight." She poured Fritz a whisky, declaring that moments like these demanded one more swig than usual, even if her husband did hold a different opinion in this one respect. "Sometimes," she confided, "he keeps himself a little too under control." She laughed. "Don't forget, Herr Kolbe: the German news we're getting is propaganda. On the ground in Berlin, things can't truly be as bad as what we're reading. People just aren't like that."

Slightly drunk and now furious, Fritz drove out of the city back to Camps Bay. He lay next to Katrin on the bed. She was breathing evenly through her straight little nose, her black hair spread out on the pillow like a fan. She muttered something and rolled her head. He touched her thin upper arm gently and, leaving his hand there, attempted to sleep.

The next morning he arrived early at the consulate. He read all the teleprinter messages that had come in overnight, then went downstairs to the little walled courtyard. He looked straight up the white-lacquered flag mast into the bright-blue sky. The swastika flag hung limp and motionless like a cadaver. He drew his pocketknife and cut through the cord. As he marched back to his office, the flag spun to earth and piled up on the lawn like a mountain diorama.

Without thinking, his head buzzing strangely now, he entered the radio and decoding room, opened the safe, took out the leather folder of radio codes, and wrote them down on his notepad before returning them to the safe. After that he called the British consulate from his office and invited a Mr. Carlsroupe, whom he knew well from his Cape Town years, to come over for a drink later that evening.

At nine a.m. the trucks that Fritz had scheduled dropped off moving crates with Reich eagles branded on them. As the staff began to arrive, he issued orders, urging them to hurry things up. When a flustered young Müller ran down the corridor, shouting, "The flag's been cut down! Our flag!" Fritz admonished Müller to get to work; they were on a deadline. Anyway, Fritz added, he should stop worrying about that flag because he was going to see enough of them soon in Germany.

"I most certainly hope so, Herr Kolbe."

What is wrong with this kid? Fritz wondered. *Not long ago he was admitting how afraid he was. A few days later he's wearing a swastika armband. And now this.*

Fritz first phoned his friends Werner and Hiltrud in Swakopmund, then spoke with the representative of a shipping line—a Dutch one, since German ships were no longer allowed to pull up anchor and leave Cape Town. He packed his photographs in old newspaper and wrapped his globe carefully, stowing it in a standing position for stability. He felt in his inside jacket pocket for the page of radio codes he'd copied.

That afternoon he left the chaos of the consulate and closed the top on his Horch—he'd always driven with the top down but didn't want to anymore. A troop of mounted soldiers was coming up the street, the horses' hooves clacking loud and metallic on the pavement. The soldiers halted at the consulate entrance and the captain shouted an order. As if a switch were turned on, the horses and men pivoted to face the consulate and stood stock still. Fritz drove cautiously past the soldiers, between the art deco buildings, parks, and florists, up to Bay Drive. At the highest point of the street, he pulled over and looked down at the surging ocean, the sky beyond it a radiant blue. Berlin was over six thousand miles away as the crow flies, yet it had effortlessly consumed the consulate and its men, now with swastikas on their upper arms, men whom until recently he'd considered reasonable human beings.

He climbed out of his car and breathed in the warm wind. Earlier, Biermann had again spoken to him at length.

"I guarantee you, Herr Kolbe, I can still make things happen in the Foreign Office. And for that, I will need you." He'd expounded on the devotion and obsession for detail exhibited by great diplomats such as Benjamin Franklin and Talleyrand, men who operated so deftly that those who signed their treaties became aware only months later of the conditions they had agreed to with their signatures. "The Congress of Vienna," Biermann gushed. "So sharp the quills, so black the ink. The situation may be dire," he said, "but together we can still stop even worse things from happening! I promise you this."

Katrin would not understand all this insanity, Fritz thought. Why should she? How could she? Consul Biermann might only be fooling himself, he realized. Maybe there was a reason they had transferred him to this faraway posting in Cape Town. And at various receptions, he'd acted more than distant to the delegations from South Africa's National Socialist Greyshirts. This would not have gone unnoticed in Berlin.

Yet the old man truly was good; he knew the history of European diplomacy like no other and was a decent person through and through. And Biermann's argument that his standing would suffer if Fritz didn't come with him had truly moved Fritz. He removed his straw hat and wiped the sweat from his brow. He felt so small. From up here he saw the ocean surge into Camps Bay and wash around Wale Rocks as a cloud-white foam. The sun was shining, and seabirds screeched into the wind. Below and to his right, the city center stretched out white and sparkling. Fritz absorbed as much of the view as he could, took a deep breath, and committed it to memory. Then he drove home down to Camps Bay.

"Herr Vice-Consul Kolbe?"

Mr. Carlsroupe, secretary to the British envoy, stood in Fritz's doorway. They shook hands. Carlsroupe had straw-blond hair with a severe part and his mustache was neatly trimmed. He told Fritz he'd always known him to be a decent fellow, adding that the British envoy sent his greetings. Carlsroupe wished Fritz the best of luck. "Though I do fear there isn't much luck to be had in Germany these days."

Fritz didn't comment. He asked if Carlsroupe felt like having that drink.

"Where shall we ever be if we start declining a simple drink?"

"Quite sensible of you."

They went into the kitchen, and Fritz grabbed a bottle of Scotch and glasses from a cabinet.

"To think that we're enemies at war, Kolbe."

"Braunwein's son, Horst, left toy pistols lying around here somewhere," Fritz said. "Perhaps we could shoot at each other a little."

They laughed and toasted. Fritz said he'd had a lovely time in South Africa, going on plenty of outings in the car with Katrin and with the Braunweins as well. He'd even gone venturing out alone despite the warnings he'd heard about wild animals.

"I never expected anything could happen to me here," he said, "until the other day."

"What day was that?"

"'As of five forty-five this morning . . .' That day."

Carlsroupe removed his panama hat and set it on the table. "The German army certainly is going all out."

"The German painter Max Liebermann commented at one point in the thirties, in response to one of those militaristic parades with thousands of flags and torches and all that silliness, that he couldn't eat as much as he would like to vomit."

Carlsroupe cleared his throat and laughed. "Well," he said, "I'm not surprised you like that quote. Despite your always elegant attire you are known on the Cape as being a strange bird indeed." He tapped Kolbe's stack of newspapers: the *Times*, *Washington Post*, and *Le Figaro*, along with papers by the Italians, Russians, Spanish, and Poles. "Still wild for the international press, I see. Even now."

"The world is big and colorful," Fritz said.

"So, why did you call me, Kolbe? It sounded urgent."

Fritz closed the kitchen door and drew the curtains, turning the room's light greenish. He pulled out the notepad page from inside his jacket. He stared only at his hand holding the paper.

"What is this?"

"These are the codes from our radio room, and the names of a few people staying behind."

"Herr Kolbe, I . . ."

"I'm no Nazi, Mr. Carlsroupe."

"Then what on earth are you doing? Did it ever occur to you that the man you wish to hand these codes to might well be a double agent? See here, everyone knows embassies and consulates are rife with spies, especially now. Yet you go around doing things like this, not knowing if you're safe? Kolbe, my dear Fritz, perhaps you should stay in South Africa after all. If you act like this back in Germany, you'll be dead within a few weeks."

Carlsroupe's words cut through Fritz like a machete. Would he do this in Germany? Fritz had heard whispers about various intelligence agencies' clandestine activities during his postings in Madrid, then briefly in Paris and Warsaw, and now South Africa. There were the British MI6, the Soviet NKVD, the French Deuxième Bureau.

"Well, give it here, Kolbe." Carlsroupe's voice had lost some of its British politeness. The Englishman glanced back and forth between Fritz's eyes and the page in his hands. Fritz slowly pushed the paper across the tabletop; it made a gentle rasping sound. Carlsroupe reached his hand, his fingers spread, a signet ring on one of them. Fritz pressed the page to the table. Carlsroupe yanked his hand back and raised his arms as if threatened.

"Can you give me some kind of guarantee?" Fritz asked.

"No, none. Surely you must know that these radio codes are already worthless."

Fritz went to stand at the window, its curtains drawn. Through a small gap he saw the sun, looking like the kind one sees blazing in the desert, more pale than yellow, masquerading as weak. *Do it,* he thought, *don't brood.* Of course the codes were worthless, since codes were changed all the time, but the gesture wasn't—not for him. Anyway, Carlsroupe clearly seemed to have more of a clue about espionage matters than he did, or the man wouldn't have tipped Fritz off to the possible dangers.

He flung the paper back onto the table; Carlsroupe snapped it up with one hand.

"Well played in any case," Carlsroupe said. "Now, do watch out for yourself. The telephones and radio traffic are bugged, and all post is being opened. You are going—voluntarily—to live in tyranny. I truly do not know what to make of you." He reached for his hat. "And, good Lord, do consider exactly what you hope to gain from this." He stuffed the paper into his jacket pocket and patted it, then shook Fritz's hand.

"Farewell to you, Herr Kolbe."

Fritz walked Carlsroupe to the door. Summer burst into the room as Fritz opened it. "We all want peace," he said.

35

"To have a roof over one's head, a family, enough to eat," Carlsroupe said.

"It's the same everywhere, no matter where in the world you look. It truly is that simple."

The Englishman set his panama hat on his head. "It will get nasty, you know. We British do not give up."

"I wish you luck, Carlsroupe."

"And I you, Kolbe. You will need it."

"Do say hello to your wife for me."

Ida had prepared braised chicken drumsticks and vegetables. Fritz ate in the kitchen with Katrin. He couldn't look at his daughter and simply chewed as she said, "*Mmmm*, tasty, Papa." His stomach had clenched up. He could hardly get a bite down.

She noticed, seeing right through his silence. "What is it, Papa?"

"I have to make a phone call," he said. He went away to his little den and called Consul Biermann.

"I'm not coming with you, Herr Consul. There's no way. I'm staying with Katrin."

His words were met by silence. Then something happened that Fritz never would have expected: the old man screamed at him.

"I'm your superior! Where would we be if everyone here simply did what they wished? Where does it end? You're my vice-consul. Berlin has been informed that I'm returning with you. Do you seriously wish to play into the hands of these philistines? You wish to admit defeat and run off with your tail between your legs like some mangy mutt off the street? I cannot believe you're telling me this." A sigh came over the line. Fritz felt small and ashamed. "I'm appalled and disappointed, Kolbe. Never, ever have I been so disappointed in a person as I am in you. But fine. Please do send this old man back to Berlin to take up a fight for which the young are too cowardly."

The line clicked and Fritz banged the handset against his temple. He cursed and punched the air. If only he could be like the rest of them. *O Reich! O Hitler, heavenly Führer! Tell me what to do and I'll do it. Take away my responsibility, and I will eagerly follow you. Take my soul, my thoughts. Take me!*

He ripped the cord out of the phone and wall and hurled it at the window. The cord stuck there a moment, like a snake, then dropped to the floor.

Fritz went back, held his hand out for Katrin, and proposed they go for a little stroll by the sea.

When he told her, she ran away, a skinny little girl with coal-black hair. He watched her go, a hook in his chest attached to a cord around Katrin's waist. He shouted her name into the wind and the coarse rushing sounds of the ocean. He ran after her, his shoes sinking in the sand, his strength draining out of him, making it hard to go on.

"Katrin! Katrin!" His daughter was fleeing from him. He pleaded with her to stand still. When he finally caught up with her and placed a hand on her shoulder, she pushed it away. Her eyes were wet, and she wore an expression he had never seen before. Katrin was grown up.

"You promised! You promised me! Fathers don't break promises!"

He knelt before her in the sand and raised his hands as if praying. Katrin punched at his chest.

"I'm coming back," he stammered, "I'm coming back, Katrin, I—"

"You're leaving me all alone." Her voice went shrill from rage and shouting against the wind. Fritz hung his head and spread out his arms. He didn't know how long he remained like that. After a few seconds, or perhaps years, he felt Katrin's body press against him firmly in that way that was unique to her, and he wrapped his arms around her, wanting to never let her go again.

"You can't just leave me behind, Papa." Her chest shuddered with sobs.

"I am coming back. I'll come get you, you're my little girl. I will come get you no matter what."

Fritz held her as tight as he could. She knew the score. She wasn't a child anymore. She read as many newspapers as he did.

"You'll have it good with Hiltrud and Werner," he said. "It's lovely in South-West Africa, believe me. As soon as it's over, I'm coming back. It won't last long, honey. There are so many horrible things going on. It can't continue to go well for them for long."

Katrin worked herself free from his embrace and pushed him away. He sunk into the sand. She turned her back to him and ran off along the beach.

Katrin insisted on going with him to the harbor. Fritz would have preferred to say good-bye at home, alone, undisturbed. He was afraid he would start crying as he watched from the railing the slight figure of his daughter disappear into the crowd. But he couldn't refuse Katrin's wish.

The throng gathered before the ship's towering hull smelled to Fritz like sunshine, flower blossoms, and sweat. A cursing man barged into Katrin and struck her shin with his suitcase. Fritz barked at the man that he should kindly watch himself and go straight to hell. He felt Katrin watching him, her eyes reflecting the sky. She had never heard him talk like that before.

Fritz embraced his daughter there amidst the heat and the ripples of overlapping voices, and she dug her fingers into his back. *I can't do this,* he thought. *I can't.* He closed his eyes, unable to budge, smelling the fumes from the ship's smokestack, the black exhaust rising straight up into the blue sky. He took Katrin's face in both his hands, felt the smoothness of her cheeks, and looked her in the eyes. *The most precious thing in the whole world,* he thought.

"I'm coming back," he said. He broke down when Katrin let go of his back to wave at Ida, who was walking toward them. The girl would be staying with her over the next few days, until Werner and Hiltrud came to take her away to South-West Africa, which had been a German colony only until 1915 and was still safe, far removed from war.

Fritz was one of the last to board the Dutch steamer *Louisiana*. The gangway seesawed beneath his feet while he looked over at the flat summit of Table Mountain. South Africa had been a paradise for him.

The crowds jostling on deck were loud and aggressive, but Fritz was able to elbow his way to a spot at the railing. He spied Katrin's fair face and the large thick figure of Ida next to her. Hundreds of hands waved, handkerchiefs fluttered helplessly, and soldiers raised fists into the air. Then the ship's horn droned and the heavy mooring cables rumbled. Fritz could feel the massive engines working away beneath the deck planks under his feet. *This cannot be,* he thought. Katrin was still so little.

She turned her back to him.

"Katrin, don't, please!" he shouted.

Ida leaned down to his girl and spoke to her. Fritz prayed. Katrin shook her head. Ida glanced up at him, then turned to his daughter again. Katrin slowly turned around. Fritz rubbed the tears from his face. Katrin was waving to him.

"I'm coming back!" he shouted. The gap between the ship and the dock grew larger. Water churned from the propellers twisting their way through the harbor. As Fritz watched, Katrin's face blurred, receded in the distance, and then vanished.

3

VOYAGE TO HELL

At sea, fall 1939

On the decks and inside common rooms, the men sang popular German folk songs. The singing unfurled over the ship like a flag. The *Louisiana* steamed on through a deceptively calm Atlantic, water heaving at the ship's sides.

Throughout the journey, Fritz often stood at the railing and looked out at the horizon's bladelike edge. A determined group of German passengers, men and women, had sent a delegation to the captain, demanding that the German flag be hoisted next to the Dutch. The captain had rejected their demand, locked up the door to the bridge, and had sentries posted outside.

Two to three times a day people pushed their way into the radio room to get news of how the war was going. Their cries of joy disgusted Fritz. "Poland's fallen!" they called out. Whenever the triumphs of German U-boats were reported, he heard a song that would haunt him in his sleep: "Today Germany belongs to us, and tomorrow the entire world." Men and women he'd gotten to know as reasonable people in

Cape Town were now constantly talking big, trying to order around the Dutch sailors. On the first day, Fritz heard that some of them had already come to blows.

He shared a tiny windowless cabin with a man named Petersen. Petersen had tried to succeed at various business ventures in South-West Africa and South Africa. It hadn't worked out, though, "all because of those half-apes down there," Petersen said. He had propped himself up on his elbows. The cabin wall behind him was greasy. Now, luckily, a whole new day was dawning for him, he said. Two more weeks and he'd be in the Wehrmacht. Was Fritz going to become a soldier too?

"I'm in the diplomatic corps."

Petersen laughed. "Diplomat? What crap. What do we need diplomats for? You look like you're quite healthy. Why aren't you fighting at the front?"

"The Foreign Office," Fritz said, "negotiated our current treaty with Russia as well as our Anti-Comintern Pact with Japan, and what's more we—"

"Yeah, yeah. Listen, that's all fine. You're not wrong there. Von Ribbentrop and the Führer are supposed to be plenty close. So if he's your superior, fine, why not?"

Fritz developed the habit of looking out to sea for hours, observing how the position of the sun changed the color of the water. He started a daily exercise routine: jog at least ten times around the decks, then do thirty knee bends and thirty push-ups. Sometimes, when all the Germanomania on deck became too much for him, he retreated into a book. One time—he wasn't sure how many days into the journey they were when this happened—he saw a vertical plume of smoke far on the horizon. A U-boat had likely torpedoed a ship, and now hundreds of people were trapped below in their cabins with the water rising, or they were treading water in the ocean until their muscles went limp and the weight of their bodies pulled them down into a world without breath. All those poor, poor people.

In the evenings Petersen droned on, delivering monologues about racial theories and how it was now being proved just how right the Führer was about everything. The peoples in the East, he said, "such as your Polacks," had nothing to counter German might. He also liked talking about how International Jewry were getting their "knuckles rapped right proper," something he said was long overdue. Fritz only felt lucky that Petersen didn't expect him to respond; the man talked on without interruption until he finally said good night and began to snore seconds later.

Fritz's sole comfort was a whale that often passed close to the ship. Its mighty gray back—slick and glossy, as if lacquered—would rise from the ocean and dive under again in one elegantly sweeping motion. The colossus then blew out water, and its huge tail flipper wound its way back out of the Atlantic, swinging as it moved, dripping wet and awe-inspiring.

Next to him Petersen said that if he had a gun right now he'd sink a few bullets into it—people were saying that these beasts could disrupt the U-boats. "The captain has to have a rifle somewhere on the bridge, don't you think?"

"That's enough," Fritz said. "You imbecile."

Petersen drew a notepad from his jacket pocket and asked for Fritz's full name and residence. "Well?" Petersen waved and two men came to his side.

"Sommer, Karl Heinz," Fritz said. "Chemnitz, Fritzstrasse thirty-three."

"There you go. People like you, Sommer, only have to be shown who's boss, and you'll knuckle under soon enough. You'll have a lot to learn in Germany. But don't you worry, we'll soon show the likes of you just how things work."

Fritz pulled his sun hat farther down over his brow and left. Karl Heinz Sommer, from Chemnitz. *Journey onward, mighty whale,* he thought. *Keep trekking on calmly through the sea. And when you pass the coast near Swakopmund, say hello to Katrin for me.*

One dark-blue and cool oceanic night, he looked to the south. Africa had long since vanished from view, and the water now surged and washed away into darkness.

Katrin! he thought. *My girl. Why do you children never know just how much your parents love you?*

After breakfast Fritz heard the sound of Therese Biermann's cane going *klock klock* against the deck as they approached. Consul Biermann was wearing a pale-gray three-piece suit, white shirt, and bowtie, and his wife wore a dark ladies' suit. Biermann again told Fritz how crucial it was for people like them to return to Germany; but Fritz was beginning to see doubt in the man's eyes—that brief glance to the side, a slight contraction of his eyelids. Ever since they'd boarded the ship, Biermann had seemed increasingly alien to Fritz.

A horde of young men in brown uniforms ran out onto the deck, red bands with the swastika on a white circle encircling their upper arms. They passed Biermann and his wife. One of the boys—Müller from the consulate—barged into Therese and kept on going. The consul wrapped an arm around his wife's shoulders and wondered aloud just who did that young ruffian think he was?

"When there's no respect left, Herr Kolbe, when books are being burned and people are hated on command just because of their religion, when decent behavior disappears, then all the rest will be gone soon too." Biermann balled his hand into a thick and wrinkled fist. "Perhaps the Foreign Office is one of our last refuges. We are simply too cosmopolitan, by the way we exchange ideas, by our very language."

"Germany is still our country, for heaven's sake." Therese reached into her jacket pocket, lit up a cigarette, and handed it to her husband. He stroked her cheek. At least she still had her cane, she said.

"We're very sorry about your daughter," she added. "But you will be surprised to see how quickly children adapt. Your Katrin is a fine girl. Try not to fret over it too much, Herr Kolbe."

Fritz left them alone in their unanimity, and when he thought of them afterward, it was in sepia tones, like an old photo. He had gotten the posting in Africa he'd desired because Biermann had made it happen—they had already worked together in Spain, where Biermann had valued Fritz's diligence. On Sunday mornings they used to meet on the Plaza Mayor in the heart of Madrid to play chess and enjoy some conversation. From Biermann, Fritz had learned a great deal about the history of diplomacy: that language was precise work, that certain treaties should be memorized, and that one always treated the opposing party nobly. Diplomacy was not the kettledrum but rather the oboe.

"And sometimes, diplomacy lies," Fritz had said.

"It's all in the language, Kolbe. The language."

Fritz stood at the stern railing looking out at the ship's white trail. Standing next to him, Petersen advised him to put his hat back on, what with his thin hair and all. Fritz didn't understand why the man kept trying to talk to him. He told Petersen he liked to get a lot of sun because its warmth traveled to his heart.

"It's time for the heart to be cold and hard, Herr Diplomat."

"Give us freedom of thought," Fritz recited.

"What kind of stupid saying is that?"

"Schiller. A German writer and poet. You do understand German? Schiller! Ever hear of him?"

"Of course I know who Schiller is."

"Born in 1620."

"I know that!"

"You can go to hell."

Petersen stayed at the railing. Fritz left. He was stuck with having to share his cabin with this man for over a week; he would have to hear his breathing and grunting at night, and in the mornings he would continue to wake to the sight of him propped up, staring at Fritz. He needed to go deeper inside himself, find somewhere he could retreat to: that whale, the radio codes now in Carlsroupe's hands. Katrin. He greeted a Dutch sailor, who angrily asked him what he wanted, saying they had too many Nazis on board who thought they could go around giving orders.

"I'm no Nazi," Fritz said. He told the man he merely wanted to ask if there was some sort of reclining deck chair on board he could use. He'd rather stick to the deck at night. "Please," Fritz added. "It doesn't have to be comfortable—only something to sleep on." He was asking from the bottom of his heart.

The closer the steamer got to the North Atlantic and the North Sea, the more men started appearing on deck wearing uniforms. Fritz wondered where they got them. He also noticed the few women on board changed their appearances. In Cape Town they had worn the top button of their blouses casually open and let down their hair sometimes. Now, every shirt was fastened up to the neck, and their hair was tight against their heads, like bonnets. Müller was in his brown uniform, baggy at his bony shoulders, the excess fabric fluttering in the wind. Whenever Fritz looked at him, Müller looked away.

During the day the Dutch crew barely showed themselves on deck. Fritz heard that arguments had broken out in the small dining room because someone had hung up a Hitler portrait and one of the sailors had taken it down. *Today Germany still belongs to us,* Fritz thought, *and this bullshit boat too.*

The Biermanns had retreated to their cabin. Fritz looked in on them now and then. "What is going on out there?" Frau Biermann asked. The consul just sat at a window, looking out over the ocean smooth as glass. His motionless face was half illuminated, like a portrait.

"I'm trusting in what you said, Herr Consul," Fritz said. "That we can do something."

Biermann turned to Fritz, who found he couldn't meet his stare. Instead, he glanced at the yellowing world map on the cabin's green wall: Africa to the east; the barren Strait of Gibraltar; Portugal and Spain, both descended into Fascism; France; the narrow channel to Great Britain. This solitary Dutch freighter was getting closer and closer to Germany, nearly in its clutches.

"Herr Consul Biermann?"

The portrait remained a portrait.

When Fritz moved to leave, Biermann said his name.

"I'm sorry about the telephone call, Herr Kolbe. I should not have let myself scream at you. One can't allow such behavior."

Out on deck, it was cold and clear. The sea was swelling just as it always would, even when the war started hacking away at other parts of the world. The ship's motor chugged on nonstop.

Lacking a warm cap, Fritz that night wore his sun hat while sleeping. Rousing him from his sleep, something hard pushed at his foot. He shifted onto his side a little in his sagging deck chair. The something pushed at him again, and grumbling penetrated his dense grogginess. Fritz opened his eyes. The dark silhouettes of several men loomed over him.

"The diplomat," one said. Fritz recognized Petersen's voice. The men looked huge against the dark-blue backdrop of sky. Fritz sat up. Someone kicked at the chair from the side. Wood cracked, and Fritz braced a hand against the cold deck floor. He pushed his blanket aside and moved as if to stand. Two hands pushed him back down.

"We got our eyes on you, asshole," a piece of the darkness told him.

"One more wise move from you, buster," said more darkness, "and you're going overboard."

Again they kicked. The deck chair wobbled, and Fritz heard the sound of wood splitting as he tried to hold on. He tried to stand up once more and was pushed back down. The chair's wooden skeleton squeezed at him.

"We'll teach you a lesson."

"Say it! Say *Heil Hitler*. Do it." It was Petersen.

The chair creaked and a gust swept cold across the deck. The contours of shoulders lined up white in the moonlight.

"Say it!"

Fritz had no chance of surviving this if he did not comply. No one would hear him cry out and even if they did, he would disappear fast in the night and would be left swimming along, one stroke as senseless as the next. The last thing he'd hear would probably be Petersen's sneering laugh.

"Say it!"

"Heil Hitler," he said. Hate and shame churned inside him, along with self-contempt and fear. The men laughed softly, one of the dark figures setting a hand on the shoulder of another.

"Do it again!"

"Heil Hitler."

"Well, well. So the diplomat does know how."

"We'll get you yet," Petersen said.

They left and the night sky opened wide again, the sound of laughter drifting off in the wind. One of the figures walking away was slight. Was it Heinz Müller from the consulate? Fritz's chest squeezed up. Never before in his life had he been so humiliated. He was small, he told himself, and a coward. He stood at the railing, gripping it hard, and breathed deep, in and out. *At least I'm alive,* he thought. He looked around him. He was all alone, his muscles so weak now that he trembled.

"Hitler," he hissed. The wind blew gloomily. The sea surged and washed up over the ship's side, the waves sounding to him like jaws ripping open. "Nazis." He cursed and pounded on the railing. *The pigs, those damned pigs. Cowards. Such big talkers in groups.*

He returned to the deck chair and pressed on its arms. It was badly damaged, but it still worked. He sat back down, pulled his blanket over him for solace, and looked up at the dark sky with its dark-blue streaks and stars like white pinpricks. The voices burned inside him. His own words burned.

With a curse, he leapt out of the deck chair and felt his way through the darkened ship to the Biermanns' cabin. He hammered on the door. He felt ashamed acting this way yet kept hammering. A strip of light glowed along the bottom of the door, and Consul Biermann opened it a crack. He had combed his hair.

"Herr Kolbe, at this hour? What's happened?"

"We can do something? You said so. We can do something? Right?"

Biermann stroked his mustache with thumb and index finger. He glanced back at his wife and whispered that he would come out on deck and Fritz should wait for him there.

Back out in the cold night air, Fritz silently begged for Petersen to appear again, alone this time, instead of with his cowardly gang of big talkers. Then they'd box. Fritz hadn't known thoughts and feelings like this before, not to this degree. Then he heard the trusty *klock klock* of Therese Biermann's cane.

"I didn't mean to disturb you, Frau Biermann, my apologies."

"It's fine, Herr Kolbe. But at the moment my husband needs to rest. He can't speak to you right now. He wishes you a good night—as much as there is of it left." The petite woman turned away. Fritz called after her.

"No, Herr Kolbe. Not now. I'm sorry. Get some sleep now. Sleep is good."

◆ ◆ ◆

Nowhere on board the *Louisiana* could he be alone. What he would've given for his own cabin, no matter how small or dirty. Petersen and his cronies watched him continually, sometimes following him down the decks, shoulder to shoulder, laughing, a surging wave of simplistic certainty. He couldn't stand it. He wanted to finish them off, every last one of them. But he didn't say anything. Heinz Müller kept eyeing him, his pale, pointy face void of expression.

Fritz didn't see the Biermanns on deck anymore, and he didn't go knocking on their door. Apart from them and the Braunweins, Fritz knew hardly anyone in his old homeland whom he could still contact. His old friend from his Spanish days, Eugen Sacher, lived in the fragile safety of Switzerland. Perhaps he would find one or two people at the Office to befriend. He couldn't possibly be the only one left who shared this view.

Sometimes he stood at the railing with his arms folded and watched the women pass, their shadows long and slanting along the deck planks. It had been a long time since he had loved a woman.

Back in Cape Town, at a small reception in the British consulate, he had become acquainted with Carlsroupe's wife, a red-haired and green-eyed Englishwoman from Cornwall who was always in a sunny mood. They enjoyed talking that evening, leaning against the wall, drinking cool champagne. On his way home he'd recalled that they had been flirting a little, their eyes lowered, sharing little double entendres.

Several days later he called her, then she him. They chatted about the city and Table Mountain, the ocean and the sun and the latest fashions. Work and the everyday receded. They agreed to meet in a café on Darling Street where they sat in the shadows of awnings, drinking whisky. Their fingers touched. Fritz felt agitated and unsure. He wondered what Katrin would think of Mrs. Harriet Carlsroupe, and he remembered that he liked her husband, Carlsroupe, who was a nice fellow through and through.

Harriet and Fritz drove in his open convertible down to the sea and walked on the wet sand with their trouser legs rolled up. Suddenly Harriet wrapped her arms around his neck and kissed him. This was an unexpected leap, a quick plunge. He held her. The kiss lasted all of thirty seconds, then she pushed him away. She shook her head, brushing one of his thin strands of hair from his forehead.

"It can't work, Fritz. It would be treason."

He looked to the ground, then let his gaze travel up her legs, along the length of her body to her face.

"Fritz, I'm sorry, but I can't. Under any other circumstances . . ." she said.

"Those are exactly what we don't have," Fritz said.

"Let's drive back. And not a word of it to anyone, ever. This kiss, this moment here, will remain between us forever. It's for the best."

"Harriet, we—"

"It can't work, Fritz."

"But don't things often work out better than people think?"

Harriet laughed into the wind, her mouth wide open. "You blue-eyed Fritzi, you," she said and tied back her dancing curls.

"I will keep this lovely moment between us," Fritz told her. "Thank you for the kiss."

"The pleasure was all mine."

He cursed this ship for carrying him steadily nearer to Germany and its red Nazi flags while at the same time dragging him miles away from Katrin. Fritz had dodged Petersen and his cronies whenever they came around to bully him, until his shame became so great he decided on another course. Now, as they came toward him on one of the well-worn decks, he stood his ground and felt his heart pounding.

The men looked at him, muttered to each other, laughed, and walked by. They were on their way to the captain again, Petersen told

Fritz in passing, to tell him he needs to raise the Reich flag. He said Fritz could come along—as a diplomat he must be real good at such things.

After a few minutes, the men came back down the tarnished steel steps that led to the bridge. Fritz held a hand to his eyes and looked up at the flag mast. No swastika.

"Strategic retreat?" he asked.

Petersen came at him, his lips pressed together. "You better be real careful." He moved to jab Fritz in the chest, but Fritz pushed his hand away. "I got your name and address, Sommer. You better watch out." Petersen waved for his comrades, and they followed him down the deck, one of them kicking at a hatch that led to the Dutch sailors' quarters.

Why did he have to go provoking Petersen? He couldn't stay clear of him or get off this ship. He couldn't ask the Biermanns to take him in either, although the elderly couple surely would have done it.

In the temporary dining hall Fritz got himself a bowl of thick pea soup and ate it on deck, his back to the wind. He then made his way up to the bridge. The sentry at the door was swinging a truncheon. Fritz raised his hands and said he needed to speak to the captain, that it was urgent.

"Another one of you?"

"Forgive me. No, I'm not another one. I'm completely different. I'm not here about a flag or anything like that. Please, tell the captain I must speak to him."

The sailor knocked on the door with its brass-framed porthole. He whispered to someone, then the captain came out. He had a firm, round belly. Fritz described his situation: that he didn't want to share his cabin with that barbarian anymore, that his life was being threatened. He couldn't sleep out on deck in a deck chair anymore either. The captain must find another spot for him—he didn't care what or where.

"What? So you can go spying around my ship?"

"Spying? Me? No, Captain, sir. Please. They'll kill me. They'll toss me overboard."

"One less to worry about," the sailor said.

"Please. I'm with the Foreign Office. I'm coming to you with a matter of international concern." Fritz had had more than enough. First those philistines had made him say *Heil Hitler*, now he stood in the sun squinting up at this man, totally dependent on his mercy. The captain wasn't wearing a uniform, only a shabby jacket with gold braids. He turned back and spoke to someone still in the bridge area. Fritz heard a man laughing.

"Is Hitler shit?" the captain asked him.

"Yes," Fritz said.

"Would you go say that real loud right now to your countrymen?"

"No. Would you?"

A grin showed through the captain's gray beard.

Passenger Fritz Kolbe, alias Karl Heinz Sommer, disappeared into the stink, noise, and shadows of the *Louisiana*'s engine room. There was no window, and the room sharply reeked of oil, coal, and diesel, or whatever was used in those pounding engines—Fritz had no idea. He used a napkin to make earplugs.

It surprised him how few men worked in the engine room. Most ignored him until he started asking them about Dutch vocabulary and basic expressions, or about which of the insulated pipes running along the ceiling he could use for doing pull-ups. At night he sometimes dared to go back up on deck, the *Louisiana*'s white walls mottled with rust shimmering in the moonlight, her floorboards a dull matte finish as if formed from dust. He looked up into the starry sky and wondered where his beloved sun must be shining now. He lived in darkness. Two of the Dutch crew members brought him something to eat in the morning, afternoon, and evening. They told him he was one odd fellow. The situation on the ship was growing increasingly tense, they said. Germany had plagued their good old Aunt *Louisiana* like a curse. If anyone was the boss here, it was their captain. No one pissed on his leg! A bunch of real shits, the Germans.

"Not all of us," Fritz said.

After the first day in the engine room, Fritz noticed that he smelled different than before. He was allowed to use the sailors' washroom, including their soap that looked like marble. Despite that, the scent of engine oil had seeped into his skin, seemingly for good, and couldn't be washed away. At least outside he had benefited from the sunshine and the robust ocean wind; down below he was breathing in things that could not possibly be good for his health.

Yet despite it all, Fritz was happy enough with his noisy cell and his solitude. Through one of the sailors, he got a message up to the Biermanns: he had backed down to the Nazis, but he still didn't know how long he could hold up.

4

More to the Story

Switzerland, a few years after the war

The memories hit Fritz more intensely now that he's telling these two strangers how it all began. When he's sitting alone facing a stack of blank paper, he turns inward and remains sealed off—feeling shattered, morose, and hostile in that way he never likes to feel. Wegner and Veronika listen attentively as he speaks and rarely interrupt him, yet he senses that they're also acting as a kind of corrective for him. At times he hears the clearing of a throat; at others, the rasp of a lighter. Wegner takes lots of notes, as does Veronika, but she writes things down at times when he doesn't.

Fritz spins his globe. "These facts that you need, Herr Wegner, are about men who stand over a man at night and threaten to drown him. Facts like those rip right through a person. I practically urinated in my trousers. Is that a fact?"

Wegner nods, hesitantly.

"From South Africa up north, then northwest," Fritz says, running his index finger over the blue Atlantic. "From the island of Saint Helena on toward Cape Verde, then a change in course to the northeast. The Canary Islands, Madeira. To the south of us lay the Sahara. These were all the sites of great expeditions focused on exploration and foreign cultures. And what was I doing? That damn ship was taking me closer and closer to Fascism."

"Do you think those men really would have killed you?" Veronika asks.

"To types like that, a life really only counts when it's their own."

"Do you have a photo of Katrin?"

Fritz opens the shabby, rustic cupboard. Its shelves are filled with handwritten papers, old folders, photos, newspaper clippings, and documents, and worn books. He knows right where to find his photos of Katrin.

"May I?"

"Please."

Veronika takes the photo and smiles. "What a cute girl," she says.

"That was taken in Camps Bay."

Veronika passes the picture to Wegner, who looks at it and then studies Fritz a moment.

"Were you able to stay in contact with her?"

"I could have."

"Where is she now?"

"This story is not yet over, Herr Wegner."

"You don't think that's overstating things a bit?"

Fritz falls silent.

Wegner lights up a cigarette. Fritz could never quite explain why, but he's always liked watching the way a person lights a cigarette— Marlene most of all. Most people look relaxed in that first moment, leaning back, growing content. He even remembers smoking himself in that secret office in Bern, and on the shattered streets of Berlin when he was facing death, his nerves wearing thinner than used wax paper.

"In 1939, you were back working in the Berlin Foreign Office," Wegner says. He's looking at his notes. Fritz can tell it's just for show, that Wegner knows the facts.

"Yes," Fritz says, "I was back in the Office on Wilhelmstrasse, in the heart of the city, in the center of power. Walter Braunwein picked me up from the port once I was finally allowed to leave that miserable ship. The Office sent a car for Biermann and his wife, all quite official. Biermann looked horrible; he was rather ill."

"Braunwein picked you up? Now there's a true friend," Wegner says.

Fritz hesitates. Then he says, "Yes, he did, along with Käthe."

"Might be another interview candidate," Wegner says.

"They don't know a thing about it."

Wegner sets his pencil on the table and looks out the window. The sky is deep blue, the meadows are shimmering green, and the mountains loom bright gray. Fritz liked to imagine those mountains making a tremendous racket as they rose thundering into the sky while forming eons ago. *The world is so lovely,* he thinks.

Veronika asks if she can have another piece of his tasty apple pie. When Fritz goes into the kitchen for a slice, he hears her whispering with Wegner. She has more patience and likely more understanding of all the sacrifices that his long-ago actions truly had required of him. He goes back in and sits down with the young reporters.

"It's so nice to see people eating all they want," he says. "As the war progressed in Germany, it was harder and harder to get any decent food on one's plate. But those aren't the sort of facts that interest you, are they, Herr Wegner?"

"With all due respect, Herr Kolbe, that—and the period where you got whatever you want to call it, scruples or whatever—doesn't play that well in print, if I may say so."

"Oh, you may say whatever you want, which is quite a good thing, isn't it? It wasn't always like that. My period of scruples, as you call it? I was torn. For God's sake, just imagine that you're working for the Devil himself day in, day out. And yet there were crucial things that occurred even before all the document smuggling. Marlene, for example."

"Marlene Wiese? You can't be serious—I mean, in regards to what we're doing here. My goal is to write an article about one of the greatest spies—"

"Without Marlene," Fritz interrupts, "we likely wouldn't be sitting here. *Definitely* not."

He carefully moves the globe to the side and pulls down a city map of Berlin from the rustic cupboard.

"This is about Berlin now. And no need to bother with my scruples. That's my issue and mine alone."

He unfolds the city map. The paper tears along the folded lines as Fritz expands the page, Berlin practically breaking into bits.

"Kurfürstendamm was where Braunwein procured a little apartment for me," he says. "And here"—he points at the map—"is the Foreign Office. Wilhelmplatz. Corner of Wilhelmstrasse and Vosstrasse."

Wegner pulls a large photo from his briefcase—a portrait. Fritz recognizes the face: gaunt and angular, with those heavy-lidded, piercing eyes.

"Hitler's Foreign Minister, Joachim von Ribbentrop," Wegner says. "Your head boss in the Foreign Office."

Fritz laughs bitterly. He takes the picture of Katrin off the table and places it on the tiled oven. He doesn't want his daughter's lovely face near this man.

"After the war, I saw von Ribbentrop one last time, at the Nuremberg Trials," he says. "I wanted him to see me. I wanted him to know what I did. Yet when we saw each other, I don't think the bastard even recognized me. Me, a minor official. He never had anything to do with regular people, our fine Herr Von. He was hanged. I'm opposed to the death penalty, but I can't say that I was sorry about him. I sometimes wonder what these men thought about in their final moments. Was there any understanding at all? Did they think of someone they loved?"

"Love?" Veronika asks. "Those people?"

"Sure," Fritz says. "Everyone loves someone, or something. Even those men loved. Whether we like this fact or not is fully beside the point."

Fritz realizes that Wegner's trying to steal a glance at Veronika's profile without anyone noticing. She too has that bold nose. Fritz likes that. The young woman radiates appeal, and he likes having her here. He believes she's a good person.

Wegner taps the photo, on von Ribbentrop's forehead. "Did you ever speak with him personally?"

"In the Wolf's Lair. And I got pretty close to Hitler."

"You passed the exact layout of the Wolf's Lair on to the Americans," Wegner says. "But nothing happened—unlike with other information you divulged."

"Why didn't the Americans bomb it?" Veronika adds.

"I wasn't ever told. I wasn't ever told much. I still haven't been."

"Everyone is just a puppet in a story like this," Wegner says.

"Not me! Damn it. Not me. What is it with you?"

"My apologies. Pardon me."

"Maybe we should give the story more structure," Veronika says. "That might work, and could be beneficial in some way."

"Oh Christ," Fritz says. "Structure? Tough to do, Fräulein Hügel. We're talking four years of keeping my mouth shut and playing along."

In hindsight, the years before the secret files came on the scene seem dull, gray, and empty to Fritz, and he doesn't know how to reassemble them. He hated himself; he *loathed* himself. Looking back now, he has no idea what he did that whole time—and he doesn't want to know. Veronika is right, though. He—they—must try to follow this story like scaling a rope, working their way hand over hand. If they don't, he'll only lose his resolve to finally get on paper everything that happened.

"I never wanted to be a hero," he says. "It's important to me that you know that."

He takes a stack of faded photos from the cupboard. He leafs through them and lays another head shot on the table.

"Ambassador with Special Duty Ernst von Günther," Fritz says. "I worked my way up to his outer office."

"You must have a picture of Marlene, don't you?" Veronika asks.

"Inside here I do," he says, and pats at his heart.

Veronika makes a camera with her fingers and says, "Click."

"The story needs a face," Wegner says.

These young people have no idea the feeling such words unleash inside Fritz. A cold shudder runs over his skin. For the longest time, when he looked in the mirror, his face contorted into a purplish grimace before his eyes. The story needs a face? Which one?

He lays the portrait of his direct superior on the city map.

"Here we go," he says, and in his mind von Günther rises from the photo paper, bouncing on the tips of his toes, marching down the long corridors of the Office, full of enthusiasm, a document in his hand as always. Eventually the day will come when he will stare at Fritz and Fritz, struck by mortal fear, will reach for the gun in his pocket. But for now von Günther is calling Fritz's name from out of the past: "Kolbe! Kolbe? . . ."

5

THE DILIGENT COURT JESTER

Berlin, 1943

"Kolbe! Kolbe?"

Fritz could hear von Günther's voice through the brown door connecting to his superior's office. He lifted his chair and pushed it back a bit. He couldn't slide it, as the rug was too tattered and fuzzy. He walked across his fastidiously tidy office and knocked on the door.

"Come on in, do come in. My dear Kolbe." Von Günther's jovial tone disgusted Fritz. He squeezed his eyes shut briefly before pushing down on the door handle.

Von Günther's office was large and bare. It had two thickly curtained windows that faced Wilhelmstrasse. A picture of Adolf Hitler in profile hung in a golden frame.

"Take a seat," von Günther told Fritz. "We have some files to discuss."

He spread out the documents. The desk lamp's glow fell on the polished wood like moonlight on a still sea. The Reich Eagle with its garland-encircled swastika was printed on the files; too much ink had been used, and the edges of some eagles were bleeding over and fraying black. Fritz's superior drummed his fingertips on one eagle at the top of a big stack of dull cardboard folders. *Top Secret Reich Matter,* Fritz read to himself. *Finally.* He didn't dare look von Günther in the eye. Fritz wasn't sure exactly when his resolve had kicked in. Up till now it had only been a plan—he'd had no idea whether he'd have the courage to follow through on what he was contemplating. He had been thinking it through for so long, feeling clear about his resolve at times, perplexed at others. He'd walk around his apartment, back and forth, his fists balled and trembling. It all led to one conclusion: if he was caught, he was dead.

"Kolbe?"

"Herr Ambassador?"

"Are you listening to me? Is something wrong?"

Ambassador with Special Duty Ernst von Günther was responsible for keeping the Foreign Office in close liaison with the armed forces—the Wehrmacht. Thousands of top-secret files crossed his desk. He was Political Affairs, Department One, Military—in short, "Pol 1 M." He was the very man whose outer office Fritz had needed to reach, which he did after years of bitter frustration and self-loathing that he'd made great effort to suppress.

After his shocking arrival in a Germany of swastika flags and goose-stepping, Fritz had gotten this far through dogged hard work and a little luck. Walter hadn't been able to do much for him, and Consul Biermann had managed just as little. Fritz had first been assigned to a position in Personnel and Visas, where he'd spent his days staring at the walls of a windowless green office.

1939. 1940. 1941. 1942. Dread, death, destruction, delusions of grandeur, war. Tyranny. There was the time two SS men had been in his

office, their black tunics open, hands in their trouser pockets. They
had fun chatting while waiting for the papers Fritz was to issue them.

"Babi Yar," one was saying. "Thirty thousand fucking Jews in one
fell swoop." He slapped his thigh and laughed as if he'd just scored a
lovely goal in a soccer match.

"Yep, that's how you do it," the other one said.

"Thirty thousand, Herr Kolbe. With one stroke. Now what do you
think of that?"

"I'm not well versed in such things, Herr Lieutenant."

"Not well versed?" Both men laughed. "It was only Jews, Kolbe!"
the first one said. "It's not like we're monsters."

"Yes sir, Herr Lieutenant."

"So are we done yet, Herr Kolbe?"

"Papers like these take time, Herr Lieutenant."

"Good God, Kolbe, just get on with it."

Fritz folded their documents, ran his thumbnail over the crease, and
slid the pages into envelopes. Once the men had turned their backs to
him, he formed a pistol with his fingers and shot them in the backs of
their necks.

Fritz had asked Walter if he could get von Günther to consider him.
Fritz always greeted Ambassador von Günther when he saw the man
dashing down the corridors and heard his loud voice in the Foreign
Office. Von Günther's outer office secretary, Frau Schmidt, was in her
mid-forties and wore starched blouses. Fritz considered ways that he
might persuade Frau Schmidt to quit her job. Death came to his aid in
the end. Frau Schmidt learned, all on the same day, that her husband
and one of her sons had been killed at the front. She crept out of the
office, someone congratulated her on her heroic sacrifice, and she was
never seen again.

Fritz was the first to respond to the internal job announcement.
He was promoted to von Günther's personal advisor the very next day.
He wasn't exactly as attractive as Frau Schmidt and was in fact a good

deal shorter, von Günther told him, but he'd only heard good things about Fritz. He was diligent, disciplined, organized—he'd made himself thoroughly well known in that regard. Biermann and that resourceful Walter Braunwein had both put in a good word for him. If the things these gentlemen said were true, he explained, then Fritz was exactly the man he wanted working for him.

Von Günther launched into a lecture about the latest crises. There was the British counteroffensive in the desert and those monstrous bombing raids. Despite the heroic nature of Germany's soldiers, they still weren't advancing any farther on the Eastern Front, and Morocco and Algeria were a disaster. But the Battle of Stalingrad—now there was greatness. "My God! Such heroism, Kolbe, such sacrifice!" von Günther said, though he admitted things weren't looking good at the moment, objectively speaking.

Fritz put on a pleasant smile, borrowed from his repertoire of lies and loathing.

"But in such a crisis, a man proves himself, Kolbe—and our system does too, yes?" Von Günther drummed on the files again. "Having to weather crisis is the only way to build character. You will see. Germany will master this."

Fritz could hear the drone of truck engines out on the street, which made the windowpanes vibrate. Von Günther was noticeably younger than Fritz, a large man with a wide face that had more than enough room for his eyes and nose.

"It's how one acts that always decides matters, Herr Ambassador," Fritz said.

"Action, indeed. Summer of '41, Kolbe—that was too late to launch a campaign against Russia. I said it back then. Spring, it would have to have been spring." Von Günther lit up a cigarette and nudged the blackout curtain to the side with a fingertip, as if touching a Renaissance painting without permission, to gaze out. Not a single light shined outside. Fritz placed a hand on the top-secret files. *All mine,* he thought. Sweat burned in his armpits. Next to the folders stood two framed photos. In one, von Günther's wife was laughing in the sunlight, holding a bouquet of flowers in her arms. In the other photo the ambassador's two daughters were sitting on a wooden fence in white dresses, their little hands clamped on the crossbeam. The wife and girls were giving Fritz admonishing looks.

"No bombers today?" von Günther asked the window. *Such is war,* Fritz thought—people gazed at the sky more than ever before.

"It's always tough on the children."

Von Günther nodded at that. "Well, I'm going home now, Kolbe. This stack of files must be destroyed. Take care of it. Our dear von Ribben-snob has signed off, all issues resolved." He laughed. "You know that snob married into money? Wife's family produces champagne. That *von* of his is yet another acquisition—belongs to some distant relative." He opened the door of his desk to pull out a green bottle of Henkell Sekt. He handed it to Fritz, saying it was a gift—the Office had enough of it. "If only von Ribbentrop were as bubbly as this champagne here, things would go down so much easier here at the Office."

"I completely agree, Herr Ambassador."

"This stays between us, naturally."

"I am always discreet."

Von Günther eyed him. "I know that, Kolbe. You could have gone far—you maybe still can. It's time you finally joined the Nazi Party. It opens doors for a fellow like you. You could get Norway—say, a lovely posting in Oslo. Consul. Ambassador. Who knows?"

Fritz pulled the stack of files toward him. It had hundreds of secret documents vital to the war effort, bearing the signatures of Hitler, von Manstein, Jodl, Himmler, and Goebbels. The cardboard covers alone made his hands itch. Ever since it had become clear to him that he couldn't keep going on as he had been, a charge of tense excitement had been running through his whole body, making him sometimes feel as though he might explode at the slightest touch.

"Ah, Kolbe," von Günther whispered with a sigh. "The women in Norway! The Führer would have no objections. Join the Nazi Party. It's only a piece of paper and a signature. Just pick up a pen."

Von Günther had started in on him early. His suggestion of a position in Norway caught Fritz completely off guard. He could get Katrin there, far away from the bombing raids and Nazi terror. A signature was all it would take. The form would be pushed along; he'd receive a number, a membership certificate, and invitations to various gatherings.

When von Günther had previously brought it up, Fritz had told him that he had to think it over. But Walter Braunwein had tried to talk him into it too. "You can be just as reserved when you're a Party member, old buddy," he'd said. Fritz still hadn't done it; he hadn't picked up the pen.

He'd tried avoiding von Günther for days, but soon ran into him in the hallway outside the Visa Department; von Günther had raised his eyebrows high on his forehead. He told Fritz he would have to consider just how much one individual mattered when compared to a mass movement—the way things stood, he could do very little for Fritz. Fritz had groped for some grand intellectual rationale, but it all came down to one simple conclusion: he could not join the Party of Adolf Hitler. It was as simple as that. Talking about it did nothing to change his mind.

Von Günther's words pulled him back into the present. The ambassador was now talking about the invasion of unoccupied southern France, where certain matters remained unresolved diplomatically. But he didn't want to make Fritz work late again.

What if I did work late, though? Fritz thought. The reality was, he told his boss, the job had to get done one way or another. He still had a few unfinished matters left on his desk.

"Well, I'm happy that you'll get a little peace and calm soon," von Günther said. "Neutral Switzerland. So beautiful and out of the way. Has Frau Hansen seen to your paperwork?"

"All taken care of, Herr Ambassador. It still might take a little while, though."

"I was at our Bern office once. Von Lützow is our man there, as you surely know. A little soft, but decent and dependable. When you have time, go see the promenade of shopping arcades—*Lauben*, they call them there; they're really quite charming." He stubbed out his cigarette until no more wisps of smoke rose up.

"It's about greatness, Kolbe. We live in horrible times, but horror produces greatness. There are awful deeds that must be carried out, just awful—yet great they are too. The Führer is the only one who's been able to create a practical plan inspired by the abstract notion of greatness. That's what we must grasp now. It is complicated. It is dreadful, yet intoxicating." Von Günther pressed the tips of his thumb and index finger together and moved his hand through the air as if sewing with a needle. "The end result will be stunning. All the sacrifices will have been worth it." He spread his fingers as if tossing something into the air. "And we? We are doing our part."

"Yes sir, Herr Ambassador."

"Greatness. Chin up. I come from the very bottom, Kolbe. Seven siblings. A sick mother. And where am I now?" Von Günther spread his arms. "It's about sacrifice. The system makes mistakes. That's intrinsic to any system. Mistakes will always happen when the goal is to motivate the political, social, and military masses. Blind obedience, for example—that's a mistake. The system should allow a little more freedom to develop, yes. I don't claim to know everything. It's tough going on intuition in times like these, to be sure, something I thoroughly regret at times."

"Yes sir, Herr Ambassador."

Fritz grabbed on to the sides of his stack of files. The stack was heavy, the paper bending under its own weight.

"Good night, Herr Ambassador."

"See you tomorrow, Kolbe."

Fritz clamped an arm around the files and pulled the door shut behind him. He sat down at his desk and pretended he was working until von Günther was gone.

It was quiet in the Office. The blackout curtains made the windows so dark, it seemed as if the Foreign Office building stood alone in a world in which everything else had been completely destroyed. Fritz stepped out into the corridor and looked around, at the rows of shut doors, the well-worn carpet, the dim ceiling lights. The portraits of Hitler, Göring, Heydrich, Goebbels, and von Ribbentrop seemed to follow him with their eyes. Von Ribbentrop loomed over Fritz from his picture frame. *High treason! I sentence you to death, Fritz Kolbe.*

Somewhere a door slammed, and Fritz jumped. Hanging his head, he went back into his office and pressed his back to the door. *Remain calm. Completely calm.* He shoved the files on the desk to the side, then he pulled them back to him and clicked on the lamp. He saw the swastika and the Reich Eagle. *Four years,* he thought. *Four years of pretending and lies, of humiliation, of work.* He was the inconspicuous civil servant Fritz Kolbe in the Foreign Office, Wilhelmstrasse 74-76, Berlin.

He poured himself a cognac. He usually didn't drink much, worried that if he got too drunk he'd end up venting all his raging hate. He took just a sip now and then to take the pressure off, to experience some inner calm, however artificial it might be. He waited about a quarter of an hour, then opened the door a crack and slipped back down the corridor, again under the gaze of Hitler and his cohorts. At the end of the hall, he looked left and right down the intersecting hallway and listened. His colleague Havermann was stepping out of his office.

"Ah, it's you, Herr Kolbe. Looks like quitting time," he said. Havermann placed a hand on Fritz's shoulder. He was saying something about music, then added that if anyone had a problem with what he'd said, they could "get in line." He kept talking until he reached the exit, where he said that he needed to get home now to his wife and daughter. "Music makes everything better, Herr Kolbe."

Back in his office, Fritz turned the key twice to lock it. He sat down at his desk and placed his hands atop the stack of files. The cardboard covers felt like a cool, compact sand. "It's your Papa here, Katrin," he muttered. He flipped open the top folder.

It was a letter. At the top of the page was written *Reichsführer-SS and Chief of the German Police, Berlin*, followed by the date and the Foreign Office's date-received stamp from one of von Günther's departments. *My dear von Ribbentrop!* the letter began. *Heartfelt thanks once again for the lovely evening at your home. You and your wife really do have a knack for such things . . .*

Fritz read about the meal served at the von Ribbentrop home and about the construction of V2 rocket facilities. The letter closed with *Heil Hitler*. Heinrich Himmler's signature was jagged, the *h*'s of his first and last names pressed hard into the paper.

Concerning the deportation of Roman Jews . . .

Concerning the development of the Messerschmitt Me 262 . . .

A general had written from the Eastern Front that morale among the soldiers was low and did not show courage. *One cannot tolerate this as it will eventually prove a danger . . .*

Fritz read about a meeting at Wannsee in January 1942, and about the practical implications of decisions made at that time regarding the Jewish Question. *Eradication. Extermination.* After that he looked in a folder with *Dear von Günther* written on it. It contained long columns of numbers listing munitions expenditures resulting from the liquidation of the civilian population and the detaining of various Jewish groups.

Fritz was horrified by the logic and consistency that was being applied across all branches of the Party in support of all the killing. "Jew-free" zones were declared once an area's Jewish inhabitants had been deported or murdered. There was a plan to let Russian prisoners of war starve to death. The stationery was divided into three columns:

men, women, and children; under these headings were four- and even sometimes five-figure numbers—a flood of horror and bloodshed.

My dear von Ribbentrop, another letter said. *A fabulous piece of work. We were able to recruit an agent right inside the British consulate in Ankara. Code name Cicero. An excellent investment of twenty thousand Reichsmarks.*

A diplomat from the embassy in Tokyo addressed von Ribbentrop as "Your Excellency" and with a tone of subservience reported that the will of the Japanese *Volk* and leadership to persevere could almost be described as German, notwithstanding the disparity in race that His Excellency does touch upon.

An SS general in Ukraine requested the support of regular Wehrmacht troops.

Fritz stumbled upon a letter classified confidential, in which his superior was addressed as *Von Günther, you old warhorse* and munitions was again the big topic. Following that was a report from a General Gehlen in Military Intelligence about enhanced interrogations of Russian prisoners in the Caucasus region, signed *Most sincerely yours, R. Gehlen, Foreign Armies East.*

Fritz read for hours. He was left speechless. The inhumane and asinine shouting of Hitler and his bootlickers would make any counterargument sound helpless and banal. He stared at his typewriter with its panzer-gray housing. It had a new key that could be found on no machines in the world but in Germany: *SS*, in runic script. Fritz tapped on it, then kept typing. He hit the return lever, the page ratcheting on to a new line. *SS*—just one stroke. He ripped the page from the roller, crumpled it up, and threw it into the trash basket.

Since von Ribbentrop had taken over the Office, more and more senior positions in various departments were being taken over by SS men. Von Ribbentrop was an *SS Gruppenführer* himself.

A few weeks earlier Fritz had, in accordance with regulations, taken on the job of ensuring that all secret files were incinerated in the sooty burn barrels down in the basement. Now, before burning these files, he locked them up in his safe, setting them alongside other secret files before rehanging a pastoral Allgäu landscape over the safe's steel door. Only with original documents would he be able to convince the British Secret Service in Bern. They would not otherwise welcome him with open arms. Old Consul Biermann had told him about the British having a station there, so Fritz had called Eugen Sacher to ask him if he still had good connections among the British, maybe even someone higher up in the embassy. Eugen asked why he wanted to know, then changed the subject to the good old times in Spain, but Fritz interrupted him.

"Do you, Eugen? Could you maybe find me a contact there?"

Eugen was silent a long while. Fritz kept the phone pressed to his ear, giving his friend time.

"What do you mean by that—a contact?"

"Can you or can't you, Eugen?" The tension made Fritz start giggling.

Eugen complained what a stubborn dog Fritz always was. He did have rather decent contacts among the Brits, he said—he even knew someone from the embassy.

"That'll do," Fritz said, and hung up before Eugen could respond. It wasn't polite, but it was for the best, all things considered.

He went into the bathroom, leaned on the sink, and took a good look at himself. His face remained calm; it didn't contort into some blue-and-red grimace. The face he saw in the mirror was the face Katrin knew—a face he hadn't seen in years.

Fritz rode his old Wanderer bicycle through the dark ruins over to the Kurfürstendamm. In the beginning he had parked his bike at the main entrance to the Office but was then informed that von Ribbentrop forbade this. He'd parked it on Wilhelmplatz ever since, at the entrance to the U-Bahn station.

The outside air and the pedaling did him good. Braunwein had set him up with a little apartment on the Kurfürstendamm, not far from Memorial Church. "Hey-ho!" he had said to Fritz, using that favorite greeting they'd shared since they were boys. "Welcome to your new domain, old buddy. Small, yet modest."

"Don't tell me—just like me," Fritz had said.

He stood his bike in the hall and made his way up the dark stairs to the top floor.

Inside his apartment's two rooms he checked the cardboard and curtains that covered the windows and then turned on the lamps. He used to hate the blackouts. Whenever the block's air-raid warden came into the apartment to check how sealed off it was, Fritz wanted to scream at him about how disgusting it was to shut out all light, but he always held his tongue. Now that his plans were coming to fruition, however, he viewed the blackout curtains as essential. He was now dark Fritz, secret Fritz. Deprivation of light and this dim somnolence better matched his life than did those grand Foreign Office windows on Wilhelmstrasse.

He boiled water, waiting till it started to bubble, and poured himself tea. His flash cards lay on the table. He'd been doing them for years to stay sharp. He read a series of numerals, turned the card over, and then went through the alphabet matching the corresponding ciphers: A=1, H=8, O=15. He wrote down twenty fictitious names on a new card, read the names seven times, and turned the card over.

He gazed at the framed photos that stood on the wall cabinet: Walter and Fritz on safari in South-West Africa, everything sunny; Käthe, Walter, Horst, and Fritz standing next to the car during their tour of the valley north of Cape Town. He had cropped the picture at his left shoulder because Katrin was standing next to him in the photo, and he wanted to keep anyone from learning of her existence, if possible.

Then there was the image of his deceased wife at a street café on the Gran Via in Madrid, her black hair full of shine. The Biermanns in the Cape Town consulate yard, elegant and cheerful. His parents in their warm upholsterer's workshop. One small frame in the back stood empty: the one that had held Katrin's photo, which he'd since put away. She must be bitterly disappointed that he hadn't written her a single letter. But his passage to Germany and those first few weeks in this hell had forced him to make certain that no censors, or henchmen, or anyone looking into either of them would have an easy time of it. He had to try, for her sake. He touched the empty center of the frame. "My dear Katrin," he muttered. "I'll explain it all to you one day."

He drank his tea and checked the card with the names—he had memorized them all correctly. Next to those he wrote aliases that he made up, read them seven times, and turned the card over.

He gazed at the photos again, at his people. He'd struck up few new friendships. The less people knew about him, the more inconspicuous he remained, the better. There was still Consul Biermann and his wife. But the old man had been booted out.

In their hypocritical thoughtfulness, the Nazis had at first assigned Biermann to a position in the Office. He was supposed to cultivate his old contacts in Spain; with all due respect to his personal connection with Molotov, others were taking over Moscow duties now. At first Fritz used to see him in the corridors of the Office, looking upright and stern, always in a gray three-piece suit and, after a few weeks, using a cane just like his wife. The more Biermann took part in conferences and meetings, the more stooped he became. Back in Africa he'd been energetic, but now he was an old man.

Biermann's pleasantly lucid voice got ignored during discussions held in the Office corridors. The young men in SS uniforms would cut him off midsentence and, laughing, leave him standing there. As they walked away, the old man would reach for their retreating backs, as if wanting to pull them back. Despite that, he didn't admit defeat, and to show his defiance he balled up his fists whenever he saw Fritz rushing from office to office with papers in his hands.

After his first private meeting with von Ribbentrop, Biermann had come into Fritz's tiny office in the Visa Department and closed the door. "I can't believe what I've just experienced," he said. "What an arrogant, ice-cold boor. Von Ribbentrop! Good God, to think he is the Foreign Minister. Why on earth does the Office, with such an illustrious history, need its own vile Jewish Department just like the Gestapo? It used to be that Berlin was swarming with foreign diplomats—and now? You have all these big-mouthed Fascist Italians, degenerate Austrians, and bored Spaniards, with occasionally a Japanese who probably feels as alien in Berlin as they would on another planet. What does Hitler need diplomats for, Herr Kolbe? We aren't diplomats anymore. Everything international has gone national. It's absurd."

The second one-on-one between Biermann and von Ribbentrop had occurred during that period of euphoria brought on by Germany's invasion and total defeat of France in 1940. Fritz didn't know exactly what had happened, and Biermann would not speak of the meeting. It was rumored that von Ribbentrop had launched into a rabid Hitler-esque tirade and then screamed at the old man. Biermann sat silently in his office the rest of the day. After that, he received a decoration and retired. There was nothing explicitly wrong with the man, von Günther had said, but he wasn't up with the times.

Months later, when Fritz's despair was raging more wildly, he had ridden over to the Charlottenburg neighborhood at night despite the curfew and glared up at the Biermann residence. "I was counting on you!" he had shouted into the darkness.

Fritz covered one side of the card and read the names out loud, then the aliases. He got two of them wrong. He pounded on the table with his fist, rattling his teacup. He read through the list of names once again and turned it over. He could see his face reflected in the glass-paneled book cabinet. Whenever he passed display windows on the Kurfürstendamm—some smeared with Jewish stars, others cracked and mended in makeshift ways—he saw a serious, forceful man who avoided his own glance. Back when this all began he had still hoped to lead a respectable life, but he quickly learned that such a life was not possible amidst this madness.

Covering one side of the card, he read the names again. This time he made no mistakes. He ate a piece of chocolate that he'd stolen from the Office, then brushed his teeth. He loosened the tongue and laces of his shoes so he'd be able to quickly slip into them should the air-raid sirens start howling in the night. He got his emergency bag ready for the bunker, and tossed the flash cards into the blazing oven. He lay down and stared at the ceiling. It would again be a long while before he could fall asleep.

The telephone rang. It could be von Günther, wanting to call him into the Office after receiving some important dispatch. Should he ignore the call? No—his cover as a particularly diligent and loyal servant had to be maintained.

It was Walter Braunwein. Walter gushed about all the good his diplomatic identity could still achieve. "To hell with curfew, Fritz. I was just in Paris, man. Listen, are you sitting down? I brought back Champagne. Genuine, real Champagne! I'll be at your place in ten minutes, old buddy. Hey-ho!"

Fritz polished two glasses, cleaned up the kitchen a little, and got dressed again. He felt his way along the dark hallway, down to the building's front door, and stepped out onto the quiet street, which smelled of grit and fires gone out. He saw a car with dimmed headlights coming up the Kurfürstendamm. Walter. He'd been on some sort of special mission again. *For the Nazis,* Fritz thought. *My friend, my good old friend.* The car stopped, and Walter climbed out waving two Champagne bottles. "Is this great or what?"

Fritz hugged him, feeling the bottles against his back.

As they climbed the steps back up, Fritz decided not to talk about the war or the Nazis. His friend was here, each day could be their last, and they had Champagne.

Walter popped the first cork at the ceiling before he'd even shed his overcoat and hat. He filled the glasses to the rim and the two of them toasted. As if reading Fritz's thoughts, Walter started talking about their safari in South-West Africa and their time together in Cape Town. They let themselves be carried away to bygone sights and aromas, revisited the safari photo, then moved on to Madrid, where Walter had become acquainted with his lovely Käthe. Fritz said he was a little worried about her. When he'd last seen her, she'd seemed nervous and a little pale.

Walter poured, sighing. He blurted out, "Oh!" and told Fritz all about Paris, about the grand boulevards and how peaceful it was there. France wasn't exactly Ireland, Walter said, but still. One barely noticed a war was on.

"In an occupied country?" Fritz said. "Filled with Wehrmacht soldiers?"

"Ah, come on, Fritz."

"Could you get Käthe out of here if you wanted?"

"Käthe?" Walter leaned back, the chair creaking. "You mean my wife. Tell me, old buddy, were you ever in love with her?"

"She is all yours."

"You introduced her to me, at the consulate in Madrid. And now here you are in Berlin, probably seeing her more than I do. But you know something? Even if you had been head-over-heels in love with Käthe, I know you never would've done that to me. You're a true-blue soul—that's what I appreciate so much about you. You're exactly the kind of man people mean when they say they can blindly depend on someone. And men like that are extremely rare in this Germany. So, to your health."

Walter set the empty bottle on the floor, paused a moment, and pulled something white out of the stove.

"Oh," Fritz said. "Give it here." He thrust out a hand for the piece of paper. It must have been from the flash cards he'd tossed into the flames.

Walter smoothed out the crumpled-up paper. "A bunch of names. Your headings are *fictional names* and *aliases*? Just the sort of neatness one expects from you. What's this about?"

"It's nothing. Give it here."

Walter looked at the list, then at Fritz.

"Just forget it," Fritz said. "Give it here."

"Why so annoyed?"

"Walter, Jesus, let's just have another drink."

"Are you doing memorization exercises? Is that it?"

Fritz didn't answer.

Walter handed him the paper, then slowly pulled the cork from the second bottle. "Don't bullshit me, Fritz."

His words receded into the corners of the kitchen. Luckily, in just that moment Fritz got the hiccups. By Fritz's third spasm, Walter started grinning. Soon they'd loosened up again, two men sitting in a tiny kitchen while a war was going on, each one trying to guess what the other was thinking. They slapped at their thighs and laughed, and the war was far, far away.

Late that night, Walter said he needed to head home to Käthe. He stared at Fritz from the doorway.

"Watch out for yourself, Fritz Kolbe."

With one hand feeling along the wall, Walter staggered down the stairs, cursing loudly when he missed a step and stumbled. "Fucking steps!" he shouted, then, "Hey-ho!"

"Be sure to tell Käthe hello," Fritz called after him down the dark hallway.

Back in the kitchen, Fritz dropped the newspaper onto the table. On the front page was a portrait of Hitler, in profile as it appeared so often. He stabbed a fork into the picture, right in the face. The fork robbed Hitler of his eyesight.

"Take that, you pig. This man is my friend."

6

Marlene and the Secret Files

Fritz had not yet dared to speak to her.

Thinking back to that time, he realized that the tiny Visa Department he always hated did have one good thing going for it: it was where he had first heard her laughter.

He had been out in the corridor. The laughter, a woman's, was coming through a closed door loud and clear. As he passed by he turned his head, hoping this unknown woman would open the door and come out before he reached his own. To him that resounding bell of a laugh represented evidence of genuine joy, in contrast to the men at the Office, whose harsh laughter carried such malice, such pomposity.

This laughter moved Fritz deeply. That a person in this world was still capable of laughing like that both appealed to him and unnerved him. It made him happy. But he couldn't just wait around to identify the source of the laughter; too many colleagues, who knew he never stood around idly, were on their way into the Office. Later, as he prepared travel visas for art experts who were being sent to requisition Göring's treasures in France, he considered asking Frau Hansen about the unknown woman, since that laugh had come from her office. Yet he also wanted to have as little contact as possible with other people at work.

As he was exiting his little office a few weeks later, he saw her: a tall woman in a dark-blue suit was just closing the door to Frau Hansen's office. He was sure this was the woman he'd heard laughing. She didn't work in the Office, or he'd have noticed her before. She wore a hat on her lush brown hair, her heels clacked against the floor, and the fabric of her suit shimmied at her hips and her shoulders. The woman had an energetic step. He followed her but realized he would need to hurry if he were to catch up. Two SS officers greeted her and watched her go by. She turned to the right, passed through rectangles of light in the main front lobby of the Foreign Office, and pushed open the heavy door to the Wilhelmstrasse. Fritz was about to follow after her when Ambassador with Special Duty von Günther and young Müller approached. Fritz had heard Müller was now working in the Transmitting and Deciphering Department. *"Heil Hitler,"* Müller said and marched on down the corridor.

Von Günther waved Fritz into his office. "Kolbe, Kolbe! Did I see you staring at that woman just now?" He laughed. "You only live once, yes?"

"I don't have time for such things," Fritz said.

"Well, in my opinion you should find some, yes? So, next on the agenda . . ."

And the horror went on. Such horror. It was so dehumanizing. Moments came when Fritz felt like he was clawing at his face, frozen in bewilderment, or screaming like a man buried alive in a collapsed mine. One such moment happened again on the day he saw the woman and, for the first time in so long, experienced feelings he thought he'd buried. As the strange woman turned toward the street door, Fritz briefly saw her profile. Her nose, straight as an arrow, gleamed in the light as if loving life with all its sensations. She was simply gorgeous.

Why now, just as he's telling them how he first met Marlene, does he have to remember the boy?

"I was riding my bike to see Consul Biermann and his wife in Charlottenburg," Fritz says. "I looked up to see men in uniform throwing a man out of a window from the third or fourth floor. At the next window, two more are forcing a little boy to watch. You hear what I'm telling you? Can you even imagine? And the boy's screaming, *Papa! Papa!*"

Fritz feels sick even now, remembering the man's frantic arm motions, as if he were yanking on cables in the air. The nausea squeezes his throat and his mouth tastes sour as he recalls the face of that little boy. No experience could've been more horrible for that child. Fritz has to blink away tears. Remembering events can hit him pretty hard, especially when they involve children.

"Did that incident make you decide to take things further?" asks Wegner.

"For God's sake, Wegner! Such decisive incidents came at us by the minute, constantly. Shit and more shit. They were laughing, those men."

He hears the screams from across time and space: *"Papa!"* He lights a cigarette, asks if anyone would like a schnapps. Veronika and Wegner nod, keeping silent. Maybe he's shocked them. It's tough to speak of something so horrific, and it must also be tough to write it all down. But it has to be done. He pours them his homemade stuff.

"Can't you just hear that boy?" he asks, feeling disgusted, angry, and bewildered. "What can a person say? What? I was also there when they were transporting Jews out of the city—women, children, men, old people, hit with clubs, spit on, and beaten to death out on the street. *Decisive incidents?* Goddamn right."

"So you couldn't do anything?" Veronika asks.

"What could I have done? Picked the man up? A hundred and seventy pounds, fallen from the fourth floor? Told the boy it'll be all right? Here's what I did: I puked. Then I rode to the Biermanns. Don't ask me what we talked about because I have no idea."

He drinks the schnapps. It is bitter and sweet in his mouth, burning at first, then he tastes the fruitiness come through.

"The people who are responsible for all this crap are now resuming their positions in the new administration, even in the newly formed Foreign Office. Do you understand what I'm saying? I ought to be sitting there! Me. Not them. But what am I doing? I'm looking out my window, never sure if the next car driving up the mountain is carrying men who've come to silence me for good."

Veronika and Wegner turn their heads and look out the window. Fritz grins. *Don't you two worry yourselves.*

"You're overstating things a bit, Herr Kolbe," Wegner says.

"Oh yeah? Do I know who tried to kill me? Has it ever come out? Gehlen's intelligence people? Russians? The old-boy network from the Office? Angry Swiss? Henchmen for that British double agent—who surely existed, even if to this day no one knows who it was?"

"Maybe we should get outside for a while?" Veronika asks.

Fritz switches to his hiking boots and laces them up firm around his ankles. The sun is high—*a sky like over Africa,* he thinks. Wegner taps his pen against his hand while Veronika gets her camera from the car.

"A few shots for scenery," she says. "It's tougher to get than people think. In the outdoors nature always looks so great, but in a photo it often comes across as terribly boring. You need specific objects as markers, trees or cliffs, to give it a certain structure."

"Like in my story?"

"Something like that, yes."

"Where is Marlene Wiese now?" Wegner asks.

"She's with Eugen Sacher in Bern," Fritz tells him, "doing a little shopping, having a nice coffee."

He leads his young visitors to a trail near the cabin that goes in a circle. They head uphill, the trail crunching under their feet, clumps of grass encroaching on both sides. Fritz loves the sound of hiking shoes on various natural soils. He's surprised at how close to the real story he's getting now that he's telling it to Veronika and Wegner. Staying sharp is vital now. He still isn't sure if he'll tell them all of it.

He plants his hands on his hips and looks toward the pointy white tips of the mountains. He plans to hike those too, to climb with a mountain guide to one of the summits and gaze down over the whole world. Maybe, up there, everything will look more insignificant somehow, and coming to terms with his past will come easier to him.

"Can I take a photo of you out here, Herr Kolbe?"

Fritz turns around to face Veronika. She smiles.

"I'd rather not, Fräulein Hügel. I'm not sure how to look into the camera."

"Do it the way you look in the mirror."

Again Fritz is amazed at how perceptive this woman is.

"That's one way of doing it, Fräulein Hügel. Let's wait on the photo, though."

"I'll be sure not to forget, Herr Kolbe."

They continue to follow the trail, which slopes down through a grove of blue firs. Around them, the branches creak and lizards scurry away into crevices seemingly too small for them. Once they're in the shadows of the firs, Fritz places a hand on Wegner's shoulder, though he's not sure exactly why.

"The closer I got to the files, and the clearer my decision became, the closer I got to Marlene."

"That's women for you." Veronika laughs.

"She was down in the air-raid shelter under the Adlon Hotel, where we always went when the bombers came. She was standing about ten yards away from me, and good old Frau Hansen from the Visa Department was right next to me. So I seized the opportunity. Frau Hansen told me the woman was the assistant for a surgeon at Charité Hospital, a professor. He traveled a lot, sometimes with her, sometimes without her. Frau Hansen thought she considered herself a little bit special. I liked that." Fritz looks up to the mountains. "But I didn't like the fact that she was married," he adds.

"But that didn't keep you away," Veronika says.

"Is that bad?" Fritz says.

"When it's love, it's never bad."

Fritz looks at her. She returns his glance, eyebrow raised. Fritz turns and continues down the path.

"When we get back I'll throw a few schnitzels in the pan," he says.

Fritz thinks about what he just told Wegner—how the closer he got to the files, the closer he got to Marlene Wiese. Wegner might think this was a fatal error. Fritz doesn't want that. Though he *should* want it, considering . . . *No!* No, he's had enough of *should*.

The trail leads them out of the fir grove and through a green meadow speckled white with stones, then swings up and around toward the cabin.

"And yet," Wegner says to Fritz's back, "couldn't you somehow have kept things from reaching the point they did?"

"No," he says, "I couldn't have. It was thousands of files, to be honest, thousands of them. It was impossible for me to pay attention to each and every detail. We always know better in retrospect. But hindsight—that's just armchair nostalgia."

"We're using hindsight right now," Wegner says.

Fritz hears the bombers over Berlin, sees Marlene's eyes. He feels the files in his hands, sees blood seeping out.

Right at that moment Veronika takes her first actual photo of him.

"Mad?" she asks.

"Yes," Fritz says.

"I don't mean at me," she says. "I mean your facial expression."

"I'd be mad," Wegner says. "I know I wouldn't be able to live with it—not with all the consequences."

Fritz jerks around and steps up close to him. He smells Wegner's aftershave. This is one of those moments where it annoys him he's not taller. Luckily Wegner isn't much taller, and Fritz is standing on higher ground.

"It could *never* have been avoided," Fritz says.

◆ ◆ ◆

Käthe Braunwein was biting at her thumbnail, a tiny crescent moon splitting apart. Fritz didn't want to watch. He was sitting with the Braunweins in their living room. Before them was a dry cake crumbling on a porcelain platter. Käthe was pasty white, and with her red-painted lips her face looked clown-like.

"So, you're here because you don't know what to say to this woman?" Walter asked Fritz.

"I wouldn't put it quite like that at this point. I'm really wondering what Katrin would think of her."

"What could Katrin say about a woman you haven't exchanged a single word with?"

"Yeah, I know. I don't know her at all, it's true." Fritz rubbed his forehead, then pounded his thighs. "But good gracious, that laugh of hers is so incredibly lovely. You have to hear it. And she looks so good."

He knew he was coming off like a schoolboy. Käthe chuckled. Fritz guessed she'd wanted to laugh outright but hadn't succeeded. She held her coffee cup with both hands and kept glancing over at the blackout curtains.

"There's so much that we cannot know," she said.

Walter's familiar face hardened as he looked at his wife. Käthe reached for Fritz's hand and looked him in the eyes. She suddenly looked quite lucid and calm.

"Speak to her, Fritz. Do it. Who knows how long any of this will be here?" She stood up and left the room.

"It's horrible to say it," Walter told Fritz, "but I don't know this woman anymore. The war and the air raids have changed her so much. Where did my Käthe go?"

"Do you even know yourself these days?" Fritz said.

"What's that supposed to mean? All I really want is to get my family to Ireland. It's what I've always wanted."

Fritz pointed at the bedroom door. Walter nodded.

When Fritz walked in, Käthe was lying on her stomach in bed, her forehead resting on her fist. Fritz sat down next to her, the bed springs squeaking.

"I could just scream all the time," Käthe said.

"Then at least one of us would be telling the truth."

She turned on her side and pulled up her legs. Fritz had often seen his Katrin lying in bed like that.

"You need to start laughing again, Käthe."

"What about?"

"I don't know. Go dancing with Walter. There's still plenty of dancing going on in this crazy Berlin of ours. Just dance."

Käthe used her index and middle finger to do little waltzing steps on the pillow.

"Forward, side, together; back, side, together," she muttered. "They first came during the night of June 7 and 8, 1940. Then January to March of '43. They unleash death from the skies, Fritz. Death. And fire—people inhale that fire."

She stared at the covers and stroked the linen like one would a child's cheek.

"Käthe?" he said. "Käthe?" She was vanishing right before his eyes, even though he could see her and his hand was resting on her shoulder.

As Fritz stepped out onto the street, a boy in uniform with bright-blond hair approached. Fritz rushed up to him and held out his arms. "Horst, my boy!"

Horst Braunwein clicked his heels together and thrust his arm into the air ramrod straight.

"*Heil Hitler,* Uncle Fritz."

Fritz's breathing constricted. He wanted to hug the boy but Horst pulled back, his glance and his eyebrows conveying resistance.

"Horst. It's nice to see you. Crazy running into you like this."

"Thanks. You too, Uncle Fritz."

Fritz reached out for the young man's shoulder. Horst pulled back again.

"Everything all right, Horst?"

"Of course it is."

"Remember us going fishing in Camps Bay?"

"In South Africa? They're the enemy, Uncle Fritz."

"Come again?"

"The enemy."

"But it was nice, though, wasn't it?"

Horst's face became expressionless. Looking at him, Fritz felt a strange sense of separation, as if the boy were standing on the opposite bank of a river.

"Your parents are upstairs," Fritz said. "Your mother's not doing so great, Horst."

"She shouldn't let herself go around like that."

"She is your mother."

"I have to go now, Uncle Fritz. *Heil Hitler.*"

"Yeah, yeah, sure."

Fritz trudged through the colorless, cratered wartime streets. *Now they've wrecked our kids too,* he thought. He sat down on the running board of a rusted-out car and looked around. In the early years of the war, Berlin had been a city of women, the men having all gone off to kill or to die, or to become crippled. Now more and more, women and children were being sent away from the city, and the men he encountered wore uniforms and were seeking things the war had already taken away. Nearby, a red swastika flag had fallen from where it had been hung. It lay on a double-decker bus, shrouding it like a casket.

It was weeks before Marlene showed up in the Office again. Fritz had made a habit of patrolling the Visa Department's hallway twice each day, hoping to hear that laugh again, or to catch at least a glance of her.

Then one day, she appeared. Fritz saw her walking down the hall and stood still, keeping a file folder clamped under his arm and waiting until she passed by.

"Good day, Frau Wiese."

She stopped and eyed him, her brows raised in amusement. "Do we know each other, sir?"

"Unfortunately, we do not," Fritz began. *Well done,* he thought, pleased with his response. She asked how he knew her name, and he told her he'd taken the liberty of asking Frau Hansen.

"Aha," she said. Fritz noticed that there were black freckles in the blue of her eyes. Her nose was straight as a ruler and her hair was the color of chestnuts.

"And why were you asking for my name?"

"I hate to keep seeing you without knowing your name. It's just not right."

"Well, now you do, so take a good look."

"May I invite you to coffee this Sunday?"

"I'm not sure."

"I am. Come on."

"This is moving pretty fast."

"Time isn't something we can take for granted these days."

With the tip of her index finger, Marlene pushed a strand of hair off her forehead. When she smiled, paper-thin creases appeared at the corners of her eyes. Two soldiers marched past her. Somewhere, a door slammed.

"A nice watery wartime coffee this Sunday, Frau Wiese? In our rather battered Berlin? Can I at least hope you will consider it?"

She turned her face away slightly and watched him from the corner of her eye. *Say yes,* he thought. *Come on, gorgeous.*

"Coffee is always nice," he added.

"Uh-huh."

"We could get something else if you'd like."

"Hmm."

"It would make me very happy." Make him very happy? What was he even saying?

Marlene smiled. "It would, huh?"

Back in his office he tossed the folder onto the desk with a flick of his wrist, danced a few waltz steps, and pumped his fists. She'd said yes.

A few days later they were sitting in a café on Mommsenstrasse. Marlene had removed her hat. Her hair was the color of fox fur, copper, and the setting sun.

She was telling him about her job at Charité Hospital, and about the internationally renowned work on creating prosthetics being done by her employer, the professor.

"He operated on his hemorrhoids," Marlene said.

"Come again?"

"My professor. He prettied up that little asshole. Himmler, I mean."

"By *that little asshole,* do you mean the man himself, or are you using it as an anatomical term?"

"Take it how you will, Herr Kolbe."

"They should have shown *that* story in the newsreels."

They laughed. Only two other tables in the café were occupied. Outside, gray heaps of debris were piled along the sidewalk, a rough path beaten through them.

"The demand for prosthetics is growing," Marlene told him. The professor traveled a lot, she said, and knew a bunch of the Nazi bigwigs personally.

"Is he a Nazi, Frau Wiese?"

"A rather accomplished one." She gazed out the low window onto the street, buried in rubble. "The man is truly good at what he does. He helps people. I help him."

"You get his travel papers from us at the Office. That's lucky for me."

Marlene lowered her head a little and turned away, smiling. Her nose looked a little broader from that angle. She took a small case from her purse, sprung it open, and pulled a cigarette out from beneath the elastic band. For the first time in his life, Fritz regretted not owning a lighter. Marlene waited a moment and Fritz patted at his jacket pockets stupidly as if a box of matches might appear. Marlene pushed her lighter across the table. Fritz clicked it and held his other hand around the flame unnecessarily as he moved it toward Marlene's face. Her lips were pale, and there were charming little creases at the corners of her mouth.

Fritz could only imagine how lovely she might look holding both a cigarette and a wineglass with the same hand. He called for the one-armed waiter and ordered her a glass of red wine.

"But I still have some coffee," she said. "You are a strange bird, Herr Kolbe."

"They used to say that about me in Africa."

"Africa? Do tell!"

She listened for a long time as Fritz recounted his memories. The streets outside turned grayer and grayer, the few other patrons left the café, and the waiter stood behind the bar, holding his arm across his body. Fritz did not mention a word about Katrin. His memories followed along two tracks, each leading away from the other. As he spoke, he realized that perhaps he should be more careful, that he was trusting this strange woman far too much, telling her too much, and that on no account should he dare reveal to her—even though he really wanted to—the plan he would soon be putting into action. In this country, a person couldn't trust anyone anymore. Not even a man like him could be trusted.

Marlene held her wineglass in the same hand as her cigarette, the white paper reflected in the swirl of red.

"Don't go getting your hopes up," she said, "thinking that I always do what another person wishes."

"That wouldn't be a hope—it would be a concern."

When they were finished, she didn't want him to escort her home. They said good-bye out on the street. After a few steps, she turned to him once more. He was certain she knew he'd be watching her go.

"I'm married, Herr Kolbe."

He wanted to say something, but didn't know what.

"This has been such a lovely wartime afternoon," she said.

"I can think of nothing better, Frau Wiese."

She smiled. "Now you're talking. I would not object if you should invite me again."

Fritz bowed. They were a sturdy, not-too-tall man in a suit and tie as always and a woman in a hat and mended dark-blue suit, standing among the collapsed buildings of a rotting city.

He watched her go. After hours spent in her company, he now felt even lonelier than before. Even if he had seen some small hints that he might be able to trust her eventually, he simply could not tell her about his plans.

7

THE FIRST TRIP

Berlin and Bern, August 1943

One day at the Office, two things happened almost simultaneously. First, a grumpy von Günther bounded into Fritz's office and tossed onto his desk more files intended for the burn barrel, then Frau Hansen knocked at his door and waved a piece of paper at him.

"You have a courier trip coming soon," she told him. "Berlin–Bern, Bern–Berlin. Lovely weather guaranteed. Say hello to Switzerland for me, Herr Kolbe. No bombs . . . my goodness, no bombs!" She placed a hand to her breast as if she needed to clutch something, and sighed.

That same evening Fritz called Eugen Sacher in Bern and told him the date he would be coming. "Listen, Eugen, tell your contact at the British embassy that an official from the Foreign Office is coming to Bern—with top-secret Nazi files for the British Secret Service."

The sound of a cough came over the receiver, then the line crackled. Eugen had probably dropped the phone, Fritz thought. Now that he was actually speaking the words, he felt his knees go weak. He sat down and pressed a fist to his forehead, as if trying to hold on to his decision with a firm grip and keep it crammed inside his head. He heard his name spoken incredulously.

"Fritz! Fritz, they'll kill you."

Fritz wanted to say that they wouldn't catch him, but the words, buried under mountains of fear and doubt, would not come out.

"You don't know a thing about this stuff!" Eugen shouted. "It won't work. Come to Switzerland—then just disappear. I'll hide you somewhere till all this crap is over. But don't be crazy. Top-secret files? Across the border? Fritz, for Christ's sake."

"Would you hide me?"

"Of course. I'd pick you up with a car somewhere in Bern. I'm a respectable citizen of good standing, beyond suspicion. No one would look for you with me."

Fritz hadn't even considered the possibility of going underground in Switzerland. He'd been too busy thinking about those swastika-bearing files. Sacher surely had a large wine cellar where he could disappear, but it was too late for that. Fritz could only laugh about it now. *Do what is right and have no fear.*

"Eugen, listen to me. The day before I arrive in Bern, make contact. That's all. The Brits will agree right away. They're good people. Churchill is the best man they could have in times like these. Eugen, old friend, you have to do this. You must do it for me. Now is the time when everything we do matters, when all the talk that comes so easily to people in peacetime means something."

"I have a wife and children, Fritz. I . . . I'll call you back."

There was a click and the line fell silent. Fritz sat on the kitchen chair as if nailed to it, pressing the handset to his temple. He wanted to climb on his bike and ride to Marlene's, to look up from the street and see if any sliver of light was coming from her apartment, maybe even ring the bell. But what could he possibly say to her?

He stood his globe next to the telephone. There, in a spot next to the broad, arching, bright-blue expanse of the Atlantic, was Katrin.

How big must his daughter have grown to be by now? Was she still so slim, her features so dainty and skin so fair below her cap of black hair? He ran his index finger from West Africa to the north, toward Europe. Germany–Switzerland; Berlin–Bern. Only a couple of inches. He'd journeyed far greater distances in his time. But this was no regular journey.

The telephone rang. Fritz placed his hand on the handset, feeling its sleek surface, then picked up. All he said was "Yes," saying it like a question instead of the exclamation he'd meant to shout.

Eugen told him he would do it.

Fritz grabbed the Allgäu landscape by the frame and carefully set it on the floor. The light from his window shimmered like gold dust on the matte-gray door of the safe. He turned the dial and pulled on the handle to open it. Inside was a stack of top-secret files and assorted pages, some corners dog-eared. Suddenly the walls of his office seemed to shift farther apart, and the room spun around him before lurching back again with a jolt.

He took out a few files and removed some papers from their cardboard covers with the red stripes. He wrapped the documents around his right calf, fastening them tight with string he had at the ready, before pulling his trouser leg back down. All this took less than a minute. Fritz felt thousands of disembodied eyes watching him. As if not quite fathoming what he had just done, he started to type a cover letter for an inspector heading to the Eastern Front. He made so many mistakes that he ripped the page from his typewriter and threw it into the wastepaper basket. The documents felt heavy against his leg. *Keep calm. Keep calm. Come on now.*

He turned out the lights in the office and stepped into the corridor, hoping not to run into anyone. His colleague Havermann said hello and struck up a conversation about music again, but it was so irritating, so odd, that Fritz found himself stammering, "What? What?" Havermann laughed and placed a hand on his shoulder. Two women from the Visa Department walked by, looking at him and smiling. Why were they all still here at this hour?

At the end of the hall leading to the Wilhelmstrasse exit stood Müller, reading a telegram. "*Heil Hitler.* You look as pale as you did back on the ship from South Africa, Herr Kolbe. Not doing so well? Think of our men at the front."

"Don't listen to him, Herr Kolbe," Havermann whispered. "Tell me, do you know Dvořák's *New World Symphony?*"

Fritz dressed himself in an ironed white shirt and black suit, and then added a dark tie and dark hat. He wanted to look as stern and serious as possible. He had arranged to have the document boxes for the German diplomatic mission in Bern brought to Anhalter train station, and von Günther had given him a briefcase with sealed documents.

Fritz could feel the documents along his right calf. He had pulled his stockings up over them.

"I've vouched for you, Kolbe," von Günther said. "You do know that everyone sent on a courier trip undergoes a thorough check? I declared you *absolutely trustworthy* and *completely beyond suspicion.* Even so, I won't be able to do a thing for you if those documents don't arrive safely in Bern."

"Yes sir, Herr Ambassador."

"Give von Lützow my best. He's always happy to hear any news from Germany—he doesn't know how good he has it in Switzerland. Between you and me, a posting there is absurdly cushy, yes? Well, then. *Heil Hitler.*"

"Hi Hitler," Fritz replied. He couldn't help leaving off the *l*, just subtly enough that no one seemed to notice—von Günther certainly didn't. The tiny acts of resistance counted for something too. "Herr Ambassador," he added.

Charité Hospital wasn't far from the Office, on the opposite bank of the Spree. Fritz asked for the office of a Marlene Wiese. He climbed the stairs and walked past operating rooms and a cabinet of preserved hands and intestines, past Hitler portraits and charts of human bodies shed of skin. Through the door he heard the staccato clacking of a typewriter and her voice, in response to his knock, saying "Come in." Marlene didn't turn around right away. She sat leaning slightly forward, bent over a page that was curling out from the typewriter. She was wearing a white blouse and he could see the clasp of her bra through the fabric. She'd tied her hair in a ponytail. Observing her from behind like this, without her watching him, made him feel both nervous and happy.

"I came to say good-bye," he said.

She moved her face away from the paper, an invisible bond seeming to sever within her, and looked at him.

"Herr Kolbe."

"A work trip to Switzerland. Can I bring you back anything?"

"Chocolate?" She offered him a seat and asked if he had time for a cup of watery coffee. He didn't, he said, but would take one anyway and could run to the train station after—he was still in good shape. Marlene left the office for a moment. Fritz looked around. There were prosthetic legs in one corner—metallic constructs with ball joints and leather parts. In a vase on the desk were dried flowers. It touched Fritz that Marlene still had that pale bouquet, its stems so flimsy that the slightest bump might break them. Old maps hung on two of the walls.

"My husband is a cartographer," she said when she came back and found him standing before the maps. *I don't want to talk about your husband right now,* he thought, but didn't say it. *Right now I want to lock this door, lift you onto the desk, rip off your blouse, push up your skirt, remove your panties, and make love to you. Tomorrow I might be a prisoner of the Gestapo.* He didn't say any of that either.

He wondered for a second why he didn't. *Do what is right and have no fear.* In a few hours he'd be risking his life at the border, and because of this shitty war he didn't dare tell Marlene what he really wanted to do. Instead he thanked her for the coffee. He looked into her eyes and tried to read her thoughts. She looked so young. Was it possible that she was thinking and wanting the same things as he?

"When I'm around you I always feel like a schoolboy," he confessed.

"I make you nervous, Herr Kolbe?"

"Isn't it a little mean for you to ask a question like that?"

"A little, yes."

A shudder of resignation rippled through Fritz. This woman was married, and there was no way he could possibly tell her what he was planning, no matter how much he would love to confide in her. She must be able to tell from the way he looked that he'd suddenly been deprived of something important.

"How do you think this all will end?" he asked.

Her face grew earnest, the muscles of her broad cheekbones tightening. She popped open the cigarette case and Fritz gave her a light with the lighter he'd bought right after they first met.

"We will pay, Herr Kolbe, everyone in their own way. My son, Hans, he . . ." She exhaled deeply as if freeing herself from more than just the smoke. "That was only 1940. Yet we keep living."

"I'm so sorry about your son, Frau Wiese . . ."

She raised her hands, a shield. Fritz couldn't imagine losing Katrin. He muttered a curse.

"Could you ever leave here?" he asked her.

"What about the patients? I'm a trained nurse, and I've been promoted to the professor's personal assistant. Also, my mother still lives in Berlin. No, I can't leave." She gazed around the office as if looking for someone else who was present. "This here, this is what I do. For me it has nothing to do with politics. I try anyway."

"I'll be coming back." He'd told Katrin the same thing, in Africa, about a hundred years ago. He looked her squarely in the eyes.

"In case we never see each other again, Frau Wiese, I'd like to tell you how very lovely it's been to at least get to know you. It was such a pleasure. I'm hoping, well . . . that you'll watch out for yourself."

"Why wouldn't we ever see each other again?"

"I'll be sure to get the chocolate."

"Then we'll certainly see each other again, Herr Kolbe."

"It's Fritz."

"Fritz. Call me Marlene."

He held out his hand. Feeling her skin against his did him good. Her hand was warm and her grip firm. From the doorway, he turned to her one more time.

"I'll tell you all about it one day."

She put out her cigarette.

"No matter what it is," she said.

The train station was bathed in a bluish light, all the regular lamps having been replaced with blue-tinted ones. The mighty locomotives bore swastika symbols. Metal grinded harshly against metal, a gigantic forge in the cold light. Women with children shoved their way into the cars, suitcases got jammed in narrow doorways, announcements were barked, and whistles sounded. Fritz's ticket was for the first car, special reserved seating. He was about to haul himself up the steps when he heard someone shout his name. The shock of it drove through his chest like the blow of an axe. He clutched the metal handrail and looked around.

"Hey-ho! I'm not about to let you go running off to Switzerland without saying good-bye."

"God, Walter."

"What is going on with you? You look like you just saw a ghost."

"You scared me to death, that's all."

"Fritz? Everything all right?"

"I'm fine, Walter. My mind was just elsewhere."

"With that woman?"

"Marlene, yes, that's right."

"You described her to me so thoroughly, I feel like I already know her. A fantastic woman, Fritz. What are your chances?"

Fritz placed a hand on his heart.

"You're alone too much," Walter observed. "You might be getting a little strange."

"Only since I've been back in Germany. Things weren't like this before."

The conductor blew into his pipe, doors were slammed shut, and the locomotive pumped out smoke.

"I have to go, Walter. It was good of you to come."

They shook hands.

"Friendship might be the only thing we have left," Walter said, looking around them.

"What kind of mess have we gotten into here?"

"I don't know. None of it should have ever been allowed to happen. And now it's our life. Not exactly heroic."

"Take good care of yourself and Käthe, Walter. And of Horst."

Fritz found an empty compartment, pulled the door shut behind him, and closed the thin curtains. At 8:20 p.m. on the dot, the train started rolling out of the station, and Fritz wanted to see nothing more of Berlin. If anyone searched him, he was a dead man. The worst part was that he wouldn't be able to defend himself. He had no weapon. Bringing one hadn't been an option. He could practically feel the Gestapo men's firm grip on his upper arms, and he had no clue how he would endure what would surely come next.

There was still time to stop it from happening. It would be easy enough: pull down the window, feel the wind and smell the steam of the locomotive toiling away, then loosen the papers from his leg and toss them out . . . Done. Only a simple few seconds, during which weakness would feel like strength. Afterward he'd be free, and his right leg so much lighter. He could stay in his job for the rest of the war, and no one would make von Günther's secretary face trial if they lost. He would make it through this—he would stay alive in order to testify against von Günther later.

He grabbed for the curtains with both hands, yanked them open, and saw his pale reflection in the glass. *Do what is right and have no fear.* He exhaled a long, deep breath, his face vanishing in the fogging glass. He pulled the curtains shut again and took his passport out of his jacket pocket. *German Reich*, it read, and below those words were the eagle with the slanted swastika and *Ministerial Passport*. He scratched at the swastika with his fingernail, harder and harder until a hint of golden dust was left on his fingertips.

He tried to read and play a little chess with his travel set. He ate his bread and cheese and drank lukewarm ersatz coffee from his thermos. At a stop in Heidelberg, a man in a suit shoved open the door to his compartment. Fritz stared at him and the man closed the door again.

As the train barreled onward, Fritz's dim and clattering cell delivered him ever closer to Switzerland.

He had to get off the train in Basel, along with everyone else. The border station there served as the final German enclave before entering supposedly neutral Switzerland, Marlene had told him. She'd once visited Switzerland with the professor, who had thought the place was teeming with secret agents—said you never knew whom you were talking to.

Exhausted, with stubble on his face, Fritz stepped from his car, glanced at the guards at the border crossing, and walked down to the baggage car. There he saw to the usual cargo boxes from the Foreign Office. Red Reich flags hung from the station ceiling, and soldiers with rifles on their shoulders stood on both sides of the checkpoint, staring at passengers, their steel helmets harshly reflecting the light.

Fritz's calf itched. His heart constricted. He tucked his briefcase up under his arm, prickling with sweat, and stepped into line with the other passengers who were waiting at the checkpoint. The border inspector was checking people quickly before bossily waving them through. There was still time to turn around, go to the toilet, consign the documents to that rushing suck of water. *No. No!* There would be no more turning back.

He heard a locomotive rumbling, giving off steam, breathing heat; he heard a woman call shrilly for her child. As he got closer and closer to the border inspector at the desk in front of the customs hut, he felt a growing urge to urinate.

When the border inspector waved papers at a little elderly man, two uniformed men stepped out of the customs hut, walked around the corner of the inspector's desk, and silently led the man back inside. They'd be conducting a body-cavity search, Fritz knew. He wondered according to what criteria the men were picking out passengers. Were they choosing based on some kind of quota, or by looking deeply into eyes that could not stay still?

Fritz's stare dug into the bright overcoat before him, belonging to a woman with a dark mole on the back of her neck. The inspector was holding her ID. For a second he glanced past the woman and into Fritz's eyes. A slight twinge happens when one person is looking at another right at the moment the other person notices. Fritz smiled. The man slapped the woman's ID wallet shut and said, "Next!"

Be calm, hand of mine, Fritz prayed. He felt the urge to twist his body somewhat due to the sweat under his arm. He showed the inspector his ministerial passport and visa without comment. The man watched him, his eyes small.

"What do you have in your case, Herr Kolbe?"

Fritz opened the leather flap, pulled the sealed folders out a bit, and let them slide back down.

"Not so fast!" The inspector pulled the case open and ran his fingertips along the edges of the folders. "You have four days in Switzerland, not a minute longer," he said. "Carry on! Don't just stand here, keep going."

Fritz didn't hear a single sound come from the hut. He hurried to the first toilets he found and urinated for so long he had to prop one hand against the wall. He stood at a sink and tore his shirt off, grabbed the bar of soap from his suitcase, and washed away the sweat. His hands still trembling, he pulled on a fresh shirt, tied his tie, and slid down along the tile wall to the floor. He stayed there, clutching at his forehead, until the washroom door opened. He fought his way up at once, whistling the overture to *The Magic Flute*, grabbed his things, and rushed out past the person entering.

Outside, the commotion at the train station spun all around him: women, children, men with hats cocked at an angle, distorted sounds, the shop windows reflecting harsh sunshine. Fritz chased down the streetcar that connected to trains of the Swiss Federal Railways and got on the one to Bern. Only when he was leaning his forehead against the cool window and saw the blue sky over the silhouettes of those striking mountains did his breathing begin to slow, and the itching on his calf lessen.

He had four days to carry out his plan. The whole first day he had to spend in the German diplomatic mission on Willading Lane. This outpost of the Foreign Office was housed in a villa with green window shutters and a yard with severely pruned shrubbery. Fritz sat with Consul von Lützow and his secretary, Weygand, in an office that smelled of freshly brewed coffee. Von Lützow, a man with very dark hair and a stature similar to Fritz's, asked about conditions in Germany and all the work being done by von Ribbentrop. Von Lützow said he'd only met the Foreign Minister once. "One does feel a bit left to oneself at times," he said.

Just as Fritz was hoping he would finally be taken to his hotel, von Lützow invited him to dinner with his family. Fritz declined, citing the long trip and the fact that he hadn't slept well.

"Come now, Herr Kolbe. My wife's German culinary skills will keep you going." Von Lützow reached for the silver-framed photo on the desk. His wife had a broad, stern face, with lively dark eyes. "It was not easy for her to leave Berlin and come here with the children to join me. Not to worry: after we eat I'll have you driven back to the hotel in my car. Do not be deceived by appearances, Herr Kolbe—we may not have to endure all those air raids here, but life is hard nonetheless. You wouldn't believe what administrative hurdles we have to jump, and one thing"—he wagged his index finger—"one thing is clear: Bern is teeming with spies. Our intelligence section never complains about having too little to do. Yet even here, Herr Kolbe, Germany remains unbeatable. Whenever Churchill, Roosevelt, or Stalin sends his agents here, we know about it. Isn't that right, Herr Weygand?"

Von Lützow's secretary hadn't yet said a word. A smile was stuck on his face. He was a pallid man with a cleft chin. Fritz noticed that Weygand balled his right hand into a fist at random intervals. Before Weygand could reply von Lützow rubbed his hands together and said, "Dining and drinking heal body and soul. Don't be shy; we have enough. And the scenery here, Herr Kolbe . . . If you had more time I could suggest several hiking routes. Splendid."

At dinner, von Lützow's wife told Fritz about the good standing German women enjoyed and the crucial role they played in raising children. Her three daughters sat lined up along the long side of the table, against the wall, speaking only when asked. Frau von Lützow's actual face was not as pleasant as the image of it Fritz had seen in the consul's office. She had something hard about her, and when she glanced at a person, her eyes narrowed to slits. Weygand eyed Frau von Lützow, sliced his roast into very small pieces, and leaned into his fork. When von Lützow asked Fritz about his thoughts on Hitler, the realization hit Fritz that he was being interrogated, and detailed questions would follow any second. They had seen right through him this whole time and knew why the skin of his calf still stung.

"Herr Kolbe? Our Führer?"

Fritz spread out his arms. "What else can be said that hasn't been already?"

Frau von Lützow nodded favorably; Weygand watched Fritz from over his fork, a piece of rosy-red meat raised near his eyes.

"We're depending on him," von Lützow said.

"Depending?" Frau von Lützow said. "My dear husband, there's far more to it than that."

"There's International Jewry, for one," Weygand said.

"Hear, hear," Frau von Lützow said. *"Heil Hitler."*

"Heil Hitler," said the three children.

"Hi Hitler," Fritz said. Weygand scrunched his eyebrows, while Frau von Lützow cleared her throat and wiped an imaginary crumb from the corner of her mouth.

After dinner, Weygand escorted Fritz to the door. A long black sedan with swastika standards on the fenders stood waiting beyond the front yard's angular shrubbery.

"Always so quiet, Herr Weygand?" Fritz asked.

"I'm waiting."

"What for?"

Weygand opened the car door for him. Darkness loomed inside. "Get in," Weygand said without looking at him.

In his hotel room, Fritz threw his suitcase onto the bed and washed his face with cold water. Putting his hat back on and pulling up his collar, he rushed back out into the night. On the drive over he'd spotted a nearby telephone booth.

Eugen answered cheerfully, but Fritz cut him off.

"I'm in the Hotel Justicia on Bubenbergplatz. Come here as soon as you—"

The phone booth lit up, a glare reflecting around Fritz. A car was coming around a curve. It passed the booth, returning Fritz to murky darkness.

"As soon as you make contact. Eugen? Are you doing this for me or not?"

The handset at his ear grew warmer and released a stammer from Eugen. Fritz gave him a moment.

"All right. I'll try. I'll come see you after. And Fritz? Have a big drink waiting for me."

"You bet I will. They have to bite. They'll be eating out of your hand. And I'll deliver too. So that all this miserable crap can end as fast as possible. I want the Nazis destroyed. I want to go to Africa. I want to see Katrin, Eugen—I want to hold my daughter again."

Fritz went to hang up the phone but had one more thing to add.

"And Eugen? Don't mention my name."

In the hotel bar a few guests, couples mostly, remained at the tables lit by little red lamps. One man in a hat was sitting alone, reading a newspaper. Fritz kept an eye on him. He drank a whisky, but even that failed to slow the beating of his heart. He smelled cigarette smoke in the air and listened to the couples around him chattering, the variety of tones blending together in a kind of gentle background music.

A car pulled into the parking lot, its headlights coloring the bushes yellow, and then the lights went dark. The car doors stayed shut. Eugen probably still had his hands on the steering wheel and was thinking about driving off.

"Come on, Eugen, get out," Fritz muttered. After a few minutes the driver's door opened slowly. The weak light of the hotel windows and streetlamps made Eugen's suit look as though it were coated in an amber powder. Fritz raised a hand in greeting but Eugen couldn't see him yet.

They hugged hello, two old friends who'd hadn't seen each other for a long time. The newspaper reader glanced at them, folded up his paper, and left. They watched him go.

"Nice hotel," Eugen said.

Fritz placed a hand on his upper arm. "It's great to see you."

Eugen only wore perfectly fitted suits and tonight was no exception. His nose looked too big for his face, and he kept his short gray curls under control with plenty of combing. Fritz wanted to ask how things were going with his friend, but now was not the time for friendly chatter.

"What did the British think, Eugen? What did they say?"

"I'd really like a whisky."

"What's wrong?"

"Yeah, well, what can I say?"

"Eugen!"

"They aren't interested."

"What?"

"It was all for nothing, Fritz."

Fritz sank down deeper and deeper in his armchair, a feeling of emptiness and the darkness of the room enveloping him. "I never even got upstairs," he heard Eugen say.

It had all been for nothing. This could not be. This simply was not true.

"Fritz, don't take this wrong—but you don't have a clue about how all this works. It's pointless."

"I'm going over there myself."

"For Christ's sake. You can't take the risk. You think the Germans aren't watching the other embassies? You can't go there, Fritz. Pull yourself together and think. You always were a dreamer—but now is not the time for naïveté."

"Naïve? Me? I have in my possession documentation on the deportation of Jews, massacres in Russia committed by the Wehrmacht and SS, agent networks in North Africa and Turkey, and tungsten deliveries from Spain, which are crucial for the war effort. We can save lives with these documents, Eugen. I don't need to tell you what the Nazis are doing to the Jews, do I? I can shorten the war. I can arrange for the Jews to be saved. So don't call me naïve. You're the one who should think. Who else do you know in Bern? What other connections do you have? Is there anyone else who can help?"

Fritz could barely restrain himself. Rage howled within him, making his whole body ache. He needed to get out of this bar. He waved to Eugen to follow and headed up to his room. So as not to cause a racket, he grabbed a pillow and beat it against the bed until feathers flew and he was left panting. He could have been bound to a chair naked by now for his efforts, beaten and humiliated, debased and then murdered. And the British didn't want to talk to him?

"The Americans," Eugen said. "There definitely are a couple of contacts I could try. I'll drop in on the Americans. All right?"

Fritz stood among the feathers, the shredded, empty pillow in his hands, feeling as grateful as he had the day Katrin was born.

"I don't have much time, Eugen."

"I'm on it, Fritz. Try and calm down now. Get some sleep."

Fritz spent half the next day with von Lützow and Weygand and, after that, worked with various consular departments, going through the bulk mail with staffers and pointing out various issues. Later, he had an appointment at the bank that arranged the Foreign Office's secret payments abroad. In nearly every room and hallway, Hitler and von Ribbentrop, in black and white, eyed him from the walls. Fritz was constantly going into the restroom to sit on the toilet and massage his temples. He could hardly bear the turmoil inside him. He was sweating, and it felt as though his heart were pounding up into his throat. He could no longer tell what acting normal was supposed to look like. Every time someone entered a room he heard handcuffs locking shut. He smiled plenty, said his "Hi Hitler"; once his agitation got really bad, he declined every cup of coffee offered him, for fear it would slip out of his fingers. At five o'clock he called Eugen from a phone booth.

"I have a contact, Fritz. Tonight. One a.m."

Fritz went into a candy shop on Rathausgasse and bought several big bars of chocolate for Marlene Wiese. In his excitement he devoured one on the spot and bought another to replace it. In the A. Francke bookstore, right behind his hotel on Bubenbergplatz, he bought splendid editions of Tolstoy's *War and Peace* and Melville's *Moby Dick*. He paged through both novels, read some passages, and thought to himself that everything he was doing here would need to be written down. He'd never written anything before, but he suddenly found himself wondering where he should begin if he ever found the spare time to chronicle his life up to this moment on a park bench in Bern. He shut his eyes and turned his face to the sun, and felt it shining through his eyelids, warming his skin and relaxing him for a few seconds.

Maybe he had drawn too much attention to himself already in the way he'd kept asking Frau Hansen about possible trips to Switzerland, by being too open about seeking contact with the Brits here in Bern. Who knew? If he were to fail at this point, no one would ever learn what he had planned. And how could he know that Eugen hadn't stumbled into a trap? He held up the novels, one in his left hand, the other in his right: books with heft to them, physically as well as emotionally. Good books. He overheard mothers speaking with their children, the street-car jingling, and the Aare River rushing by, flowing around Old Town in the shape of a *U*—no soldiers, no swastika flags, no air-raid sirens turning people into wide-eyed, scampering hordes disappearing deep underground through some bottleneck of an entrance. Peace. The sky above was that same African blue. Flowers bloomed in window boxes and the shop windows were full of cheese and sausages, fresh fruits and bread. If only the tip of Marlene's lovely nose could touch one of these shop windows. Berlin was a pestilent boil compared to this town.

Fritz crept into the car and gently shut the door as he turned to Eugen in the driver's seat.

"Who are we meeting?"

Eugen, not quite hearing Fritz, only stared as if he still couldn't believe this was happening. Fritz cleared his throat and repeated the question.

"Officially, an American trade representative. I was on the phone for hours and met with people I'm sure weren't really who they claimed to be. Still, I get the impression the Americans are somewhat more interested."

"Were you on the phone with a lot of people?"

"Several, yes."

"And you're certain they were all Americans?"

"Yes. Well, I mean, how was I supposed to know?"

The car rolled quietly down the narrow, old lanes, the buildings drifting by Fritz as if on film, dreamlike: stretches of wall yellowing in the headlights, hundreds of dark windows eyeing him.

"I wrote my will, Eugen. Here. Open it only if something happens to me. There's a letter to Katrin. But only send it once Hitler is dead."

Eugen slid the envelope inside his coat. "If something happens to you," he said, "I might not learn of it until years later."

"Katrin has to know why I never got in touch with her."

"Everything is going to be fine."

"A nice saying. But only when it's true."

Eugen slowed the car and let it roll to a stop along the sidewalk, looking around them. "How are things in Germany, by the way?"

"Horrible as ever. Hitler keeps an iron grip on everything and everyone. Do you know how he does it? Give the petty dumbshits some power, just a little, then let them go order the others around. They'll all crawl so far up your ass, they'll never get out again."

"You never would have talked like that in the old days."

"They threw a man out a window right in front of his son, Eugen. Just like that. Such things are allowed now. It's completely out of control. Inhumanity has become a virtue. It's madness, old friend. Madness."

Together they looked out onto the street, at stately homes forming dark silhouettes in the night, the overhangs of windows and doorways tawny in the streetlamp glow.

"See that lovely mansion there, Fritz? Herrengasse 23. You're supposed to go around back to the right and through the yard. Someone's expecting you at the back door. If you think you've been followed, you're supposed to stay away. You have the documents?"

Fritz pulled up his trouser leg, loosened the string, and held up the papers. They smelled like him and were shaped like a plaster mold of his leg.

"I'll wait here," Eugen said. "Doesn't matter how long it takes. Really a lovely mansion."

Fritz wiped sweat from his forehead. "A car only makes us stick out more. But have it your way."

He climbed out of the car and quietly closed the door. He looked around, the night pressing at him from all sides. He tapped gingerly on the side window. Eugen leaned across the seat and rolled down the window.

"What if we have it wrong, Eugen? What if it's a trap?"

"You don't have to do this," Eugen whispered, cupping his mouth. Fritz took a deep breath. The air was nice and cool. He could feel fear battling to keep him from taking action.

The city was still, the shadows deep and never-ending. He walked down the street until he reached the three-story building, then stopped and looked around. He saw blackness enveloping the street, places to hide, ribbons of light from windows above. He turned down the narrow lane along the side of the building and found a wooden garden gate.

It was dark in the backyard, the shrubs forming black talons against the gray-lit lawn. A door was opened and dim light rolled a yellowish carpet onto the steps. Fritz saw the silhouette of a slender man in the doorframe. Was this his contact? Was this shadow the person he would be trusting with his life?

"Are you the official from Berlin?"

Fritz felt the gate's wood grain, dry to the touch. Who was this shadow man?

"Well?"

"I am."

"Come in. Quick."

Fritz pushed the gate open and walked toward the light. The American shut the door and looked out its round window into the backyard. Then they faced each other in a narrow hallway that was tiled halfway up the walls. The man was young and wiry, and had brown hair. He stared into Fritz's eyes, his features unmoving.

"Arms up."

"What?"

"Arms up!"

Fritz only raised his hands.

"Mister, you don't need to go surrendering just yet. I need to search you for weapons."

"I'm not carrying a weapon."

"Arms up."

The American felt under his armpits and around his hips and upper thighs. The search was intimate and offensive.

Another man emerged from a cellar door, yanked up his overcoat collar, and slipped outside.

"He's going to make sure no one's followed you."

"There wasn't anyone."

"If there was, you definitely wouldn't have noticed. Now follow me."

"Please."

"What?"

"Now follow me . . . *please.*" On top of his fear, on top of the sweat and the nerves burrowing inside him, Fritz was in no mood to be ordered around in Bern too.

"Listen here. You might be some kind of joker but don't go getting funny on me. You Nazis—"

Fritz shoved him up against the wall. The young man freed himself from Fritz's hold in a split second and yanked his arm up behind his back. Fritz's right shoulder strained against the man's grip, the joint wanting to pop. He groaned with pain and anger.

"Don't ever call me a Nazi again. You hear me? Never again. You asshole."

"You don't want to pick a fight with me."

"Let me go, for God's sake."

The young man pushed him away and plucked his lapels to straighten them. "If I may introduce myself, Herr . . . ?"

"Kolbe, Fritz Kolbe. I'm bringing you important intelligence."

"We'll see about that, Herr Fritz Kolbe. Now follow me, *please.* With plenty of sugar on top."

Furious, Fritz followed him down the hallway. They walked up a wide and echoing stairwell to the second floor and entered an outer office. Inside, a woman was sitting at a desk. When she saw Fritz, she let out a puff of cigarette smoke. She wore her hair up and had on a white blouse. On the desk stood a bouquet of flowers in a crystal vase. The young man knocked on the only other door in the room, then opened it and waved Fritz through, the woman watching him go. Fritz wasn't sure, but he thought she'd just winked at him.

The office was lit by two floor lamps and the desk lamp. The fireplace held an unusually large amount of ash for summertime. The man behind the desk looked big. He had a mustache, wore glasses, and was dressed in a three-piece suit. He was puffing on a pipe.

"This is Fritz Kolbe," the younger man said. He had left the door open and Fritz could hear the woman rustling paper in the next room. The older man came around the desk and shook Fritz's hand, his grip as firm as Fritz's. No one said anything. No one moved. The whole scene seemed frozen in time. The younger man walked around Fritz like a museum visitor around a statue. He exchanged glances with the older man. Were they about to start laughing? Would they pull out their Gestapo IDs? Had poor Eugen already been arrested down at his car? Fritz cleared his throat. The older man smiled, offered him a seat, and asked him if he'd like a drink.

"I am Mr. D," he said. "The young man there is Mr. P, trade representative."

Mr. P poured three glasses of whisky. Mr. D leaned against the desk and watched Fritz. They toasted.

"Our Mr. P here gets a little forceful," Mr. D said. "Don't take it personally. He's a good man. I only have good people here, Herr Kolbe. We're constantly exposed. International trade. Such are the times. Business is not exactly easy. Now, this contact of yours—"

"Sacher," Mr. P said. "Born February the third—"

"Okay, Mr. P, okay," said Mr. D. "This Sacher fellow has indicated you might have something for us. Something important."

Fritz hesitated. It was maybe five steps to the door, then the woman's office, then the stairwell.

"Well, Herr Kolbe?" Mr. D asked.

The details of Fritz's whole life blurred into this one moment; the past and future were pulled into a whirlpool, small and dark. He took the smuggled documents from his jacket pocket and handed them to Mr. D.

"These are secret documents from the Foreign Office in Berlin, Mr. D. I work there as secretary to Ambassador with Special Duty Ernst von Günther. I have access to many top-secret files—they cross my desk daily."

Mr. D folded up the papers without looking at them, then rubbed his mustache and glanced at Mr. P. He held the folded papers up to his temple. "So these are what, exactly?"

"A Nazi agent in Ankara, plans for deporting Roman Jews, memoranda about tungsten deliveries to Germany from Spain, along with documentation about other matters."

The woman stepped into the doorframe and crossed her arms at her chest. Fritz saw Mr. D exchange a lightning-quick glance with her. "That's quite a lot," she said.

"If it's even real," Mr. P remarked.

"Oh stop." The woman pointed to a black-and-white framed portrait of President Roosevelt. "Just what would the man think of your behaving like this?"

"You young people today," Mr. D said. He placed a hand on Mr. P's shoulder and smiled at the woman. "I don't wish to be impolite, Herr Kolbe, but Mr. P and I would like to have a look at this alone a moment. Do have a seat with our Ms. S in the outer office. Surely there's still coffee, Ms. S?"

"I'd like to get my eyes on those myself at some point, sir. Herr Kolbe, can you come in here? I'm guessing our coffee is better than what you get in Germany these days."

Mr. P shut the door behind them. Fritz sat at the desk across from Ms. S and thanked her for the cup of coffee.

"Coffee's always good," Ms. S said. "Perks you up, keeps you alert. I need it for the work—which I do love, by the way. I'd love to be back in the States, holding down some nice job. You ever been before? Washington or New York maybe? Maybe you know what I'm talking about: the sun shining on the Empire State Building, or Times Square on New Year's Eve."

"Unfortunately not," Fritz said. "I've gotten around a bit, but had to pass on America."

"You don't get the sort of things there that you get in Europe—your old fortresses, knightly castles, and medieval towns. I find that all quite adorable, but I grew up in America. Sure is funny how strongly a person can feel about their own country."

"That's probably true." Fritz took a sip of coffee. His hand was shaking. He knew that Ms. S was questioning him. Charmingly, courteously, but she was indeed questioning him. Mr. D had likely sent him to her for exactly that purpose. She was sitting remarkably upright, her shoulders pulled back severely. Ms. S was slim but Fritz could see she was in good shape, her body tight as a bow.

"Berlin must have been lovely before the war," she said.

"Used to be, before the Nazis. We had such great theater, cabarets, dance halls. The streets were filled with people."

"The Nazis didn't just show up all on their own, Herr Kolbe."

"They won't be going away all on their own either, miss."

"All right, you can stop with the *miss* now. It's okay that I tell you: my name is Stone, Greta Stone. Those boys in there are Allen Dulles and William Priest."

She's throwing me a bone, he thought.

"Are you an adventurer, Herr Kolbe?"

"Hardly."

"The ancient Romans said everyone loves treason but no one the traitor. Believe me, Herr Kolbe, these are very different times. I'm going to bet that you have at least some idea where you are. Do you know

113

what our business is? It's betrayal." Greta opened her hands up wide, as if holding a globe. "That's our profession. If one does it well, one achieves a great deal. It's a fine profession, provided a person is on the right side. Maybe that's the nature of these times—right and wrong, good and evil. We, the Americans, are always the good guys."

"Good and evil is how you see it?"

Greta slid a cigarette between her lips and clicked on her lighter. The flame lit up her face.

"You speak English remarkably well, Herr Kolbe. Do you like the German language? It's tough to learn."

"In German you can express yourself with both precision and remarkable poetry. A wonderful language. That's all getting raped by the Nazis as well."

"Fritz Kolbe, employed by von Ribbentrop, loves the German language. You're working for Uncle Adolf."

"I'm employed as a civil servant."

"For Adolf Hitler."

"I'm not even a member of the Nazi Party."

"Well, I'm not so sure I believe that."

"I give you my word of honor."

"Word of honor? Around here? Oh please." She smiled. Her face retained a strange clarity no matter what expression she used. "You're not in the Nazi Party, and yet you have the job you do?"

Fritz placed his passport on the desk. "Try finding a Party-member number, Ms. Stone."

She picked it up and waved it in the air. "We have people who can make me IDs like this in an hour."

The door opened and Dulles and Priest approached the table. Dulles laid the documents before Greta and set his pipe on the ashtray. The man radiated authority. In the face of his calm assurance, Fritz didn't know how he was supposed to act. He felt nervous and worked up, and could not keep his eyes still. He looked at the ashtray, the typewriter, the flowers, Greta's long fingers, Dulles's elegant suit, a map of Europe. It was all unsettling.

"According to your papers you only have two more days here in Bern, Herr Kolbe. Therefore, I suggest we meet again tomorrow, perhaps earlier. Say, nine p.m. Will that work for you?"

Priest pointed at the documents. "These are good. Ending up on the gallows is not so good. You got tired of living, is that it?"

"I want to stroll with Marlene in a Berlin that's whole again." Fritz would have liked to say more, but he couldn't. Again the thought nagged at him that he didn't really know who Dulles, Priest, and Stone actually were.

"These documents are good," Priest repeated. "So good they smell like forgeries to me."

"They're real."

"You have proof?"

"No."

"How did you get the documents out of your office?"

"Around my leg."

Dulles cleared his throat and looked down at Fritz's legs.

"And Uncle Adolf just lets a man in a job like yours travel to Bern?" Priest said.

"Courier trips are assigned by rotation. I'm considered absolutely trustworthy—besides, I'm not a top diplomat."

"You sure aren't," Priest said.

"Easy, Will," Dulles said.

"A source right inside the Foreign Office on Wilhelmstrasse? It's too good to be true," Priest said.

"Too good," Greta said. "Not necessarily too good to be true."

"How much do you want?" Priest asked.

"How much money? Not a cent, Mr. Priest."

"Ah." Priest, Dulles, and Greta eyed each other, a triangle of glances across the desk, a sworn society. Despite their different personalities,

Fritz sensed a solidarity and a great trust among them—so unlike the Office in Berlin, where mistrust was seen as a virtue.

"Not one cent?" Greta said. "Gentlemen, honor does still exist."

"Come along, Herr Kolbe, I'll take you down," Dulles said.

Priest and Greta reached for telephones and started working the dials.

"It's going to be a long night," Dulles said. "But we're used to that."

Dulles led him back the same way he'd come with Priest. At the door to the backyard, Dulles stopped and looked Fritz up and down.

"We're going to have to look into a few things. It's never very easy. Phone calls are being monitored, so we have to do things in a roundabout way: middlemen, alternate routes, technical stuff that I know works, though I couldn't tell you how. Be careful, Herr Kolbe. If things seem like they're going wrong, disappear. Never try to fix the matter. Find an excuse and disappear. Do you understand me?"

"I believe so."

"Good. How are you getting back?"

"Herr Sacher's waiting in the car."

"Right nearby? Don't do that tomorrow. Have him wait farther away. Agreed, Herr Kolbe? See you tomorrow evening. And if you find the time, do go and see the famous shopping arcades here in Bern, *Lauben*, they call them, they're quite charming."

"So you trust me?"

Dulles smiled at Fritz and pushed his glasses back into position before opening the door. "You Germans are a strange people. You're capable of outperforming anyone, culturally as well as technologically. Truly exceptional. And then you go plummet like this. How does something like that happen?"

"I don't know," Fritz said. "It's either highly complicated or disturbingly simple. Either way, it must be stopped—at all costs."

"It will be very, very costly, for all involved."

Dulles waited until Fritz reached the garden gate. Fritz nodded at him, seeking some token response of accord or faith. Dulles's silhouette, broader yet more welcoming than Priest's, remained motionless.

Fritz walked out to the street and turned toward Eugen's car. He heard a sound behind him, like something being dragged. He looked around. A shadow in an alley appeared momentarily to have an arm, and then it was slowly pulled back into darkness. Fritz walked faster and scrambled into the car.

"We're being watched," Eugen said.

"Someone's following me."

"So now what, Fritz? What now?"

"Drive, Eugen. Just drive."

"They know who I am."

"Good Lord, just start driving."

Eugen started the engine. The car jerked forward, metal grated against metal, and the car lurched back to a stop.

"Eugen?"

"Yeah, yeah." Eugen started the car up again and stepped on the gas. He wiped sweat from his forehead and lost his glasses doing so. Fritz groped around and found them next to the gas pedal.

"They're—they're behind us," Eugen stammered.

Eugen drove along the wide streets, turned off hastily into narrow lanes, then crossed the Aare and steered back toward the city center. After a few minutes Fritz had no idea where they were. Who was in the car behind them? Were German intelligence men following him, or had he fallen into a trap by going to Dulles and his people? Fritz couldn't think straight. He kept shifting in his seat, and he could smell Eugen's sweat.

After about twenty minutes, the yellow cat's eyes in the rearview mirror faded. Eugen was making strange noises, his breath rattling as if he'd just done a sprint. Fritz had Eugen let him out far from the hotel and told his friend he'd be in touch if he needed him. Otherwise, Eugen should keep a low profile, and go about his daily routine.

"Why did they stop chasing us?" Eugen asked. "This isn't good, Fritz. This isn't my kind of thing."

Fritz wanted to say something, but his heart beat so heavily in his chest, he couldn't get a word out. He gave Eugen's shoulder a squeeze and climbed out into the warm night.

"What's the best way back?" he said.

Eugen told him the route.

William Priest was waiting at the entrance to Fritz's hotel. He had his hands in his pockets and was looking far more relaxed and casual than before. Fritz felt like punching him, more out of hostile rage than fear.

"That was a pretty amateur tail," Fritz said.

Priest laughed.

"There are always two teams, Herr Kolbe: one that you notice and a second that someone like you never will."

Fritz cursed.

"The most important thing to know is this: we tailed you, but no one else did. That's one good thing. Well, see you around."

Priest stopped a couple of yards away and turned back to Fritz. "You're certain you don't want any money? We could pay you in dollars. There's no end to the funds we have at our disposal. Our organization, the OSS—"

"OSS?"

"Office of Strategic Services. We're a big deal. See, the OSS is booming with the war on. Washington showers us with dough. The Russians are our brothers-in-arms for now, but that will change at some point. America hates communism. *I* hate it. So, let's say a thousand dollars per delivery?"

Fritz shook his head.

"Five thousand?"

"Why don't you use that money to go buy your wife something nice instead," Fritz said. He liked giving such a sharp-witted reply.

"Don't try and kid with me, Kolbe."

"You think Dulles has something going with Greta?"

Priest laughed and pointed at Fritz. Then he headed off into the darkness, a blur in the night.

He wanted to call Marlene on the phone so badly—and Katrin. He wanted to tell them what he'd done; he wanted to imagine them with their ears to their handsets, to let them play a part in his work. He was dying to tell even one person about his meeting with the OSS. But that couldn't happen. He had to think of their safety, and of his survival; it was better they didn't know anything if ever questioned. It was bad enough that Eugen knew the small portion he did. He had to keep his story to himself, completely and utterly. Having to do so hit him low in the gut, just like the act he put on in the Office did.

Fritz stood before the mirror. He looked tired—but he grinned. He pressed his hands over his mouth and committed the image to memory. The skin of his skull shimmered under the glow of the light. If he only knew how to calm himself. He still felt as if he were running far and fast, his heart racing.

He went down to the bar and had them pour him a glass of champagne. The waiter asked him what the celebration was for. "You would never believe it if I told you," Fritz said. He looked through the bubbles rising in the glass at the red lighting of the hotel bar, and laughed.

Back in his room, he spread a map of Bern out on the table and memorized the main traffic routes and landmarks: the stretch of Old Town that ran east to west with the Aare River flowing around it, the cathedral, the Kramgasse and Schmiedenplatz, and Kirchenfeld Bridge which led to the other side of the river, where the German diplomatic mission was. He ran his finger over the various routes to the clandestine office of Allen Dulles and his team. Priest showing up at the hotel like that had angered him, yet he felt certain he'd landed in the right place. One Fritz Kolbe was passing explosive Foreign Office documents to US intelligence.

He called down to the hotel bar. "You know what? Go ahead and bring a bottle of that champagne to my room."

"For that thing I wouldn't ever believe, Herr Kolbe?"

"The very one."

Fritz set his bare feet on the window ledge and looked out over the Bubenbergplatz, at the circles of yellow light around the streetlamps and under the shopping arcades, and drank his bottle of champagne. It was almost light when he went to bed. The mattress was hard, the way he liked it, the duvet thick yet lightweight, and he smiled because he sensed that weariness was finally winning out over anxiety. He felt his limbs becoming heavy and his breathing steady, then he twitched a little, his eyes snapped back open, and he experienced that wonderful moment when a person is able to sense, as clear as the day, that the warm cover of sleep was taking him away.

At nine in the morning, the car from the German diplomatic mission pulled up to the hotel. Weygand was inside. He grunted hello to Fritz and instructed the driver to take his time so that he and Fritz could talk.

"Do you have any contacts in Bern, Herr Kolbe?"

The question caught Fritz by surprise. Why was Weygand asking that? He might not know about Eugen, yet it was no secret back in Spain that Fritz had been the one to process the documents necessary for Eugen to give up his German citizenship. Had Weygand gone digging back that far? If so, why? Could this seemingly subdued man know something about Eugen and his contacts in Bern?

Fritz was looking out the window. "A very pretty town," he said.

"Herr Kolbe! Do you have any contacts in Bern?"

"There's a man named Eugen Sacher. A merchant. I met him many years ago now. He lives here in Switzerland, as far as I know."

"Did you happen to see him?"

"I don't know where he lives or where I can reach him. On top of that I hardly have time—when I get even an hour to spare I'm exploring the town. You've heard about those famous shopping arcades, the *Lauben*, surely?"

Weygand rested his fist against the window. "They're all going to get a big surprise one day," he muttered. Then he raved about Hitler and grand new weapons and big strategic moves, about how weak the British and American armies were and how primitive the Russians.

As he spoke, Fritz imagined Weygand dressed in pink underwear. That was another idea his father had come up with. Hierarchies had their place at work and in school. There was a place for recognizing other peoples' achievements too. *But as soon as someone abuses his position, even for a second, imagine him in pink underwear,* Fritz's father had said. *Whether a king, a general, or anyone else: pink underwear!* Where had the man gotten all his ideas? Fritz's mother had been fond of saying he was practically swimming in them, and she loved that about him. She said she would have loved to be able to read his mind as he worked away for hours in his workshop.

The car pulled up and parked before the diplomatic mission's front yard. Frau von Lützow was standing at the gate, her daughters lined up along the varnished fence. Fritz said hello. Weygand begged Fritz's pardon and said that Fritz should go on ahead because he had a small matter to discuss with the madam. Fritz thought he heard Frau von Lützow say, "Make it snappy" but wasn't sure if he'd understood correctly.

The polished scent of the diplomatic mission's foyer met Fritz as he walked in and entered the first office. Its window overlooked the yard and quiet street. Frau von Lützow was looking around and talking with Weygand. She got up close to him and pinched the man's chest real quick. Then with a snap of her fingers, she ordered her children in their white dresses to follow her.

As Fritz went to leave the office, he caught his foot in the kink of a telephone cord. The phone clattered off the table onto the floorboards. He cursed and picked it up. When he'd finished, Weygand was standing in the doorway. The two men looked each other in the eyes a moment. Then Weygand came in and looked out the window through which Fritz had been watching.

"Someone gave away Citadel," Weygand blurted.

Fritz wanted to ask what he meant, but decided to keep quiet.

"The assault on Kursk—Operation Citadel. Someone gave it away. That means there's a leak somewhere in Berlin. If the Russians hadn't known about our plans for deployment, they never would've been able to stop us. Model, von Manstein . . . none of those Ivans could have stopped our field marshals. Isn't that right, Herr Kolbe?"

"They would've had no chance," Fritz said. He did not say, *You Nazi asshole.*

Weygand was eyeing him as if searching for something in Fritz's face.

"All of Russian history shows that those people are born only to serve. If I may: Why are you not at the front?"

"I'm exempt."

"As *indispensable to the war effort*? You? Why aren't you a Party member? I find that a little disconcerting—like so much these days."

Here we go again, Fritz thought. *Personal Record Form, entry 27.*

"I'm about to apply soon."

Weygand smiled, took Fritz by the arm, and led him out into the hallway. "People are always so quick to draw the wrong conclusions, aren't they?"

"That they are, yes."

"A person has to proceed carefully. At the gallows, they slip that noose around a traitor's neck very slowly. Then, while he's still twitching, they pull down his pants. All of that gets filmed."

"I think Herr von Lützow is waiting for us."

"Ahem . . . right. Then we probably should get going."

Allen Dulles and Greta Stone were standing in the doorway to the backyard, watching Fritz as he pushed open the gate. He approached and they did not budge, two statues halved by shadow and the glow of the orange summer sunset.

"Nice to see you again," Fritz said. Dulles and Greta glanced at each other, that same deep trust passing between them. Fritz wanted to exchange glances like that with these people; he wanted to finally be acknowledged someplace where he could truly be himself. Where else could that happen but here in this clandestine OSS station?

"Hello, Mr. Wood," Greta said.

"Wood?"

"From now on," Dulles said, "your name is George Wood. There's no Fritz Kolbe anymore."

"Fritz Kolbe is dead," Greta said. "Long live George Wood."

"Fritz Kolbe is not dead," Fritz said.

"He's deader than dead," Greta said.

William Priest was waiting for them up in the offices. He pointed at Fritz. This was likely some American form of greeting, so Fritz returned it. Priest grinned.

"I think I can trust you, Mr. Wood," Dulles said.

"Me, I'm not so sure," Priest said.

Fritz looked to Greta, who was leaning in the doorframe. She wiggled her hand. "I'm just so-so."

"You went to the Brits before you came to us," Priest said. "You should've told us that detail."

"The Brits declined."

"Wood, you have to tell us such things," Dulles said.

Fritz was surprised by how easily these people had switched to his unfamiliar new name. Greta, seeming to notice this, told him the name Kolbe would never be uttered again in these rooms, nor would the name ever get mentioned at any other OSS post.

"You remain unknown," Priest said.

"These documents of yours"—Dulles patted the files—"they're outstanding. I want to come clean, Wood: there is immense mistrust of you. It will be tough getting you established."

"Can you do something for the Jewish people mentioned in so many of the reports?"

"Let what we do be our concern," Priest said.

Greta was pouring whisky, while Dulles stuffed his pipe, then held a match over the tobacco as if in deep concentration.

"We can't guarantee your safety, Wood," Dulles said. "You're traveling back to Berlin tomorrow. If—and I stress *if*—something happens to you, we will deny ever having heard of you. On the other hand, we'll do all we can to protect you, though there's not much we can do after you switch trains in Basel."

"Nothing at all," Priest said and toasted Fritz.

"You want to continue with the deliveries?" Greta asked. She placed her slender fingers on his shoulder and looked down on him as he sat there. She was wearing a black turtleneck sweater. Fritz had never seen such a thing on a woman before.

"Yes," Fritz said. "I do."

Dulles sat behind his desk, his pipe sticking out of the middle of his mouth. From Fritz's angle it looked like Dulles had a thick dark-brown nose that was pumping out clouds of smoke.

"You bring us the reports, Wood," Dulles said, "and we'll assess them."

He leaned back and stared at Fritz, then exchanged those dueling glances with Priest and Greta. Fritz understood that the moment had arrived for him to convince the OSS once and for all. He reached into his inside pocket and pulled out more documents he'd transcribed onto thin paper.

"One of your diplomatic dispatches from Cairo was intercepted. So you can assume your State Department code has been cracked."

Greta ripped the page of codes from his hand. She rushed into her office but stopped in the doorway. "This your handwriting? It's awful. We'll practically need a cryptographer for this."

Moments later, Fritz heard her swearing at someone on the telephone.

"German and Japanese U-boats meeting near the Cape of Good Hope, and plans for the Wehrmacht's retreat in Russia, and here—the exact position of the Telefunken factory in Berlin. They make targeting devices for the Luftwaffe."

"Good man," Priest said.

Dulles, not even glancing at the rest of the papers, removed his glasses and eyeballed Fritz again. It was the first time Fritz thought he saw the man look perplexed.

Someone knocked. Priest went to the door in the adjoining room, spoke with someone on the other side, and came back. He said it had been one of the Brits, coming to have a word about Wood.

"Don't tell me, Will. We shouldn't trust him, right?" Dulles said. He bumped his pipe and tiny dim particles rained onto the files like ashes onto Berlin after an air raid. "Quite the drama going on over there, I imagine. Wooldridge from MI6 called me; he was downright furious. Now they want to bad-mouth our Mr. Wood here."

"It's a home run," Priest said.

"I would say so, yes."

"Is Eugen Sacher in any danger?" Fritz asked.

"What kind of question is that?" Priest said. Dulles gave him a disapproving glance and Priest shrugged. "Tell us something about your life," he said. "And tell us about the mood in the Foreign Office as well as here at the German diplomatic mission."

As Fritz talked, Berlin seemed far off. He talked about his father's workshop and quoted him: *Do what is right and have no fear.* Nearly forgetting where he was, he lost himself in the soft clouds of reminiscence until Priest interrupted him.

"What's your greatest secret, Wood?"

"What's yours, Mr. Priest?"

"Not your concern. Well?"

Fritz stared at Priest standing to the right of Dulles. Greta had come back in and stood to the left of her boss, who was puffing on his pipe.

"My daughter, Katrin, is with Werner and Hiltrud Lichtwang in Swakopmund. I left her behind in 1939. Ever since . . . I haven't spoke to her once. I haven't written her a single letter."

Greta and Priest wrote everything down as he spoke. They looked at him from over their notepads as if wanting to snap up his words before he got them out.

"Katrin cannot be dragged into this," Fritz said.

"Of course," Dulles said.

"What about von Ribbentrop—is he really as dense as you've described?" Greta asked.

"He just parrots everything Hitler tells him, from what I hear. Horrible. The man is completely vacant. When he was posted in England, he greeted the king with a *Heil Hitler*. It doesn't get much ruder than that."

"You appreciate that, don't you? Politeness," Priest said.

"I don't know any other way to be, Mr. Priest. Do you?"

"I certainly do."

"Okay," Dulles said.

Okay—this little expression was ingrained in all of their speech, it seemed to Fritz.

"Now, let's discuss ways you can make contact with us," Dulles continued. "I assume you can't be taking trips to Bern at will, whenever the situation demands."

"One more thing," Greta said. "It might be best, if the British do approach you now—"

"Don't tell them a single word," Priest cut in.

"Don't give me orders." Fritz managed to keep his voice clear and firm. He was feeling more assured during this second meeting. He knew his smuggled documents were explosive in content, and it was increasingly apparent just how crucial Dulles considered the files to be.

"I think I like you, Mr. Wood," Greta said.

Fritz felt a warmth creep over his cheeks.

"All I meant," Priest added, "is that it's highly advisable you have nothing to do with the British. Nothing at all. You're our man."

Fritz had to admit, he did admire the man's tenacity. These people were not to be toyed with—and neither was he, not anymore. Not ever again.

That same night he called Eugen and told him he shouldn't attempt to get in touch with him, nor should he come to the hotel or the train station to see him off. Fritz said he might still use him as a contact, maybe even for sending things in the mail. Could he agree to that?

"But no one's in danger, are they, Fritz?"

"I told Weygand I know you, but we haven't met up and I don't know where you live. I had to, just in case. Listen, Eugen, there are dangers. I won't try and convince you, let alone force you."

"I know, Fritz. It's fine. After the war, they will celebrate you as a hero."

"They can keep their celebrations."

"You can count on me."

"Does your wife know?"

"I haven't told her."

"But she's noticed something's up."

"Of course she's noticed."

"Don't tell her. Don't tell her a thing. Only once this is over."

"When will that be?"

"I don't know." Fritz pressed a fist against the phone-booth glass. "I provided them with intelligence, Eugen. These documents will shorten the war. We did it."

The next morning Fritz packed his suitcase, walked through Old Town, and turned at the Theaterplatz, heading north for the Aare. The river below coursed around the columns of Kornhaus Bridge, the water dim in the shadow of the bridge and rippling with gold in the sunshine. The mountains were sending down a clean, fresh breeze, and for a moment Fritz felt content and calm. Langmauer Lane ran along the bank; he stepped off and gathered some earth and a few pebbles for the tin he always carried. He pushed its lid down tight and wrote *Bern* on the tin. "For you, Katrin," he muttered.

But now, he had to return to the hell that was Berlin.

8

MARLENE AND HEADQUARTERS

Berlin and Rastenburg, 1943

At home, within the safety of his blacked-out apartment, Fritz danced. He was alone. He hopped and swung his arms. Joy filled his kitchen. He held his globe up to his face, spun it, and raised it high into the air.

Marlene, Katrin—your Fritz will finish them off!

Over the next few days at the Office, many of his colleagues asked what was going on with him—he'd always been polite and obliging but why was he now in such a remarkably fine mood as well?

"Well, when you're doing what's right . . ." he said and waved files at them. He did not add that these were going directly to the Americans.

Von Günther notified Fritz that he'd be sent to the Wolf's Lair next—von Günther was going there himself and needed Fritz's assistance. They would be in close proximity to the Führer, he said, and would get to experience the man's aura. It would be an honor, Fritz said.

That same day he got himself a map of Rastenburg and its vicinity from the Office's archives. The Wolf's Lair was Hitler's headquarters. After the trip, he would hand over the precise coordinates, down to a hair.

Dulles would have it bombed! He was doing this; he really was. The war would end. Katrin would arrive back in Germany. And Marlene Wiese?

At the lunch break he walked down Wilhelmstrasse and crossed the Spree. Flak guns threatened the skies at the ramps to the bridge. At the doors to Charité Hospital, cool gusts of wind made the red swastika flags swell, collapse, and swell again as if they were having trouble swallowing something. He approached Marlene's office as a rather tall man was just leaving, his doctor's coat all broad shoulders. Fritz saw him only from behind. He went inside. He was a spy bringing Marlene Wiese her chocolate.

"This is so wonderful," she said. "And so much of it." It was nice seeing her laugh, her cheeks forming creases like little crescents.

"Who was that man just now?"

"The professor." She smiled. "Jealous?"

"Me? No. What did he want?"

"To chat a moment, Fritz. With me."

Fritz moved some prosthetic legs to the side; they rattled in his hands. He sat down and tried to force himself to look at more than just Marlene.

"So how was Bern? No war going on?"

"There really wasn't, no."

"Really?"

Fritz ran a hand over his bare forehead and thinning hair. In Africa he'd never left the house without a hat, and he rarely did here either. They glanced at each other, stalling.

"Did all go well in Bern?"

Fritz coughed. "Of course, yes," he said. "I did what I was supposed to." He looked at the clock and said he had to get going, but kept sitting there. Marlene offered him some of her chocolate, saying he looked like he could use some.

"It's all for you."

"Do it for me," Marlene said. She pushed the chocolate across the desk and broke off a piece, leaving little brown splinters on the silver wrapper. "I've almost forgotten what it's like to do some proper cooking," she said. "And afterward, to get all snazzied up for dinner and drink a schnapps and smoke a cigarette. To live. Go swimming. Be happy. Read a good novel, see a pretty landscape—it's really not all that much to ask."

"In Spain," Fritz said, "we always had fresh tomatoes and eggplant. That was marvelous."

"Don't they have a really good oil there?"

"Olive oil. It's wonderful. Smells completely different than ours."

"I've never been abroad. But I do have a large atlas." She held up her index finger. "Along with this here."

"Does it get around much?"

"All around the whole lovely world. When your husband's a cartographer you . . ." She let the words trail off, lifting her feet and staring at her shoes.

She's married, Fritz thought. *I have enough problems. Someone else's wife—that's the last thing I need right now.*

"I'd like to see you more often," he heard himself saying.

Marlene pulled a handkerchief from her jacket and polished the toes of her shoes.

"Me too," she said.

He wanted to say *we only live once*—but the saying was too silly, too corny and feeble, and it gave too much homage to war.

"We only live once," Marlene said.

It didn't sound silly or corny coming from her mouth. It sounded good and simple and right. She laughed her resounding bell of a laugh, the first thing about her that had sucked him right in. He wanted to make a playful remark, but then he pictured those secret files on the desk of Allen Dulles in Bern, and Greta Stone with her arms crossed, and he heard William Priest saying a man like Fritz would never notice someone actually tailing him. He could not get Marlene involved in this. He forced himself to remember that he hardly knew this woman. Marlene said nothing, watching him as she slid a piece of chocolate into her mouth.

He leaned back. "Tell me something about your life," he said. "What do you love to do?"

"Cook. I mean, cook well. To do it right. Apart from that—"

"What dishes do you like?"

"I don't know. In times like these, anything you eat can remind you of the past. Though sometimes not." She gazed at him. "This is all so insane."

"Well, I'm off to a good start. I'm traveling to the Wolf's Lair."

"Oh. I didn't know you're such an important man."

A laugh burst from his mouth. "As a matter of fact," he said, "it seems that I am."

The heat was oppressive out in the country near Rastenburg, the forest air thick with amber light. Fritz tried in vain to shoo the mosquitos from his face. He was billeted in a hunting cottage outside the outer security zone of the Wolf's Lair. Tasked with keeping an eye on von Günther's documents, he had plenty of time on his hands. He'd been told he could be called at any moment and should always stay near a telephone. Nonetheless, he roamed the nearby fields and birch groves, liking the feel of his feet sinking into soft natural ground. He frequently ran into soldiers on patrol; one always aimed a rifle at him while another checked his papers. The notion that only a couple hundred yards away, Hitler was expounding on his ideas about the world to his generals and subordinates left Fritz feeling strangely empty, a feeling that seemed to lift only out amid the heat and scent of the woods. He spread out his handkerchief at the foot of a birch tree, sat with his back against the white trunk, and lifted his face to the sun. He felt at the bark's rough crevices. "Sit down, Marlene," he muttered. It was so hard to imagine her free of the war, even for a moment. He could barely grasp this moment of peace and calm. He felt as if he were totally alone on earth and his heart seemed almost to laugh with glee. He dug up a little dirt and pressed it into his tin. He wrote *Wolf's Lair* on the lid.

When he returned to the cottage, the other lodger, a man from the Security Service of the SS, clicked his heels and told him the world hadn't experienced anything like this since Alexander and Napoleon.

"Alexander was a drunkard," Fritz said. "And Napoleon failed miserably in Russia."

"Neither of which have anything to do with the Führer," the SS man replied. "We're doing our part too."

"That we are," Fritz said.

The SS man switched on the radio. Zarah Leander was singing, "This Is Not the End of the World."

"That song came out during the Battle of Stalingrad," Fritz said.

"So heroic," the SS man said. "Such a sacred honor, giving up one's life for the cause. It must be a great feeling. Men getting to experience such hatred and fanaticism till the very end. Faces of doom. People will still be singing about it a thousand years from now."

"Sure they will," Fritz said. "You bet."

The SS man sat on the veranda's wooden railing and stared resolutely out into the woods. Fritz didn't know anything about the young man, but something made him think of Marlene Wiese's dead son.

"It's rumored they resorted to cannibalism," Fritz said. "At Stalingrad."

The SS man glared with his mouth open, his face filled with horror and rage. "Soldiers of the Wehrmacht? You believe such a thing?"

"Me? What do *you* believe?"

"If certain elements of our Volk are spreading such ideas? Eradicate them, I say. Get rid of them."

Fritz had brought along several books. He went into his corner of the cottage now and lay in bed reading Sophocles's *Antigone*. He liked to imagine all this as a Greek tragedy or one of William Shakespeare's tales. It truly did help, and he didn't consider the practice outlandish or silly. Why shouldn't he reach for a crutch in times like this, to help him find his bearings?

When he was growing up his parents didn't have much money for books. They never had much schooling either, yet one of his most cherished memories was of his mother reading out loud to his father in the evenings. The story had to be something with adventure in it, so she read Schiller's *The Robbers* and *William Tell*, and at one point his mother mentioned someone called "Suffucles" because she thought that was the correct pronunciation in Greek. His father said he'd have to hear some of that fellow before deciding whether he was worth reading, but once he did, he liked *Antigone* a lot. Brave woman, he said. Most women are silently braver than men, Fritz's mother replied, the men always needing to bluster so much.

Antigone stood all on her own against the powers that be, against her king. *"Say, wilt thou aid me and abet? Decide."* Fritz knew Antigone ended up paying bitterly for her deeds, yet it was still comforting to read the play. He often wondered how dramatists figured out how to leave the reader feeling better, despite all the horrors in a story. *Antigone,* he thought as he closed the book. *She did what is right.*

When Fritz came back out, the SS man was sitting on the veranda thumbing through documents, smoking a cigar. "Keeps away mosquitos," he said.

Fritz handed him his book. The SS man told him he didn't read, and when he did he read German books.

"Like Heinrich Mann?"

The SS man put on a sullen face that he likely imagined was that of the doomed men in Stalingrad. "They should've burnt Heinrich Mann along with his books." He stood up and towered over Fritz, the corners of his mouth turned down severely. "I'm going to remember your name, Herr Kolbe."

Fritz heard a car engine and tires crunching on the forest road. A sedan pulled up, the sun reflecting on the long hood and the woods in the windows, like in a movie.

"I'm leaving to meet with Foreign Minister von Ribbentrop and the Führer," Fritz said.

"The Führer? Personally?"

"Should I tell him anything for you?"

"I, I didn't know . . ." The SS man stretched his right arm in the Hitler salute. *"Heil Hitler."*

"Hi Hitler." Fritz took his book back into his room, locked the door on his way back out, and climbed into the too-hot car next to the driver. The young man turned the car around, leaving the SS man standing there with his arm still raised.

Fritz acted excited to be at the Wolf's Lair, asking all about the place and inquiring just whose billet was where. The young driver, surely prohibited from giving out such information, was nevertheless infected by Fritz's cheerful enthusiasm. He told Fritz where the barbed wire and the power lines ran, and talked about the sentry units and guardhouses and which particular luxury car was used by Himmler, Göring, and others. Foreign Minister von Ribbentrop resided in Lehndorff Mansion on the east side of the compound, he said.

In his mind, Fritz made little marks on a map, taking note of every fork and turn-off, the flak positions with camo netting, the gray tops of the bunkers and the dark-green rail coaches parked on short stretches of tracks that led nowhere. He saw the future blowing up before him— relentless, blazing, and vital explosions in all their beauty, the rail coaches springing into the air, bursting apart. The clean-shaven kid driving him would probably end up lying in his own blood. It wasn't the first time such a thought had hounded Fritz. He let it lie. He did not pursue it.

Fritz sat in a compartment of the rail car, looking out at the compound through a crack in the curtains. Von Günther had told him he couldn't appear at the Wolf's Lair in civvies, so he was dressed in his uniform, which was too tight under the arms and made the sweat in his armpits burn. Somewhere a dog was barking. Two truckloads of military passed by the rail car, and then farther off, through a gap in the trees, he thought he briefly saw Goebbels, the Nazis' mouthpiece, in his brown uniform.

Then von Ribbentrop and von Günther were approaching Fritz's rail car, and Fritz heard the rustle of sentries saluting and the door opening. He heard von Ribbentrop and von Günther go into the car's conference room, right next to his compartment. Von Ribbentrop was talking about Japanese Foreign Minister Oshima and the military setbacks in the Pacific. Military Intelligence was asking how the British suddenly knew about Japanese and German U-boats meeting off the coast of South Africa. In addition to that, von Ribbentrop said, the Jewish Department in the Foreign Office needed to become more effective, as the work of exterminating the Jews was not moving forward fast enough. Himmler had personally expressed his displeasure, and that meant the words were coming right from the Führer's mouth. Fritz couldn't believe how many times von Günther said, "Yes sir, Herr Foreign Minister" and "Agree completely, Herr Reich Foreign Minister" and "Very good"—it was too many to count. Next von Günther asked the orderly about Fritz and soon was pulling open the door to Fritz's compartment.

"So you're already here," he whispered. "If you do not mind, Kolbe, yes? The Herr Minister does not like to be kept waiting."

Fritz straightened out his uniform and von Günther grabbed him by the arm.

"Don't ever forget the *von*, Kolbe. The man's name is *von Ribbentrop*, yes? Understood?"

Fritz followed von Günther into the other compartment. Bottles lay dripping in a silver ice cooler. The place smelled of stale cigarette smoke. Fritz wondered whether he should click his heels together but didn't know how. Von Ribbentrop watched him, his high forehead creasing, that face stern as always, his skin white like paper. Fritz had never seen any other expression on his face besides haughtiness. Even sitting, von Ribbentrop looked down from above.

"Hi Hitler," Fritz said.

"You are?"

"Kolbe, Fritz. I'm the—"

"Yeah, yeah, right. You have the files?"

"As instructed, Herr Reich Foreign Minister."

Fritz unbuckled his briefcase and pulled out the documents, feeling von Ribbentrop's eyes on him the whole time, as if he were waiting for Fritz to make a mistake.

"I hope you're aware of the privilege you have been given, Herr Kolben. The Foreign Office, gentlemen, is without a doubt the most important government office in the Reich. When Herr Himmler or Goebbels gives orders, we are the ones who act globally and, as such, are the ones who maintain an appropriate view of things. I am the one in charge. Our ministry is far greater than it has ever been, you understand?

"When the current crisis is overcome, we'll be the first to make governing the new territories a reality. We are the ones; no one else. I was in America, England, and Russia—I know them all. It astounds me to this day that no one truly comprehended our nation's will, nor did they anticipate it. The British think their Churchill is such a great man. Gentlemen, please. Churchill is a fat, cigar-sucking drunk, Roosevelt a puppet of International Jewry in America, Stalin a monster and a Bolshevik. Our enemies' alliance will crumble just as the Führer predicts—thanks in no small part to me and my efforts. Now, you two are to understand the following . . ."

Fritz stood next to a motionless von Günther, who followed von Ribbentrop's monologue as if mesmerized. Von Günther was sweating but apparently didn't dare wipe the sweat from his face. Fritz pulled out a handkerchief and patted his own forehead. Whenever von Ribbentrop paused, von Günther said, "That's right, sir." When the Foreign Minister ordered that his car be called, von Günther left the room quickly and shouted for an orderly.

"I won't be needing you anymore, Kolben."

"Hi Hitler," Fritz said. He was looking von Ribbentrop in the face. The man always had faint dark circles around his eyes.

"Something else?"

"No, Herr Reich Foreign Minister," Fritz said. "It's just that, well, I so seldom see the Herr Reich Foreign Minister in the Office. I want to say that I'm proud to be able to serve him." He felt the sweat in his eyebrows. "I do my job well, Herr Reich Foreign Minister."

"Of course you're proud of it. Of course you do your job well—otherwise you would not be in my ministry. So get accustomed to conducting yourself more appropriately to your position, Kolben."

"Certainly, Herr Reich Foreign Minister. Hi Hitler."

Fritz found von Günther outside in the heat, standing near the rail car. He was smoking a cigarette, the cloud from his mouth leaving pale gray streaks in the sunshine.

"So pompous. The man's just a door-to-door salesman. My name is *von* Günther, Kolbe—and it's always been *von*. Unlike that ridiculous champagne merchant! Well, I can tell you one thing . . ."

Von Ribbentrop was stepping down from the rail car, adjusting his uniform collar. "Where's my sedan, Günther?"

"Coming any moment, Herr von Ribbentrop. Such a shame our meeting has come to an end so soon."

"Yeah, yeah. I'm heading back to the mansion. You know what to do. Send Kolben here back to the Office with the files."

"Yes sir, Herr Reich Foreign Minister."

"And make sure that your subordinates conduct themselves more appropriately in the future."

"Yes sir." Von Günther turned to Fritz. "Again with this, Kolbe? Did you fail to show proper respect toward the Herr Reich Minister? I'm always having to hear this about you. No more of it—understood?"

A black and highly polished long sedan with swastika standards rolled up. The driver rushed out and opened the door. It was the same kid who'd previously driven Fritz. Von Ribbentrop tapped a fingernail on his watch.

"You do understand you can always be sent to the Eastern Front?"

"Yes sir."

"Gentlemen . . ." Von Ribbentrop climbed in, thrusting out his chin like a dictator.

"Watch out for yourself," Fritz said to the young driver as he rushed, cowering, back around the car. Fritz and von Günther watched the sedan drive off, turning left at the bombproof barracks and disappearing in the woods' sunny haze.

"I'm not afraid of the boogeyman," von Günther said. He placed a hand on Fritz's shoulder. "I was only putting on an act, Kolbe. No offense?"

"I understand putting on an act," Fritz said. "I understand it very well."

"Listen up. The man gave me a lot of documents that need to go back to the Office. Your plane takes off at five p.m. Once you're back in Berlin, here is what you must do . . ."

One part of Fritz was well aware of precisely what he had to make happen back at the Office; while another part of him felt strangely amused, was laughing even, because a certain Fritz Kolbe now had the upper hand and soon would be putting a detailed map of Hitler's headquarters into the hands of the OSS.

Back when Sigmund Freud left Vienna, Fritz had read articles about the fellow in the international papers, and in the process he had stumbled on a story about mental disorders. He couldn't remember what Freud called it, but there actually was such a thing as a split personality. Fritz Kolbe had been declared dead in that office in Bern, and he and George Wood could only become one again the moment that stooping, mustachioed Hitler was caught, dead or alive.

Fritz listened as von Günther talked but looked beyond him, toward the camouflaged main complex of the Wolf's Lair. Between the barracks and bunkers a group of uniformed officials was walking down an asphalt path about a yard behind a dumpy-looking man in a brown uniform tunic. The man was wearing a military cap with a shiny visor and walked bent forward, one hand behind his back. Fritz stared at the figure, far off, partly in shadow, partly in sunlight. The man turned in Fritz's direction, and that pale face seemed to grow larger, until for a moment it seemed to Fritz that he and Hitler were peering into each other's eyes. Then Hitler pulled his gaze away and turned back. Fritz imagined himself drawing a pistol from a holster and running straight at the man, aiming his gun, and in his mind he kept on shooting, always at that face, kept shooting until it was no more, and still he ran onward, out into the country, aiming for the lakes and woods in the sun.

The man and his entourage vanished into the mottled shadows under a stand of trees.

"Kolbe, are you listening to me?"

"What?"

"Kolbe?"

"Apologies. The Führer was just back there."

"Ah, right. I understand. It can render a person speechless to see the man personally—something quite different than the usual hustle and bustle. Well, pull yourself together, Kolbe. He'll fix things soon enough."

"As will we."

"What's that?"

"As will we, Herr Ambassador. We will too."

Fritz sat at a window in the Junkers Ju 52 and looked out. The engine was droning loudly and everything was rattling and vibrating in the cabin. Below him lay forests and lakes that reflected the greenery and sunshine, and sometimes he saw the plane's shadow sweeping the tree-tops, dropping into a yellow field, or crossing a river. It would be so nice to fly over South Africa in such an airplane, Katrin next to him, and with the Braunweins and Marlene Wiese too. Below, a road glimmered with the strange whiteness of tanks and trucks heading east—where only death and destruction awaited.

The closer Fritz got to Berlin, the grayer and more scarred the landscape became. Then he saw the city's devastation from above for the first time. *The apocalypse,* he thought. He could detect nothing but ruins spiking upward like so many crooked fingers. Where there once had been housing developments and streets there was now nothing but barren deserts of rubble where tiny people scurried along, stooping in their efforts to find even one item left of what had once been theirs. *They won't find even a pot,* Fritz thought. Family photos, books, an oven, clothes—all of it was gone, and wherever they searched lay only a steaming wasteland. This plane was plunging into a hell that no longer wanted any humans.

The Junkers bounded along the battered landing strip next to the buckling flight tower, where the only splotches of color to be seen were those red Nazi emblems with the swastika. Gray and red were now the colors of a Berlin that had once shined so brilliantly and been so full of life. This urban corpse, devoured down to the bone, was where he would again see Marlene.

The footsteps coming down the corridor sounded like drums beating, countless hard soles striking the Office's polished floor in a steady rhythm. Fritz froze at his desk. Soldiers. Had he been found out? Had Weygand noticed something in Bern?

He watched the closed door to von Günther's office. He heard no sound coming from inside. The footsteps grew closer. Fritz crept over to the window and looked out over the Wilhelmstrasse drenched in sunshine, a military truck out in front of the Office, the Propaganda Ministry on the opposite side of the street with its windows always dark. Over there in its basement, people were tortured. Where was he supposed to run? *For God's sake. Katrin. Marlene.* Were they coming for him already?

He squeezed his hands into fists till they hurt, and listened. The beats became muffled, as if the drums had been covered with blankets. They had passed. Fritz opened the office door. At the end of the corridor, he saw a group of soldiers following an officer in lockstep, rifles on their shoulders. More and more doors opened to frightened looks and expressions of uneasy questioning.

Fritz followed the soldiers. The officer instructed two of them to open a door, then stormed into the office behind them. Fritz heard him screaming orders. Something clanked. Then calmness reigned, as if time suddenly stood still. Soldiers guarded the door, their rifles lowered in front of them. Müller stood out in the corridor with his arms crossed and grinned. Fritz heard that lockstep again, then the officer came out followed by two soldiers, then Franz Havermann, with more soldiers behind him. Havermann was white as a sheet. He tried making eye contact with those standing around, but everyone looked at the floor or turned away. As the column marched by, Fritz heard Havermann muttering and their eyes met. Havermann's were wet. "I was only listening to music, Herr Kolbe. Music." The officer barked at Havermann that he better shut his trap.

"Halt!" The order rang out down the corridor. The officer called his men to attention. Von Ribbentrop, presumably arriving from his office upstairs, came down the hallway with his personal secretary in tow and stopped before the man in custody. He stared at Havermann, while the officer said nothing. Havermann was trembling. *The poor man,* Fritz thought. Von Ribbentrop reached back and slapped Havermann across the cheek. Tears fell from Havermann's eyes.

"Filth," von Ribbentrop said. "Take him away, Lieutenant."

The column marched on with Havermann in the middle, his hands clasped at his chest as if bound there. *Better you than me, Havermann,* Fritz thought. He was ashamed of the thought, but he meant it.

"He'll be bawling soon," Müller said. His thin arms were still crossed and he was looking over at Fritz. Fritz wondered again if this lost young man had been among those who had accosted him onboard the *Louisiana*. Was he there when they made him say *Heil Hitler*?

Von Ribbentrop pivoted on his heels, adding, "Don't you all have anything to do?"

Everyone standing around vanished immediately and closed their doors behind them. Fritz silently went back into his office. Poor Havermann had probably been listening to an enemy broadcast. *Music. It was only music.*

Later that evening, Walter Braunwein entered Fritz's office and uttered a gentle "Hey-ho." He pointed at the door to von Günther's office. Already left, Fritz told him.

"Shitty business about Havermann," Walter said. He ran his fingers through his unruly hair. "Goddamn it," he said. "Is there anything we can do for him, Fritz?"

"Not a chance."

"None at all?"

"No, Walter. Not me. That's not possible. I have to . . ."

Walter folded his arms and stared at Fritz, his eyes conveying skepticism and curiosity.

"You have to what? Something's going on with you."

"Hardly. There's nothing going on with me at all." There was the sound of arrogance in Fritz's voice, that old protective wall used by the insecure and by those seeking something to hide behind. He didn't want it, especially not with Walter. Fritz was guilty of having acted conceited before, but that was just a matter of him thinking they could all go kiss his ass, and so was something else entirely. But this—fending off his old friend this way because he didn't know what else to do—genuinely pained him.

"How is Käthe?" he tried.

Walter didn't respond.

◆ ◆ ◆

The Americans had heavily bombed the Messerschmitt factory in Obertraubling. Fritz looked in the mirror above the sink in his office and squeezed his eyes shut. Back in Bern, he had given Allen Dulles the exact coordinates of the factory.

More Gestapo men started showing up in the Office, many in stiff leather overcoats. Every government office with information about Obertraubling was being examined. The factory had been considered top secret. Air raids had hit V2 facilities on the coast before, but the latest bombing seemed to have been more precise, von Günther told Fritz.

That was me, Fritz did not say.

"Maybe that was Havermann too," von Günther said.

"But Herr Ambassador, how could someone get information like that from our offices and pass it to the enemy? It's just not possible."

"You're quite right there, Kolbe. It could not have come from the Office. But you try telling these people that, yes? Sure, we need them—but between you and me, these fellows are suspicious to the point of being pathological. One must understand the Führer's greatness, and in so doing accept certain conditions. The man puts a good deal of thinking into everything that he does. Yet, some people become like dogs in the way they follow him. Speaking of which . . ." Von Günther stood at his office window, one hand in his trouser pocket, one on the windowsill. He spoke as if to the glass, something he often did when he thought he had something important to say.

"There will be a few changes in the process for destroying files in our office. From now on you'll have to countersign when you take documents down to the basement for incineration—you'll sign a log down there, witnessed by the man in charge."

"Yes sir, Herr Ambassador," Fritz said.

He went back into his office, set the Allgäu landscape on the floor, and looked into the safe. All files for Dulles. He immediately knew what this news meant. He'd have to bring the documents home, transcribe them, and then take them down to the burn barrels to have all the files signed off. Everything would be recorded—hundreds of pages—which meant he'd have to act faster in the future. He'd have to pick and choose his intelligence now and summarize it. He couldn't do it all alone.

The office door jolted open and Fritz started. A Gestapo man strode in. He was small and nondescript.

"Fritz Kolbe?"

"Yes?"

"You were in Switzerland recently."

"At the diplomatic mission in Bern, yes. What can I do for you?"

"Your assignment was?"

"I supervised the transport of documents and delivered them to Herr von Lützow at the diplomatic mission."

"Did you have contact with anyone apart from the staff at the diplomatic mission?"

Remain calm, somehow remain calm. He had no time to think.

"No, none."

The Gestapo man stared at him, his left eyelid twitching. Without asking he sat down at the desk across from Fritz. A classified folder lay on Fritz's desk. The Gestapo man turned the folder his way.

"This is top-secret material, Herr Kolbe."

The words *stay alert* popped into Fritz's head. He reached for the folder and turned it back so it was facing him. The little man placed one hand on top of the other.

"Who is Eugen Sacher?"

Why had he ever mentioned Eugen to Weygand? How could he have thought being open would divert suspicion away from him?

"Madrid, 1935," the Gestapo man added. "It had to do with his giving up German citizenship."

"If you say so."

Von Günther came out of his office. Seeing the stranger sitting at Fritz's desk, he planted his hands on his hips. "What's this all about?"

"I'm questioning your secretary."

"If you want to question any of my subordinates, you contact me beforehand."

The little man looked as surprised as he was angered by the snub. His people weren't used to such pushback. For a moment, Fritz felt respect for von Günther.

"Herr Kolbe is one of my most trusted staffers. He is diligent, loyal, and never hesitates to work overtime."

"That's neither here nor there."

"Do you wish to go upstairs with me to the office of Foreign Minister von Ribbentrop? Herr Reich Foreign Minister is always willing to hear my concerns."

The little man stood up and looked von Günther up and down. *Go ahead and tear each other to shreds,* Fritz thought.

"I know Herr von Ribbentrop quite well," von Günther said. "I cannot imagine that he would be pleased about this. Why exactly are you here?"

"I owe you an explanation? That's certainly news to me. Havermann worked here too. Isn't that right, Herr Ambassador?"

"Then interrogate Havermann. He wasn't even in my department," von Günther replied.

"We already interrogated him."

"How is he?" Fritz asked.

The two other men, their cheeks flushed from anger, looked at him as if they'd forgotten he was there at his desk.

"Dead."

"His family?"

"Nothing will happen to the daughter. The wife is being questioned."

"Kolbe!"

"Herr Ambassador?"

"Go destroy those files now. You can show how it all works."

Fritz took out the stack of folders piling up in the safe. There was nothing to do about it now. He thought of all the information that was in there: the transport of Jews, shipyard reports, supply routes to the Eastern Front, documents on combating partisans, talks with the Japanese ambassador Oshima, assessments of Roosevelt's health, agents in Spain. All going into the fire, instead of to Allen Dulles.

"Wait," the little man said. He shouted down the corridor, "Corporal Schulz!" A young soldier came running up to the door holding his rifle to his chest. The little man ordered him to escort Fritz on his task.

Fritz was back in his office ten minutes later. He didn't know what von Günther and the Gestapo man had been doing while he was gone, but they were still standing across from one another. Von Günther held out a hand. Fritz handed him the page with the document numbers and the signature of the man in the basement who oversaw incineration. Von Günther held the page up to the Gestapo man's face.

"We're not close to finished here, Herr von Günther," the little man said. He saluted. *"Heil Hitler."* He left without shutting the door behind him. Von Günther tapped on the door and it swung closed but didn't catch. He pushed again and the latch clicked in place.

"If you encounter these secret-service types, Kolbe, just get clear of them. You really must be mentally ill to devote yourself to such a profession. Types like that only ever see things their own way, you know. They see ghosts, in the truest sense of the word. Very well, Kolbe, next thing up is . . . Is something wrong? You look pale."

Fritz again saw the wispy flames engulfing the documents, discoloring their edges before flaring into a bright blaze. Death sentences. And the noose around his own neck grew tighter the closer to him the questioning got. He had to get to Bern. He had to have Dulles, Greta, and Priest tell him what to do in dangerous situations. He also needed a weapon. He would never let himself be tortured in a Nazi prison.

He said he wasn't feeling too well. Von Günther handed him a glass of water from the office sink and said he should go home and get some rest. God knows, he said, Fritz was working too much. "Call it a day early, just this once. That's an order, Herr Kolbe. I am your superior."

Once Fritz was at the door, von Günther called after him. "Don't go getting scared, Kolbe, yes? Look at me. I am not scared. You still have some things to learn." He smiled with sympathy. "Well, go on. *Heil Hitler.*" Von Günther returned to his own office.

Fritz took him up on the offer. As he left, he carried the chair from the other side of his desk under his arm and, once outside, threw it onto one of the piles of rubble. There was only one chair in his office now, and no one would be able to sit and face him there again.

Fritz checked the blackout cardboard and curtains in his apartment and pressed them closed. *That'll do,* he thought.

On a map, he drew in the exact layout of the Wolf's Lair. He circled Hitler's bunker and the mansion where Ribbentrop resided. He kept thinking about Dulles, Greta, and Priest, and he worried about Eugen. It was highly likely Eugen was being watched. Fritz knew he had made mistakes. He couldn't attempt any more contact with Bern, not via Eugen at least, and he had to find some new way of working with the OSS. Dulles would know how to accomplish this.

He ate a piece of brown bread with a little butter and a pinch of salt. The rationing was growing worse, and he reminisced about plates full of Spanish tapas, Polish *bigos* smelling of bay leaf and sauerkraut, French cheese on bright-white bread, a steak at a restaurant in Cape Town down along the promenade, and that *Schweinebraten* stuffed with herbs his mother made. How had Marlene put it? Do some proper cooking, then get all snazzied up and smoke a cigarette after dinner. If only there were a single person he could talk to, one single soul he could tell what he was doing.

He heard footsteps out in the stairwell. Hurriedly, he folded up the map and slid it under his bed's worn-out mattress. Someone was knocking on the door. He stepped up to his front door and stared at the shabby wood. The person knocked again. He could act like he wasn't home.

"Fritz? It's me. Marlene."

She'd come to visit him—unannounced. How wonderful. How dangerous. He opened up.

"I got ahold of some cookies at the hospital. And—now brace yourself—they have chocolate on them!" She tilted her head sideways. "Fritz? How about a *please come in?*"

He so deeply yearned for her. He was just aching to pull her close right now. But the incident in the office weighed heavily on him—the officer's questioning, the destruction of those files whose contents he would never know, his fear.

"I can't right now," he said. He did not say, *Come in, sit down with me, let's eat the cookies, kiss me.*

"I don't understand," Marlene said. She fell silent, letting her head hang. He wanted to tell her so much. He didn't want to tell her a thing. Her shoes were old but well cared for, her suit worn but elegant. He heard her breathe through her lovely nose.

"What is it, Fritz? I was so happy about this. It wasn't easy for me, coming here."

He kept silent.

"Should we go somewhere else?"

He pressed his hands together and bit his lip. He held on tight to his resolve, snuffing out any resistance.

"It can't work," he said in a strange voice. "You . . . you're married."

Marlene straightened her shoulders. "That's for me to deal with." After a moment she added, "I was just fooling myself," and left.

He threw the door shut and cursed. He punched the wall. *Goddamn it!* He ran down the stairs and out onto the bomb-shattered Kurfürstendamm. The sky was as gray as the scarred city. He caught a glimpse of Marlene's blue suit and could see rage and disappointment in the way she held her back. He caught up with her and grabbed her arm. She yanked it away.

"What?"

"Marlene . . ." He waited until a woman and her child had passed by them.

"What?"

"It's difficult."

"Things like this always are."

"There is more to this."

"Watch yourself, Fritz Kolbe. I'm in no mood for nonsense. I don't care for it one bit."

"Sometimes I imagine that I'm with you in Africa," he said. "It's so lovely there. They have fresh-caught fish."

"I have no idea what you're saying."

"Come back to my place. Let's eat those cookies."

"I don't want to anymore." She walked on. Fritz watched her as she sidestepped a mound of debris and passed a burned-out car, becoming smaller and smaller amid the rubble. It was a sad sight. She walked through the dying city and, at one point, looked up at a weather-faded, reddish swastika flag that dangled limply from a scorched wall.

Come back.

Marlene.

Come here.

He dragged his bicycle from his building's foyer and rode to the Braunweins with his head down. Cursing with anger, Walter told Fritz that they now had to sleep with a little too much fresh air. He showed Fritz the bedroom—the outer wall had a nearly circular hole in it, over which Walter had nailed boards and a gray blanket.

"You don't look good, Fritz. What's the matter with you?"

My friend, Fritz thought, *my old buddy Walter. And I can't tell you a thing. I can't explain it to you any more than I can to Marlene.* Walter had never once brought up their tense encounter in Fritz's office. Walter was good at such things; he had always been so adept at letting things go. Just like that.

"The Gestapo came to your office, I hear?" Walter placed a hand on his shoulder. "Those types can really scare a person. But hey-ho, Fritz, it's not like you have anything to hide."

Fritz cursed himself for having come here at all. There was no point.

"I have to go abroad soon for a few weeks," Walter said. "Could you check in on Käthe?"

"Where to?"

"Fritz, please. The people in Intelligence found a way to send me overseas—a pretty risky way too."

"Walter—where? Give me a compass direction, at least."

"North. East . . . South. West."

"Are there any memos about it at the Foreign Office?"

Walter's brow pinched, and he smoothed out the blanket on the wall. Had Walter noticed something different about Fritz? Could Walter see through him?

"Does this assignment you're going on have an official name?"

"That's quite enough, Fritz."

Käthe pushed open the door, which dragged on the floor, likely from the blast. She'd made coffee, she said.

They sat down at the table. Nearby, the Braunweins' People's Receiver radio played the music of Franz Liszt. Fritz asked Käthe to turn it off. Käthe looked at him and didn't budge, her eyes blank. *For heaven's sake,* Fritz thought. He turned the dial until it crackled and Liszt faded into silence.

"Turn down the assignment, Walter. And you, Käthe—leave Berlin, once and for all. Get out of here for good." He stood at the table and stared at his friends. No one spoke. The wall clock ticked on listlessly.

Fritz couldn't stand it. If only they could all return to a life without Hitler.

"Get away from here, Käthe. Your husband will be leaving you all alone."

"Fritz, have you lost your mind?" Walter shook his head.

"It's his job," Käthe said gently. "He can't take me along with him like he used to. I'll be here when he comes back. I'll be here when Horst has to leave again."

"The two of you know as well as I that the war is lost."

"Goddamn it, Fritz," Walter said. "You're saying too much. People are getting killed for outbursts like this."

"What, are you going to turn me in?"

Both men stood. Walter stepped up to him. They stood inches from each other, sharing the same breath.

"I would never turn you in, Fritz. That kind of betrayal makes me sick." Walter placed a hand on Fritz's arm. "We're all too worked up. Is it any wonder? I say we drink a schnapps."

Have a few minutes of peace, Fritz told himself. *Relax a little, have a schnapps.*

"I'll get the nice glasses," Käthe said.

"You stay there, I'll get them," Walter said. The glasses were small, with thick stems. The light from the floor lamp glistened in the cuts of the glass like ice crystals, and the glasses felt nice to hold. The schnapps was the color of water and smooth as silk.

"Where are you off to, Walter?" Fritz asked.

"I'm not saying. You know there are things I can't tell you."

"More schnapps," Fritz said. He was feeling far too reckless. He desperately needed to find a better way to navigate between the two worlds in which he drifted. At the moment, he was doing a balancing act with one foot in each and it was threatening to rip him apart. "Let's do another," he said.

Walter laughed. "You sure?"

"Sure I am, come on. Käthe too."

"I'd rather not."

"Oh, come on, Käthe."

After working a few hours the next morning, Fritz adjusted his tie and headed out down Wilhelmstrasse. He had to get to Charité Hospital, to Marlene.

The door to her office was shut. He wanted to knock but couldn't make himself. He walked down the gray hallway, passing stretchers and nurses in worn-out smocks, then turned around and headed back, facing the dark door like a wall before him. He raised a fist to his ear, ready to knock, but stopped his hand inches from the wood. He cursed, then knocked.

"Come in."

He opened the door.

"Out!"

He shut the door. He never thought Marlene capable of such a harsh tone. It hit him hard, squashing his will to fight. He nudged the door open and said, "I'll return later." He only got Marlene's back.

He headed back to his office. Von Günther was standing at his desk with another man and asked where he'd been. "Work, work, work," Fritz said.

"Where's the other chair?" von Günther asked. His open hand gestured at the empty spot in front of Fritz's desk. Coin-size imprints in the carpet showed where chair legs had stood.

"It's *kaput*. I'm sorry, Herr Ambassador."

"This is?" The stranger's words sounded more like an order than a question. He was short and wore a general's uniform that gathered in folds over his flat stomach.

"My secretary, Fritz Kolbe, Herr General. Herr Kolbe, may I introduce General Gehlen, Foreign Armies East. Head of Military Intelligence on the Eastern Front. One of our best men."

Gehlen eyed Fritz up and down. The man was slender with a pointy face and had thinning hair, like Fritz. "Fritz Kolbe, secretary to Ambassador von Günther," he said and tapped at his forehead. "Best notepad ever invented, right up here," he said. "You only have to keep it sharp. Did you know you can train the memory, just like a muscle?" He continued, "Von Günther and I have been going through some documents. We want to deposit certain papers at the diplomatic mission in Bern—the reason does not concern you. Von Günther tells me you are absolutely trustworthy; you even did the Switzerland run once, to his utmost satisfaction."

"Yes sir, Herr General."

"I never forget a face," Gehlen said. "And I appreciate loyal staffers. It's of great importance to us that we have von Günther here, acting as the Foreign Office branch of the Wehrmacht. You are aware of the position you're in, Kolbe?"

"Of course, Herr General."

"Von Günther?"

"I would entrust my children to him."

"Always be watching out, Kolbe. Always be looking around you. Be attentive, listen to details. In tense times people become weak—it's unforgivable. But if you're capable of recognizing others' weaknesses, then you're already well on the road to success. Like I am. Weakness, Kolbe—it's everywhere. Well, I'm flying back to Russia today. Von Günther will give you your instructions, and you are to tell no one."

"Yes sir, Herr General."

"Gentlemen."

"Heil Hitler," von Günther said.

"Heil Hitler," Gehlen replied.

Once the general had left, von Günther rubbed at his chin. He looked tense.

"Perhaps, Kolbe, perhaps that man has just the sort of greatness that our system and the Führer need. I do wonder sometimes . . . How should I put it? If a person is just one individual, right in the thick of things, then that person loses sight of the whole. It's about the mass movement, Kolbe. The masses are about size; masses are great. As an individual, one is nothing.

"Now, I can tell you that other departments here don't work the way they would if I were running them—and that's not even taking into account any questions of competence. So, Kolbe, you should organize the following files according to this formula I have here . . ."

Von Günther explained the system to him. He had sealed the folders for travel as usual, so there was no way Fritz would be getting at any of this material. They spoke a few minutes more, then von Günther went back to his office—but first he stopped in the doorway. "Gehlen thinks big," he said. He made a circular motion with his index finger as if winding the hand of a clock. "We should keep in good standing with that man. He's actually a fairly agreeable fellow, all things considered. Tell me, Kolbe, can Weygand be relied on more than von Lützow, in your view? Over in Switzerland, I mean."

"No."

"No?"

"No."

"Very well. So then, it's off to Bern at the end of next week. You arrange it."

"Herr Ambassador, one last question if I may: Do you know where Walter Braunwein is being sent?"

Von Günther planted his hands on his hips. "What's this about?"

"He said something to me about a new assignment abroad. I was just thinking, well, maybe I could ask him a little favor. Maybe he could bring me some—"

"Have you gone mad, Kolbe? A little favor? Bring you something? It's not a trip to some beach resort. Sometimes I don't understand you at all."

"Pardon me, Herr Ambassador. It was just a question."

"We live in an age of answers, Kolbe."

Fritz worked until von Günther had left for the day. Then he opened the safe, stuffed into his briefcase as many files intended for incineration as possible, and rode his bicycle through Berlin's battleship-colored streets of rubble.

At home he checked the cardboard and curtains on the windows, sat down at the table, and began looking over the files. It was a thick stack. He searched for clues that pointed to Walter's trip but found nothing.

He began to write: about rail networks to Auschwitz, Treblinka, and other camps; about secret munitions depots in the East; about infiltrating the Vatican; about a secret transmitter near Dublin used to support Irish Nazi sympathizers against the British and to notify U-boats; about ship sections being manufactured in the Ruhr region; the restructuring of combat divisions in France; spies in Italy; ongoing diplomatic efforts in Franco's Spain; advisors in Japan; and insights straight from General Gehlen himself about Stalin's secret service. It went on and on. He wrote the whole night through, until a pumpkin-tinged sun rose above the ruins and undamaged buildings that made up the chaos of Berlin.

9

SECRET MARLENE

The people were standing and crouching, shoulder to shoulder, head to hip, clinging to one another, as if they could protect each other from the thing intent on devouring the city and its inhabitants. They were staring at the concrete ceiling of the air-raid shelter under the Adlon Hotel as if their gazes alone could keep it from collapsing. Fritz could practically touch the fear that permeated the commotion in the bunker. An old man was ranting and pointing: he had told them all! And now when the phosphorus bombs came, the air itself would burn.

In the flickering light Fritz saw Marlene standing a few yards away, her back pressed against the wall. She was holding her hands to her cheeks, her elbows pinned to her sides as if lashed down. Von Günther was kneeling with his wife and two daughters, who had been visiting him at his office, von Günther being one of the few who permitted himself such visits. He was stroking his girls' flat, dull hair, looking to his wife now and then, fear filling every corner of his broad face. Fritz smelled urine and rotten apples. Some soldiers were smoking cigarettes, the glow of burning tobacco the only color down here among the dusty shapes. He pushed through to Marlene. She was as pale as the cement powder fluttering down around them.

"I'm sorry," he said to counter the force of the hammering bombs. A brutally near miss rocked the bunker, scoring the old masonry with glowing-hot embers that floated down from some crack or crevice above. Screams rang out. Someone wailed that they'd all be buried alive. Fritz placed his hands against the quaking cement to either side of Marlene's face. The bridge of her nose was shiny, her lips dry and chapped. The tears from her eyes were gray and bleary with grime.

"They just need to stop." Her voice trembled.

He bent down close to her face. "You want the Nazis to win this war?" he whispered.

The bunker swayed like a ship in a storm, throwing Fritz against her. He felt her body, damp with sweat, beneath his and her hair against his cheek. He lowered his head onto her shoulder. If he died on one of these air-raid nights, it would have all been for nothing. No one would ever know what he'd done, and Katrin would remain in the dark about his absence for the rest of her life. He had to survive. His story had to survive. Marlene had to survive.

A great crack sounded from farther back in the bunker. In seconds, all went dark around them. Thin voices shouted for help, then matches flickered and, after that, the timid flames of candles. Fritz felt Marlene wrap her arms around his back and he pressed himself to her. Why hadn't they all been holding each other this whole time? He put one hand on the back of her neck, feeling the muscles below her hairline.

"I have to tell you something, Marlene. It's important. It's dangerous."

Her arms squeezed tighter. He'd made yet another mistake. He could not tell Marlene a thing. Nothing.

The bombing strikes ended. Things grew calmer in the bunker. The stench of feces mingled with the dust, sweat, and breath, and voices somewhere were arguing over a bucket. The old man's gravelly words penetrated the dark chaos: "We've all been betrayed . . ." Fritz heard an odd sound, like a sack collapsing. He couldn't quite make out what had happened but thought he'd seen someone punch the man in the stomach.

They would have to stay down in the bunker awhile, so that the fires up above didn't consume them as soon as they unbolted the steel door. Every one of them knew what awaited them outside.

Von Günther stepped next to them, wiping grime from his forehead sticky with sweat. "Yes, I always say this job does have its good side. You're that professor's assistant, aren't you? Well played, Kolbe—in an air-raid shelter."

Both of von Günther's girls were clutching at his legs, so Fritz squatted down to ask them their names and told them this would all be over one day.

"But there aren't any playgrounds left," one of the girls said.

"We'll build plenty of new ones," Fritz said.

"Heil Hitler," said the girls.

Von Günther rubbed the fear from his face. "It's always tough on the kids," he whispered into Fritz's ear—Fritz should be glad he didn't have kids.

Eventually, the fearful, stinking throng slowly made its way toward the bunker exits, to climb the stairs up to the unknown. Marlene took Fritz's hand. They didn't take the underground tunnel back to the Office like von Günther and the other officials and staffers did.

Above ground, Fritz glanced only briefly at the corpses, the shreds of clothing, the final embraces between mother and child. Marlene's eyes reflected the churning, fiery glow. Fire trucks tried to make their way through the smoking rubble of crushed pots and chairs and all the usual nonsense that got hurled from smoking homes. The Brandenburg Gate stood dark and shattered, while farther north flames soared between earth and sky, the air itself burning. A soot-black man with singed hair came up to them. He carried a dead child, her arms and legs swinging. "Good evening, name's Jaschke, this is my daughter." He moved on, speaking to the next person he saw. "Jaschke, good evening. Pardon me. This is my daughter." An invisible cord tightened around Fritz's neck, and his heart felt too dry to perform its bloody chore. The man walked on through the fiery glow and the stinking refuse of war, and disappeared into the darkness.

"For the love of God . . ." Marlene began.

Fritz grabbed her upper arm.

"I'm smuggling secret files from the Office for American intelligence in Bern."

"What?"

"I'm spying for the Americans."

Marlene pushed him away. The crackling fires exhaled, a hot wind battering the blackened square before the Adlon.

"What are you talking about?"

Marlene looked to the sky burning in the north and in the east, at this turbulent panorama of war with its muck and filth and ended lives. She struck Fritz in the chest with her fist.

"I know," he said.

About a hundred yards away, a building welled up golden with a fiery glow and then gave way, sending a cloud of dust flowing down the canyon of streets already buried alive. Flames raged in the skeleton of the building next door, rolling out of windows and doors. More fire trucks and ambulances rumbled up and stopped at angles among the craters and debris, soldiers laden with rattling gear running and disappearing into the smoke.

"I'm taking you home," Fritz said. One side of Marlene's face flashed brighter whenever the flames welled up and set the grimy sky on fire. The sun was about to rise beyond all the smoke but it remained stubbornly pale, as if trying to stay hidden and not have to come out.

"Don't touch me," Marlene said. "You are completely out of your mind! How could you tell me that? They'll kill the both of us."

She walked off and Fritz knew better than to follow her. On she went into the night sizzling from the fires, inhaling all. After only a few yards she blended in with the murky, thick air. The last thing he saw of Marlene was the flickering outline of the handkerchief she held pressed to her face, and then she vanished into a city that was devouring its people.

Fritz trudged home. He squeezed his eyes shut when passing streets where the asphalt had melted and rehardened over human extremities. He covered his ears when he encountered people trying to clear piles of rubble many feet high with their bare hands while screaming for those crushed somewhere underneath. He passed trees that had become torches and were now thin as arms and dry as stone. He did not look at the parts of corpses he stumbled over, or at the evidence of what a hellish blaze did to a body. He tried to hum the chorus from Beethoven's Ninth Symphony: *Joy, lovely divine spark, daughter from Elysium . . .*

How can we do these things to one another? he wondered.

He didn't see Marlene for nearly a week. Some of his colleagues hadn't turned up at the office again, making everyone wonder exactly how the latest air raid had devoured them. Müller said the Luftwaffe would inflict retribution and it would be fearsome, *Heil Hitler.*

In Fritz's office, von Günther touched his fingers to his forehead and mused out loud whether such an attack wasn't in the end something "great" after all. "You must abstract," he said. "Understand, yes? Abstraction is the root of a true people's movement. The individual as a concrete object does not hold top priority. It's complicated . . . a complicated yet fascinating subject."

You have gone truly and completely nuts, Fritz thought, but didn't say a thing.

When he saw Marlene in the Office again she passed by him without a word, giving only a curt nod and walking around a ladder that was leaning against the corridor wall. A staffer was standing on it, hammering a new nail into the wall to rehang the portrait of Hitler that had fallen. Everything within Fritz told him to follow Marlene, urged him to embrace her. He waited outside Frau Hansen's office until she came out.

"Can I talk to you? Please."

She pushed by him, her shoulder brushing the wall. Fritz followed and grabbed at her arm.

"Please, Marlene."

"Do you want to kill me?" she spluttered. Two men in uniform were watching them.

"This evening, Marlene. In that café where we sat for the first time. At eight. Please."

"And if they're already after you? I'll be arrested right along with you."

Fritz looked down the corridor, waved to a colleague from the Jewish Department, and tried to look Marlene in the eyes. He couldn't do it.

"This evening. Please, Marlene."

Not caring whether anyone was watching, she hit him in the chest with her fist and left.

"Herr Kolbe, could you please hand me that picture of the Führer?" Fritz looked up at the man on the ladder. He had turned in Fritz's direction and was holding a hand out. "Herr Kolbe?"

Fritz went back into his office.

The front façade of the café on Mommsenstrasse was gone, but a sign hanging from a scorched beam read "Still Serving Drinks." Fritz sat at a table, the debris grit on the floor crunching underfoot, and ordered a bottle of red wine. "Provided you still have any," he said. The one-armed waiter served the bottle with two mismatched glasses. Fritz was a half hour early. He hoped that this was why she was not yet there.

Marlene came down the street, now only wide enough for a hand-cart, making her way between the slopes of rubble, and sat down across from him without a word. Fritz poured the wine, its bright red astounding to him in this city that had been robbed of all color.

"The head of American intelligence in Bern is named Allen Dulles. He has two colleagues working closely with him: William Priest and Greta Stone. The cover address is Herrengasse 23 in Bern."

Marlene lit a cigarette and turned her face to the side without taking her eyes off him. "You know what they do to people like you?"

"I had to tell someone—you. Who else could I tell?"

"Himmler, Kaltenbrunner, the SS, the Gestapo. These are ruthless mass murderers. Have you gone crazy?"

"I'm not the one who's crazy."

Marlene laughed bitterly. She looked for the waiter, who was paging through a newspaper at the bar.

"You are. You're stealing documents from the Office. You know people in American intelligence? Seriously?"

"Yes."

"My God, Fritz." Marlene placed a hand over her eyes and shook her head. Fritz wanted to stroke her hair, or touch the tip of her nose. He clutched his wineglass.

"He agreed," she said.

"Who agreed to what?"

"The professor. They're doing experiments—on Jews, in the camps. They're using them as human research subjects. He told me about it. He's not taking part, but he did sign his name to a paper. It's for science."

"The documents I'm compiling have to do with criminal acts. They all must stand trial one day. When they do, there will be firm evidence against them."

"Isn't this weird? Here we sit, no one listening in on us—we can say what we want, having a glass of wine. One little bit of happiness. My God, Fritz. It's all so unreal."

"You have such a lovely nose."

She laughed. It sounded just like that first laugh he'd heard from her: clear and resounding and completely honest. Laughing like that made her lips all smooth.

"Fritz Kolbe, just what am I supposed to do with you?"

"Whatever you want?"

She raised her eyebrows, staring at him. "I have to give this some thought—about you, about us. Thank you for inviting me." She looked out over the street. "Berlin can still be nice sometimes, I have to say."

"It will be again," Fritz said.

"We met amid such misery."

"But we did meet."

Marlene dropped her head to one side and watched him from the corner of her eye. "Yes, that's the one nice thing about it. Wait till I tell Gisela about—"

"Who's Gisela?"

"A girlfriend. When I tell her about us—"

"You're telling her about us?"

"Hey, when did you start interrupting? When I tell her about us, I'll . . . It's just so odd—meeting amid the rubble, having a quarrel in the ruins. Romance really is something else."

"Is she a Nazi?"

"She works in a munitions factory. She always came in second in swimming, behind me. Yet she could joke about it, even slapped my butt in the shower after. Gisela understands me."

"Don't talk to anyone about us, Marlene."

"This is coming from little blabbermouth you?"

"I've been so damn secretive, it's practically a sickness."

"That's what you think, Fritz."

He didn't get to see her for a couple more days. It was another air raid of all things that sent her to him. The knock on his door came at that very moment of the morning when the air was cooling down, when the filth and dust had settled on the downtrodden city and the fires had burned themselves out. At the sound of the knock, he gathered the files into a pile and hid them under the mattress. Fatigue had dulled the fear he felt every time someone showed up at his place unannounced.

He opened the door.

◆ ◆ ◆

"And there she stood," Fritz says. "In that strange light—for some reason, it was always dim in those days. On the ground at her feet was an old bedsheet tied into a sack. In it was everything she had left after the air raid."

"We didn't come to hear a love story," Wegner says.

"Herr Wegner, tell me one story that doesn't include love. Such a story wouldn't make any sense at all."

"Touché," Veronika says.

"I want to write about Fritz Kolbe the spy," Wegner says.

"Reducing people down like that just doesn't work," Fritz says. "It never works. No person is just one thing, certainly not me. Maybe some dreary religious guru sitting around out in the desert, but a real human being? A complete human being? *My name is Legion, for we are many*—isn't that how it goes?"

"That's it," Veronika says. "I like that one."

"The facts, Herr Kolbe," Wegner says.

"The fact was and is that we were in love, that we wanted each other. Desire isn't a privilege limited to youth. We went right at each other. We were opposing the war and the destruction and the fear through our acts of love." Fritz hesitates. He's all for granting erotic latitude but is not so interested in publicizing the details. Scrutiny takes the magic away. His story of espionage should not be filled with magic, yet his story of Marlene must.

Fritz says he's going to throw those schnitzels he promised in the pan. On his way to the kitchen, he hears Wegner mutter, "Typical." After a few minutes, Veronika leans in the doorway and asks if she can help.

"Keep me company," Fritz says. "I rarely get visitors up here. It's probably going to stay that way awhile."

"Except for Marlene, right?"

"Except for Marlene, of course."

"It was nice hearing what you said about love still being so exciting, even when . . . um, I'm not sure how to put it."

"When a person already has a few years under their belt?"

"That, yes. Pardon."

"It's completely all right," Fritz says.

He holds a wooden spoon in the fat drippings, and little bubbles form; the fat is hot enough. He coats the pinkish schnitzels in the breadcrumbs he's made and places them carefully in the pan. They sizzle, and the schnitzels' flavorful aroma fills the air immediately.

"Herr Kolbe? What are you not telling us?"

"Why are you here exactly, Fräulein Hügel?"

"Me? Oh. Well, I want to make something of myself. Hardly any women are working journalists—not in Switzerland, and not in your Germany. I'm one of the very, very few. I won't deny I've had good support. My father might have had a hand in opening doors. After Martin—Herr Wegner—started speaking with Herr Sacher, he talked to our main editor, then to me. He told me everything he knew about you, from Herr Sacher and from that early article that came out about you, as well as from his own intense research. I don't know how to put it, Herr Kolbe, but I was quite excited. A spy, opposing the Nazis. That impressed me. I come from a small village. All I remember from my childhood is the smell of cows and tight confines. I hope to meet interesting people and . . ." She forms a camera with her fingers and says, "Click."

"Plenty of people are interesting," Fritz says, "provided you take time to listen. What's your colleague's story?"

"Martin? He likes biographies. He says history is made by people, not by some connecting forces that historians think they recognize in hindsight. By people, individual people. He reads a lot, but only biographies. Otherwise nothing, almost nothing."

"Reading novels is good," Fritz says. "Reading them makes your life better, even in tough times."

"You're avoiding my question, Herr Kolbe."

Fritz turns over the schnitzels. One side is golden brown now, tiny bits of fat jumping up in the pan. "There's salad as well," he says. "You do know he keeps eyeing you?"

"He's married."

Fritz's laugh is partly bitter, partly amused. "Doesn't matter," he says. "What was the question again?"

"What are you not telling us, or not telling yourself?"

He stares at the woman. The thought occurs to him that he looks older than he is. Who does she see at this moment? Her glance echoes her question. He wants to tell her, he really does. He can't do it.

◆　◆　◆

"I don't have an apartment anymore. This"—Marlene pointed at the dirty sheet—"is all that's left. A few pots, Fritz. Not one book, no pictures, not my favorite flower vase or dishes. Not the letters from my son." She put her hand to her mouth. "Just a few pots."

"Pots are good, Marlene." Fritz hugged her and she began to cry. He took her into the living room, poured her a cup of tea, and set some more chocolate from Switzerland on a little plate.

"Both those lovely books you brought me from Switzerland are gone too." She sobbed and said nothing more, just sat there with her head hanging, and he let her cry. He got the files back out and continued writing. Once she had calmed down a little, he asked about her mother, who he remembered lived in Berlin. Marlene said she'd been evacuated to Southern Germany.

"I'm from Munich," she said. "I was born there. Mom and Dad had a men's clothing shop. Actually, it was more Mom's. My dad was a dreamer. He wanted to write novels. I liked that."

"So, did he?"

Marlene smiled and shook her head. She sipped tea, ate chocolate, and began to look around the room. Fritz pulled a pile of photos from the cabinet. "Africa," he said.

As he worked, Marlene looked at the photos, pausing at some pictures, turning others over. When she was done she tapped the pile into a neat rectangle on the table. She slowly reached for one of the documents, turning it her way. Her wedding ring twinkled. He slid paper and pencil over to her.

She read. "Fritz, my God." Her voice conveyed recognition and despair.

"It's the right thing to do," he said.

"The French Resistance," Marlene murmured.

"I only summarize the most important things."

"Methods used by the SS in Russia, and by the Wehrmacht. The Wehrmacht too?"

"September 1941. Babi Yar, a ravine near Kiev, I think. Over three thousand Jewish women, children, and men were shot to death by units of the magnificent Wehrmacht. General Field Marshal von Reichenau welcomed the measures and requested that radical methods be used. Disputes over whether too much ammunition is being used on Jews instead of at the front are still going on today."

"Measures? Radical methods?"

"Yes."

"But, Fritz, if you . . . what if you hand over, say, a secret U-boat route, and the Americans or British go sink one of those U-boats?"

"Yes," he said. "That's exactly what this is."

He'd mostly avoided thinking about it up to now. Now he pictured the childlike, beardless young man who'd driven him to the Wolf's Lair, the driver he'd told to "watch out for yourself." He'd been pushing any true consideration of the deadly consequences of his actions deeper and deeper into the darkest dungeons of his soul, knowing full well that they were to reemerge one day—yet not what they were to inflict on him.

"You're fine with that?"

"No."

"Yet you do it?"

"Yes." He clung to this one little word.

"You must never repeat one word about any special cartography units, Fritz. Not one word! My husband is a cartographer."

He pushed the pages and pencil away and stared at Marlene. If only her husband had died years ago, like hundreds of thousands of others in this war. He placed his hand on hers.

"I promise," he said.

"Your word of honor?"

"Yes."

"So no information about—"

"Yes. Jesus."

"He's my husband, Fritz."

"He's the other man."

They gazed at each other. Marlene was twisting her wedding ring on her finger. Was she only here because of the war? What did an attractive and energetic woman like Marlene Wiese want from a too-short, staid-looking man like him? How much time and room was there left for them?

"It's so nice having you here, Marlene."

She smiled and put one hand over the other, hiding her twinkling wedding ring. "So, how's it going there?"

"Uh, what do you mean *going*?"

Marlene tapped on the paper. "Penmanship isn't exactly your strong suit."

She reached for more paper, but before long she said she had to lie down and shut her eyes. She didn't have any other clothes to wear, she muttered, and no pajamas either. He got out one of his shirts. Marlene undressed. He saw her naked for the first time. His desire for her was gentle and calm. She pulled on the shirt, and he stepped before her and fastened the buttons over her breasts and her stomach, feeling her pubic hair at the lowest button. When she leaned over his cracked sink while brushing her teeth, the flesh of her bottom shined. He brought her into the bedroom.

"Nice place you have here," she said. Fritz drew the covers over her and stroked strands of hair from her face. "When you come in later, hold me tight."

"I will be sure to," he said.

When he came into the bedroom later, she was sleeping on her side, her legs pulled up to her stomach. Fritz undressed and carefully climbed into bed. He nestled up to her creamy-white back and didn't know what to do with his arousal. He had yearned to make love for so long, and so deeply, yet she was already anxious, and he didn't want to burden her with his erection. He carefully placed his arm around her chest, then laid his head against the back of her neck and pulled his lower body away from her. It was impossible to sleep like this. He pressed his cock into the warmth between Marlene's thighs. She shifted, murmured something, and turned her face deeper into the pillow. Fritz held her tightly to him. He could feel his own heart beating, and Marlene's heart too, under his hand in that shadowy crease between her breast and ribs.

He had overslept; he was supposed to have been in the Office over an hour ago. He rushed into the kitchen and stopped in his tracks. Marlene was standing naked at the oven, wearing his felt slippers. She hadn't

170

combed her hair, her gaze was not yet wakeful, and her salmon-tinted nipples looked cool and small. Fritz looked at her. His eyes filled with desire. He wanted to cling to this image of her, wanted it never to disappear from his mind.

"I could stand here for hours," he said. "For days."

She smiled, calm, satisfied, maybe even happy. She'd found some coffee, she said, and handed him a cup. Her fingers gleamed against the porcelain, the glow of her skin traveling along her outstretched arm, her shoulder, her collarbone, and the curves of her breasts, along her ribs, and down to her hips and her upper thighs.

"Can you go in even later?" she asked.

She had tiny creases in the corners of her eyes, and when she laughed deep lines etched curves in her broad cheeks. Her jawbone was set hard, and the skin over her collarbone stretched taut. Her nipples reached out to him when he kissed her. She had a deep, dark navel in her tummy, a little burrow into the very heart of her. Her privates smelled of flesh and lust. A thick, long scar ran across her left knee, and her toes were big. "Aren't they awful?" she asked.

"Nothing about you could be awful in any way," he said. He kissed her on the mouth. With her eyes so close to his, he could see the tiny black dots sprinkled within the blue. "I want to be the breath that flows through that wonderful nose of yours," he said.

"I have a wonderful nose?" she asked.

"You do," he said. She asked him to hand her a cigarette. Today she was going to take care of the administrative details. She would give Charité Hospital as her new address; the professor had nothing against her doing so, and she had everything there she needed. She didn't want to be living with someone, so moving into Fritz's place permanently wouldn't work either.

"Because you're married," Fritz asked.

She blew smoke out. "I've betrayed him. We promised each other that such a thing would never happen. I didn't want it."

"You wanted it with me."

She pushed him away, her arms out stiff. He pressed his weight against her, squeezing his eyes shut because he couldn't bear to see her looking at him like this, then he felt her elbows begin to give way, her arms going limp. He slumped against her and there they stayed: still, just breathing.

A few minutes later they got dressed. Fritz watched how Marlene put her bra on backward, fastened the hook, turned the bra around, and pushed her arms through the straps, her breasts rising and then vanishing behind the white fabric.

"I don't want to do anything that's bad for you," he said. "Ever."

"You already have, Fritz."

Von Günther was standing in Fritz's office holding files.

"You're in far too late, Kolbe."

"I'm so embarrassed," Fritz said.

"Stop." Von Günther slammed the files on the desk, a little blast of air shifting papers.

"Our Führer," he began, and another of his lectures came whooshing at Fritz, one about "greatness" and "will" and the giant, concrete-abstract machine that defined modernity. "You are a trusty little cog in this large powerful machine. You must comprehend that."

"Yes sir, Herr Ambassador." Fritz so hated this. His heart seethed.

Von Günther turned on his heels. He exhaled loudly, the heavy, responsibility-laden sigh of an important man.

"Tell me one thing, Kolbe: Did this have anything to do with that woman?" Von Günther circled two breasts on his chest.

You bastard, thought Fritz. He wouldn't be able to keep Marlene a secret now that von Günther had seen him with her in the air-raid shelter.

"Frau Wiese was bombed out of her home."

"She's staying at your place right now? Temporarily."

"Yes sir."

Von Günther laughed. "Just don't be late again, Kolbe. All right? No one will find out a thing from me."

"Thank you very much."

"Women, yes? Good, now listen. These files here are for von Lützow's secretary, Weygand. Only for him. He will pick you up at the train station in Bern. You'll give him these documents—the rest goes like usual. Don't say one word about this to von Lützow. Understood?"

"Yes sir. Is something wrong?"

"I can't tell you, Kolbe. I'm not allowed to tell anyone. I don't want to either."

"No, of course not. By the way, does anyone know why Havermann was arrested, Herr Ambassador?"

"He was listening to enemy broadcasts. His daughter reported it."

"His own daughter?"

"This girl already senses greatness. As it should be. It's a good thing."

"Havermann was listening to music."

"Broadcast by the enemy."

"Music doesn't have a nationality."

"What was that? Kolbe, are you crazy? I never want to hear such things coming from you. What is wrong with you?"

After having spent so many years alone in his apartment, it felt strange to open his apartment door and know that Marlene would be sitting on the sofa, reading something, or maybe cooking a frugal meal in the kitchen. Marlene had gotten some clothing from a donation held on the square at Gendarmenmarkt. She used to hire a Jewish tailor to do her sewing for her, but he was long gone, along with his whole family, so she stitched up the skirts, jackets, and blouses herself. The tailor's name had been Liebling. "I couldn't do anything for them, Fritz."

On the last night before his second trip to Bern, Marlene held out her hand to him as he came into the living room. They knew every day, every night, every time they touched could be their last. The notion was nothing new during wartime, yet no matter how many times the words were spoken, the sentiment never lost its spark of urgency. Perhaps this was the one headline that applied to all of their lives.

After they made love, Fritz told Marlene about Katrin, and she told him about her dead son.

"He was such a lovely boy. He should have lived," Marlene said. Fritz was holding her in his arms. "It's so horrible when children die before the parents."

Fritz would have loved to say something nice to cheer her up. But what?

"We're going to finish off everyone who's responsible. We'll hurt them wherever we can."

The next morning, she helped him bind the thin pages around his calf. Her hands were shaking. She asked if it pulled at the hairs on his leg and laughed uncertainly.

"If they catch you," she said, "I do not want to end up in their hands. I don't, Fritz. I want to live."

Marlene pulled open a drawer and took out a butcher knife. She stood there, tall and strong, her thick hair undone, her nose flushed a little. Fritz didn't know what he was supposed to say. He cradled her hand that held the knife and caressed it.

"I'll go right now and take these files to be incinerated as ordered and have it signed off, all completely normal and according to regulations."

"You're dreaming."

"Of a better world, yes."

She hugged him. He felt the knife flat against his back and her breasts against his chest.

"Will you bring more chocolate back?"

He smiled. "Yes," he said, "I'll be sure to."

"I'm not going to the train station, Fritz. We'll say good-bye here."

They hugged again. The knife fell and Fritz heard it cut into the floorboards.

"And ham, Fritz? What do you think? Or a little cheese?"

"I love you," he said. From the doorway, he turned to take a look at her. She was standing in the kitchen, the cool light finding one side of her, and next to her stood the knife in the floor, its blade a gleaming gray. He put down his suitcase, went back in, and kissed her lips.

"Now it's even tougher traveling to Bern," he said. "Yet easier."

"Both?"

"Yes," Fritz said. "Life seems to be that way."

He telephoned Käthe Braunwein from his desk at the Office. She answered sounding faint and weary.

"Käthe, where is Walter supposed to be sent?"

"You remember when we went hiking? In the Allgäu? It was spring then, those big Allgäu meadows full of flowers and—"

"Käthe! Käthe—where to?"

"Ah, Fritz."

Fritz cursed. He could have screamed.

"Käthe, listen, I . . ." Right then someone knocked on his door. "Yeah, yeah, come in!" Fritz shouted. It was Heinz Müller in his baggy uniform. Fritz put a hand over the receiver. "What, Müller?"

"*Heil Hitler.* I have some teletypes here for Ambassador von Günther."

"Fine, yes, just leave them here. I'll take care of it."

Young Müller left the papers on Fritz's desk, saluted, and left. Fritz waited until the door was shut.

"Käthe, where is Walter going?" he shouted.

The door pushed open again. Müller was staring at him.

"What now, Müller? And kindly knock before you enter."

"I heard you shouting, Herr Kolbe. Who are you speaking to there?"

"Get out!" He pressed the phone to his ear, feeling the hands of those men onboard the *Louisiana* on him again. He still didn't know for sure if Müller had been among them. He scratched at his calf strapped with papers. He needed some clue about Walter Braunwein.

"Käthe, please . . ."

She'd hung up.

Using a false name, Fritz called the field office where Walter was working. He got right to the point and asked for a Herr Braunwein, but got rudely rebuffed.

And his death sentence pressed tight against his calf.

The border checkpoint inspector at the train station in Basel was the same one Fritz had encountered the first time he crossed the border. This time the man had dark circles under his eyes, and he was thinner. Fritz thought too that he could see more soldiers patrolling under the station's dark roof than before. The man ahead of him in line had glanced around and noticed the diplomatic pass in Fritz's hand. He asked Fritz if he was also from the Office, which would be quite the coincidence considering that some people who worked in the same ministry never once ran into one another even in Berlin. He said he was heading to Zurich for two days of work, then some rest and relaxation in Switzerland, wonderful indeed. He handed the border inspector his papers, turned Fritz's way one more time, and laughed—somewhat too loudly, Fritz thought.

The border inspector slapped the man's papers against his palm and waved over two soldiers. "Go with these men."

The previously unknown colleague looked back at Fritz, confused, his eyes blank with fear. *Better you than me,* Fritz thought. The inspector took Fritz's passport and visa from his hand and thumbed through a list.

"Have you crossed the border before, Herr Kolbe?"

"Yes sir."

The inspector pointed at Fritz's briefcase. Fritz set it on the table and pulled out the documents. The inspector raised one of the official stamps close to his eyes, shuffled through the other files, and again read the memo about the document box being transported on to Bern. Fritz felt his left knee trembling and hoped it wasn't visible through his wide trousers. He began to sweat despite the cold wind blowing through the station hall, and he could smell the oily smoke from the locomotive on his clothes. If he were led off into that customs hut now, it would all be over. On that safari he'd taken with Walter a hunting guide had told him never to look a wild animal in the eyes. How did it work with wild humans? *Defend yourself,* he thought. *If it happens, defend yourself. That's the one final thing that you can do.*

"All right." The inspector held up Fritz's papers but moved them just out of reach when Fritz reached for them. "Don't let all this go to your head, Herr Kolbe."

This ate away at Fritz. It nauseated him to have to constantly swallow such comments. *I could vomit,* he thought. Having to keep silent was going to kill him.

On the platform in Bern, Weygand stood leaning against a steel girder. He was in uniform, his boots polished to a high gloss. Close behind him, two men in rigid leather overcoats were looking around intently. When Weygand saw Fritz stepping down from the train, he rushed over to him and held out his hand.

"Give me the files!"

Fritz handed Weygand the sealed papers from General Gehlen and von Günther. This seemed to satisfy Weygand—their encounter was brief, but he left looking considerably more self-assured.

"Not a word about this," Weygand said and waved for the two others to follow. After walking a few yards, he turned back to Fritz. "Not about *anything*, Herr Kolbe."

Fritz didn't answer—he just shoved his hands in his trouser pockets and recalled the way Frau von Lützow had pinched Weygand's chest. He bet it pleased madam that Weygand was now wearing a uniform.

Fritz arranged with the diplomatic mission driver to have the document box brought to Willading Lane, then had the driver drop him off at the Hotel Justicia on Bubenbergplatz. He got the same room as on his last stay. He locked the door and shut the curtains to the windows that overlooked the square and statue monument—he'd been so nervous his first time in Bern, he hadn't even noticed that armed man of stone in the middle of the square.

He sat on the bed, pulled up his trouser leg, and untied the string. Going back through all his notes, he found nothing that could connect Walter to any of it. He gathered the thin pages into a neat stack, folded them twice, and stuck them in the inside pocket of his jacket. He then shoved his map of the Wolf's Lair site into his outside pocket. Thick raindrops burst against the window, and the Bubenbergplatz with its monument gleamed gray and wet as if poured from lead.

He ate meatloaf in the hotel restaurant. It came with croquettes, sauce, and salad. *My God, Marlene,* he thought and imagined her sitting next to him here, imagined watching her as she ate a meal just like this. When was the last time she had smelled a piece of meat, let alone ate one, or felt a knife travel through it?

From a telephone booth he called a number Dulles had given him. "Yes?"

"I don't smoke cigarettes."

"I wouldn't have a light for you either."

"In Rome there were eternal flames burning."

"What do you want?"

"It's Wood here. I must speak to Dulles."

"One moment . . . Tonight, nine p.m., the same entrance as last time."

Fritz hung up. He went back to the hotel, took a bath, and then had the diplomatic mission car called over. He'd sure like to know what was going on there, and why the powers that be were bypassing von Lützow.

Fritz sat with von Lützow and Weygand in the vast office, glaring at yet another portrait of Hitler, right in the eyes. *I got you,* he thought and felt at his sketch of the Wolf's Lair in his jacket.

Weygand was talking about the extermination of International Jewry and Bolshevism, and again Fritz thought about how these fellows were always saying the same thing, again and again and again, each one just like the next. They repeated whatever Hitler told them to repeat. The very thing that made a human being human—individual thought—was dead and cremated.

Fritz wasn't that smart of a man; he was moderately educated, but attentive and curious, and he had a phenomenal memory. Whenever he'd chatted about literature or music with Consul Biermann, he'd left impressed by how much the man knew, and had listened intently to him and learned things. One time in a Madrid café, Biermann had talked about Greek drama with him, specifically *Antigone*, the very play Fritz's father had enjoyed having read out loud to him. Biermann had mentioned *catharsis*, and Fritz had felt ashamed he didn't know the word. That evening he'd looked it up in his one-volume dictionary: *a cleansing and purification of the soul after or despite suffering and abject adversity*—like martyrdom, a moral victory that you sometimes pay for with your life. Catharsis—*do what is right and have no fear.*

To Fritz, it appeared that Weygand's offensive behavior and constant talk annoyed von Lützow. Von Lützow smiled at Weygand pleasantly and said, "A lasting peace suits the Führer. That's what he actually wants. He was still stating that clearly in March of '42, in his speech for Heroes' Memorial Day."

"It's not to that point yet, not by a long shot," Weygand said.

Late in the afternoon Fritz returned to the hotel, pulled on his overcoat, and asked the hotel staff to set a chair out by the door to Bubenbergplatz. It had stopped raining, a cold wind was sweeping across the cobblestones, and Fritz didn't see a single Nazi flag hanging anywhere he looked. He thought about smoking a cigarette and had to laugh. Marlene said smoking was enjoyable, and that anything enjoyable couldn't be that bad—and didn't always have to be so healthy. So he got a cigarette from reception and puffed on it a little and enjoyed the taste of the tobacco, which was a little like coffee. Katrin would definitely scold him if she knew.

He saw a man on the other side of the square glancing over at him. When Fritz stared back, the man moved to the right along the square and disappeared into the nearest alley. At the same time another man in a hat with his overcoat collar pulled high appeared at the corner of the building to the left of Fritz. He was making an effort to conceal himself. Dulles's men? Men checking to see if he was being shadowed by still others? Fritz stubbed out the cigarette. What was it Priest had said? *There are always two teams, Herr Kolbe: one that you notice and a second that someone like you never will.*

A black sedan rolled onto the square from Laupenstrasse, its rear windows rolled down. From inside the car, Weygand made eye contact with Fritz, and then the two men who'd been with him at the station stepped out. They each went in a different direction across the cobblestones, looking around. They turned down side alleys and came back out others, then got back into the car and drove away.

Fritz left the hotel in darkness and headed north toward the Aare. The river rushed loudly and ran higher than it had during the summer. He walked along the bank until reaching the rise where City Hall stood and then turned toward the city center, stopping repeatedly and looking around. Sometimes he changed direction and holed up for a few minutes inside a building's doorway. The Herrengasse was dimly lit, yellowish and shadowy. He turned for the rear door of the OSS's secret main office, stood near the garden gate a couple of minutes, and entered the yard when he was certain he wasn't being watched.

Priest was standing at the door.

Dulles and Greta Stone were sitting in Dulles's office. Low purplish flames were burning in the fireplace, the remains of incinerated papers lying beneath them like shadows on stone. Just like last time, Dulles was wearing a gray suit and smoking a pipe. Greta's blouse was the color of fresh snow, and she looked immensely self-confident. Skipping the small talk, Fritz pulled his map of the Wolf's Lair from his pocket, unfolded it, and set it on Dulles's desk.

"This is Hitler's headquarters, the Wolf's Lair. Go bomb it, Mr. Dulles. Kill him. Call for the raid at once." Fritz wrote the coordinates on a piece of paper and pushed it across the table.

Dulles looked up at Greta, Greta looked at the map, and Priest stepped behind the desk and bent over the squiggles, arrows, and names Fritz had jotted down on the map.

"The latest from Berlin," Fritz added. He was feeling good.

"It's difficult, Wood," Dulles said.

"There are very, very few men in Washington who know about you," Greta told Fritz. "Your information is classified, codename Kappa—it's more secret than secret. That's already saying something."

They circled around him. He knew full well they were cunning and committed to their cause; did they still harbor a mistrust of him too?

"You had the V2 site bombed, a mission that succeeded. And you scored a direct hit on the Messerschmitt factory too, using my information."

"How do you know it succeeded?" Priest asked.

"Got it straight from the Office."

"Is that so?" Priest said.

"Listen to me. You're dropping tons of bombs on Germany anyway. Why not there—now?" Fritz stabbed at the map. "I saw that pig there. Blow him away, goddamn it."

Dulles rubbed at his mustache. Greta poured four whiskies.

"What would it take to convince you of my sincerity?" Fritz asked.

"Pretty absurd, isn't it, someone like you trying to convince anyone of anything?" Priest asked.

"You bastard."

"You'd better watch yourself," Priest said.

"Says who? Some American sitting in Bern picking a fight with me? If I'm caught, I'm a dead man, Mr. Priest. If your cover's blown, it's off to America. Just what do you want from me?"

Dulles placed a hand on Priest's forearm.

"This whisky would love to be killed," Greta said.

This wasn't how Fritz had imagined it would go. He tipped the whisky back and held out the glass to Greta. She laughed, shrugged, and poured another.

"I want to have a pistol," Fritz said.

"What for?" Priest asked.

"William," Dulles said calmly.

Priest left the office and came right back. He laid a snub-nosed revolver on the desk and set out three little gray boxes of ammo. "You know your way around a gun?"

"Don't worry," Fritz said. "I went on safari with Walter Braunwein a few years before the war. I shot a buffalo and a lion." It was easy to tell a made-up story, and by this point he could come up with one real quick. For a few seconds he even believed what he'd just said. He could smell the bullet hole in the animal's skull.

"A lion, sure you did," Priest said.

"That's enough now, gentlemen," Dulles said. "What else do you have for us, Wood?"

Fritz pulled out the papers from his inside pocket.

"The Leuna Works factory in Berlin. Plans from a man named Eichmann for murdering even more Jews. A secret transmitter near Dublin. And here are estimates concerning American naval forces in the Pacific, from the Japanese."

"That's interesting," Dulles said. "Washington has been asking if you could deliver more intelligence about the Pacific Theater."

"Sounds like they aren't prepared to believe me when I do."

Dulles smiled and stuffed his pipe. "Believe, disbelieve—both work. Before Pearl Harbor, MI6 smuggled a team into the US to spread false information. They wanted to get America to join the war faster. An ally was working against its own partner—that's what this was. Was it betrayal, or just another form of sincerity?"

"These things are complicated," Greta said.

For nearly two hours, they went through the notes Fritz had smuggled into Bern. Priest and Greta wrote things down. Now and then one of them left the office and made a call. They discussed what resulted from Fritz's previous notes: breaking the radio code, the agent in Ankara.

"What happened to the man?" Fritz asked.

"We took care of it," Priest said without looking up from the notes.

"How?" Fritz asked.

"No idea," Priest said.

"If I wanted to get someone out of Berlin, can that person hide out here?"

"No," Priest said.

"We don't have the resources for that. Not at the moment," Dulles said. "How are things at the Foreign Office?"

Fritz told them about Havermann's arrest and the interrogation.

"If you're questioned," Dulles said, "look your interrogators in the eye or look at the floor, but not to the left or right—that's like trying to escape. Looking them in the eyes is bold and inspires trust, while looking down can indicate you're trying to think. But never to the sides."

"What's Berlin like?" Greta asked.

Fritz saw the smoldering soot-gray man with his dead daughter coming at him. *Name's Jaschke, this is my daughter.*

"Are the air raids breaking the people's will?" Priest added.

"People have had enough. They want this all to be over. But the Germans are a long way from any mass uprising against the regime. They have too many other things to worry about. Destroying Hitler will have to come from outside. Militarily."

"Would you shoot Hitler if you could get close enough?" Priest asked.

"No."

"Why not?"

"Because I'd be dead right afterward."

"You won't go so far as that then, huh?"

"Tell you what: *you* go and shoot him."

Fritz and Priest stared at each other. Fritz had pleasantly surprised himself with his quick answer—and he'd made an impression on Priest. Priest gave a hint of a nod.

"Can you two drop your little boy games?" Greta said. "I'm going to make coffee and find some chocolate. You take milk and sugar in your coffee, right, Mr. Wood?"

Before Fritz could answer, Dulles dispensed with Priest and Greta with a nod.

"We've got the same problem as last time," Dulles told Fritz. "Your intelligence is so good, so secret, that a bizarre sort of mistrust prevails.

184

I've seen to it that only a tiny circle has access to your case. President Roosevelt knows about you."

"The president?"

"He is skeptical—not in the same way William is, but skeptical still. On top of that, MI6 keeps trying to foul up the works for us. Something about their outfit doesn't add up. You remember Wooldridge? The Brits' head man here locally, the one who called the first time you visited us and was so angry that his men let you go? Well, Wooldridge is a pro and one experienced and prudent fellow. We've been meeting off and on for months. He thinks a double agent has infiltrated the London office. Not from the Germans—he suspects someone is working for the Russians.

"He suspects that this agent, provided that he does exist, wants you all to himself—for the Bolsheviks. For Germany the war is lost, Wood. Hitler is beaten. But afterward? For a source such as yourself, it becomes tricky. You have to understand that rumors are going around about you and at the highest levels. That's not good. If there is a leak anywhere, God forbid. Now, do you know anything, even just a hint, about German agents in London or even Washington?"

"No. Nothing."

"Our psychological assessments of Hitler lead us to believe he would never consider surrendering. How do you see things?"

"Bomb the Wolf's Lair, Mr. Dulles."

Dulles leaned back and gazed at the shut curtains. "This person you wish to get out of Berlin—who is it?"

"Her name is Marlene."

Dulles smiled and raised his cement-colored eyebrows. Marlene— her name alone was enough to rise above issues of war and mistrust. Marlene—if only Fritz could have her here, whatever the conditions; if only she were in Bern, in the pleasant air, under bomb-free skies. And Katrin too. Fritz choked back his longing and blinked away the strain in his eyes.

"There must be a way to get her out of there," he said.

"Let's wait and see, shall we?"

"I've never demanded anything in return."

"Patience. Wait and see. You remain undercover."

"Weygand, from the diplomatic mission, is watching me."

"The weakest link there is von Lützow. Weygand is more dangerous, or at least that's what we're guessing. You'll have to tread very carefully."

It gradually dawned on Fritz what Dulles was implying: the American president knew about him, and possibly so did a British double agent; rumors about the name George Wood were spreading down the carpet-soft corridors of the White House and through Whitehall in London.

"The flow of information cannot be impeded," Dulles said. "We've set up a second cover address at Brückenstrasse, in Marzili here in Bern. The story is, you got to know one Elenor Pfäffli, and you write to her now and then. Tomorrow night we'll brief you on cipher writing, letter and number codes, invisible inks, and other tricks."

"I can only do so much by mail," Fritz said.

"What else can you tell us about the Russians?"

Fritz recalled from his notes: "The Wehrmacht is committing huge numbers of crimes on the Eastern Front. There are several references to that, from a man named Reinhard Gehlen."

"You mean the general with Foreign Armies East?" Dulles asked. "He's with German military intelligence."

"I've met Gehlen personally," Fritz told him.

"What's your take on him?"

"Cold. Intelligent. Completely devoted to his cause."

"Nazi?"

"Through and through."

"Recently became a general, right?"

"Why are you so interested in Gehlen?"

Dulles waved away the question, sucked on his pipe, and, looking annoyed when he realized it had gone out, put it aside.

"One more question for today, and then I think we'll all need to get some sleep. Have you ever heard about the Germans' so-called Alpine Redoubt? Bunkers deep underground, supply passages, radio installations? Essentially a self-contained facility in the Austrian or Swiss Alps."

"No. Never heard of it before. Do you have any people in South-West Africa? My daughter—"

"That's not my game to play, Wood. Keep your eyes and ears open. We'll see each other tomorrow at nine p.m., all right?"

Fritz slid the pistol into his jacket pocket and the little ammo boxes into the large pockets of his overcoat.

"Bomb it," he said. "Kill him."

In the other office, Fritz found Greta and Priest bent over his papers. They were smoking, the air billowing gray and smelling to him like coffee.

"Your coffee's gone cold," Greta said. "Great stuff here." She stood to say good-bye.

Priest rose too, holding one of Fritz's pages. "Penmanship's not exactly your strong suit, is it?"

"A smart guy like you can surely figure it out."

Priest gave him a probing look, something Fritz was used to by now, but this time he seemed pensive too, as if working something out in his head. Unsurprisingly, whatever it was, he kept it to himself.

The night was black and starless and clung to the cold walls of the surrounding buildings, and Fritz could hear his footsteps echoing off the cobblestones. Washington was six hours back—people were just settling in for the evening. He wondered if at this very moment someone could be putting a Kappa report on George Wood before the President of the United States of America. Crazy. He was stepping out onto increasingly bigger stages; he was no longer a minor player.

Soon, American B-17 or British Lancaster bombers would be emptying their payloads over the Wolf's Lair. The Nazis would be running and squealing, then dying and disappearing from the earth forever. His first mission had already been a success—now it would be crowned with a bang of explosions brought on any second. Hitler's Reich would be swallowed up whole by a huge sucking crater, and a new Germany would emerge, a good Germany. And he, Fritz Kolbe? He would receive a nice posting in the Foreign Office. He would help to make diplomatic relations bloom once again. He would get Katrin back and marry Marlene Wiese and never have breakfast without her again.

My God, he thought as he passed under the golden glow of streetlamps on Bubenbergplatz. He pictured a Berlin without war, with skies free of that rumbling, metallic hell game played by the bombers, where lovely buildings rose again out of the decaying jaws of rubble, the streets were again full of people and cars, and there was not one single red flag bearing the black swastika. He had never strolled down a single intact street with Marlene; the only Marlene he knew was one who lived among the rubble and its stench. *I'm doing what is right,* he thought.

At the front door to the hotel, he rang for the night porter and invited him to have a generous shot of whisky.

The following afternoon, he spent an hour at the diplomatic mission discussing Switzerland's tighter customs regulations with several officials. Then Weygand told him to go.

He walked from Willading Lane with its villas and quaint old front yards over to the Kirchenfeld Bridge. Strips of blue sky poked through gray-and-brownish clouds, the river under the bridge ran dark, and the glittering sun danced on the water like a swarm of tiny birds. From a butcher on Münstergasse Fritz bought a vivid red ham with bright trimmings of white fat and had it wrapped in three layers of paper after ensuring it had been cured well enough to keep for a long time. Such an item hadn't existed in Berlin for an eternity. The butcher had a severe part in his hair and wore a blue shirt and tie and a white apron smeared with bloodstains. *What an absurd man—very much like a German,* Fritz thought.

He could picture it precisely, as if it were happening before him right now: the way he would cut off a nice piece of the ham for Marlene and lay it on a white plate—in his blackout-darkened apartment amid the rubble of Berlin. He would cut his slice into little pieces and feed her each one slowly, bite by bite, letting her get a whiff of every morsel with that lovely nose of hers. Why were such true moments of happiness always so brief?

In a small cozy restaurant on Amthausgasse, he ate a fresh-caught trout with potatoes sprinkled green with parsley. Gray clouds were rushing in to blot out the blue sky. He wanted to get back to the hotel before it started raining, so he thanked the headwaiter for the fish and hurried out into the damp wind.

Right before he reached the slick cobblestones of Bubenbergplatz, a black car stopped close to him, its paint gleaming wet, and two men got out. They grew larger the closer they got, and then they dragged him by one arm into the car and started talking at him. Their English was strongly accented. Fritz tried to break free, but the men pressed his hands to the seat and covered his eyes with a scratchy blindfold. He heard the driver step on the gas and felt the car traveling fast through the city.

This was it. Over. Dead.

"Do not have worry, Herr Kolbe. We do nothing to you," said the voice to the right of him. He could feel the men's thighs against his legs. The abduction had gone down so fast, it was only now becoming clear to him what was happening. He was sweating. All was black behind the blindfold, but he could sense the people active around him, their breathing, their hostility.

"Who are you?" he squeaked, then cleared his throat and repeated the question.

"Friends, Herr Kolbe, friends."

Fritz breathed in and out, trying to quell his urge to gag. The rain struck the roof with full force now, and the car drove over a pothole. They weren't in Bern anymore. They had to be out on a country road. His pistol was lying in a drawer in his hotel, and he had a ham on his lap instead. What did they want from him? For heaven's sake, what? He couldn't give anything away now, nothing at all. And yet his fear was overwhelming. He told them he needed to get out. He needed to piss? they asked. He did, yes—and how. This is not a problem, they said. So nice when a fellow can take a good piss.

The car stopped. Fritz felt a hand on his head, then the blindfold was removed. He found himself looking into a rugged, smiling face. The man had black hair and hadn't shaved. His companion was smaller and gestured kindly to the door. The winding road was hemmed in by dense forest on both sides and smelled of wet bark and good soil.

Fritz asked the man if he would hold this and handed him the wrapped-up ham. The man weighed it in his hands and raised his eyebrows approvingly.

Fritz moved a few yards away from the car and sought out a tree. Flee now? Run with long strides along the blackberry-colored forest floor? No, that was pointless. He looked back down the road to see if another car was behind them, but the wet gray route looked empty. Taking into account the facial features and the accent, he deduced that the men were probably Russian.

He climbed back into the car and saw one of the men holding the black cloth stretched between both hands, then all was dark again.

Some time later the car turned off the country road, down what Fritz guessed to be a forest lane, the tires rolling more softly. He could remove the blindfold now, the man on his right said. They climbed out of the car. They were standing before a hunting cottage, its low roof dripping wet. A man with a rifle was walking back and forth before the door. The men led Fritz into the cottage, where a fire burned in the hearth. Sitting at a wooden table in the middle of the room was a man in a stiff brown suit. He faced Fritz and extended his hand.

"Herr Kolbe, what a pleasure." His accent was better than the other men's, his English good. "Please, sit down. A drink?" The man reached for an earthenware liquor bottle and poured two little glasses full.

Fritz set the ham on the table. "To Hitler's downfall."

The two men from the car stood on either side of the hearth, warming their hands and watching him.

"You work in the Foreign Office in Berlin, Herr Kolbe."

Now what? He had to do something, say something. Fritz stared into the low flames. He wanted to drink the liquor but knew that his hands would tremble.

"I don't think that men like us, men of action, need to play any games," the Russian said. "Do you?"

"Who are you?" Fritz sputtered.

"Someone who comes from a long way away."

"That must be nice." Fritz's voice was growing firmer. Where did he get that? How did he manage to sound so forceful all of a sudden? Within Nazi Germany he constantly had to disguise himself, always had to pretend to be someone other than who he was. He did not feel like having to hold back on smuggling missions too.

"Allow me to come right to the point, Herr Kolbe."

"You can do whatever you wish. As can I, by the way."

"What do you know about General Reinhard Gehlen?"

"Don't know him."

"Now look here, if you're going to be—"

The door flung open with a gust of cold wind. In came William Priest and Greta Stone, each holding pistols, their backs straight, eyes alert, both looking confident in their victory. "Gentlemen," Greta said. The men at the hearth reached for their pockets, but Priest warned them not to even try it. Fritz blinked with relief. He was saved. He felt lighter, a laugh ready in his belly. He heard the rain outside and the splattering of water running off the roof, then the sound of someone coming in and shutting the door. Everything fell quiet. Allen Dulles sat down at the table and set his pipe before him.

"Mr. Musky."

"Musorksky, Mr. Dulles, it's Musorksky," the man in the brown suit said.

Fritz was certain Dulles knew the man's correct name. Dulles apologized and began stuffing his pipe. "What is that?" he asked.

"A ham," Fritz said.

"Ah. Lovely. So, Herr Musorksky, what do you want with him?"

"A chat, Mr. Dulles. A nice talk between men who are on the same side."

"Which side is that?"

Musorksky looked at Dulles but said nothing. Fritz wondered how Greta, Priest, and Dulles had found him and what had happened to the Russians' driver and guards. Priest had disarmed the men at the hearth and ordered them onto two stools in the corner. Greta added more logs to the fire and looked at Fritz, adding a quick wink.

"Tell me, how did you know about him?" Dulles added.

"A little birdy told me."

"Amazing, what all the little creatures can do these days. Tell me . . ." Dulles held a match over the pipe's bowl and puffed until a thick cloud of smoke the same color as his mustache billowed from his mouth. "Tell me, does this little birdy possibly perch in Whitehall, London?"

"There are so many little birdies."

"London is a lovely city. Ever been there?"

"For work. I know London well."

"The British will not be pleased about this."

"Today we are brothers-in-arms. It's been ages, Mr. Dulles."

"If we only had more time to chat about the good old days. But I'm afraid we'll have to resolve this situation here and now. So, okay. I've sent for Dollmann. Does your superior know about this operation, Musorksky? Or were you trying to collect points by doing this on your own?"

"You're the one who is trying to make a career for himself, Mr. Dulles. It's no secret you view Bern as your personal springboard, regardless of how many casualties pile up. Washington offers a much bigger stage, though, isn't that right?"

Greta looked at Priest, Dulles looked at Greta, and Priest glanced at Dulles while keeping an eye on the two men on the stools. Fritz always noticed their glances, but what were they saying?

"Do you think it helps your career," Dulles asked Musorksky, "to carry out an operation like this in broad daylight, starting right in the middle of town? I certainly don't. It's rather amateurish, if you ask me."

Anger twitched in Musorksky's face for the first time, but he kept himself from reacting.

One of the men on the stools started to say something. "Shut your trap," Greta said. The man fell silent. Fritz had never met a woman like Greta Stone before. Standing there, she looked as natural and casual as if she were at home in America somewhere, making a pot of coffee, and just happened to be holding a pistol in her hand.

Priest pulled up a chair and sat down next to Fritz. He kept his pistol trained on the men. "Doing all right?" he asked quietly and, to Fritz's amazement, with genuine concern. Fritz was so flustered after listening to the two intelligence operators' ludicrous conversation that he blurted out something or other about a drive in the country always being a pleasant affair. Priest laughed and placed a hand on his shoulder.

The door opened again. A very tall and pale man, presumably Dollmann, entered and calmly shook Dulles's hand. He looked down at Fritz. Then he inhaled sharply through his nose, glaring around him.

"That's my ham," Fritz said and gave the butcher's address. Priest giggled, something Fritz had never heard the young man do. Dulles left the cottage with the man and stood under the porch's splintery awning. Fritz could hear that they were having an intense discussion but couldn't make out what they were saying. Musorksky had gone quiet and was looking at his fingernails. After a few minutes, Dulles and the man came back in. Dulles nodded for Priest, Greta, and Fritz to go outside. Fritz grabbed his ham from the table. "Good-bye," he said to the Russians.

Outside, Greta and Priest laughed. "What was that for?" Priest asked. "Did you see no better option than being polite?"

Fritz climbed with the others into a long black German sedan. The Russians' guards and driver were nowhere to be seen.

"They're still alive, don't you worry," Priest told Fritz. Fritz was sitting between him and Greta. Dulles, who'd rejoined them, was up front next to a driver who wore a peaked cap.

"I don't think they'll be bothering you anymore," Dulles said.

Fritz felt Greta's hand on his. She squeezed tight.

"You are my Fritz, after all," she whispered. "My dear, dear Fritz."

"Once the Russians reach Berlin," Dulles said, "once that curtain rises for the final act—that's when we'll have to exercise even more caution. But we're not there yet."

"How did they know about me?"

"Dollmann is dangerous—but in line. I think Musorksky was operating all on his own," Dulles said. "Don't worry, Mr. Wood. It's in no one's best interests for you to get found out."

"No one's but the Germans," Greta said.

"What's that supposed to mean, *don't worry*? How, goddamn it, do the Russians know about me? Goddamn it!"

"We'll find out," Priest said.

"What did Musorksky ask you about?" Dulles asked Fritz.

"Can we discuss my situation first?"

"What did he ask you?" Dulles sat there motionless, all of Fritz's objections seeming to glance off the back of his gray head. He repeated, "What, Wood? It's important."

"I'm important too."

"What did he ask about?"

"Without me, none of this would even be happening."

"What did he ask about?"

"About General Gehlen."

"So, them too," Dulles muttered.

"What does that mean?" Fritz asked. No one replied. Dulles, Priest, and Greta simply looked out the windows. "I see," he said and breathed in the aroma of his ham. "This is mine. Mine alone, Ms. Stone." Greta turned her face to him and smiled wryly. "Mine and Marlene's."

Once the rooftops of Bern showed above the trees, the driver stopped the sedan along the side of the road and had Fritz get out. Greta gave him an umbrella. Then the sedan started off again, little threads of water squirting up under the tires as it sped up and disappeared into the drizzle of the next bend. Fritz headed toward town, a burbling trickle of water running along the road next to him, his feet getting wetter with each step.

His cover was full of holes, Fritz feared, his skin too thin. Back in Berlin he was facing mounting distrust, and the small sense of security he'd felt since making his first move in Bern was evaporating. It was becoming increasingly clear to him that Dulles and his people weren't anywhere close to telling him all he needed to know. Why the strange reaction from Greta and Priest when Musorksky verbally attacked Dulles? Why would Greta make such a claim to him in the car, saying he was hers alone? Dulles's allusion to London must have had something to do with the rumor of a potential Russian double agent. Most importantly, if, as Dulles as well as Priest had implied, it were really true that the war could continue unabated even with Hitler destroyed, that meant Fritz was stuck between the front lines of the Western Allies and those of the Russians. He cursed. He didn't want to be a cog in their absurd machine, didn't want to become someone's plaything. He wanted Hitler dead. He wanted to be happy, with Marlene and Katrin.

He heard a car behind him. The Russians' sedan drove slowly past him. Dollmann stared out the sopping windshield. Musorksky turned his ashen face to Fritz and pointed at him in a threatening manner.

"Leave me alone," Fritz said. The sedan sped up. Fritz loosened a rock from the roadside with the toe of his shoe and threw it at the car. The rock clacked onto the road, bounced twice, and tumbled off into the ditch. The sedan disappeared into the rain-glossed city.

At the hotel, Fritz dropped onto his feathery-soft duvet. He hugged the pillow as if it were Marlene. *What are you doing this very moment? Think of me, Marlene, think of me as I think of you. Eventually, we'll escape the death and the destruction, somehow.*

Greta Stone was sitting at Allen Dulles's desk wearing a light-gray turtleneck sweater. Dulles and Priest weren't there, and Fritz's question about the gentlemen's whereabouts went unanswered. Greta described to him how to make invisible ink from either urine or lemon juice, then explained how to figure out whether he was being followed without the trail noticing he was doing so, as well as how to disappear into a crowd of people. "You consider yourself an inconspicuous man, Mr. Wood, isn't that right? You don't think you'll have any problem being inconspicuous?"

"No, none at all."

She leaned toward him and touched her fingertips to his lips. "You're deluding yourself, I'm afraid. You're not that inconspicuous at all."

Fritz didn't know what he was supposed to say. He could smell Greta's perfume.

"Okay, then," she said. "Now, a few ways of communicating." She taught him some astoundingly easy codes. She told him that these ciphers couldn't be broken so long as the enemy didn't have a snitch on the inside. She laughed.

"Reminds me of good old Ancient Rome," she said. "They'd shave some young associate's head and then write a secret message on the skin of his bald dome. The boy gets a break from the action, long enough to grow his hair back. Now with flowing locks, our courier hurries to the message's recipient, who shaves off those very locks again and, ta-da, now reads the message. Brilliant, right?"

"I love simplicity."

"That can be pretty tough to maintain in our line of work. Be that as it may—you got it all in your head now?"

"Yes."

Greta raised an eyebrow at that. She gazed toward a window. "You know, Washington has the same crummy weather as here," she said. "But you wouldn't believe how impressive the Capitol and White House look with the sun shining on them, and with the American flag flying on the roof. There's something quite extraordinary about that country of mine."

"You should have seen Berlin before the war," Fritz said.

"We Americans won't ever experience air raids like you get. Ever. What's it like being in an air raid?"

"Afterward, men come up to you carrying the corpses of their daughters in their arms. You have children, Ms. Stone?"

"Do I look like I do?"

"A husband? Dulles likes you."

"Allen? I'm not so sure about that. You pay attention to such things?"

"Always. On that note, I think that our good Herr Weygand likes to have Frau von Lützow pinch him."

Greta laughed out loud, her mouth open wide like an opera singer's. Her teeth were snow white. "A slave to lust? That's a good one." Fritz shrugged at her.

"What will these men do when the end comes?" she said. "Goebbels, Göring, Himmler? Uncle Adolf?"

"They'll try to run, maybe assume new identities. Or they'll kill themselves. None of them will defend what he's done. How could a person defend such a thing?" Fritz glanced out the dark window. "That is the question: How can I defend what I do?"

"Ah, well put. You know anything about that rocket scientist von Braun?"

"Not a thing. Well, not much anyway."

"Washington wants more intelligence on the Pacific Theater."

"I can't always just go picking and choosing."

Greta laid her pencil on a folder and eyed him. "I understand that, Wood. I truly do. But there are people in Washington who still don't trust any of this."

"That's your issue to resolve, not mine. Give me one logical reason for not trusting me. I'm risking my life here. If I were going to blow the OSS's operation in Bern, it would've happened long ago. And I've never asked a single one of you for information, not one time. So why the runaround?"

"That's just the way it is, okay?"

"No, not okay."

"The highest levels of the intelligence services are a little like some absurd stage play. There are no clear lines. An intelligence service is sort of like the subconscious of a society or of a political system."

Greta lit her cigarette and slid the pack over to Fritz. Fritz had Greta light his, their hands touching.

"You've changed," she said.

"I'm from Berlin, Ms. Stone, Berlin at war. That's enough to change any human being. I need something in return."

"So William was right."

"Her name is Marlene."

"Like Dietrich? Is she good looking?"

"You have to help me get her out of Berlin."

"I'll see what can be done. Meanwhile, don't forget you're operating all on your own. Just make sure you go west when things get too dire. To the south works too. Just not to the east."

"I'll see if I can't get more about the Pacific," he said. He glanced at the portrait of Roosevelt. "What kind of man is he?"

"Some men become greater in wartime. He's such a man. It's the same with you. The way I hear it, you admire chubby Mr. Churchill? Now I ask you, where would Churchill be without Hitler? Where would *you* be without Hitler?"

"You can't be serious."

"You are the Kappa spy. You will go down in history, whether you survive or not. Without Hitler you would still be a minor German official."

Fritz realized that Greta meant all this nonsense. He had to laugh. They were all crazy. Greta Stone was crazy. *Whether he survived or not?* Good God.

"A minor official who could be with his daughter," he said, "who could be strolling through a lovely Berlin with Marlene, drinking a beer in the Tiergarten, ambling down the boulevard Unter den Linden, well dressed, holding his woman's hand. Reading books, listening to music. I shit on your history books, Ms. Stone. I shit on Hitler, whether I'm nobody without him or not."

"Please, Mr. Wood. A man who doesn't want to become the hero? There's no such thing. You're the one making it all happen."

"Not me, Ms. Stone."

Greta stubbed out her cigarette, confident in her assessment. Fritz could see she felt she was in the right and that no one would convince her otherwise. Many men in the Foreign Office had the same attitude.

"I'm doing what is right," Fritz said. "What are you doing?"

"Being an American."

Fritz laughed. Greta raised both eyebrows. She either didn't understand his reaction or she disapproved of it.

"I'd like to say good-bye to Mr. Dulles and Mr. Priest before I go," Fritz said.

"That's not possible."

"Where are they?"

"Not here."

He and Greta said their good-byes. She told him to be sure to watch out for himself and to keep his head down in Berlin.

"Actions have consequences. If you keep going as you are—and I really hope you do—you'll eventually have to make the sort of decisions you wouldn't want to make for anything in the world."

"Why are you telling me this?"

"It's my job. One other thing: the smartest thing a traitor can do is make the world believe he never existed, even afterward—for a long time afterward."

"But a person has to talk about it at some point."

"Don't! For her sake too—what's her name again?"

"Marlene."

"For Marlene's sake too. Just don't."

"Do you have any idea how much ridiculous bullshit I'm already forced to say *yes* and *amen* to?"

"I do not. Not interested either." Greta held her hands to her forehead, then let them fall to her sides. "Just know this: if you're not capable of doing what I've told you, it could be curtains for you."

She escorted him through the other office and was just opening the door to the stairway when the telephone rang. Greta picked up and said something in Italian, her brow furrowed. Then she held a hand over the receiver, looked at Fritz, and glanced toward the door. Even this rude gesture looked charming coming from Greta Stone, and she had the air of one who assumed no one could really hold such a thing against her. Fritz wondered if she had taken acting lessons in America.

He nodded and left.

The next morning he had breakfast with von Lützow and his family. "You're such a pleasant guest, Herr Kolbe," von Lützow said. Weygand was wearing his uniform. Von Lützow's wife told them about theatrical productions in Berlin starring Heinrich George and Gustaf Gründgens, and how much she regretted not being able to see them. "My husband ended up out here, unfortunately. But don't misunderstand me, Herr Kolbe; Bern too has its benefits." Weygand reached for the knot of his tie. Von Lützow gazed at his three daughters as if they were about to vanish and he would be left all alone.

"The fight is going to get even tougher," Weygand said. "But the best will prove themselves. I like that more drastic measures are being taken now. Soon, every last man will grasp what this is all really about. It's the final sanding, polishing to perfection."

Frau von Lützow fingered her neck. The chain she wore had unusually large silver links. "My husband's secretary," she said, gesturing at von Lützow. "Now there's a man who truly understands matters."

"One cannot shy away from our heroic mission," Weygand said. "This is a Wagnerian opera in its most potent form. We will wade in the blood of our enemies and destroy the hordes of subhumans."

"Peace would be nice," Fritz said. Everyone, including the three girls, looked at him. He could feel the tension that had entered the dining room, just because he had uttered the word *peace*.

"Well," von Lützow said.

"Until that happens," Weygand interrupted, "we still have much to do, Herr Kolbe. It surprises me that you would even think about peace at a time like this. This is a sacred battle."

"Horrible and wonderful," Frau von Lützow said.

"Indeed," Weygand said.

Von Lützow was turning a jar of red jam and looking at it as if something were moving inside. It seemed that all the man had left in this moment was a jar of preserves, the thickest chunks glistening like ice.

"Madame, this jam is outstanding," Fritz said.

"Would you like to take a jar back to Berlin, Herr Kolbe?"

"The woman I love would be beside herself with joy."

"It's so lovely when even from hundreds of miles away a man thinks of the woman at his side. Is she holding down the fort in Berlin?"

Fritz put a hand over his mouth. He shouldn't have mentioned Marlene. These people were getting too close, reaching down into even his deepest thoughts.

"Who is this woman?" Weygand said.

"The best there is. For me, that is."

"*Heil Hitler,*" Frau von Lützow said.

"*Heil Hitler,*" the girls said. They were watching Fritz, their faces fair, eyes bright, everything about them clear.

10

The Price of Secrets

On the table are wartime maps of Berlin and of Bern. The light reflects off photos of von Ribbentrop, von Günther, and Käthe Braunwein. Postcards from Bern and Berlin lean against the scarred globe, and obituaries on yellowed, dust-dry paper soak up the sunshine.

"So the Russians were onto you," Wegner says. "I'm unclear about how that could happen."

"Unclear is better than clueless," Fritz says. "I'm afraid it's going to stay that way."

"And good former-general Gehlen is about to become a real big shot in your new Germany," Wegner says. "Both the Russians and Americans were asking you about him before the war was even over."

"There was also that ham," Fritz says.

"Ham again? Herr Kolbe, come on. Please."

"You keep thinking the story is about great events. The story's never about that, except perhaps in hindsight. Great events piece themselves together from many everyday occurrences—and from lies. My God, man, do you have any idea how important a ham was at that time? In Berlin? I used to feed Marlene little pieces of it and she took a good whiff of every morsel."

"Back to Gehlen," Wegner says.

Fritz grabs another box of photos. He selects a portrait of General Gehlen and lays it on top of the papers. The slender man stares up at the ceiling. "A Nazi," Fritz says, "is about to become the head of the first intelligence service in the new Germany."

"That must drive you nuts," Veronika says.

Fritz lights himself a cigarette. *Yes*, he thinks. *That it does.*

"A person gets used to it," he says. He looks at Veronika, sitting with her back to the window, her hair shimmering like metal in the sunlight, her fingers making a little camera. "No," Fritz corrects himself. "That's not true. A person does not get used to it. I was hassled so much about never having joined the Nazi Party—and now it doesn't matter at all whether someone was a Party member or not. This cannot be happening."

He pounds a fist on the table. Papers flutter, a cup jingles on its saucer.

"Adolf Eichmann," Fritz says. "One of the top-ranking annihilators of the Jews. I was the one who gave the Allies his name for the first time. I read letters Eichmann wrote to von Günther, requests for assistance to the Wehrmacht and the like. Eichmann was able to flee. I'm telling you, more people than we think know where he's hiding. I'm certain the pig has a real nice life now. I mean, how could a man like that go underground without help? He'd need expertly made counterfeit papers, he'd need money, he'd need people to cover for him and provide him with a hideout, and on and on and on. It was I, you understand, who told the Americans who this man is."

"That all said, let's get back to you . . ." Wegner reaches for a pencil. "After your second trip to Bern, you go back to Berlin. And no one in the Office ever caught on to you? The situation there must have been getting worse and worse, the way the war was progressing. There had to be even more suspicion and lies and fear, right?"

"It was hell. Silence and pretending—those were the tricks that got me through. Pathetic. You try doing that for years on end, acting against every one of your convictions. It would kill you."

"After the second trip, and after what happened as a result, you must have felt so—"

"Did Sacher tell you about that?"

Fritz goes through one of the photo boxes until he finds a picture of his friend. He lays Eugen Sacher's face on the table—that sympathetic smile, so content—and one corner overlaps the picture of General Gehlen. It's just as Fritz suspected: Sacher told Wegner more than he should have.

"Click," Veronika says.

"Let's not do that. Please."

"Your face was so candid just then."

Fritz needs to have a talk with Eugen. He shoots up out of his chair and goes into the bathroom. His mirror image contorts and blurs before him. He's back in Berlin, during the war. *Heil Hitler. Calm down. Stay calm. It's over, it's over.* He considers canceling the rest of his interview with Wegner and Veronika and tries to find the right words to send the two away.

He doesn't want to be rude. But just what was Eugen thinking? Sympathetic to everyone, and so uncorrupted himself, Eugen has a hard time seeing that others might try corrupting him. He only wants to feel safe. Good people like him—they tend to think everyone else is like them. For such bourgeois types, maintaining harmony always comes first. They cannot, nor do they wish to, comprehend that life can treat others far differently than it does them.

Fritz turns on the faucet and cups his hands to run cold water over his face. He feels it run down his cheeks, his goatee. It always felt so lovely when Marlene stroked his face or Katrin placed a hand on his cheek. Marlene. *Mar-lay-nah.*

How could I?

◆　◆　◆

205

Along the corridors of Charité Hospital, there were even more wounded on cots and the floor than there were the last time Fritz visited, their bandages oozing red. A man with his head fully wrapped in bandages like a mummy was smoking a cigarette and muttering to himself. Moans carried throughout the building and joined the stench of bodies shredded by bullets. Fritz knocked on the door to Marlene's office, his briefcase bulging from the ham, his heart swelling with agitation and delight.

"Come in."

Luckily for him, he always made sure never to speak before knowing the score. Any "Darling" or "Hi, sweetheart" or "I missed you so much" would have been a huge mistake. In a fraction of a second, a gate shut inside him and he became not who he was to Marlene but what he was to all others: an upstanding, smartly dressed, not-very-major official from the Foreign Office.

The man standing behind Marlene's chair with both hands resting on her shoulders was noticeably taller than Fritz. He wore a Wehrmacht uniform, a strand of hair forming a comma on his forehead. He smiled at Fritz. Fritz had feared they would encounter each other at some point. *Hopefully the man is unpleasant,* he had thought.

He wasn't.

"Ah, Herr Kolbe," Marlene said.

"Frau Wiese, nice to see you."

"Let me introduce my husband. Gerhard, this is Fritz Kolbe, an acquaintance of mine."

Gerhard Wiese shook Fritz's hand.

"Pleasure," Fritz said.

"Likewise. Always good to make new acquaintances in times like these."

"I know Herr Kolbe from the Foreign Office. He handles the professor's visas."

So she was going on the offensive. She was disguising herself. Marlene glanced right at him, and her look of recognition receded.

"Yeah," said Fritz, "and I was just on an official trip to Switzerland. I took the liberty of bringing your wife some chocolate. I hope you don't object."

"Chocolate for my Marlene—you don't say? Give it here. But do keep some for yourself."

"Sure," Fritz said, and opened the briefcase. He reached past the ham for the chocolate bars and handed them to Marlene.

"Oh, how lovely," she said. Their fingers brushed as she reached for the gift. More prosthetics than usual were leaning against the wall behind her: a row of metal legs, with and without knee joints.

"I go on a whole week's leave," Wiese said, "and my Marlene ends up living here. This woman is an angel, Herr Kolbe. An angel to her husband, an angel in her work."

Just get the hell out, Fritz did not say. He cleared his throat. "It might be nice if you could get your wife away from Berlin."

"That won't happen," Marlene said.

"You see? That's the way she is." Wiese leaned over her and kissed her hair.

Don't you try that again. Take your fucking hands off my woman! "I know," Fritz said.

"What did you say?"

"Oh no," Fritz said. "Duty calls. I have to get back to the office. Frau Wiese, do enjoy the chocolate. Herr Wiese, it was a pleasure meeting you."

They said good-bye. Just as Fritz closed the door, wanting to scream, Marlene called him back in. Her schedule showed an appointment in the Visa Department tomorrow at ten thirty.

"Perhaps we'll run into each other," Fritz said. Gerhard Wiese's hands, which had been resting on Marlene's shoulders, moved lower down her front, nearly touching her breasts. Fritz could feel the hard metal of his revolver in his jacket pocket. He was sweating, his heart cramping. He thought he might be sick.

He headed back through the mourning city to the bombed-out Wilhelmplatz, unchained his bicycle from the U-Bahn entrance, and rode home, snaking his way around the craters and rubble, around the black holes and the tar flecks from burned tires, and around trees, their charred remains mere splinters pointing into the gray sky. Most streets were getting hammered so badly, bicycling them would soon be impossible.

In his apartment, he lay on the bedsheet, smoking. In his mind, Marlene was here, her body, her blue eyes, that resounding laugh. *My God,* he thought. A husband away for so many months coming back to a woman like that—he would sleep with her. That mouth Fritz loved so would moan for another.

Stop that! Stop doing that!

He slapped his beloved globe off the table with an angry swat and the earth split apart, continents and oceans flying away and teetering on their curvatures along the floor. He let the multicolor pieces lay there and reached for a cognac bottle he'd stolen from the Office. The alcohol burned his throat. He turned on his People's Receiver and waited for news of the bombing of the Wolf's Lair and the death of Adolf Hitler. It did not come. He shook the radio, trying to wrest the news out of it. Nothing.

He gathered up the remains of the world, piled them carefully in his hands, and placed them on a piece of paper. Tears were squeezing out of his eyes and he couldn't stop them. All this *Heil Hitler* shit, this revolting game that never ended—and now Marlene's husband was back in Berlin as well. He clutched his forehead with his hand and cursed. *I can't do this much longer,* he thought. *I just can't.*

The next morning he walked into his office without greeting a soul and slammed the door shut. Von Günther was in Paris and von Ribbentrop had withdrawn to his mansion again. Fritz stared at the dozens of swastika-marked documents on his desk, then pushed them aside and looked at the Allgäu picture over the safe. He tried not to think of Marlene but only ended up thinking even more frantic thoughts about her.

Someone knocked. "What is it?"

The handle turned and the door opened to reveal a fair hand with long nimble fingers, a dark-blue suit, and chestnut hair. Marlene slipped inside. She used her back and both palms to push the door shut, her body bent forward a little like she was about to jump. Fritz could read her face: the despair, the worry. Was there love there too? Deceit?

"Lock it," he said.

Without turning, Marlene felt for the key in the lock and turned it twice. Fritz heard the lock click. She removed her hat and let the pins out of her hair.

She came to him. Fritz lifted her onto the desk and pulled her overcoat off her shoulders. He pushed up her skirt, tugged on her panties, heard the sound of tiny seams splitting. Their breathing merged, they kissed greedily and deeply, clawing at each other's bodies as if climbing down a mountainside. The folders slid around under Marlene's behind, her flesh pressed to the table, tearing a swastika on a folder in half.

"You," he said.

"You," said she.

Afterward, they lay with his body against hers, her arms around him, their clothing damp with sweat and the scent of love. Marlene giggled, saying her leg was going to fall asleep in this position. Fritz glanced down at his trousers, which lay wrapped around his feet like a cloth figure eight, and laughed.

They looked at each other, holding each other's hands.

"Let's not talk about anything right now, Fritz."

"Okay," he said. "Okay."

When it was time to go, Marlene put her hand on the door handle and looked back at him.

"I love you," she said. She'd never spoken these three words—the most important in life—to him till now.

"Are you sure?" he asked.

"No," she said.

"I love you too," he said.

Marlene looked pale against the green walls of his office, her hair darker.

"I just love looking at you," he said.

"My husband's waiting."

"God."

Her kiss was a bite.

"Are you doing all right, Marlene?"

"No. You?"

"No."

"But we're doing it. Doing something. That's a good thing."

Once she was gone he grabbed a handful of the Nazi documents and pressed them to his face. They smelled of Marlene's skin, of her dampness, and a little bit of her perfume. She had told him she had only a few drops left and had put it on for him. The documents had absorbed it.

One by one, Fritz worked his way through the files. A spy in Rome was reporting in about the Vatican: the Pope had openly stated that he was hoping the Wehrmacht would hold its ground against the Russian onslaught. In addition, no resistance was expected from the Church regarding further deportations of Jews from Rome. *Such holy fucking clerics,* Fritz thought.

A man in Washington—codename Willi—had sent a report on the state of President Roosevelt's health. He estimated the president's condition would only worsen and agreed with the Führer that the alliance of Germany's enemies would fall apart should Roosevelt die, *Heil Hitler*.

Fritz read a list of places where Winston Churchill stayed when he traveled, to be forwarded to a commando unit in Plön along with recommendations concerning an operation to eliminate the prime minister. Then he stumbled on a letter from some blowhard writing to his *Dearest von Ribbentrop*, extolling the complete freedom they were enjoying in the East. *Fabulous! You really won't come visit even once? You're gathering dust there in your office. Do come out and watch how we work.*

The areas where Hungarian partisans were in retreat had been marked on a map. Someone was complaining about the precarious situation in Italy and ranting about the weakness of the Führer's friend Mussolini.

Page by page, Fritz learned about reorganizing deliveries of parts for Messerschmitt Me 262 aircraft, repairs to rail lines, postponements in production, and growing suspicions about certain aristocratic, intellectual Wehrmacht officers. Jewry. Bolshevism. Obliteration. A subservient type addressing von Ribbentrop as *Your Excellency* respectfully took the liberty of describing the situation in Tokyo as *not completely clear*.

There were assessments of the American armaments industry and secret reports on damaged U-boats that were supposed to anchor in Spain, and *Dear von Günther* was informed about espionage activity in Franco's Spain.

The documents sent by General Gehlen were written in the neatest hand. He reported at length on tactics, strategy, and Soviet partisan activity behind the front lines.

The longer Fritz sat going through the files, the more Marlene's scent faded. He addressed a letter containing the most important information he'd found to a certain Frau Pfäffli at the cover address in Bern, stuffed his notes into a pocket, and then carried the documents down to the basement. He watched the paper get devoured by the flames. Would Marlene's love wither as quickly? Had their time together been nothing more than the adventure of a war wife who, like everyone else, didn't know if she'd still be alive tomorrow? Her husband was a cartographer and a surveyor. Where were men like him stationed, exactly? Fritz watched through the holes punched in the burn barrels as the papers burned out, an edge glimmering here and there like a single thread running through it all. The room smelled of ash. *I have the power,* Fritz thought. It occurred to him that power might be the worst thing that could happen to a person.

He went into the Foreign Office's cartography archive, his head lowered. Metal lamps hung from the concrete ceiling, their glow muted like powder. The man at the desk told Fritz how nice it was to see him down here.

"What can I do for you, Herr Kolbe?"

Fritz planted both hands on the table. "It's about one of your . . ."

"Herr Kolbe?"

"You know what? It's fine. Pardon me. It was just an idea I had. A stupid idea."

Back at home, standing in his blacked-out rooms, Fritz called out her name. This was where he belonged. Marlene. *Mar-lay-nah.* He stared at the kitchen chair she always sat on, at the pillow she'd propped up, the imprint of her body still upon it. *My God,* he thought. *In front of your own husband, you disguised yourself so expertly, so callously. You are doing the same as I, Marlene.*

Nervously scratching at his thumb till it bled, he asked von Günther if there was any news from the Führer's headquarters. Visiting there recently for the first time, he said, had left such a big impression on him.

"Yes," von Günther said, "being close to such a historical phenomenon—and that's what Hitler is, a phenomenon—does leave a deeply lasting impression. What will must reside inside that man. Especially now, yes? Surrender—now that's a word the Führer does not know, Kolbe. After all that had to be done in Germany's name over the course of this war, how do you think the enemy would treat us if we gave up now? No, we must stay the course." Von Günther turned to the window overlooking Wilhelmstrasse, stroking the glossy white sill. Fritz was certain the ambassador realized that defeat was coming. Many were starting to realize that victory was impossible.

"Listen to me, Kolbe." Von Günther turned to him, his expression earnest. "That woman, the one I saw you with? Well, I happened to notice she was wearing a wedding ring. Don't look at me like that. Pay attention to what I'm saying: no one is going to hear a word of it from me, you understand, no one. Not even my wife." Von Günther slid a cigarette into his mouth and looked at Fritz from over the flame of his lighter, his eyes flickering. "You can rely on me, yes? As I do on you, Kolbe. I can indeed rely on you, can't I?"

"Completely, Herr Ambassador."

"And in every respect?"

Just what was von Günther driving at? Why was he asking this? *Go on the offensive,* Fritz told himself.

"In every respect, Herr Ambassador."

"You know, Kolbe, there's simply too much talk going around, even here in the Office. I'm very glad you're my secretary." He chuckled. "You certainly are not a blabbermouth. When I tell you something, you always keep it to yourself." He turned away, probably because his sudden openness embarrassed him. "Nothing else for now," he said. "Back to your work, Kolbe."

◆ ◆ ◆

At home, he now kept his hated People's Receiver on constantly. All that came from it was contempt, rubbish, barbarity, the thunder of jubilant masses. Fritz sprang up every time Franz Liszt's music came on to signal a special announcement. "Why are they not bombing the Wolf's Lair? For fuck's sake!" He slammed both fists on the table.

Marlene kept calm. On the very evening of the day her husband departed, she showed up at Fritz's apartment door. She had never seen him as enraged as he was waiting for the news of the bombing of the Wolf's Lair. She reached for his hand. "Let's go for a walk," she said.

They went out into the rubble and walked along paths that wound between hills of debris standing where there once had been streets, down to the Spree River where soot-black barges bobbed along on water gone filthy from war. On Marienstrasse they saw soldiers shoving a man in a torn shirt into a car. An officer in a leather overcoat stretched out his arm in the Hitler salute, laughed with one of the soldiers, and climbed into the vehicle. The overcoat gleamed like it was made of liquid metal. Marlene's grip on his hand tightened.

The Capitol Movie House in Charlottenburg had not yet been pounded into the earth by bombs. Marlene asked Fritz if he'd go to the cinema with her and Fritz accepted at once. Marlene was surprised, since he hated the films that came out of the Nazis' studios.

"But I'd gladly go to the movies with you," he said. "We get to hold hands. I also learn things from actors. Things about becoming completely absorbed by a role. About acting like a different person than one actually is."

"Just don't forget who you are," Marlene said.

They watched *I Entrust My Wife to You* with Heinz Rühmann. Fritz's heart leapt as Marlene lost herself in the film, especially its scene of a chase through Berlin in a double-decker bus—a Berlin that was still so luminous. *Why not,* he thought as she laughed. *Don't stop—keep laughing, Marlene.*

During a visit to Fritz's office, Walter Braunwein sat on the edge of his desk, causing the folders to slide out of place. "What do you think you're doing?" Fritz said and put them back in neat order. Walter laughed.

"What am I supposed to do?" he said. "You appear to have gotten rid of your other chair—which does sound like something you would do, Fritz."

"These documents are important, Walter. I need them organized, spotless, and easily accessible."

"You need them? I don't understand."

"It's not for you to understand."

Walter stood and looked at the Allgäu picture, then glanced over his shoulder at Fritz. Not for the first time, Fritz considered that Walter might be seeing right through him. But the question remained unspoken, despite their friendship—or precisely because of their friendship.

"The two of us went hiking there," Walter said and tapped on the picture. Fritz was flooded with memories of fresh air and of looking out together over the green sea of the Alps.

"We definitely have to do Ireland together. Bantry House, or the Cliffs of Moher. Man, that would be something. With Käthe and Horst and . . ." He pointed at Fritz. "Hey-ho. I still have not met your girl. Käthe really wants to as well—in her own way. Come by tonight for dinner. I could get ahold of something special for us to eat."

"When do you have to go abroad?"

"We could really stuff ourselves."

"When do you have to go abroad? And where to?"

"Stop with that, Fritz. Just stop."

When Käthe saw Marlene, her hands flew to her cheeks. Even though Marlene was a complete stranger, Käthe wrapped her arms around her. "Oh, okay," Marlene said and laughed.

"So this is the mysterious Marlene," Walter said. He kissed her hand. "Our Fritz here is just crazy about you."

"He better be," Marlene said.

Walter invited her to the table. Fritz smelled onions and something tart, the scent making his mouth water. He slid his chair closer to Marlene's. It was so nice visiting his best friend with her.

"I was in Kiel on official business," Walter said, "and guess what I got ahold of? You won't believe it." His hands hovered over the two covered porcelain bowls on the table. He let out a loud "Hey-ho!" and lifted the lids.

"Pickled herring," Marlene said. "I'll be damned." The fish had been browned and were swimming in stock along with thin rings of onion. Fritz fanned the aroma toward Marlene.

They drank white Mosel wine that Fritz had stolen from the office. Only Käthe declined, saying it didn't agree with her anymore. She stared at Marlene the whole time, and squinted when Fritz and Marlene touched each other. She kept turning horribly pale and looking as if her thoughts were a long way away. Walter tried entertaining the others with stories of Ireland, reaching for Käthe's hand where it rested, next to the silverware. Fritz hoped to preserve their little get-together by telling stories about remote lands, but the mood kept spoiling, the specter of war and death showing itself in the white face of a distressed Käthe Braunwein. Fritz noticed that Marlene drank a lot, and he thought this fitting.

"You're married," Käthe said. She looked at Marlene but held her glance for only a few seconds. No one spoke. Walter poured more wine. Käthe held a hand over her glass again.

"She's my one and only," Fritz said.

A smile twitched on Käthe's face. "That's nice," she said.

"Do you know what else Fritz is up to?" Marlene asked them.

Fritz grasped her arm tight.

"No, what is he up to?" Walter asked.

"Nothing," Fritz said.

"You sure about that, old buddy?"

Marlene took a big gulp of wine. "He keeps stealing alcohol from the Foreign Office," she said. "He does it all the time. He's become a real expert at it." She held her glass up for Walter to fill and then drank the contents down in one chug. "Fritz takes plenty of risks," she told Käthe.

As Fritz and Marlene staggered home, Marlene said Käthe was a stupid cow.

"Naw," Fritz slurred, "she's a great gal."

"Yeah, before maybe," Marlene said. "But that doesn't count."

"She can't help it."

"That's what they're all going to say, after the war."

One cinema after another was disappearing. At night their chilled ruins reflected the color of a full moon. Now movies were sometimes shown in darkened cellars, where Fritz and Marlene could hear the spooling noise the projector made and the sickly breathing of people who had to live in this ailing city. Marlene whispered to Fritz that Heinrich George really was a good actor, that Fritz could learn a thing or two from him.

One time, Marlene's friend Gisela came along. Fritz was meeting her for the first time. Gisela was a sturdy woman with full cheeks and unruly curls. "Nice to meet you. Marlene told me lots about you."

"Oh," Fritz said.

"Don't worry, little guy. Gossip doesn't matter. All that matters is how you live your life."

Once Fritz and Marlene were back home, Fritz complained that Gisela kept calling him *little guy.*

"Don't take it personally," Marlene said. "She didn't mean anything by it. Gisela decided long ago to do whatever she wants—usually for pleasure. She sleeps with quite a lot of men."

Marlene sat down on Fritz's lap. She gave him one of her puckered-up girl kisses. "We only live once, after all." She stroked his head.

"I would never betray you," Fritz said.

"Ah, Fritz, but betraying people is what we've been doing this whole time. All the way down the line."

When Von Günther went along with von Ribbentrop to attend a meeting with the Japanese emissary, Fritz used the time to take even more file notes and sent them in code to the cover address for Dulles and his team. Sometimes it was all he could do not to grab for the telephone and call Bern to ask, "Why are you not bombing the Wolf's Lair yet? Wipe them all out!" He kept asking himself the question, again and again. And after the war, when the attempt was made on him and Marlene, he was still asking himself why the air raid had never happened.

Fritz saw General Gehlen speaking in the hallway with von Ribbentrop, looking white as a sheet. Shortly afterward, Gehlen came into Fritz's office and said he was there for an appointment with von Günther.

"Intelligence work," he said, "is the best work there is."

Von Günther came out of his office, saluted, and disappeared inside with Gehlen, but soon opened the door again.

"Kolbe, I'll need the files on the Warsaw situation—we got them yesterday or the day before."

Something caught in Fritz's chest. He could hardly breathe.

"Kolbe?"

"Yes sir, Herr Ambassador."

Von Günther shut the door. The files were at home under Fritz's bed. He left his office and hurried down the corridor that stretched on and on. His footsteps echoed as he ran down the stairs.

Down at the entrance Heinz Müller was talking with a courier. "What's the rush, Herr Kolbe?"

Fritz threw on a borrowed smile and said, "Work, work, work."

On the Wilhelmplatz he climbed onto his bicycle and pedaled, steering around the scars of war and sliding into curves. He stormed up his stairs but couldn't get the door unlocked, then saw he was using the wrong key. He stuffed the files in his inside pocket, hurried down the stairs three steps at a time, and rode back to the office. He was wet with sweat. Did they finally have him? Was it over now?

He hurled his bicycle against the railing for the Wilhelmplatz U-Bahn station and ran for his building's entrance, gulping down deep breaths. He hurried into the Office with lungs pumping. Müller was standing in the doorway of the office next to his, arms crossed at his chest as if waiting for Fritz. He said nothing, but watched Fritz pass. Officially, Fritz was senior to the scrawny-shouldered Müller, yet the balance of power between them remained unclear. One day, though, he would find out for sure whether Müller had helped the others attack him aboard the *Louisiana*. Fritz smiled at him, saying there was always so much to do around here.

If von Günther was waiting in Fritz's office, Fritz would hardly be able to pull the files from his jacket. Luckily the room was empty. He made it to the safe just as von Günther came into the room, and he made a show of having just pulled the documents from it.

"Kolbe? What's going on? The Warsaw folder. The general is waiting. Where were you?"

"My apologies, Herr Ambassador. I must have eaten something bad. Here's the folder."

General Gehlen was standing in the doorway. Fritz hoped he didn't notice the sweat on his face or any specks of grime on his shoes and trouser legs.

"Forgive me, Herr General," he said.

"This doesn't happen with my people, Herr Kolbe."

"It doesn't normally happen with mine either," von Günther said. "You can be sure that there will be consequences, Herr General."

Gehlen waved von Günther back into the office. The general was looking Fritz in the eyes.

"I'm very sorry, Herr General," he repeated.

"You were abroad a long time," Gehlen observed. "And you're not a Party member."

"Yes sir, Herr General. No sir." Fritz hated this. He was disgusted with himself. Gehlen was untouchable—Fritz saw no way of going on the offense, no way out of this at all.

"Nothing escapes me, Kolbe."

"Yes sir, Herr General."

Gehlen glanced into von Günther's office, then at Fritz again, resting a finger on his lips as if pondering something. Fritz struggled to keep his composure. He wouldn't be able to take much more of the general's scrutiny. His chest was heaving too hard, his breathing too fast.

"Everything all right, Kolbe?"

"Yes sir, Herr General. I'm really awfully sorry."

"As you should be. Right?" Gehlen whipped around and closed the door in one calm, fluid movement.

Fritz staggered over to the sink and scooped handfuls of water over his face. Someone knocked. Fritz cursed. "What is it now?"

It was Müller. He wanted to speak with von Günther.

"The Herr Ambassador has a visitor," Fritz said.

"It's important."

"It's not possible right now, Müller. I'll let him know you were here."

"Heil Hitler."

"Hi Hitler."

"I'll wait here."

"No, Müller. I have things to do. The Herr Ambassador has things to do. I'll tell him that you'd like to speak with him. You might tell me what it's about while we're at it."

"Certainly not, Herr Kolbe."

"I can't do this anymore," he said.

"You have to hang on," Marlene told him. "Everything worked out all right in the end. Now come here, you. Come here and take me in your arms."

Fritz came to Marlene so forcefully, she stumbled backward against the kitchen cupboard, a little concert of porcelain clanging as she bumped it. "Ah, Fritz. It makes me so happy to sit at the table with you in the evening, copying files. Even with this war, I'm happy. I'm proud of you. We will live, Fritz. Live! And now I'm going to cook us these four potatoes, but not the onion."

"An onion?"

She lifted it as if she'd conjured it up by magic: a medium-size onion with a light brown skin, its outermost layer peeling in one spot. Fritz watched as Marlene carefully peeled the onion so that not one single shred was lost and then cut it into fine, translucent slices the color of vinegar.

The debacle with the folder had hit him hard, and he was still worked up about it. All his worries had mounted inside his head, and his thoughts kept turning to the sky over Africa, to the parks in Madrid and the boulevards of Paris, to foreign languages. He went back over in his mind what had happened earlier. As he had been getting ready to leave for the day, General Gehlen had come out of von Günther's office and passed quite slowly through Fritz's outer office, keeping an eye fixed on him the whole time, or so it seemed to Fritz. Once he was gone, von Günther stood in the doorway and eyed Fritz. He didn't budge. He didn't do anything. He just stood there, looking at him.

Fritz's embarrassment made him want to scratch at his forehead. He had smiled and made notes until von Günther shut the door again, and then Fritz went completely weak at his desk.

"I love you," he said now without looking at Marlene. He said it earnestly, his voice sounding strange in the shadows of his darkened apartment. He'd just told her he couldn't do this anymore—now he was telling her he loved her. Such fundamental declarations these were, full of trust and complete devotion. He looked into her eyes. She smiled, and started blinking. "Must be the onion," she told him.

"They're watching me, Marlene. Von Günther is still partly blind, I'm hoping. The man trusts me, for whatever reason. He hates intelligence officers, he hates the Gestapo. There's something about their deep mistrust that revolts him. But—"

"But what, Fritz?"

"Müller. Müller saw me. That scrawny son of a bitch has been watching me for years."

"Is he a threat?"

"No idea."

Marlene went into the bedroom, came back out, and set the revolver on the table in front of Fritz.

◆　◆　◆

We've reached that point, thinks Fritz. *I must say something now. I want to say it now.*

"Roughly seventy million died in the war," he says. "That's just a number. But there's more to it than that. That's seventy million human hearts, seventy million screams. Everyone lost friends, family members, sweethearts. If only Marlene and I and Walter and all the others had never had to experience such complete and utter hell. The war had such power to destroy, you cannot imagine. Total madness."

"If it weren't for the war," Wegner says, "you never would've gotten to know Marlene."

"Not true. No, no matter what, Marlene would have crossed my path at some point."

"That's a nice thought," Veronika says.

"He would have crossed your path no matter what too," Fritz says to her.

Wegner leans back and looks out the window.

"I couldn't help what happened," Fritz says. "I didn't want that. No one can blame me for it. Doing so is impossible. You understand me? It's impossible. A series of events unfolded, that's all. There's no way I could control all that. Write that down, Herr Wegner. Make a note of it. It's important. In such times there's no one who can control everything, no one who can account for it all. It cannot be done."

"That's already quite clear to me, Herr Kolbe."

"Oh really?"

"Yes, really. At least you did something. Others did not."

"Perhaps I . . . I shouldn't have done anything, after all."

"You can't be serious?"

"I'm not sure anymore."

◆　◆　◆

Von Günther was the one who told him.

The rain was hitting the office windows at a sharp angle, obscuring the view of the building on the other side of the street. Below them, the street was still.

"Herr Kolbe . . ." Von Günther looked around for the chair that no longer stood opposite Fritz's desk. Without a word, he went back in his office and returned with a lightweight green armchair. He sat in it and folded his manicured hands.

"Churchill and his goddamn commando missions," he said.

Fritz didn't understand. He set his pencil down on the desk pad. "What's wrong, Herr Ambassador?"

"You're good friends with Walter Braunwein, isn't that correct?"

"Yes. Since—well, as boys we went hiking together in the Allgäu."

"Like in that picture?" Von Günther pointed at the gold-framed landscape covering the safe.

"Reminds me of better days," Fritz said. "Why are you asking me about Herr Braunwein?"

"The Office often sent Herr Braunwein away on special assignments. He had good connections in Ireland. You probably know that."

Fritz picked up his pencil again, wrapped his fingers around it, and pressed his thumb against the end until the narrow wood bowed with tension. Had Walter defected? Without Käthe? No, that could not be.

"We had a secret transmitter near Dublin. Well, somehow the British must have gotten word of it. They . . . you know, these things do happen in war—"

"What happened?"

"They attacked the transmitting station."

"Was Walter there?"

"Herr Braunwein was, yes. One of the men was able to get away, and three days ago he established contact with us." Von Günther looked at his hands.

"Walter's being held captive?"

"No, Herr Kolbe."

"He . . . he's been wounded."

"No."

The pencil cracked, sending splinters of wood across the desk. A coarse noose was being pulled around Fritz's neck, choking him.

"I'm very sorry, Herr Kolbe."

Fritz grabbed his overcoat and hat off the hook on the door and walked out. He heard clattering behind him as his superior rose to call after him.

"Kolbe! Kolbe!" Von Günther was bellowing at his back. "Don't storm out like that! Kindly keep your composure. Others have lost comrades too. We're at war. Kolbe! Kolbe!"

Later, he couldn't have recalled where or for how long he wandered in that brittle, crippled city, nor could he have recounted how many ashen, starving faces he saw or which debris heaps he climbed over.

He had been the one. He was the agent who'd given Dulles the memo about the secret transmitting station in Dublin. A brief mention, one of hundreds passed along inside a clandestine office on the Herrengasse in Bern. He had done it. He should have known better. Ireland, Walter's dream. His friend Walter Braunwein with his disheveled hair. *Hey-ho.* Käthe. Horst.

Fritz stood before a building with a sign nailed to it: "No Entry, In Danger of Collapse." He climbed through the fangs of the busted door, pushed himself along sooty walls, and climbed a stairway that was missing its railing, the grit-covered steps crunching under his feet. He found the top floor rotting away under the cold gray sky and sat down on a wooden chair next to an oven that was collapsing in on itself. He looked out over the monstrously violated city now nothing more than stone stalagmites: an endless, grotesque apocalyptic wasteland. The wind tugged at the brim of his hat. He had killed Walter. Käthe would never again hold her husband in her arms. And Horst, oh Horst—yet another boy without a father.

He took the revolver from his jacket and set it in his lap, the metal cold and dark like the sky. Walter! His name was all that was left, written on the ruined walls in blackest soot. It was a name that encompassed everything, and Fritz was a small man in a dark overcoat inside a decrepit building, a face wet with tears in the wind. Only one thought was clear: he had betrayed Walter. Fritz Kolbe, the spy, the man who wanted to shorten the war. He was the one.

Please, please, don't let it be so, he thought. And yet another thought was clear: the Wolf's Lair had not been bombed, but the British had sent one of their special commando teams to Dublin. Those men were lightning fast. They had gone because of information Fritz provided to Dulles, who would have shared it with the Brits, with their well-oiled boots, automatic weapons, and blackened faces in the night. Walter would have looked up when he heard the noise. Fritz pictured the flash of gun barrels and bullets piercing his friend's body. The bullets would have gone right through him, maybe even through his face, his stomach. In the front and out the back, if no bones were in the way. This was it. It was over. *Katrin.* She'd turned her back to him at the harbor in Cape Town. He'd cried out for her, but she wouldn't turn around, her black hair a shiny curtain down her little back. Fritz Kolbe did not exist anymore. George Wood did not exist. Nor did the Walter Braunwein he'd hiked with and raced to the buoy with in the sea off of Cape Town. It was all over. He wiped at his eyes, writhing in pain.

What was Walter's final thought before all went dark? Was it of Käthe? Horst? Fritz slumped down on the creaking chair and curled into a fetal position. He wanted to crawl into a gash in the earth like some tiny louse, to feel nothing but cold rock all around him. So this was the end. He stood up and stomped and stomped on the gritty floor. The building kept standing.

Fritz stared at the door to his apartment, at the finish that got rougher and rougher each day. He turned the key. He could see Marlene down the hall, sitting in the kitchen. He couldn't bring himself to step over the threshold and say to Marlene's face what he had done. Marlene came to him, the golden light from the kitchen illuminating her profile and shining against her lush hair. She went past him and locked the front door, then clasped her hands behind her back and leaned against the wall.

"What happened?" she asked.

Fritz felt himself shaking his head wildly. Marlene went into the kitchen, and out of the corner of his eye, he saw her busy with something. Then she came back and handed a glass to him. Cognac, she said, that he himself had stolen from von Günther. They drank, leaning against the walls across from one another. Fritz couldn't return her stare.

"Fritz?"

"It was me," he said.

She fell silent. At some point—seconds or hours later, or in some other age—she told him she had made something to eat.

She had made him something to eat.

Tears welled in his eyes.

"Fritz, what's happened?"

Hand in hand, they went into the kitchen and sat down at the table. A folder from the Office labeled *Top Secret* lay next to a plate of bread with sausage. Fritz stared at the Reich eagle and the swastika and swept the folder off the table. It landed at Marlene's feet, which were dressed in her thick stockings.

"I wanted to do what's right," he said.

"Please, tell me. Tell me what happened. Don't leave me in the dark. It doesn't matter what it is. Tell me."

Fritz grabbed the safari photo from the picture shelf, handed it to Marlene, and touched the face of Walter Braunwein.

"I passed the information to Dulles. I did it."

She said nothing. Maybe she didn't know what she should say. Maybe she was scared of saying the wrong thing and hurting him or making him angry, or maybe it was simply that there was nothing to say. She stepped close to Fritz and pulled his head to her chest. He clawed at her back. Then he wailed. Into her body he wailed it all: every *Heil Hitler*, every *Yes sir*, the hate, the self-loathing . . . and the death of Walter Braunwein.

The next day, Käthe shot herself dead.

In the Office, he now started taking folders down to the basement at the earliest possible opportunity. He'd have the man at the metal table sign off and then watch as the flames in the burn barrels devoured potential intelligence for the OSS, all orange and red, the papers' edges turning blue. Bern might assume that he was dead. Dulles might have deduced from his silence that he'd confessed under torture and would already be taking certain countermeasures.

Fritz decided to send a message to him. He kept Berlin-themed postcards in a desk drawer—the boulevard Unter den Linden in sunshine, men wearing hats, women holding flowers, gleaming cars. He put one in his typewriter and typed a coded message to the OSS in Bern on a margin, then slid it into an inside pocket. At home later, he handwrote some lines on the card, telling his imaginary friend in Bern that he would not be writing to her anymore. When Marlene saw him with the postcard, he told her he'd found it with the margins already like this, probably someone trying to learn how to type. Marlene snatched the card from his hand and tore it down the middle. She then ripped those halves in two and kept on ripping until fingernail-size shreds were falling to the floor.

Fritz went into the bedroom and slammed the door behind him. How could Marlene do that? Who did she think she was? He glared at his bed where he slept with her night after night. He heard the sound of something being slid along the floor. The strip of light below the door was obscured by something in the middle. Fritz reached down and felt that dry card stock he knew so well. It was the folder he'd pushed off the table. He picked it up and opened the door slowly. Marlene was standing before him, holding a pencil in front of her face.

"I'm not betraying anyone anymore," he told her.

"You didn't."

He flung the folder to the floor and twisted his foot on it like it was a cigarette butt. "No one can stop this slaughter."

"So the British and Americans shouldn't even bother fighting, is that it?"

"I don't care."

"You've always cared, about everything."

He grabbed a chair, raised it above his head, and smashed it over the table. Pieces of wood sailed through the air, fell to the floor, and tumbled away. Marlene had thrown up her hands to protect her face. The sight of that shocked him. He had only wanted her to relent, to agree to leave him alone.

"He was my best friend."

"He worked for the Nazis."

Her words sat between them like a stone.

"Walter was no Nazi."

"I work for the Nazis too at Charité Hospital. You told me what you're doing. You told me right after a man came up to us holding his dead daughter. And in that moment the world was saved a little. It was a tiny bit better."

"It's over."

She went into the bedroom and locked the door. Fritz stared after her. How could she be so hard on him at a time like this?

He gathered up the pieces of busted chair and laid them next to the oven. He considered opening the folder. What information did it hold? Details of yet more Jews being annihilated? Names of spies? Evidence of secret weapons?

In those dramas Fritz's mother read aloud to his father—and that Fritz himself later enjoyed reading—the writers often jumped back and forth between different characters' points of view. In such a tale, it would have been possible to read what Allen Dulles was doing now, or what was being said about the spy George Wood in Washington, to see just who was putting what actions into motion as a result of Fritz's treachery. But in real life, there was no such option. He had only his own limited perspective.

Whenever Fritz thought about the possibility of one day writing down what he had done—or having someone else write it down for him—he hoped that he would be able to keep it all to one point of view. He would be sure to focus on the events of the war at a human level, something that could only work if the story was told from one person's perspective. Anything else would be a lie, an amalgamation of events combined for the purpose of giving them meaning—an approach that might be artistic, but was false.

He had killed Walter and Käthe. If Käthe hadn't killed herself first, would he have one day told her the truth about what he'd done? Fingers trembling, he lit up a cigarette. And then there was Horst. If Horst somehow made it through the war unscathed, would he be able to tell Horst what he'd done? Look him in the eyes? And what about the girlfriends and wives of the U-boat crew members whose mouths were ripped open and filled with water because of his treachery? How would he face them? Loving people. Human hearts.

"And me too, Fritz," said a blood-smeared image of Walter. Walter pointed at Fritz's chest, kept coming closer. "And my Käthe." Fritz threw his hands to his face. *Do what is right.*

He knocked on the bedroom door.

"Marlene? I love you. I just can't do it anymore."

"Then come here to me, Fritz. Get in here."

He didn't see her. He only heard the covers rustling, like footsteps across a forest floor covered with leaves. He stood in the darkness and tried to make out her shape in the bed. A wave of her hair shimmered faintly; the light caught a part of her hip. She sat up, one shoulder higher than the other.

Fritz felt completely lost and harbored no hope of that changing. The Allies were advancing up Italy and the Eastern Front could not be held, yet because of the Nazis' lunacy and Hitler's rabid and relentless mobilization, the dying and mutilation would continue for a long time. What people were finally hearing about the extermination camps, where

Jews were being abused and killed, was beyond comprehension. Yet here he sat, holding in his arms a naked woman who, just a few days ago, had been as happy as a child when he brought her a pear, a simple piece of greenish-red fruit. The world was completely coming apart at the seams. Fritz didn't know what he was supposed to do. It seemed absurd to him that he was even living at all, that in this moment he could feel Marlene's breath rising from beneath her smooth ribs. He slipped out of his own body a moment, hovered above it, and returned only when Marlene sat up straight and kissed him deeply on the mouth.

When he came home to her at the end of the day, she had the table cleared off and a sharpened pencil set out for him. He responded by picking up the pencil and placing it on the windowsill. Night after night.

"There are no innocent people anymore, Fritz," she told him. "What will Mr. Churchill, whom you respect so much, say when the war is over and he sees the bombed-out cities? When he learns how many civilians were killed during the air raids? In this time, it is impossible to live completely right."

He fumed at his indecisiveness, at his apathy, and at his agony over every day of the war passing just like the last. He detested himself in the way he had during those first few years in Hitler's Berlin—though, at least back then, he had begun to feel the first sparks of a fire igniting inside of him. Now, he felt paralyzed by the deaths of the Braunweins and by his fear that von Günther was watching him. He was beaten. He knew, logically, that one should never admit defeat, but his heart felt strongly otherwise.

He could not sleep, and he often became sick when he ate. His nerves were strained nearly to the breaking point. Von Günther, quite correctly, reprimanded him for making careless mistakes and told him things couldn't go on like this. "Think of the men at the front," he told

Fritz. "They're losing friends too. Don't let yourself go. Pull yourself together!"

"That young man from the Transmitting and Deciphering Department came to my office recently," von Günther said one day. "Müller."

"A pain in the neck. What did he want from you?"

Von Günther didn't answer.

"Herr Ambassador, I could see how nasty Müller was even before leaving South Africa. He is utterly lacking in any sort of class."

"That's not the impression I got."

"With all due respect, Herr Ambassador, Müller and I butted heads a few times in Cape Town. The boy is insolent and thinks he's entitled to things he's not."

"That's enough, Kolbe. I'm completely capable of judging for myself. I am not at all pleased at the way the Braunweins' deaths have knocked you so far off course. I'm telling you for the last time: pull yourself together." He rapped on Fritz's desk with his knuckles.

"Listen to me," he continued. "You have a thoroughly attractive woman by your side. Indulge yourself. Know what I mean, yes? You must understand me. It's not as if I don't know how bad it is to lose a friend. And his wife, killing herself? Well, I've heard of that too. Horrible. I'm not one of those National Socialists who dares to make nasty comments about that poor woman. I don't do such things, Kolbe, and you know that. Walter Braunwein died for the Führer, Volk, and Fatherland. His wife as well. That's the way I see it."

I should shoot you dead, Fritz thought.

"Yes sir, Herr Ambassador," he said.

"Müller says that you did not behave like a committed National Socialist on your journey from Africa back to the Reich."

"Complete nonsense, with all due respect. Who painstakingly organized and carried out the consulate's move out of Cape Town? Who made sure everything came out in tip-top shape? Müller? No. I was the one. You should send Müller to the front, sir."

"Müller is still exempt. He's too skinny to fight." Von Günther laughed. "Unlike you. Rumor has it you have something of a knack for boxing."

Fritz wished he could respond like a real man, wished he could say, *You don't wanna pick a fight with me,* or *Go ahead and try it.* He kept silent.

Von Günther waved off the subject and rubbed at his broad chin. "You know that we have to remain tough in the East. That greatness I speak of depends upon it. It's ultimately about combining the abstract and the concrete, all in the service of . . . Well?" He pointed at Fritz and smiled.

"Greatness, Herr Ambassador." Fritz took a deep breath, trying to suppress his urge to retch. Under the table he pressed one foot into the other.

"And in taking part in greatness." Von Günther nodded, pursing his lips. "There are reports that on the Eastern Front, some officers are still expressing misgivings about the way we deal with Jews and partisans. Not just in private letters from officers and enlisted men that are intercepted and must be censored—no, there remain those who dare to criticize openly. So. Von Ribben-snob drafted a document that again expresses the Foreign Office's full approval of measures being taken in Russia. He would like our branch here, as intermediary between the Wehrmacht and the Office as a whole, to add our endorsement. I wrote the piece myself. Now, as you well know, I'm frequently away on official business. So, let's put you down as signing *On behalf of* and put it under your name."

Von Günther pulled the page from inside his jacket, unfolded it, and placed it on the desk before Fritz.

"Give me your signature, Kolbe."

"But I'm not at all authorized."

"Oh, Kolbe, it's perfectly fine." Von Günther unscrewed his fountain pen, laid the shiny black cap on the desk, and handed the pen to Fritz. "To counter any pangs of doubt I might have. Sign your name to the document below. You are an insignificant official. Signing won't cost you anything—no one will look at this signature. Besides, my good man, you have such a sloppy scrawl that no one could actually decipher your name anyway."

"Herr Ambassador, I'm not permitted to—"

"You're refusing, Kolbe?" von Günther cut in. "You're refusing an order from the Führer?"

"No. No, it's just that—"

"You do agree with me, though, that our Lebensraum policy in the East means that areas must be seized using all our greatness of force, and that such areas should be cleared out for the German Volk? You do also agree with me that this requires special methods which send the clear message that, yes, drastic measures must be taken. Or do you see things differently?" Von Günther held the fountain pen closer to Fritz's hand. "Well?"

Fritz lit a cigarette. He knew that if he hesitated too long, von Günther would bellow and order him to obey—and would eventually enforce the command. He let this, his last shred of freedom, linger a moment. Then he took the pen and signed. He tried to disguise his handwriting but it didn't work. Von Günther patted him on the shoulder.

"Now, I must go. I have a visitor arriving any moment. A lady. She's an acquaintance who is coming to see me about a few, um, concerns. As for what we've just discussed, let's not breathe a word about it, Kolbe." Von Günther held up the page with Fritz's signature. "Betray a secret to a woman and it'll be all over the papers the next morning," he said.

At the door to his office, von Günther turned around one more time.

"We really should talk about private matters now and then, yes? Most people hardly know each other, even when they see each other every day." Von Günther laughed. "Don't look so peeved about it, Kolbe. Go to that lady of yours. Take her. And this here . . ." He held the page in the air again, waving it, a glowing white. "This here? Bah. It's nothing."

The Braunweins were dead; music-loving Havermann was dead. Apart from Marlene, Fritz had no one left to talk to. When they were together, Fritz tried to speak about nice things, about books or films or the outdoors. He told Marlene about the long conversations he used to have with Consul Biermann in Madrid.

"Biermann was why you came back to Berlin, right?" Marlene asked.

He was, Fritz told her. He could still hear Biermann screaming at him on the telephone.

Marlene had lots of work friends at Charité Hospital. She was an open sort of person and often tried to steal away from the chaos and misery for a few minutes to rest on a stool with a nurse or lean against a wall out in the courtyard and smoke a cigarette. Every two weeks she'd visit her friend Gisela, who told her plenty about her erotic adventures, which Marlene then passed on to Fritz, uncensored. Fritz wondered if that was all right with Gisela, and Marlene said Gisela didn't mind one bit. Fritz, on the other hand, was considered a lone wolf at his office—polite as ever, but more insulated than before. That was just fine with him.

Still, Marlene proposed he get on his old bicycle and pedal over to see the Biermanns. Talk with them, she said, see somebody different. Have a simple chat. It would do him good.

The Biermanns lived in a four-room apartment in Charlottenburg; they'd rented out one of the rooms to a mother and daughter whose place had been bombed. The apartment smelled like coffee as Fritz looked over the spines of books on shelves that filled one whole wall. A private library—such a thing did still exist! Frau Biermann offered Fritz a seat while he waited. When Consul Biermann entered the room, Fritz greeted him with a heartfelt handshake reaching all the way back to their time together in Madrid and Africa.

"You look terrible, Herr Kolbe." The old man lowered himself into an armchair. "So nice of you to come visit us."

"It's grown rather quiet around here," Frau Biermann said. Fritz took the tray holding the coffee pot and cups from her, and she leaned her cane against the sofa and sat down.

"Would you be so kind?" Frau Biermann gestured at the tray. Fritz poured the coffee and handed them their cups. No sound could be heard from the street below; the traffic in Berlin was disappearing.

In this apartment Fritz felt a little like he was in Switzerland—on seemingly neutral ground. It felt good to sit here and drink a cup of coffee and look into these trusty old faces. The bond between the Biermanns was different than the one between Dulles, Priest, and Greta, but it was just as strong, made of love rather than professional duty. Biermann and his wife would stay with each other until the very end, Fritz knew, something he'd heard people say about couples onboard the *Titanic*.

"Someone was here," Biermann said. "A colonel. He was making insinuations, asking about my connections in the Foreign Office. He said something about treason—a putsch—against the great you-know-who, that monster. We're too old for such things. Besides, I have to think of my wife."

"Herr Biermann, please, there's no need for you to justify yourself."

"When should one justify oneself, Herr Kolbe, if not in times like these?" Frau Biermann asked. Her thin hand was grasped around the knob of her cane.

"Words, Herr Kolbe," Biermann said. "What use were all our diplomatic efforts? All those words, all our fine talk? Sure, we were over six thousand miles away then. But diplomacy—the great tradition of diplomacy—is the exact opposite of what's happening here. We have failed all the way down the line. What's happening is absurd. Why even have a Foreign Office in this Germany? For what purpose? We should've quit the service back in 1933."

Sure, we should've, Fritz thought. This wasn't what he had come here for. He didn't want to be polite anymore. He wanted to tell Biermann that he was disappointed in him and point out that the consul hadn't been able to keep any of the promises he'd made in Africa. But wasn't there enough goddamn shit piling up all around him already?

"Nice books you have there," he said.

No one spoke for a time.

The consul pounded feebly on the arm of his chair. "Should have done it back in 1933," he said.

"But we didn't, Herr Consul."

Biermann looked out the window.

"Anyway, what if one *did* do something," Fritz said, "and people ended up getting hurt?"

The wall clock ticked. Frau Biermann stared at her cup, lost in thought. "It's the same old story, Herr Kolbe," she said. "One always blames oneself."

"Walter and Käthe Braunwein are dead."

"Oh. Oh, I'm so very sorry," the old man said.

"Käthe was so lovely, wasn't she?" Frau Biermann asked.

"She shot herself when she learned of her husband's death."

"If you were to go, I'd follow you," Biermann said to his wife. The elderly couple gazed at each other. Fritz knew they would never leave this city again.

"Well," Biermann said, "I am very sorry I convinced you to return to this country. That was one of the biggest mistakes of my life. Yet I do hope you can forgive me. And I fervently hope you survive all this madness here."

"Perhaps there is something good to my being here. Good—and bad."

"Good and bad, it's the—"

"No more philosophy," Fritz said. He heard Frau Biermann draw a sharp breath.

"But there's still music," Biermann conceded. "I have a lovely recording of Beethoven."

"Music can never hurt," Frau Biermann added. She cranked up the boxed gramophone, slid a record from its paper sleeve, and put it on the turntable. She lowered the tone arm, knowing just the right groove for the chorus . . .

> *Joy, lovely divine spark,*
> *Daughter from Elysium!*
> *We enter fire-drunk,*
> *Heavenly one, your shrine.*
> *Your magic binds again,*
> *What custom has strictly parted.*
> *All men become brothers*
> *Where your tender wing lingers.*

Fritz began to hum. Biermann joined in, then so did his wife. They sang together, poorly and feebly, but they didn't mind. They sang, and the tears ran down Fritz's cheeks.

"It's all right, Herr Kolbe," Frau Biermann said. "It's quite all right."

"Have you heard from Katrin?" the consul asked.

Fritz wiped at his eyes and shook his head. "I've abandoned her."

"No," Frau Biermann said, "you've kept the girl away from all this. That's good, Herr Kolbe. Do not go blaming yourself."

After their visit, the consul escorted Fritz to the door. Walking was tough on Biermann, his knees and hips stiff. His beard had grown long. In the hallway hung gold-framed landscapes: rustling woods, splashing streams. It was his opinion that nature was always there to console, and he said he knew Fritz saw things the same way. On the wall beyond Biermann's head, a mountain range basked in sunlight, its snowcaps as white as the consul's hair. Only now did Fritz realize that he couldn't be absolutely certain Biermann would approve of his treason. The word might not even have entered the elderly man's head.

"Is it that bad, Herr Kolbe?"

"Yes."

"You must sit tight," Biermann said. "You can withdraw within yourself, and perhaps you should in times like these. But there is no other alternative to sitting tight. Don't try any nonsense. Don't go down the wrong track. I understand that you were alluding to something earlier, but I don't want to know the details. Stay at your post and raise your hand once this is all over. Then you'll be well positioned. You'll understand what to do then. If you try the wrong thing now, who knows what will happen. Your character will be marked irreparably. Farewell, Herr Kolbe." In their handshake, Fritz sensed an assumption of how he would respond. "And please, do not come here anymore."

"No," Fritz said. "Why would I ever come to you again?"

The old man jerked back. The back of his head tapped the landscape behind him.

As he rode home, Fritz clung to his bicycle. Biermann had noticed. The old consul had seen right through Fritz and had turned his back on him. Fritz couldn't take this. He couldn't stand it anymore. It would always be unbearable, but never more so than now.

"The British Secret Service were good," Fritz says. "It's possible that they located that transmitter in Dublin using intelligence other than mine. People in MI5 and MI6 could have gathered their own clues by listening in on U-boat radio traffic, or whatever. Who knows."

Fritz has taken more photos out of the box. He's fastened them to the lime-washed cabin beam with little nails: the picture of him and Walter on safari in South-West Africa; a photo of the car he and Marlene were riding in when they were attacked; and an image of the smoking remains of the Leuna Works in Berlin, the factory halls nothing but blackened carcasses, the giant steel lathes twisted into tentacles by the force of the explosions.

"I gave the coordinates of the Leuna Works to the Americans," he says. "I thought about going over to the factory right after the air raid—I could see the fire when I came out of the shelter. I didn't do it."

Veronika looks at Wegner, who makes a note and mutters that he understands.

"You didn't make contact with the OSS for a long time."

"I was fed up—up to here, for God's sake! Can you imagine the pressure I was under? And letting Marlene in on it only made things worse."

Fritz's heart is pounding. He rubs his forehead as if this could somehow suppress his thoughts. He's exhausted and feels empty and depleted. The weight of the past is great.

"The air raids on Berlin got worse and worse. Refugees from the East started streaming into the city. Hell finally broke loose at the hospital where Marlene worked."

"But where is she right now?" Veronika asks.

Fritz looks past her, out the window.

"She's probably out getting something to eat with Eugen Sacher and his wife," he says.

The sun has passed its highest point, and the shadows of the mountains are starting to settle into the valley closest to the hillsides, turning groves a bluish color and dimming the light along the stream as it winds around the mountains.

Six years of war, Fritz thinks. Six years of living a double life. He hasn't stopped lying since. The lies and parallel worlds have become so much a part of him that he keeps losing his way, again and again. Sometimes it's as if he has amnesia, and he has to rediscover his identity through the photos and notes, through his globe he's repaired, through the folds of torn city maps. He wants to be rid of the past, wants to get it onto the page, truly and finally. The impulse to be rid of it is as strong today as it was on the day someone violently banged on his door and Marlene demanded that he do the unimaginable. "Marlene was the one," Fritz says. "I kept going for her sake."

"The fact is the Americans sent someone to talk to you," Wegner says.

"Perhaps he shouldn't have come," Fritz says.

"Let's stick to the facts," Wegner says.

"You really don't get it, do you?"

"Oh, I do, Herr Kolbe, I get it completely. But there are certain facts. Period. There was a Hitler, and there were mountains of people gassed and starved to death, whether we like it or not. These are the facts. And just so you know, it's very clear to me that each and every one of these people once had a living, beating heart. But we have to make progress here. I'm writing an article about possibly the most important anti-Nazi spy of the Second World War. So, your OSS contacts did send someone to Berlin, is that correct?"

Fritz pulls the photo of Eugen Sacher from the stack. Gray suit, white shirt, smiling as always.

"They weren't at all shy about exposing Eugen to danger. That was when he got to know Marlene. And me."

"What do you mean *and me*?" Veronika asks.

"This whole time, it's as if I've been talking about someone I don't know. About someone I never wanted to be. Not Fritz Kolbe, and not

George Wood either. I'm not sure how insane a person has to become to be able to cope with such a situation. I was completely at wit's end. Did you know that Eugen wanted to send me to a psychiatrist, no matter what happened? No? Well, now you know."

◆　◆　◆

For a time Fritz and Marlene tried to keep Fritz's blackout-darkened Berlin apartment a place free from war, resolving that when they were together there, they would not talk about all the horror and death and destruction.

Whenever she came to the apartment, Marlene made a habit of jingling her wedding ring in the cutlery drawer. She'd open the front door, pass by him into the kitchen without a word, splay out her ring finger, and tug on the gold. She only let Fritz embrace her once the ring had disappeared between the forks and knives.

When they had time, they would go strolling through the rubble. They shared their love at busted railings along the Spree River, where scorched wooden planks bobbed in the water; on the inexplicable remains of barges; and upon mountains of debris, where they lost their footing on slopes they'd climbed in order to look out over the shattered city. Their walks, taken hand in hand, led them down former streets that were now only paths and onto badlands where buildings had once stood, before being blasted away by doomsday force.

Marlene sometimes went for weeks without mentioning his inaction regarding matters of espionage, leaving him in peace. Then all of a sudden she would allude to it in the middle of conversation, wondering aloud how much her love for him had to do with his working for the OSS. Wasn't that the major difference between him and her husband?

Every time Fritz took files down to the basement for incineration, his stomach burned, as if the flames in the burn barrels were igniting within him. What might Dulles have done with the material he was destroying right now? He kept picturing von Günther sitting at his desk, telling him Walter Braunwein was dead. Instead of running straight to Käthe, he had let sorrow overtake him, had told himself, *Tomorrow I'll go to her, tomorrow I will.* But tomorrow was too late. Tomorrow, Käthe was dead, the knowledge of that shooting a hole straight through all of Fritz's memories of her.

After one of their scenic strolls, Marlene turned to face him in the kitchen. Holding a cup of tea in one hand, she asked him about the secret files.

"I wanted to do what is right," he told her. He balled his fists and held them to his eyes. "What is *right* supposed to mean anyway? You tell me. What?"

Marlene set a chair before the kitchen cabinet and climbed atop it. He rushed over to support her, holding her hips. She reached into the top of the cabinet, felt around, and handed down a yellowed page, curling along the edges. She stared down at him from up on her perch, her broad jawbone and her nose looking unusually attractive from this angle, even a little arrogant.

"A German spy in southern England, codename Brandt. You wrote about it in that crazy handwriting of yours."

She reached into the cabinet again.

"A report from General Gehlen that you transcribed into concise notes. Take it!"

He was holding the pages in his left hand, his right resting on Marlene's hip. He grumbled that she needed to come down from there.

"Why don't *you* come back up?" she said. "My son is dead. My boy, Fritz. I'm deceiving the man who married me. You confided in me. Our life is hanging by a thin thread. And all for nothing? Did we do all that just so you could stop now? You can't stop, Fritz. Not something like this. It would—that would be treason. *Real* treason."

Someone knocked on the door. Fritz stared down the dark hallway and handed Marlene the papers. The knock was gentle, friendly. It was funny how a person could read so much into such small things.

"Who's there?"

"An old friend."

Fritz recognized the voice immediately. Eugen Sacher.

They hugged, Eugen smelling of aftershave and cleanliness, not like war and hardship. Fritz pulled him into the apartment. He could hardly believe it—he had an actual friend here with him in a Berlin that was more flattened and hollow than ever.

"Nice place," Eugen said.

When Eugen saw Marlene leaning against the kitchen cabinet, he gave her a little bow and a kiss on the hand, his big nose brushing her wrist. Fritz introduced them. Eugen said he'd brought chocolate and Marlene sighed with pleasure. Fritz got a bottle of Mosel wine from the cabinet.

"Fritz is quite good at stealing booze these days," Marlene said. She polished three water glasses, held them up to the lamp's caramel glow, and passed them around. She told Sacher he was only allowed to tell them about Bern, please; she only wanted to hear about a city no bombs fell on. Sacher could take her on a little imaginary stroll through his city—please, please, she said. They toasted and Eugen took them there. Marlene shut her eyes and tilted her face up as they listened to descriptions of shop windows full of sausage and cheese, Marlene breathing it all in.

When Eugen asked why Fritz had broken off contact with Bern, Fritz stammered something about the Braunweins dying. They fell silent awhile and listened to banging from the neighboring apartment, sounds like furniture being rearranged.

"Eugen, did anyone see you coming here?"

"No, I don't think so."

"Why would they take a risk like this?"

"I'm afraid you have to choose which side you're on," Eugen said.

"Says who?" Fritz asked.

Eugen raised his hands in defense and apologized.

"I've chosen sides," Fritz said. "It's just that I've had to choose more than one of them. Is that clear enough for you, Eugen?"

"Yes. Yes, it's fine, Fritz." He drank a gulp of wine and smiled at Marlene.

"Easy for you, coming from Switzerland."

"Fritz, please," Marlene said. "That's unfair."

"Listen to me," Eugen told Fritz. "No harm done, everything's all right. I do understand what you're saying. But here's what Dulles is asking: troop movements westward, out of Russia and Italy; restructuring of forces in France; supply routes, coastal defenses, and divisional commanders."

"The invasion!"

"We can hope. This madness does have to end at some point."

"My God," Fritz said. "A landing in France! That'll break that pig's neck. Finally."

"Dulles told me next to nothing, of course."

"They're good at saying nothing."

"Yet you think a great deal of Dulles."

"That amount has been reduced considerably."

"They provided me with a first-rate fake Swiss passport. And they didn't force me at all. They asked. I'm here on business with a trade delegation. I don't have much time. What should I tell Dulles?"

Fritz looked at Marlene, her gaze forceful, demanding. She opened the kitchen cabinet, pushed a few things around inside, and pulled something out. She set the globe on the table. She had glued it back together.

"My globe! It's whole again. You even repaired Germany."

Eugen ran his fingers over the resinous scars of glue. "It's not like the world's as smooth and round as portrayed anyway."

"How much time do I have?" Fritz asked.

"One hour."

"Fine. I'm going out for a bit."

"It doesn't look good out there," Eugen said.

Fritz left.

He sat down on a pile of rubble and it gave under his weight, dumping grit and little bits of earth inside his shoes. At one point a truck drove by, then a man on a bicycle, now and then a dusty car. He had one brief hour in which to decide. Fritz felt the weight of his revolver in his jacket pocket. He looked both directions down the destroyed street, past the gray debris and the buckling buildings, some bulging out into the street, as if trying to topple one on the opposite side. He would never get used to witnessing such horror.

He lit a crooked cigarette and blew out smoke. *Katrin, what do you think? The ones I've killed, my girl, are not all Nazis; they are not all swine. I always wanted to be decent, to keep my composure. But how do I do that here? Take a look around here, Katrin, and see for yourself! It's unbelievable.*

He heard the low drone of an engine, a double-clutching howl: that first grumble of a new gear and then the motor running at speed. Fritz looked up. A military transport was rumbling down the street, its grayish camo tarp raised, dull and sucking away light. Fritz drew his revolver. "Bang," he said. A woman was staring at him from across the street, her daughter holding her hand. "Get out of Berlin!" Fritz shouted. "Take the girl and leave—now!"

The girl glanced at her mother and said something; the woman pulled her onward by her thin arm. The little girl was limping, her right leg stiff, her shoulder lifting with each step. *The children are suffering too,* Fritz thought. He put the revolver away.

How could he continue to live with Marlene if he was no longer spying for Allen Dulles? How could he live with himself? It was awful to imagine British, American, Canadian, Russian, and French soldiers shooting at their targets when their targets were German men. Fathers, sons, husbands. Cartographers. Walter Braunwein. It was that bad. And that irreversible.

Fritz flicked the cigarette, white and smoking, onto the street. It landed in a crater and disappeared, only a thin string of smoke rising from the churned-up earth. In the books he'd read, there always came those dramatic moments when a decision loomed. He was at such a moment now: he and his thoughts, with his bad luck and with his good-luck charm Marlene, and a stiff-legged girl who will find no luck in love, and the dead Braunweins. He lifted his hat off his forehead, surprised at how easily the decision came in the end. *I'll finish you all off,* he thought. He went back to his apartment.

"Tell Dulles I'll start delivering again. Not a word about anything else, nothing of what we discussed here. Nothing about the Braunweins. Just tell him Wood is back. A different Wood."

"Wut?" his friend said, pronouncing the German word for *rage.*

"Not *Wut*—Wood," Fritz said. "But in my case, it's one and the same thing."

11

Invasion and Assassination

Berlin and Paris, 1944

"Madam, if I may?" Fritz held out his arms for Marlene to dance with him in the kitchen. It was the night of June 7, 1944. The Allies had landed in Normandy.

"You may, sir."

They moved the table aside. Marlene was humming a waltz. "Singing is nice," she said. "It makes me happy. I used to be in a choir. Don't go thinking I'm too bourgeois, though."

"I don't," Fritz said. "Music is never bourgeois."

"Oh no, then what about the Nazis' music?"

Fritz sighed. "The Nazis can kiss our asses."

Marlene giggled. "Absolutely not," she said. "You can kiss mine, though. But no one else's."

Fritz laughed bitterly about the announcers on the People's Receiver, who were constantly worked up into a state of excitement. It didn't matter how badly Hitler's armies were defeated; their battle results were always depicted as victories, brilliant military maneuvers that would cost the enemy dearly. Everything worked to the Führer's advantage. Goebbels was screaming into the microphone, his voice breaking. Fritz watched Marlene through a cognac glass, saying that maybe he too had become a fanatic—at least, about her.

"I can live with that," she said.

The little creases at the corners of her mouth had deepened over time; sometimes, when she stood before the mirror, she said that seeing all the maimed people and dealing with all those clanging prosthetics were going to do her in. She bent down close to the mirror as if searching for something on the surface of her face. The use of prosthetics was decreasing, though. "It's all about amputating now, saving lives in any way possible. Nothing gets replaced anymore." No one was discussing research either. Or human experiments.

"He's nice," Marlene told Fritz. "The professor, I mean. A pleasant person, polite, educated, humane to his staff. It's almost as if—I can hardly believe it myself, but I actually . . . Oh, I don't know what I want to say."

"It's as if you like him?"

She raised her hands, perplexed, skeptical of her own feelings. "I have to think about it first in order to detest him. When I'm not thinking otherwise, I like him."

"I don't understand it either, all that makes up a person. It's not easy to see."

"He's been secretly drinking. He pours cognac into his coffee cup."

That night Gisela came by. Marlene had told her that Fritz recently stole more wine from the Foreign Office, a practice that was becoming his specialty. Gisela laughed after almost everything she said. Her way of remaining so unaffected by life's troubles both irritated and amused Fritz. He didn't have the slightest idea where this plump, robust woman found reasons to laugh. *It just comes naturally to some people,* he thought. Maybe she was dumb—but she was good at remaining upbeat, so good that she always brightened things up with her presence.

"Now that the invasion's over—I for one am excited about these American boys," Gisela said. Fritz still felt a tinge of self-consciousness around her.

"It has to be a good thing," Gisela continued, "when a country has so many nationalities mixed together, right? What do you two think? All these borders led to all this crap in the first place."

"We're going to put an end to the crap," Fritz said.

"Ya don't say? Well, sure would be nice. Leni, cutie, you reckon it's true what they say about those Negroes having such big penises?"

Marlene laughed. She looked at Fritz. He slapped a hand over his eyes in resignation.

Fritz wanted to travel to Bern at the earliest opportunity, but the courier trips were being cut back and carefully watched. When he learned that a colleague would soon be traveling to Switzerland for the first time, Fritz tried to talk the man into letting him make the trip instead. The man laughed, saying, "The hell you will." Fritz couldn't insist too strongly. He considered shooting the man at night, or pushing him down stairs at the Office, but he couldn't bear to stoop even lower than he had already. The OSS could pull off deeds like that. He couldn't.

Von Günther, looking nervous and pale, sent Fritz to Paris. This trip is semiofficial, he said, adding that he knew he could always depend on Fritz. The assignment could do Fritz no harm. He was supposed to personally hand over a document to a man in the consulate there, have the man sign off on the delivery, and then return.

"If abstract greatness comes up against concrete reality . . ." von Günther started to say, but didn't go on. Out in the corridor some men were standing around and laughing hard, something about bleeding the Americans and British to death. Fritz could see the fear, worry, and insecurity on each of their faces when they sauntered down the hall.

Now and then he heard people whispering, and then someone would pass by and call out, *"Heil Hitler."*

In Paris, Fritz was sitting at a street café on the Champs-Élysées when he heard about Count von Stauffenberg's attempt to assassinate Hitler with a bomb. Again Hitler had escaped death. Fritz pounded on the little round tabletop, the tableware clanking and catching the light. Soldiers and officers looked his way. "Those pigs," Fritz said. *"Heil Hitler,"* said one of the officers.

Stauffenberg. It was all over the news. Someone had stood a radio on one of the café tables, and everyone listened in suspense, sunlit ears turned toward the speaker, eyebrows stern. The announcer spoke of a small clique of arrogant officers and of a leadership taking fervent revenge. In Berlin, it seemed, confusion had reigned for several hours until Hitler called the city's military commander and reported himself safe. "Our Führer cannot be killed," an officer said.

His fists buried in his trouser pockets, Fritz wandered off into the sunshine as military boots hammered the asphalt of Paris's broad avenues. He had always thought the Reich would collapse immediately if Hitler died. Comradeship, unity, solidarity—these were words only. The Nazis would tear each other to shreds once Hitler was finally dead and gone.

At the Eiffel Tower, he peered at the sun through the steel beams. He had summarized as concisely as possible everything he could learn about troop movements in the West and sent the information on to Bern by courier mail. Perhaps this intelligence had helped. It must have helped.

He stood at the foot of the tower looking up. A column of military trucks rumbled by, and he heard the clattering of heavy panzer tracks, felt the earth vibrating beneath him, but he didn't look around. Why had the Nazis still not given up? This was sheer madness. There was nothing but destruction left. Was it a love of death, the hero's death as a great event—as if dying under tank tracks or in a burning airplane gave death some special quality? How had Stauffenberg and his people managed to place a bomb next to Hitler and yet not kill the man? Things were only going to get worse. There were rumors that people were being arrested all over Berlin, that the first executions already happened. The brutality had reached the Foreign Office as well. All Office employees who were abroad during the assassination attempt would be investigated thoroughly. He had to get back. Back to murderous Berlin, back to that stinking hell. To Marlene.

Fritz rode the Metro to Jardin du Luxembourg, hoping to steal an hour of peace and feel the sun on him a little before it was time to leave. To some, on the surface, Paris might have looked virtually unchanged. But Fritz saw armed Wehrmacht soldiers patrolling among the civilians, and Nazi flags hung at the entrance to Boulevard Saint-Michel. A woman in a dark suit and hat was sitting on a park bench, smoking a cigarette and watching two German soldiers pass. Once the men were a few yards past, she spat in their direction. Fritz grinned at the incongruence of seeing such an elegant woman spit. He turned toward the soldiers and spat onto the path too. The woman smiled. She said she'd thought he was a German, that he looked like one.

"I am a German."

The woman raised her eyebrows. "You should be ashamed," she said. Then she stood and passed through the shadows of trees at the park's ornate iron gate.

No matter what you do, Fritz thought, *it's always wrong.* He scooped a little soil from a flowerbed, dumped it in one of his tins, wrote *Paris* on the lid, and pocketed it.

At the train station, soldiers swarmed under the tall vaulted ceiling. Out along the tracks, where the sun softened the edges, Fritz noticed smoke, then a Nazi flag ablaze, the flames advancing up it in a zigzag pattern. Soldiers carrying rifles ran out into the light, chasing a man.

"Good luck to you," Fritz muttered.

◆ ◆ ◆

The last air raid had hit the Office. When he got back from Paris, Fritz asked around anxiously to find out if Minister von Ribbentrop had been in the building.

"No, fortunately not," Müller said. "Come to think of it, where have you been this whole time, Herr Kolbe?"

"What's it to you, Müller?"

The young man stepped up close to Fritz. "I'll get you yet, Herr Kolbe." He straightened his body inside his baggy uniform and stretched out his right arm in the Hitler salute. The more disastrous things looked for Germany, the greater Müller's confidence seemed to grow. For a fraction of a second, Fritz nearly felt sorry for the boy.

The upper floors of the Office were no longer usable. Debris from the bombing got dumped into the inside courtyard. Most windows had been blown out from the blast, and the glass had been replaced with cumbersome plywood sheets, making it dark in the corridors even during the day. The radio transmitters were moved into various basement areas, communication lines were regularly disrupted, and officials were constantly seen running down the damp hallways, seeking the recipients of various telegrams. Müller, trying in vain to make his office the collection point for all incoming messages, kept shouting at grit-dusted motorcycle couriers out in the corridor. Von Günther was away somewhere again.

Fritz saw to it that the office ran smoothly. On his desk, more dispatches were stacking up than ever before. Von Günther congratulated him over the phone after hearing reports that Fritz had the situation under control and was handling things with a typical German official's diligence.

"You bet I have things under control, Herr Ambassador."

With Marlene's help, Fritz transcribed documents about the satellite states of Bulgaria, Romania, and Hungary, where attempts to topple the governments were continuing—intelligence that would be quite crucial to the Americans. He wrote in code the names of Japanese divisional commanders and sent that information by courier mail to Bern. A majority of department heads had removed themselves to Salzburg, one had disappeared without a trace, and three or four were arrested after the attempt on Hitler's life and never seen again. Müller reported that many colleagues had been interrogated. "You're still due, Herr Kolbe."

"Müller, I have nothing to hide. Nothing at all. I'm loyal."

"To the death, Herr Kolbe?"

"No. You?"

"What kind of question is that?"

"What kind of question, indeed."

12

WEAKENING COVER

Berlin and Bern, early 1945

Von Ribbentrop released dozens of decrees concerning the Foreign Office. One that was of particular significance, and that he said was wholly in keeping with the Führer's wishes, involved recruiting more able-bodied men into the Wehrmacht.

"Naturally, this doesn't affect you," von Günther said, and personally saw to it that Fritz remained exempt. Other men packed up their belongings with heads hanging and disappeared from their offices. Von Günther was only seldom in his office, and during one of the rare times that he was there, Fritz saw him chewing at his thumbnail. He smelled like sweat now, despite the great emphasis he put on personal hygiene. He rambled on and on about the power of fanaticism to succeed in seemingly hopeless situations, about the power of the will and recent tragedies that cried out to be celebrated in song, now and a thousand years from now.

"Perhaps, Kolbe, fanaticism is a form of—"

"Greatness?" Fritz interrupted.

Von Günther stared at him, the corners of his mouth turning up with appreciation. "Yes, Kolbe, yes. You have indeed learned something." He raised a finger. "The subject is quite interesting, yes?"

After a while, Von Günther had all his private things removed from his office. In the inner courtyard the barrels blazed constantly now, flickering orange under the gray winter sky. The only thing Fritz heard about Hitler was that he was having one attack of rage after another up at the Berghof, his home in the Alps. Fritz figured his monologues were undoubtedly growing longer and longer. One thing Fritz knew about Churchill was that he'd regularly joined the people out in the rubble of London after the German air raids. Hitler had shown up only during the early days of his victories.

When von Günther wasn't in the office, Fritz often locked the door and shadowboxed until he felt queasy. He punched out as much as he could of what was inside him.

As he boxed, he pondered. He had to get Marlene out of Berlin. Just as strongly as he wanted Hitler dead, he wanted Marlene Wiese to live—at any cost. At home he stabbed at Hitler's picture in the newspaper with a meat fork until the fork bent, then he scraped at the black-and-white face with its stupid mustache until only thin curling strips of paper were left. Time was getting short, the Nazi regime's stranglehold tighter and tighter. The number of executions was rising quickly. This capital had once had streetlights that glowed; he now saw men, their heads limp, hanging dead from those lamps, often with a sign on their necks reading, "I am a coward." Some had their pants pulled down and there they hung, their faces blue and aghast, their bodies robbed of all dignity.

At some point word leaked out that Hitler had come to Berlin and retreated into the bunker under the bombed-out Reich Chancellery.

Fritz was now very close to him.

◆ ◆ ◆

Von Günther called him into his office. The doors to the file cabinets stood open, and the rug was gone.

"I had my wife and children taken out of the city, Kolbe," he said. He was biting on his thumbnail. His eyes darted around as if he were watching some absurd tennis game. "The Führer says the new weapons for overcoming this crisis will be finished soon enough. I think we should be prepared for unpleasant times nonetheless, yes? It would be nice if Ribbentrop could be here." Von Günther's eyelids twitched. *It must be clear to him,* Fritz thought. *He must know that the end is coming.*

"Listen to me, Kolbe. You'll have to go to Bern again. I have certain documents ready for Weygand. Only Weygand, understand?"

"Yes sir, Herr Ambassador."

"Come back as fast as you can afterward. I'm going to ask a favor of you, one that can't do you any harm. You are to get out of this city. That's all I can tell you now."

"Where will you be, Herr Ambassador? What if the enemy makes it to Berlin?"

"He won't make it. But assuming, purely hypothetically, that he does, then we'd have to look to the West. To the West and the future. Have you ever met an American personally?"

"An American? Me? No, Herr Ambassador."

"They're not so evil. And they're essentially enemies of Bolshevism too. You and I, Kolbe, we are diplomats. Always have been. Always will be, yes?"

Von Günther handed Fritz a brown envelope, a Foreign Office stamp smeared on it. Frau Hansen wasn't with the Office anymore, von Günther said, so he'd issued Fritz's visa himself.

"It won't be easy getting to Bern. The special compartments and other privileges have been dropped. Trains must roll to the front, Kolbe. But one train is still running, and it leaves at eleven thirty tomorrow from Anhalter station. By the way, according to the new decrees, you aren't allowed to travel alone anymore. Müller will escort you to Bern."

"Müller?"

"You have a problem with that?"

The windowpanes began to vibrate, and dust floated down from the room's battered ceiling. Von Günther stepped over to the window. Three worn-out panzers, tracks wobbling, rolled down Wilhelmstrasse. A ragged crowd of refugees had gathered outside the U-Bahn entrance, their eyes searching the skies in all directions. Across the way at the Propaganda Ministry, faded Nazi flags hung heavy with grit on bent poles, the only flags left out now. He pulled his cigarette case from his jacket and offered it to von Günther. They smoked at the window while looking out over the bombed-out square.

"This favor you're to do for me . . . Well, Frau Wiese, that's her name, right? She can benefit from this too. Trust me. Just like I always and unfailingly have trusted you. And I"—he raised his cigarette high—"I've always had your back, yes? Don't forget it. You never became a Nazi Party member. You're the only one here who didn't. You have me to thank for things, Kolbe. You have me to thank for plenty."

"I could take Marlene along. Tomorrow."

Von Günther's eyes narrowed to slits. Fritz wondered if he'd gone too far. He read mistrust in his eyes, but didn't feel ill at ease.

"Have you gone mad, Kolbe?"

They had crossed over some kind of line. Maybe it had to do with the end of the war approaching, but Fritz couldn't hold back anymore, not completely. They were no longer the subordinate facing the ambassador, nor the actor and the liar facing the ambassador—this was Fritz Kolbe the man facing Ernst von Günther the man. Fritz tried with all his might to put on his "Yes sir" face, but he couldn't do it. Von Günther said nothing, holding a fist to his lips. Did he finally see through him now? Then something in von Günther's eyes drew back.

"Off you go!" he said.

I'll see you again, Fritz thought, *after the war.*

As he placed his hand on the door handle, von Günther called after him, his words echoing in the empty office.

"Weygand is one sharp attack dog, Kolbe. We have plenty of people in Switzerland. Certain people are getting strange ideas."

"Yes sir, Herr Ambassador."

"It would be a shame to lose our good little civil servant, yes?" Von Günther showed how much of a shame it would be by holding the tips of his thumb and forefinger about an inch apart.

"This good little civil servant will survive this war, Herr Ambassador. Marlene Wiese will too." Fritz tapped the envelope to his forehead.

"Go to Bern. Don't worry, I'll see to Frau Wiese. Off you go."

Fritz walked back into his office, closed the door behind him, took the Allgäu picture off the wall, and opened the safe. After he'd stuffed secret files into the inside pockets of his jacket and overcoat, he left his office. He ran into no one in the corridor and heard nothing but two people screaming at each other inside one office and the pounding of a typewriter in another.

He stepped out onto gritty gray Wilhelmstrasse and pushed through the refugees at the U-Bahn entrance to his bicycle. He looked into all the pale faces around him, smelled the people's filthy clothes and their weak and hungry breath. He ran back to the office, grabbed the rest of the chocolate, and handed it out to some of the children. It was cool outside, the sun shining on the dusty rubble and the children's pitiful wool caps. Farther to the east a black pillar of smoke billowed sideways into the sky. Passing ragtag troops, he followed the street until he reached the bank of the Spree. The bridge was destroyed, and he pedaled along the water to the nearest temporary crossing. The Spree was brown from floating debris and earth that had been churned up by bombs, and on the opposite bank was a row of corpses.

Trucks with Red Cross tarps were parked around Charité Hospital, and hundreds of people with crude bandages lay on stretchers out in the courtyard. The dark building had become an orchestra of moaning and pleading. Fritz pushed his way down the halls to Marlene's office. She was not there. Cases of bandages were stacked up in her office, and prosthetics were piled on her cot. He asked a sobbing nurse where Marlene was, and he was told she was in the operating room, helping the professor.

"Which OR?" Fritz asked. The whole building was an operating room.

"In the cellar," the nurse said. "The professor only operates down in the cellar now."

Marlene was sitting on a wooden chair, her surgical gown pink where she'd tried futilely to wash out the blood. She let her head hang, a cigarette between her fingers. Fritz crouched before her. At that moment, someone pushed a curtain to the side and passed by them carrying a bucket. When the bucket swayed, several severed hands within seemed to beckon to him.

"Nice place," he said. He reached for Marlene's shoulders. When she looked at him, the black freckles in her eyes seemed far away.

"How I love you," he said.

She blinked away tears.

"I have to go to Bern one more time, Marlene. Tomorrow. When I get back, we're disappearing from Berlin. I'm obtaining the necessary papers. For you too. We're getting out of here. I'm bringing you to safety."

She inhaled on her cigarette. "Take a look around you, Fritz."

He gazed around at the stooped wounded, at the nurses' legs rushing by, at the leather-strapped backs of heavily armed soldiers.

"Berlin cannot be held, Marlene. The chaos will be unimaginable. A massacre. We're getting out of here, you and I. It's time for us to disappear."

She dropped her cigarette to the floor and ground out the stub with her filthy shoe. Then she glanced up and down the cement-gray hallway. From somewhere came a sound like a person's screams, muffled by a towel. The place stank of disinfecting agents, tobacco smoke, and feces.

"I'll pick you up here this evening," Fritz said. "Tonight we're sleeping side by side. In our bed, Marlene. Do you hear me? You and I."

"I don't know if I can get away."

"I'll be here at eight o'clock."

She hugged him tightly. When he looked up again, he saw the broad back of a man in a white surgical coat hurrying past. "The professor," Marlene said.

"What do you want more than anything, Marlene? Tell me. I always love to hear you say it."

"To live," she whispered. His ear was damp from her tears.

"*Live,* she always said. *Live.*"

In his mind, Fritz still hears her screams. He tried to turn around but all the damn bent metal wouldn't let him. The car had rolled over.

"The fall of Berlin," he says. "That final trip to Bern, then our escape. Our suffering should have ended along with the war. It didn't, though. It got even worse. We'd survived air raids, we'd survived my espionage work—and then what?"

Wegner looks at him and his eyes give something away. Fritz guesses that Wegner is just now beginning to understand what he's saying.

Fritz grabs three bottles of beer from the well alongside the cabin and wipes the water off, the labels slipping under his fingers. "It's about that time," he says, and they pop the hinged lids and toast, the bottles clinking together. Wegner looks deep into Veronika's eyes and she smiles at him warmly. Fritz thinks of Marlene. Often when he made her laugh or gave her a compliment, she would turn away slightly, lower her head, and look at him from the corner of her eye. He always found that so lovely.

"You're a long way away," Veronika says.

"I'm constantly going back and forth," Fritz admits. "There was this one time when someone was knocking on our door like crazy, screaming my name. Marlene and I were just about to copy some documents. We thought: this is it. Gestapo, SS . . . we had no idea. Marlene . . . she wanted me to shoot her. I threw the files in the oven, then went up to the door holding my revolver. I was terrified. I almost fired. But then I realized the Gestapo or SS wouldn't ever knock. It turned out to be the new block warden—that brown-nosing Nazi pig. My blackout curtains weren't straight! That's all it was. I'd gotten home before Marlene and had moved the cardboard slightly so I could peek onto the street. I wanted to see her coming home to me. I wanted to gaze at her as she made her way to me."

"Being in love under such high-pressure conditions . . . Does it feel different somehow?" Veronika asks.

"Yes."

"You haven't shown us one single photo of her," Veronika says.

"Later."

Wegner underlines something in his notes, circles a couple of other items, then loosens his tie. "My father was taken from Switzerland by the Gestapo," he says. "We never found out why. It must have been a mistake. He was just a regular person."

"So am I," Fritz says.

"He never did anything illegal. Ever. He never would've dared. Not that I'm blaming him! Even so, a good friend of his . . . people said he was spying. We never heard from my father again, not even after it was all over. He disappeared without a trace. It was like the earth had swallowed him whole. My mother later married the friend."

"I'm very sorry about your father," Fritz says. "It's tough, not knowing what happened."

He takes a drink of beer. It's strange how much good it always does him to raise that cool bottle to his mouth and let the bitter flavor flow out, to gulp it down and feel it relax his body and soul. "A lot of alcoholics got started under the Nazis," he says. "If you got a bottle of beer in your hand, you drank it right down. When Berlin was falling, people held these bizarre orgies of all kinds—no one wanted anything more to do with discipline or order or standing at attention."

"After your third Bern trip, a death occurred," Wegner says, "one that made you realize that in the new Germany you were . . . how should I put it?"

"Persona non grata. In the new Germany, I was just as much a thorn in their side as I had been in Cape Town. They would've preferred that I never existed. My presence was a reminder that they had done nothing to stand up to Hitler. They still can't bear to have a man like me around. There are some who are steadfast Nazis, of course, but there are far more who simply went along with it. They couldn't tolerate sitting in an office next to me. And the ones who are now slowly inching their way back into positions of leadership? They would never permit it."

He lays a photo of the Nuremberg Trials defendants on the table among all the overlapping faces and maps.

"All pleaded innocent. Many lower-ranking Nazis were acquitted; others were given sentences far more lenient than they deserved, including von Günther. The detention he served while awaiting trial counted toward his punishment. They're being received with open arms. And me? They consider *me* the traitor—the one responsible for fatalities. How many murders are they guilty of, for God's sake? One of the men who took part in the Wannsee Conference is now a tax consultant living right in Berlin. You do know what happened at the Wannsee Conference?"

"Of course," Veronika says. "Top Nazis planned the Final Solution for exterminating the Jews."

Wegner looks at Fritz. His eyes convey both recognition and disbelief, reminding Fritz of the way William Priest looked at him years ago in Bern.

"Is conscience a provable fact, Herr Wegner?"

"I'm not sure. I'm starting to think so."

Veronika runs her fingers over the photos and city maps. She looks von Ribbentrop in the eyes, turns General Gehlen toward the light, and smooths out a newspaper clipping that shows a photo from Auschwitz of a gray heap of bones and skulls crying out.

"The photographer who took that was good," she says. "But where's the photo of you, Herr Kolbe?"

"Of me?"

"You have so much to be proud of," Wegner says.

The young man's compliment moves Fritz. Who doesn't like to receive a compliment? Yet inside, he is still crashing against a blood-smeared wall, something inside him still fighting this connection to the present. He is in the past: the filth of living in Hitler's Germany, and the dead; Marlene screaming; Katrin at the dock.

"There is a price to pay," he says, "for doing what's right."

Wegner writes down Fritz's remark. Veronika slides off her seat and walks out of the cabin. The men watch her go.

"Are you in love with her, Herr Wegner?"

"I'm married."

"People aren't always married to the person they want to be with."

The door scrapes against the wooden floor as Veronika comes back in a few minutes later. She is holding her camera.

"It's time, Herr Kolbe. Please."

"Okay—I agree."

"Can you repeat what you just said? The part about having to pay a price?"

"There is a price to pay," he says, "for doing what's right."

The camera clicks, its shutter working away. All Fritz can see of Veronika's face is her jaw and forehead.

He sits down at the table, his hands on his box. When all he takes into account are the facts, it's impossible to sort out what happened. Yet the past *can* be explained. Photos, he thinks, are just frozen moments in time, without a history. No lies, no betrayal in them—or is there? He lays a picture on the table.

"Having a drink in von Günther's office, after the defeat of France," he says. Veronika looks at the photo and Wegner leans her way, their shoulders touching. Fritz doesn't need to look at this picture; he knows them all. In this one, he's standing right next to von Günther, wearing a suit and tie as always, not exactly looking tall—he chuckles at that. He's never described himself as short, he says. Maybe medium-size. He never did like looking up at a person. There are only men in this typical Nazi-era photo. Their arms are cocked and they hold champagne flutes. There's a picture in the background of Hitler in profile. All the men are laughing, but Fritz is smiling with his mouth closed, showing no teeth.

"Looking at this photo, one might think you don't belong there," Veronika says, "especially knowing what we know now."

"What can a photo tell a person anyway, Fräulein Hügel?"

She raises her index finger and wags it left to right, like a metronome. "Photos don't lie," she says.

"Sure they do," Fritz says.

She smiles at him. "That's a whole other discussion," she says.

Fritz sets out another photo: he's sitting on the bench in front of the hotel in Bern, legs crossed, a cigarette in the hand on his knee. His hat brim casts a shadow over his eyes. Eugen Sacher took this one.

He doesn't set out the photos that come next—he looks at a photo of the smashed car and again hears Marlene screaming, even after all these years. He turns the picture over and picks up the next: von Ribbentrop, in a black SS uniform, receiving an Italian delegation. Von

Günther is laughing in the picture and Fritz stands at an angle behind him, looking like he might be gazing at von Ribbentrop.

"You really were in the thick of it," Wegner says.

"No other intelligence source got as close," Fritz says. He's never expressed it quite like that, never said it so directly. It does him good, feels good, to say it.

"Here's one," he says. "Allen Dulles and I met briefly in Berlin, after the war. The good man barely had time to see me."

"He abandoned you too?"

Fritz flips the photo onto the table like a playing card.

"Dulles has risen to the top of his field. He's the big boss now in America. He was also the one who made General Gehlen palatable to his fellow Americans. It would be laughable if it weren't so horrible. And this one here: William Priest and I, also in Berlin. He was a good guy whom I did grow to like, later on. Around this time, he was going crazy for German beer—thought it was splendid. Don't get me wrong: the man was no drunk. Drunks are a lousy sort. Another beer?"

His young guests nod. The atmosphere between them has changed, and an unspoken, delicate understanding is beginning to emerge. Fritz has told them a lot—he finally went on record with the Braunwein story—but he keeps leaving things out too. Something is working away on him, eroding his walls of resistance, and he's yielding. It's doing him good.

Outside, he grabs three more bottles of beer from the well and looks toward the mountains. The sun hovers at the peaks, the rock face illuminated on one side and looming dark on the other, the shadows growing longer. The valley below spreads out gray-blue, and the river is now dark with white spots where the water gushes over stones.

Fritz turns on the lamp above the table. Streaks of gloss appear on the photo paper, shining on different parts of the prints as he moves his head, adjusting his perspective.

"So then," Wegner says. "That final trip to Bern. The escape from Berlin."

"The final chapter, Herr Kolbe," Veronika says.

"The attack on you, Herr Kolbe," Wegner says. This time he looks right at Fritz when he says it.

Fritz shakes his head. "The final chapter is nowhere near written," he says. He leans back, stretches out his legs, and lights up a cigarette. "You simply can't let things get you down," he says. "Now *that* would be betrayal—a betrayal of life itself. I don't care how pathetic that sounds. I mean exactly what I said."

◆ ◆ ◆

Outside his building, Fritz stood with his back to Marlene, slung her arms over his shoulders, and picked her up.

"Fritz," she muttered, "I'm bigger than you."

"I'm an athlete. And now I'm going to carry the woman I love up the stairs, no matter how uncomfortable it makes either one of us."

"Well, when you put it that way . . ." Marlene giggled. The steps creaked under their combined weight, Fritz laughing from the strain and their love. Once they were inside the apartment, Marlene dropped her overcoat and shuffled into the kitchen. Fritz made her tea and a slice of bread with jam and cut an apple into slices for her.

"Let's get you out of those smelly work clothes," he said. He helped her undress, hung her blouse, skirt, stockings, and underwear in the window, and heated more water in the kitchen. "While we're waiting for that to get hot," he said, "let's waltz." Standing naked before him, Marlene laughed and opened her arms. Fritz placed his right hand on her back and took her hand in the other. "One, two, three," Marlene said. He kissed her. "We're really doing it, my belle. We're getting out of here." She linked her fingers at the back of his neck and held him firmly, pressing herself so close to him that he ached. He knew that she'd closed her eyes and was holding on to this moment of calm and togetherness just like he was. "You," she was saying, "you, you."

Once the water was hot, he washed Marlene's neck with a damp washcloth, and then her armpits, her breasts, and the inside of her thighs, all sticky with sweat, before covering her up with a blanket. When he kissed her, he kissed her all over her back so she could finish her food and tea. He longed to sleep with her and she surely wanted him too, despite her exhaustion and extreme fatigue, but in this moment, too much stood between them. Marlene smiled at him sleepily and he kissed her nose, her cheeks, her mouth. She fell asleep as he sat with her. Carefully he cradled the back of her head, settled her among the pillows, and turned off the light.

A pile of secret documents lay on the kitchen table, dull and coarse in the lamp's glow. Why in heaven's name did all those Germans want to die? What honor was it supposed to bring, to die for those butchers who despise life itself? Life—not some Kaiser or Führer, and certainly not some ideology—was the source of honor. The fanatical Japanese were being beaten just as badly as were Hitler's troops, so how were they surviving?

Fritz flipped through the pages and laughed: just look at that! The Japanese owed the German Reich sixty million marks.

He paged through reports on Japanese weapons and read that the Taisho machine gun was performing at five hundred shots per minute.

Any reverses that were suffered in certain areas of the Eastern Front could be viewed as more or less final, he read. It was beyond Fritz how someone could write such a thing.

A report to von Ribbentrop, addressed *Dearest Reich Foreign Minister*, claimed that the Allies' invasion had in fact been welcome. *It's not the material resources that decide matters, as you know, Herr von Ribbentrop, but rather the troops' fighting spirit.* Naturally, the writer said, Germany's foreign posts had known about the invasion beforehand, as it would have been impossible for the enemy to keep such an undertaking a secret.

Fritz put his hand to his forehead, shaking his head. He could not believe what he was reading. He continued to thumb through the pages one by one. *Drastic measures.* More Jews would need to go into individual rail cars. There was a need to free up more trains for the front. *Dear von Ribbentrop, if the Jews arrive at the camps already dead, so much the better.* Fritz wrote down the number of armored reserves and armored training battalions in the West. Someone calling von Ribbentrop *Your Excellence* wrote subserviently from Tokyo about *a gratifyingly high level of fanaticism.*

Dear von Ribbentrop, just between you and me: are you sure you know what General Gehlen of Military Intelligence is up to?

There followed a circular marked *Secret,* and issued by von Ribbentrop himself, which said that no negligent behavior by female receptionists would be tolerated.

One report said that Churchill's assessment of the situation was wrong.

From another: bank gold reserves were to be sent to various locations in Switzerland as directed via X2Z. In Switzerland, operatives were waiting. Check courier trips closely. Hail victory!

Fritz raised the page off the table. *Check courier trips.* His mind ran through what that could mean. Check Fritz Kolbe. Apprehend Marlene Wiese. Leave Katrin in the dark forever. He cursed, pulled the page closer to his eyes, and read about alleged secret negotiations in Italy. The traitors, he read, must be liquidated at once with no consideration given to name or rank.

General Gehlen was haranguing von Ribbentrop for not having his ministry under control. No one else would dare take such a tone with von Ribbentrop, but Gehlen sounded quite sure of his rebuke. *Read this carefully, Ribbentrop!* Complete with exclamation point.

After that followed a more recent letter from Japan; in this one the sender didn't address the Foreign Minister as *Your Excellence* anymore. Then Fritz stumbled on yet another report about gold being transported into Switzerland.

They're bringing the money to safety, he thought. *By the millions.*

He summarized as much intelligence as he could, focusing on the state of the Western Front, assessments of Allied forces, and the Pacific Theater. He included details from the memos about gold transfers between the Reich and Switzerland and noted down agent activities in Spain, Italy, and France, as well as the names of leaders in Eastern Europe who were operating more or less openly against the Nazi factions in their own countries.

Later, he stood in the bedroom doorway, glancing back and forth between Marlene and the folders. On one side: top-secret Reich matter. On the other: top-secret woman, asleep.

Fritz was riding to Bern in a cold freight car. When he climbed onto a crate and peeked out through the bars of the window slots, he could see fields passing before him, white with snow and marked by stretches of brown earth. One swastika-flag-bearing train station had been bombed into ruins and was populated by cowering refugees, their eyes aghast and weary.

At one point the doors were yanked open to the sounds of scraping metal, and Gestapo men with hungry German shepherds entered the darkening car in order to inspect the papers of the people within. Müller stood up at once. *"Heil Hitler."* One man was tossed from the car by two Gestapo men and put into handcuffs out on the rickety platform. Fritz held his diplomatic ID and visa at the ready. The officer checking him didn't even bother looking him in the eyes.

"Fucking diplomat."

Fritz said nothing. He knew one false word would cause the men to haul him out of the train and frisk him. Once again he had to keep silent, hide himself away, show his subservience. He didn't know this officer who wouldn't look at him, didn't know anything about his inner life, whom he loved, the things he'd done—but he hated him so much that he instinctively felt for his revolver inside his overcoat pocket. The man returned Fritz's papers and barked for the next one. As he began to examine Müller's papers, Fritz saw Müller lean toward the man and whisper something to him. "Don't tell me what to do!" the officer retorted. Fritz grinned at Müller. All the malice and brutality of their time were on full display right here, in the tight spaces of this one train car.

Fritz had a good sense of direction, yet wasn't able to tell what route the train followed as it zigzagged through Germany. It took over fifty hours to reach the border, and sometimes at night they saw the glow of fires in the distance and heard the rumble of air raids. At one point the train traveled backward, then it halted somewhere and stayed there for hours, the people in the car reeking of sweat and thirsty breath. To Fritz, it felt as though Germany were suffocating under a foul gray mantle.

"We won't let this get us down," he said. The others glanced at him, then looked away.

"Heil Hitler," Müller said.

Fritz went and stood close to him, the edges of the young man's paper-white face blurring in the dim car.

"Were you with them then, Müller? On that ship? Did you want to throw me overboard?"

Müller smiled.

"My position has allowed me to do more for the real Germany than you ever could."

"Heil Hitler, Herr Kolbe. Just say it."

271

"I feel like I'm on a ship from South Africa to Germany again."

"I don't know what you mean, Herr Kolbe."

"Oh, Müller. You're not really very smart, I'm guessing."

The checkpoint inspector at the station in Basel was the same one Fritz had encountered on previous crossings. The tracks were cold, the lines of steel deserted, the station quiet. Only four people stood in line before the inspector's table, their tensed-up backs to Fritz.

"Ah, Herr Kolbe, heading to Bern again?" The inspector's voice was friendly. He had grown a mustache. He looked over his shoulder. Two sullen Wehrmacht soldiers in worn uniforms walked back and forth, their rifles shouldered, boots crunching on stones.

"Not far now. Just a few more steps," the inspector said. "Then you're in Switzerland." He swallowed, his Adam's apple shifting. "You're staying . . ." He looked at Fritz's papers. "Three days. Then you're return-ing? To Germany?"

"Of course."

The inspector held Fritz's visa up close, turned briefly toward the two soldiers again, then checked the document's other side. "How one piece of paper can be so important, isn't that true? Herr Kolbe, I was only doing my job. Whatever has happened back there"—he gestured at the customs hut—"is not my responsibility. I never did a thing to anyone."

"Pardon me, but I really have to get going."

"Yes. Of course." The inspector held the visa to his eyes and smiled at Fritz. Fritz knew this expression so well—it was the look of someone who wanted to say something, but couldn't do it.

Fritz didn't know what the inspector had to fear. He certainly wouldn't be tried as a war criminal when all this was over. Perhaps he feared revenge from people he'd sent away for cavity searches, though why he'd plead his case to Fritz was a mystery—Fritz had no idea whom this man had handed over, or why. One thing he did know was that revenge would keep swinging at Germany like a scythe, and for years to come. So much unpunished barbarity. Drag the concentration-camp guards through the streets, let the SS officers starve, lock the Gestapo members in cells for twenty years—it was all the same to him. People liked to wax philosophically that revenge was immoral, that taking revenge made the avengers no better than those they sought revenge on. Fritz could care less about that. He understood the feelings and arguments for revenge all too well. It was his ardent hope that not a single camp commander would be spared. He hoped Goebbels, Göring, von Ribbentrop, Kaltenbrunner, and the rest would be forced to stand trial and account for what they'd done.

"I'm sorry if I was ever rude or disrespectful, Herr Kolbe. I'm under so much pressure here."

"Under pressure? I know what that's like." Fritz almost reached out to give the man a derisive pat on the shoulder. He leaned in close instead. "Now give me my papers, you asshole. One false word from you and I'll blow your balls off. I'll be back through in a few days, you miserable little prick. Have I made myself quite clear, or do you have some trouble understanding I should know of?"

The man suddenly turned even paler. His eyes pleaded. "No, Herr Kolbe. Sorry."

"In line after me is a man named Müller. He was giving me a bad impression this whole trip, making defeatist comments. I strongly suggest you search him thoroughly."

"Yes sir, Herr Kolbe. *Heil Hitler.*"

Fritz used a telephone booth in front of the station in Bern to call the OSS team, using the usual code. He didn't ask for an appointment; he just told them when he was coming. Next, he called Eugen Sacher.

Fritz stood at the hotel-room window, smoking a cigarette. The Bubenbergplatz lay under a blanket of snow, dark dots of cobblestones shining through, like holes for ice fishing. The monument was surrounded by scaffolding, the fog-colored tarp that covered it shifting in the slight breeze, shaking off drops of water. The sky over the mountains was gray. Fritz had lain in a hot bath for a long time, washing off the smell of the trip and his thoughts of revenge.

At the arranged time, he waited for Eugen at the hotel's rear entrance. Eugen had his hat down over his face and his overcoat collar turned up. Fritz pulled him into the hallway and the two embraced. Up in the room, Fritz poured them whisky.

"It's nice here," Eugen said.

"Has anyone come to your place?"

"A captain in the Swiss police. He asked if I know you."

"And?"

"I said I used to, back in Spain, but that I hadn't seen you here."

"You volunteered that you hadn't seen me here? Even though he didn't ask you that?"

Eugen hesitated. "I guess so."

"Eugen, what am I going to do with you?" Fritz muttered. He looked out onto the square, at the people ducking into the shopping arcades to escape the weather, the cars passing, a newsstand with papers waving like feathers in the cold wind.

"It's almost over," Eugen said. "The Nazis have to surrender."

"You may be right."

"So stay here."

"I'm going to get Marlene out of there, Eugen. I have to go back."

"But they're just getting more insane. They won't keep buying your act much longer. You can't hide who you are anymore."

"Nonsense."

"You've been really good at it. I can hardly believe it. But you look different. Something's changed." Eugen drank his whisky down and poured himself another. "Tell me you're not getting reckless."

Fritz was definitely not becoming reckless, but Eugen was right about one thing: the emotional shield he put up was growing unavoidably thinner. Week by week, his act was becoming less believable. With every tank that neared Berlin, with every man who disappeared from the Foreign Office and every office that was cleaned out, his cover was crumbling. The most damning thing was that it made him feel so good.

Pull yourself together, he thought. He dragged a chair up to Eugen and sat next to him. "I have to go soon," he said. "But before I do I want to sit here with my old friend and drink this whisky."

"Have you heard anything from Katrin?"

Fritz looked out the window. He placed a hand on Eugen's shoulder.

"Eugen, old boy, tell me about your last hike. Tell me what you saw. I used to go hiking with Walter a lot, like I did with you. Outdoors, for hours on end. Katrin never liked that very much." He laughed. "Marlene will like hiking, though. She has these long, muscular legs— you really have to see them."

Not as many people were working in the diplomatic mission on Willading Lane now. The hallways were lined with nailed-up crates, many without the swastika emblem. One office Fritz passed had been completely cleared out. An empty schnapps bottle lay on the floorboards, and a portrait of Hitler was on the wall.

Weygand intercepted Fritz in the hallway. He asked where he'd been and held out his hand for the envelope from von Günther. Weygand waved the letter in the air, murmured, "Good, good," and threw his door shut behind him.

At just that moment, Müller walked into the diplomatic mission. He stared at Fritz, his lips pursed and drained of blood. Fritz told Müller that he'd already taken care of what they were sent to do and if Müller had any complaints about it, he could take them to Herr Weygand. He pointed at Weygand's office door.

Müller, overcome with rage, knocked and flung the door open. Fritz waited. In just seconds he heard Weygand screaming. Once Müller had stepped back out into the hallway, Fritz handed him his return ticket.

"Your job was to escort me and the documents to the diplomatic mission. That is what you did, efficient as ever. Go get something to eat. There's time to rest up for an hour or so before your train heads back to the Reich. Oh, by the way: What was that business back at the station?"

Müller ripped the ticket from his hand and stomped down the hallway for the gray daylight. Fritz felt at the revolver in his overcoat pocket.

Von Lützow, looking pale, sat at his desk signing documents.

"A face from the Office in Berlin. How nice," he said. He was sweating, and his hand holding the fountain pen wouldn't keep still. At his temples his black hair had turned gray, the color of rock. He asked Fritz to report on the latest decrees from von Ribbentrop concerning communications between Berlin and Bern and the reorganizing of the courier service. Von Lützow felt that he was clearly being ignored—something was going on behind his back between von Günther and other officials in Berlin and Weygand here in Bern. And it wasn't about Final Victory and Hitler's secret weapons anymore. It was about money, nothing more.

"So how is our Herr Reich Minister von Ribbentrop doing, Herr Kolbe? I must say, it would be nice if we heard from him now and then here in Bern. One seems rather left on one's own, if you get my meaning." Von Lützow pulled the framed portrait of his wife closer to him.

"Von Ribbentrop withdrew to his mansion long ago. No one sees him at the Office anymore."

The corners of von Lützow's mouth twitched like those of a small child trying not to cry.

Without asking permission, Fritz lit himself a cigarette. "No one hears anything from Hitler anymore either," he said.

Von Lützow let out a sound, and Fritz briefly thought he was going to reprimand him. But the man seemed to have lost the strength to do it. This told Fritz that von Lützow was finally a clear target. "But aren't people in Berlin still of the opinion that . . . I mean, their faith in Final Victory still remains. Does it not, Herr Kolbe?"

"In Berlin? People are starving. After one air raid, I ran into a man carrying his dead daughter in his arms. People don't want words; they want warmth. They want food and a roof over their heads. And . . ." He paused a moment. "They want peace."

Von Lützow screwed the cap onto his fountain pen and looked out into the diplomatic mission's wintry gray yard. They heard a truck pulling up, and soon afterward orders were echoing through the villa.

"Think of your wife and three girls," Fritz said.

Von Lützow stood and planted his hands on the desk as he watched Fritz leave.

Weygand was waiting out in the hallway, several files tucked under one arm. He nodded his chin toward von Lützow's door. "He's shitting his pants."

"It happens, Herr Weygand."

"What about you, Kolbe? You're not going to get any funny ideas here in Switzerland, are you?"

"I'm going back to Berlin in two days. The home front—soon the front lines. The Volkssturm militia would accept someone like you right away."

"My post is here."

"Are *you* getting any funny ideas, Weygand?"

What was wrong with him, for God's sake? How could he take risks like this? How could he forget the role he was playing? He listened as

Weygand droned on about Final Victory, Fatherland, Führer, fighting to the last bullet—all the usual shit he kept hearing, over and over. He abruptly turned and walked off down the hallway. Weygand called after him but he didn't turn around.

"Kolbe. Kolbe!"

Von Günther used to yell at him like that. Fritz turned back. The hallway separating them was long and dim, the wooden crates absorbing the light. A man with a typewriter in his arms crossed their line of sight.

"Heil Hitler," Weygand said.

"Sure thing," Fritz said softly.

He went back to his hotel early that evening. The porter who met him at the door said he was sorry. Fritz rushed into his room. Shirts and underwear lay on the floor like a patchwork rug. The closet, the chest of drawers, his suitcase—everything had been ransacked. His editions of *Antigone* and *Michael Kohlhaas* had been ripped apart. Such a hatred for books—the fear of foreign ideas and viewpoints, so common to small minds. He gathered up the pages, smoothed them out, and put them back in order. Then he stuffed the pages back into their covers and ran a hand over them. No one had found anything suspicious here—he'd carried the secret documents on his person the whole time. But who had come here to try?

Fritz crossed the Bubenbergplatz in the dark, the square silvery in the winter night, his shoes splashing through the soft, wet layer of snow that was gradually freezing back over. He followed the Amthausgasse, keeping close to the walls of buildings, crossed the lane multiple times, and plunged down a dark alley near the casino. This was where he first heard his tail, even though he'd had a feeling he was being shadowed when he first left the hotel.

The fear in his heart stayed minimal; Fritz kept his fist around the grip of his revolver. He did not assume that he was targeted to be killed.

His room had likely been searched by Weygand's people, maybe by the Swiss police, perhaps the Russians. He guessed it was Weygand's men because the books had been torn apart. He walked down to the Aare, the river rushing dark and loud, and scurried into the shadow of a column under the Kirchenfeld Bridge. He heard the other person's steps and waited until the figure passed.

"Evening." Fritz's voice sounded loud and rough-edged under the bridge.

The man slowly turned to him. Fritz saw him in shadow, a silhouette against the river's flat glaze. He thought he saw the man nod. Then the stranger moved on, heading east, blurring into the blackness of night.

When Fritz reached the cathedral he turned toward the city center, doubled back, and went down the Herrengasse. He fired up his lighter three times below the OSS's windows, as if his cigarette just wouldn't light. As previously arranged, after the signal he walked down the street toward the casino. He waited five minutes, came back, then stepped into the side lane and pushed open the cold garden gate.

William Priest stood in the doorway.

"Mr. Wood."

"Mr. Priest."

Priest shook his hand warmly. "So you were followed?"

"And my room was ransacked. They destroyed two of my books."

"Such bullshit," Priest said. Fritz felt himself loosening up and began to chuckle. Priest placed a hand on his shoulder and the two laughed in the tiled hallway.

"*Antigone* and *Michael Kohlhaas*," Fritz said.

"*Antigone* I know. Who's Kohlhaas?"

"German literature, by Heinrich von Kleist. It's very good."

"I'll give it a go."

"An excellent book. You should definitely read it. Kohlhaas rebels against state authority after facing great injustice. He does make a few small mistakes, though."

"Such as?"

"I think he might have burned down a couple of towns."

"That doesn't sound so bad these days. Does he succeed?"

"Absolutely. Yet at the end, he loses his head."

"In that case, we should probably keep a real close eye on you. Come on," Priest said, and they made their way up to the secret office of Allen Dulles.

It was as if Fritz had seen Dulles just yesterday. He was wearing the gray three-piece and smoking his pipe. He greeted Fritz and the two of them sat in armchairs by the fireplace. Priest got them their whisky. "Where's Ms. Stone?" Fritz asked.

"Washington," Priest said. "We're to send her regards. She wishes you all the best."

"That's all?"

"She also said that no matter what happens, you should persevere."

"That's nothing new," Fritz said.

"She liked you," Priest said.

"Greta Stone? Me?"

Priest raised his whisky glass.

"She just wanted me wrapped around her little finger," Fritz said.

He had learned to trust his OSS triumvirate so well. He had never imagined attending one of these meetings without Greta Stone taking part. Although he never quite knew what to think of the woman, he did miss her—her upright bearing and that coolness about her that was strange, but never unpleasant. He asked what she was doing in Washington. "Furthering America's cause," Priest said. "We miss her too, you know."

"Let's get to business," Dulles said. "Do you have any idea who was following you?"

"Do you?"

Dulles smiled and pointed at Fritz with the stem of his pipe.

"Weygand's people, I assume," Fritz said.

"They're getting increasingly nervous," Dulles said. "Now, there's one other thing Ms. Stone was wondering about, and it's something that interests me too. And that's how did Hitler carry out domestic surveillance of the Germans? According to our assessments, the Gestapo and other agencies ran a cleverly thought-out, highly efficient system of total surveillance. We disapprove of such a thing, naturally. But it interests us just the same."

"I can't tell you much about how the Gestapo is organized. It functions. They terrorize people, and they have immense authority. They don't ask permission. They're allowed to do anything. That in itself makes them powerful."

"They don't ask. Everything's allowed." Dulles sucked on his pipe, crossing his legs. "Interesting, the way you put it. Purely hypothetically, Wood—you think they've been gathering material on every citizen?"

"They threw a man out of a window right in front of his son. They didn't need any material on him to do that."

"Fair enough," Dulles said. "Okay, so you brought us something?"

"Plenty," Fritz said. He pulled pages from the pockets of his jacket and overcoat, from his socks and his waistband.

"Good work," Priest said, scanning the documents. "Wehrmacht armored reserves on the Western Front. Restructuring of units, German generals under suspicion. Good work, good work. And here, oh yeah, that jet fighter, the Me 262—outstanding! Though this handwriting of yours, Wood, is one of the war's true disasters. Can you even read your own writing?"

They'd been reviewing the documents for barely five minutes when Dulles looked at his watch and said good-bye. He had another appointment. Priest saw the way Fritz watched him leave.

"Top-level stuff, Wood. Allen's meeting with an SS general from Italy, Italian aristocrats, a Wehrmacht colonel, and a high-ranking exile coming from Sweden. Real big fish."

Fritz held up his pages. "What about this here?"

"You're his best informant. But Allen is moving in higher circles now. They're polishing up a desk for him in Washington. A real big desk."

Fritz glanced around the office. He listened to the logs crackling in the fireplace and looked President Roosevelt in the eyes. Now only two actors remained to perform this clandestine chamber play of theirs.

"Don't take it personally," Priest said.

"I could lose my life, that's all. That's pretty personal."

Priest grinned at him. "Dulles is simply playing on multiple fields now, and, well, some happen to suit him better than others. Listen. I've seen plenty of intelligence pass through this office, more than you would probably think, from men and women alike: everyone from anti-Nazis and common traitors to probable double agents. But you? You're the only one whose conviction I truly bought."

"Eventually."

"In the beginning, I thought you were a crackpot, or worse. All the others at least attempted to seek protection for themselves, or they took our money—plenty of it, by the way. But you came in here and just handed us the most confidential intelligence we've ever gotten our eyes on—and you didn't want a thing. Greta really was fond of you, by the way."

Fritz ran a hand through his thin hair. "Does she have a husband?"

"If she does, I wouldn't want to be in his shoes."

They laughed. Priest put more wood on the fire.

"You can call me Fritz."

"William. My friends call me Will."

"Sounds good, Will. You know, some people in Germany are trying to transfer huge amounts of gold into Switzerland."

"We already got wind of it. Am I right in thinking von Lützow is a weak link? That we can soften him up?"

"I've already started working on that."

Priest chuckled. "That's okay by me. But don't tell Allen about operating on your own like that."

"Weygand has his eye on von Lützow."

"That problem will be taken care of."

"And what about the banks?"

"Without them, this war wouldn't have happened. There's nothing new there, Mr. . . . . Fritz."

"Mr. Fritz. The way that sounds!"

"But you do have a very German name."

"I'm a very German sort. Glad to be, at that. German literature, German music, German philosophy. The Nazis aren't Germans at all. They have no culture. They burn people; they burn books. All they have is their miserable screaming. If I hear one more time about how Hitler is supposed to be this great orator—what a load of shit. That's absurd, just garbage. Churchill is an orator. Hitler's just dull, a bawling baby. No substance at all. He's always hiding away somewhere."

"You lived abroad for years. Maybe that's why you see things differently than other Germans do? There was that safari in Africa. How was that?"

"It was in South-West Africa, with my good friend Walter Braunwein." Fritz drank his whisky, the memories sloshing down his throat with the liquor: conversations, Walter's laugh, *hey-ho*, Käthe in South Africa wearing her sun hat in the car next to Katrin. "My best friend. He's dead now, Will. You know why? Because I betrayed him. Here in this very room, without even realizing it. That secret transmitter near Dublin, you remember? Walter was there."

"Goddamn." Priest rubbed at his chin. "Fritz, I'm so sorry. Your best friend?"

"His wife then killed herself. Käthe."

Priest stared into the fire. Fritz knew that look, saw the moment when Priest's cheeks warmed and all of existence seemed to shrink into the pull of the flames. It was the look of someone who was losing himself and concentrating, all at the same time.

"That was the disruption?" Priest asked. "The reason we didn't hear from you for so long?"

"I couldn't do it anymore."

"Yet after all that, you keep going."

"Marlene convinced me."

"What kind of a woman is she?"

"The very best."

"I'm going to make sure Allen knows all this."

"Let it go, Will. I told you about it. I'll tell others, the ones this actually concerns. But leave Dulles out of it. Please."

"We all pay such a high price."

"You too?"

"Not as high as you, Fritz. Nothing like that. But I haven't seen my wife for three years. And she isn't exactly one to stay sad, if you know what I mean."

"The first sound I heard coming from Marlene," Fritz said, "was a laugh."

They sat together awhile longer, watching the flames grow tall around the black logs. Finally, Fritz said his journey had been exhausting and he needed to get to bed. They agreed to meet the following evening. Fritz asked if he should be worried because of his room and his tail.

"I have no idea," Priest said.

"Yes or no, Will."

"Yes. You should. Not one of these Nazis now wants to have been a Nazi. They're all starting to evade, cover up, look for escape routes. If word gets out about what you've done, Fritz, some people will start to realize what you must know. They'll ask themselves what happened to all the secret files, how much you've seen. They'll wonder if you maybe even kept copies."

"Wonderful."

"I promise you one thing: we will watch out for you. I will, personally. You can depend on it. You still have the revolver?"

Fritz patted his jacket pocket.

"If it ever comes to that, always aim for the center. Not the arms or legs, not the head. Shoot at the middle of the body, always at the middle. Don't hesitate. Pull that trigger, then turn around and get out of there. Can you do that?"

"I never would have known all that, Will. Good God. Hopefully, I won't ever have to."

There was a knock at the door. A young man wearing a winter coat and hat entered, whispered something in Priest's ear, and left again.

"Your tail's still out there."

"Shit."

"When you leave tonight, don't worry about that. I have my best men on him. The best anywhere, period. The OSS keeps growing. Our people are getting special training, really good stuff. The OSS is going to become a pillar of America. The country can't stay secure without us. It's all very exciting and pretty incredible. You, Fritz—you were a big part of this."

"I want Marlene and Katrin. That's all I require. Will, Marlene has to get out of there."

"I'll do everything that I can."

"My daughter, Katrin. She's the finest girl there is. Could you get a message to her? One that can't be traced back? Can you get in touch with her somehow? Please, Will."

"I'll see to it."

Fritz told him more about Swakopmund and about Hiltrud and Werner Lichtwang. "Perhaps Katrin's sitting on the beach right now,

Will. She likes to sit with her knees up and her arms wrapped around them. She always wears her hair down."

"I'd like to have a kid myself," Priest said.

"It's the best thing a person can do," Fritz said.

The telephones at the diplomatic mission were ringing nonstop, yet few staff were left to answer them. A Mercedes limousine had pulled up to the villa, and men in leather overcoats were carrying crates from the building and stowing them in the trunk.

Fritz wanted to speak to von Lützow, but the consul said he didn't have time—he was on his way to an appointment. He couldn't tell Fritz what the appointment was about. Then Weygand told Fritz that "I myself" will deal with "the likes of you, Herr Kolbe" and very soon.

Then something happened that deeply amused Fritz. Right in the middle of the hallway, amid the clamor of the telephones and the clack of the typewriters, von Lützow shouted that Weygand should kindly come with him and that was an order. Fritz never heard von Lützow talk like that. But it worked, even on a bastard like Weygand. Rage filled Weygand's face, yet he said he was coming at once and added, almost as a reflex, "Yes sir, Herr von Lützow." Fritz grinned at Weygand, who marched out into the gray daylight behind the consul, swinging his arms far too aggressively.

Fritz gathered the communications staff around and briefed them on the current routes to Salzburg. Many sections of the Foreign Office were to transfer operations there, he said, including the following departments . . .

He bought a black bra and chocolate for Marlene on Marktgasse, and the British *Times* and the *Washington Post* at the train station. In his hotel room he lay on his bed, smoked, and read the news. In that moment he desired nothing more than for Marlene to be with him, to caress those cheekbones of hers, and to be standing on the train platform, reunited with Katrin. He let the newspaper fall and looked out the window into the powdery sky. Was it possible that no one in the Office was onto him yet? Then why had his room been searched, and by whom? It seemed inconceivable that he could be peacefully lying in bed like this: his body free from harm, blood flowing through his veins, the paper in his hands. What did it all mean?

He folded up the newspaper, stood at the window, and looked out over the black, white, and gray city. How long had it been since Marlene had seen a city at peace? The life he shared with her was all war and secrets.

Outside, a solitary man in a black overcoat was crossing the square, looking up at the veiled monument.

◆ ◆ ◆

"Individual Nazis had tried to move between five and seven thousand tons of gold into Switzerland—per month," Fritz says. "Weygand never had full authority in such matters, so he couldn't just oust von Lützow over it despite developing his own contacts in Berlin. I'm not entirely sure how von Lützow kept his position until the end. Probably cronyism. A person always knew someone who knew somebody else." He sighs. "Will Priest ended up telling Dulles that I'd started working von Lützow on my own initiative. Dulles was appalled. His face went pale, but he didn't say a word about it."

"Fritz Kolbe had emancipated himself," Veronika says.

"William Priest told you he would look out for you personally after the war, is that right?" Wegner asks. "Did he mean nowadays too, or only right after the war ended?"

"It was his voice. I heard his voice when . . ." Fritz falls silent.

"When what? Herr Kolbe?" Veronika is holding her camera ready.

He goes into the kitchen, the dusk carving the shapes around him into silhouettes. He prepares a plate with cheese, radishes, onions, and dark bread. Then he goes outside and grabs three more bottles of beer from the cold water of the well. He looks around. Such a view, such fresh air. He hears the sluggish clanging of cowbells and the rushing of the stream in the valley, and sees the mountains going blue like the meadows now in shade.

He's held things in for so long. His pathetic attempts to write things down have all failed because he hides certain truths, just as the Nazis did. Eugen Sacher has been worried about him, and surely still is. Fritz remembers sitting outside the cabin with Eugen before Wegner and Veronika's visit.

"I'll be the one to tell him, Eugen," Fritz said. "Me. Not you."

"Are you really going to? You'll tell him everything? Because if you don't, it's going to crush you."

"Yeah, yeah."

"With all due respect, Fritz, what you've written—and in English at that! *The Story of George. George was an ordinary German boy* . . . Sorry, old friend, but you're no writer."

"It wasn't that bad," Fritz said.

Eugen laughed and threw up his hands. "It's a disaster. But you'll do what you want. You always do. You have to."

"True." Fritz gazed at the mountains, thinking he must get up there soon. "You know, Eugen, so many people want to be something special. I just want to be normal again."

"Then tell him, Fritz. About everything."

He is gripping both hands so tightly that one of the damp bottles slips through his fingers and hits the ground. It doesn't break; the glass is thick and sturdy. He looks down at himself, at his strong legs. He thinks of Marlene's legs. He remembers the prosthetics in her hospital office: in hindsight, such foreshadowing, yet he didn't recognize it as such at the time.

Ah, Marlene. My love.

He picks up the bottle and leans against the cabin. He hears footsteps and sees Veronika looking around the corner.

"You look like you could use a drinking buddy," she says.

Fritz raises the bottles. "Drinking together like this is nice."

"I think so too." Veronika walks over next to him, and they look out at the mountains across the valley, the sky growing dark. Fritz hands her a bottle. The beer makes a gurgling sound as they drink.

"Do you have a man in your life, Fräulein Hügel?"

"Oh, Herr Kolbe. Sure, there's been a man here, another there. But I'm not really sure what I want."

Fritz studies her: such a young woman, her skin so smooth, even when she smiles. When Marlene smiled she got little creases on her cheeks. He loved that, and often placed a hand on one of her cheeks while kissing the other all over, that straight nose of hers so close to his eyes. *Oh, Marlene,* he thinks.

Down on the road something yellow flashes, like a cat's eyes. A car is driving across the bridge. It stops at the fork where Wegner halted this morning. The headlights make it tough to make out any details, nothing seeming to move, inside the car or out. The car pulls back a bit. If it takes the turn-off, Fritz knows, it's coming up here. The road doesn't lead anywhere else.

"Anything wrong?" Veronika asks.

"We'll find out," Fritz says.

Whoever is down in the car must see the cabin clearly, given all the light glowing in the windows. Then the car's lights go off, the darkness throws a black blanket over the vehicle, and two people step out. Fritz can't tell what they're doing—they're too far away, and it's too dark.

"Who are they?" Veronika asks.

"No idea. The thing is, in novels and plays everything tends to make sense. It's not like that in life. Not everything lines up; not all the loose ends get tied up. It would be nice if they did, but that's not the way it works. In novels, guilt eventually comes back to claim the guilty. In life? Sometimes, maybe—but God knows, it doesn't always."

Fritz sees movement down at the car. Then the lights come on again and the car drives off down the road, spreading a fan of yellow light before disappearing into the valley.

"We're being rude to Herr Wegner," he says.

They go back inside. Fritz grabs the cheese he prepared and sets it out on the table. Pictures and documents are strewn about the living room, and photos, news clippings, and city maps hang on the walls. Wegner has filled many pages of his notepad and is now looking through Fritz's documents. Fritz opens the door to the woodstove and holds a match to the paper already crumpled under a pyramid of kindling. After a few seconds the wood starts crackling, and warmth flows from the stove. He waits a moment, then adds some larger pieces.

"Files were incinerated during the war," he says. "The Nazis had filled so many pages with ink. They recorded everything: every bullet cartridge, every conversation. Every person. Himmler very publicly stated his pride at having mastered so well the logistics and intellectual challenges which ensured that . . . Jews were incinerated. Though he didn't actually say *intellectual*, since Hitler detested intellectuals. They're capable of thinking in multiple ways, whereas Hitler only thought in one way. Actually, I'm not sure if he was truly able to think at all."

"What great cheese," Veronika says. This annoys Fritz for a moment, and then he sees her young cheeks bulging as she chews. He laughs. Try a little of the radish with that, he tells her. They're fresh picked.

Wegner taps a pen against his notepad.

"That was your last visit to Bern before the end of the war," he says.

"And the worst," Fritz says. "No bombs were falling, no panzers rolling in. And yet . . ."

13

A Silent Shot in Bern

Fritz spent only an hour at the diplomatic mission the next day. Most of the staff looked ashen and hopelessness showed in their faces. Fritz overheard them feigning loyalty to one another and lying about their belief that Germany would triumph. *They're all doing the same as me now,* he thought. Only the doors to Weygand's and von Lützow's offices remained shut. Out in the yard, flames flickered in burn barrels, their intense orange a sharp contrast to the gray sky and moss-covered tree trunks. Hundreds of pages of damning material were curling to ashes and drifting out from the barrels, now just little black particles on the air.

Dulles had told Fritz he should dangle the bait of asylum in Switzerland before von Lützow. Fritz wasn't sure if the offer was a serious one, but he could care less either way. He just wanted to complete his work here and return to Berlin as fast as possible so he could get Marlene out of the city.

Out in the hallway, Fritz chatted with a woman from the Visa Department about flowers in South Africa, waiting until Weygand left the office. When Weygand did leave, it was in the company of a nervous-looking Swiss customs official. Fritz thanked the woman for the nice chat and knocked on von Lützow's door. He sat at the desk across from von Lützow and gestured toward the window.

"Lovely country, Switzerland," he said.

"Oh indeed," von Lützow said. "Especially the lakes. Quite wonderful."

"It would be even lovelier in peacetime," Fritz said.

Von Lützow didn't respond. Unease showed itself in his eyes.

"Asylum, Herr von Lützow? In Switzerland? Security for you, your wife, and the children. All you'd have to do is prevent files from being destroyed."

"Come again?"

"All around you, people are starting to defect. Negotiations are being conducted in secret at the highest levels. Your superior, von Ribbentrop, is sitting in his mansion, drinking his family's own champagne and pissing his pants real good. You don't owe him any accountability."

Von Lützow stared at Fritz, the pomade in his black hair mixing with sweat.

"Work with me."

Von Lützow bent down, pulled the wastepaper basket toward him, and vomited. Fritz looked out the window at a stripe of blue sky between two long and drawn-out banks of clouds.

Von Lützow patted his mouth with a white hanky. "I could have you arrested on the spot." He was out of breath, as if he'd climbed up one of the nearby hills without stopping.

"You won't do that," Fritz said. "Nothing will happen to you. Roosevelt, Churchill, and Stalin are demanding unconditional surrender and won't negotiate with the Nazis. The Wehrmacht is beaten. And our so-called Wonder Weapons aren't coming, Herr von Lützow. You sat here in Bern during the whole war. You haven't done anything wrong—or at least, not much. They're offering you a hand."

"What have you done, Herr Kolbe?"

"I can guarantee your safety."

Von Lützow leaned over the wastebasket again. A sour odor permeated the office. Fritz took official Nazi letterhead off the desk and pitched it past von Lützow's face into the wastebasket. *Puke and swastikas*, he thought.

"I'm calling von Günther."

"Von Günther is about to make his own escape from Berlin."

Fritz had seldom seen a human being look so stunned. Von Lützow seemed to go utterly weak. He appeared as devoid of bearings as a man who'd suddenly found himself left exposed naked and alone in the middle of the desert, or atop some high mountain peak.

"Do you seriously think all those funds being transferred to Switzerland are stockpiles for the Final Victory?"

Von Lützow tugged at his tie, then reached for the phone; but the handset tumbled from his shaking hands and banged against the desktop. Fritz picked up the handset and hung it up. He knew he was taking a big risk, but he'd been doing plenty of that over the last few days. He was getting so close to that showdown he had wanted for so long. Von Lützow might not be a criminal, but he was still an emissary of Hitler, dutiful and subservient—and now out of his depth. Fritz guessed the man had never really bothered to take a good look at what was happening in the world created by Hitler. Still, Fritz didn't have the time to make allowances for him now.

"If you tell anyone about our conversation, I'm done for," he said. "But, Herr von Lützow, if that happens, my friends will learn of it. And if anything happens to me, you're a dead man." Fritz drew the revolver from his jacket and waved it in an arc. Acting like this seemed immensely fitting, considering the game he'd been playing for years. Not for a second did he think he might look silly.

"Have you gone crazy, Kolbe? Did you lose your mind?" Von Lützow's stare was fixed on the gun. "You miserable traitor."

Fritz laughed bitterly. "Gas chambers, a war of extermination, the eradication of human beings. Herr von Lützow, you're clearly a civilized man. So, who's a traitor to Germany? Me?"

Von Lützow uttered a sound that seemed to come from deep within his heart and gut and mind. His shirtfront was wet, and his eyes darted around. Fritz kept playing his game. He played it meanly and viciously, startled by the nasty pleasure it gave him.

"And if anyone hears about our little get-together? You won't be the only one who's done for. Your family will suffer. Greatly." The lies came easily to him. He'd have to tell Marlene about this. Then again, maybe he shouldn't.

"You . . . You . . ." Von Lützow's intended epithet became a question, expressing all his astonishment about Fritz Kolbe. "You?" he blurted, as if he still couldn't comprehend it was Fritz who was sitting across from him, holding a gun.

Fritz put the revolver away. "It's out of my hands, Herr von Lützow. If it were up to me, your family would be left out of it."

"You're a paid errand boy."

"Not paid, Herr von Lützow."

"A real man does not betray his country."

"These people you depend on are going to leave you out in the ice cold. Weygand calls the shots here now. He is the one Berlin talks about when the conversation turns to Bern. Not you. So don't go telling me you still trust a man like Weygand."

"He stands with Germany and our Führer."

"Please. Stands with the Führer? I highly doubt it. Now, here's what I need you to do. By tomorrow morning, write down everything you know about any funds being transferred. Banks, middlemen, addresses, figures, routes—all of it. Think long and hard. Ask yourself where your future lies. Speak with your wife." Fritz paused. *Speak with your wife?* It was one of those sayings a person hears so often they utter it absent-mindedly, without recognizing any emptiness or falseness in it.

"Maybe not with your wife," Fritz added.

"I talk over everything with my wife."

"She doesn't with you, however."

"What—"

"It doesn't matter now. That's your problem. It's nothing that concerns me. Whoever you do speak with, do not mention my name. Understand?"

"How can a person be so depraved?"

"Christ, von Lützow, the war is almost over. Something new will come. We can play a part in making it better—far better. Starting now."

Fritz stood and looked down at von Lützow. The man had spread his arms out wide on the desk.

"Think it over. Use reason."

When Fritz reached the doorway, von Lützow ran after him.

"Germany isn't just Hitler. It includes Hitler right now, but that's just a phase. But . . . treason? Just what are you thinking, betraying a whole system? You're handing people over to the enemy."

Fritz pictured Walter at the campfire during their safari. He saw Käthe's cracked skull, and Katrin's little back on the dock.

"We'll see each other tomorrow, Herr von Lützow," he said. "After that I'm traveling back to Berlin, to the Office, where there's hardly anyone left. Come with me. See for yourself what's become of Berlin, of all those trusty servants in the Foreign Office and everywhere else. Come with me."

"My post is here."

"Don't let any more files be destroyed. Cases are being prepared to take the Nazi leadership to trial."

Von Lützow ran back over to the wastebasket and retched again.

"My God, man, you'll come out of this fine. Get control of this place. You're the boss here! So pull yourself together. Those money transfers. The files. You'll figure it out."

On the sill of the window looking over the yard stood a bottle of cognac next to some balloon glasses. Fritz poured a glass half full and placed it on the desk before von Lützow. Light from the window found the glass and cast a swirling shadow of cognac on the desk pad.

Fritz headed north. He left the street right before the bridge and made his way down to the bank of the Aare. He smoked a cigarette and wondered whether the river might have any trout. He thought about Horst Braunwein. It seemed decades ago that he'd gone fishing with that young towhead in South Africa. Cape Town, Katrin, peace—all so long ago. It had been a whole other life.

He scrambled back up to the street and kicked off the mud that was starting to dry into a crust on his shoes. Several passersby looked at him. "You have to go off the beaten path sometimes," he told them. "It does a person good."

Musorksky was waiting in his hotel room. Fritz recognized him at once. The man was pale. His thick, dark overcoat spread over his body like a blanket.

"What, you haven't been shipped off to Siberia yet?"

"The Soviet Union is prepared to pay you much money for information on General Gehlen. Very much money. If you wish, a peaceful life in Moscow. A wonderful city with a great history."

"One can't serve two masters at the same time, Herr Musorksky."

"Herr Kolbe, listen. It is very important to us. The class enemy is—"

"Important for *us?*" Fritz interrupted. "Or for you?"

"There are rumors of major financial transactions between German and Swiss banks. Do you not grasp what is going on here? The capitalists work together, always. Even in this war. America and Germany. You are not the sort of man who plays along, Herr Kolbe."

"Perhaps I'll go back to Africa."

"Where the black race is being exploited by Western imperialism? What did you fight for anyway?"

"Look here, Musorksky. I'm fed up to here with all the speeches and lectures, all the lofty ideals—the whole damn mess. I'm sure the

Soviet agencies are doing just as much as the Americans or British. But don't count on me to be part of it. I've never claimed to work for anyone. I work *against* someone. So any *for* there might be is my affair, and mine only."

"I could resort to violence."

Fritz laughed. He leaned against the wall, genuinely amused. With a naturalness previously unimagined, he drew his revolver for the second time that day. He looked down at his hand. It was steady. His momentary doubt was swept away by one crystal-clear thought: *You've already come all this way.* He sighed.

"You really think I've gone this far just to let myself be sidelined by you and your bullshit ideas?"

Musorksky looked unimpressed by the gun. He pursed his lips as if sucking on a bitter lozenge.

Would he really be able to shoot Musorksky? Sink a bullet into the man's gut?

"How did you get files here?" Musorksky said. "Courier mail, that right? We can do that too. An envelope gets sent to us at a cover address, a completely safe affair. All we need is one file, one envelope—information on Gehlen and his cutthroats. And put the revolver away. That's an American model, they're good. But you can't keep going around pulling guns on people like that."

"Just go nab Gehlen. He's always out East somewhere."

"He is long gone. Say you don't deliver us the goods on him. Say you don't pass us material so we too have something in our hands—as soon as the war's over, your American friends will start working with that very same General Gehlen. This I guarantee you."

"Nonsense."

"Do not be naïve, Herr Kolbe. Just a few documents on Gehlen's activities in the East, for us, back in my homeland. Say, ten pages of damning details. That would be enough."

"Who put you on my trail, Musorksky? Who? How did you find me?"

Musorksky rubbed his forehead. Fritz could see the man was under great pressure. Maybe he had been given this one last chance to get Fritz on board, after his previous capture of Fritz backfired.

"A whisky?" Fritz asked. Musorksky gazed out the window and nodded. Fritz poured two glasses but kept his gun hand free, picking up only one glass and handing it to Musorksky.

Musorksky gulped greedily. He watched the gun from a corner of his eye. "Your hand's shaking," he said.

"Nonsense."

"If you say so. The Americans are going to work with Nazis, Herr Kolbe. You must be clear on this."

"I won't be coming to Bern anymore, Herr Musorksky. This is my last trip here. I'm returning to Berlin tomorrow morning. I leave all this to you."

"And what if I saw to it that Berlin learns of your activities?"

Fritz sat down without taking an eye off Musorksky. A sudden wave of weariness washed over him. "Keep on threatening to expose me in Berlin and I'll have to shoot you right here, Musorksky. An intruder in my room . . . Dulles will make sure the story sticks."

"Allen Dulles is keen on building the world's greatest intelligence service. You don't figure into those plans much."

"The President of the United States reads my reports. I have Dulles to thank for that. I count plenty. So. Who told you about me?"

"A little birdie—"

"*In London.* All right, you bastard. Have yourself one more capitalist American whisky and then disappear."

Fritz tossed the bottle across the room. Musorksky managed to snatch the missile from the air with both hands. He opened the cap and drank straight from the bottle. Fritz was now certain the man had been given an ultimatum. His threat must have been a bluff—if Fritz were dead, they couldn't get their information on Gehlen.

"You have no idea what you've gotten mixed up in, Herr Kolbe. People like you, no training in this field—they get trampled on." Musorksky pressed his hands together and rubbed them as if about to squash something.

"You should escape to the mountains, Musorksky. I hear Siberia is freezing cold."

"The SS and other German units butchered so many in Russia. You know that? You have any idea the damage they inflicted? And the Wehrmacht as well."

"You know quite well some of the intelligence I delivered to Dulles went straight to Moscow. What do you want from me?"

Musorksky pounded his fist on the arm of his chair. "Gehlen. Gehlen, goddamn it! You're making him a nice and cozy bed to lie in, Kolbe."

"Rubbish."

"The man possesses extensive intelligence about the way our country wages war. About our armaments, our strategics. He'll tempt the Americans. He'll make them an offer. You really don't understand that?"

"He'll rot in prison."

Musorksky buried his face in his hands. "He will not!" he screamed. "Someday you'll be horribly sorry about all this. A man like you—it will affect you brutally. Someday it'll hit you. The blinders will be taken from your eyes. I offer you my hand, Kolbe. Grab hold. We take care of our friends. And if you wish to live in the West, please do. That's not a problem."

"Feel free to keep the bottle."

"Kolbe!"

"You're just another of those, those—"

"What about Allen Dulles? What makes him any different than me?"

"Take the bottle when you go."

Musorksky did. Fritz stared at the door through which he disappeared. *Better you than me,* he thought.

He went down to the little hotel restaurant and ordered trout with boiled potatoes. He thought about what Musorksky had said, about Dulles's questions regarding surveillance in the Nazi state, and about Priest's reference to a new war beginning after this war ended, as Musorksky had just implied would happen. He'd stopped deluding himself that the Americans would not cooperate with Nazis subordinates. But surely they would stick men like Gehlen in prison. How could they cooperate with men like that? They couldn't. No, it was impossible. Such a move would hurt the Americans' standing in international politics. Wouldn't it? And no new Germany would reintegrate a Gehlen. The idea was ridiculous.

He sliced through the crispy skin of the trout and separated fillet from bone. If Marlene were sitting here across from him, he would still be able to look her in the eyes. The Marlene Wiese who was married. Marlene, naked on the kitchen table, swastikas under her back or chest. Marlene, exhausted. Marlene, brave. Marlene in his apartment, Marlene at Charité Hospital, Marlene on the street. *Mar-lay-nah.* Her maiden name was Martens, Marlene Elisabeth Martens. Then Katrin would come out of her room in this adorable hotel, rest a hand on his back for a moment, and sit with them, paging through the menu and calling out all the things she did not like, and Fritz would laugh.

At the reception desk, he asked to be connected to Charité Hospital in Berlin. He spoke to seven different harried-sounding people before finally getting Marlene on the line.

"I love you," he said. He heard an ungodly scream in the background, then the sound of metal rattling.

"I love you too," she said, and then her voice sounded more distant. "No, no, bring him in back here. Right, I'm coming at once. Fritz? Fritz?"

"Yes."

"The Gestapo came to see me."

Fritz pounded on the front counter. The man at reception gave him a look. Fritz held a hand over his eyes. "Good God. Did they do anything to you?"

"They were so cruel, Fritz. So disgusting. Wait, you can't go in there yet. Back there, yes. Yes, I know. I don't care what you think about it. Just do it. Good. Fritz?"

"I'm here. Did they hurt you?"

"No. I'm not hurt, no. They know about us, though. They know. They wanted to know where you were when Stauffenberg tried to kill Hitler."

"I was in Paris. All official."

She was sobbing into the phone. A dark gloom shot through Fritz.

"I'm going to get you out, Marlene. Just hold on. I'll be back in Berlin soon."

"My God, Fritz. I was so scared."

"I'll kill them. I'll blow them all away."

"Yes, do that. Look—I have to get back to work here. Take care of yourself, Fritz, just . . . take care."

"Marlene, I . . . I . . ." he stuttered, picturing Marlene's face close to his. He wanted to touch her lovely nose. Somebody started to pull her away from the phone. He screamed for her.

"Fritz. Don't come back. Stay there." The line crackled and went dead.

Fritz wanted to smash the telephone against the counter's hard wood. He rushed back to his room and screamed as loud as he could at the landscape portrait above the bed, yet no sound came out. He struck the mattress with a chair with such force, it bounced back and hit him over one eye.

Marlene. For God's sake. He rushed to the train station, searched the cold newspaper rack for a German paper with Hitler's portrait printed in it, and ran back into the hotel. He barked at the man at reception to give him a fork immediately. In his room he stabbed so long and violently at Hitler's face that the fork busted in two, causing him to accidentally cut his own cheek.

That evening Fritz told Dulles and Priest about his confrontation with von Lützow. He also reported on Musorksky and asked whether the OSS had been watching when the Russian entered the hotel. That they had, Priest said. He asked if the Russian had hit Fritz, because of . . . Priest pointed at Fritz's cheek.

"That was something else. What if he had shot me?"

"That was never his plan, Fritz," Priest said.

Dulles looked back and forth between them, but said nothing. Fritz smoked one cigarette after another. He felt Marlene screaming at him from Berlin. *Live, Fritz, live!*

"Goddamn it," Fritz said.

"What's wrong?" Priest asked.

"Forget it. Musorksky said the same thing you did, Will: that the war is going to continue even after Nazi Germany ends. He also thinks the Americans will be working with high-level Nazis."

Dulles and Priest looked at each other.

"We have to concentrate on the here and now, Mr. Wood," Dulles said. "Once again, the material you've provided is first-class. Your final chance to work on von Lützow comes tomorrow, midmorning. Here is the card of a man who works at a bank here in Bern. This is all the information I can give you, for your own safety. Assure von Lützow that this contact is secure and serious, and that he has nothing to fear. Hopefully von Lützow will hand you the documents. You will then leave those behind in the hotel, after you stop there on your way to the train station. What's the matter?"

"Does Weygand need to be taken out, Fritz? Is that it?" Priest said. "Tell us now."

"Oh please. No."

Priest laughed. "You're too good for this world. We are at war."

"That saying has been used to justify far too much."

"Gentlemen, please," Dulles said. "There's no time for philosophizing. Once you're back in Berlin, Wood, you'll be all on your own again. Don't stay in the city if you can help it."

"The Russians really are keen on you," Priest said.

"This will likely be our final meeting of the war," Dulles said. "A drink wouldn't hurt, I should think."

Priest poured the whisky.

"How much longer will it keep going?" Fritz asked.

"Resistance is pointless, but the Germans can get fanatical. A number of days ago, some prisoners were taken near a German village. Their lieutenant had been hanged from a tree. The SS had ordered the lieutenant to attack an American unit with his armored assault gun. According to the prisoners, he told the SS that he would do so at once—if he only had ammunition. But he didn't have any. Not one shell, not even a round for the tank's machine gun. The SS repeated the order to attack. 'With what?' asked the lieutenant. That was his death sentence. They hanged him. Given events like these, well, it seems the war is going to last much longer than it should."

"There are also whole units giving themselves up to us," Priest said.

"Gentlemen," Dulles said and raised his glass. "To the deaths of Hitler and the Emperor of Japan." They toasted, the whisky sloshing in their glasses, its color like liquid honey. The alcohol burned in Fritz's gut.

"I won't try to hide it," Dulles told Fritz. "My department has profited enormously from all that you've done. Your efforts have made our team in Bern stand out from the others. I made the president take notice of you, and in turn, he naturally took notice of me. I'm climbing the ladder, Wood. In America. For America. The best country in the world. I want you to know that I'll be indebted to you my whole life, and indeed am honored to be so."

"That's nice to hear," Fritz said. Dulles's words left him cold. He thanked them for their trust and cooperation, but said that it was not yet over and Berlin was still a den of murderers.

The time had come. He had wanted to lure Dulles in, to ensnare him. Fritz cast his line out with his heart thumping and Marlene's sobs in his ears.

"I must get out of there. Marlene as well. I've never demanded anything of you before. Now, I have one demand. The Gestapo came to see Marlene. I want you to get my Marlene and me out, now. Help us."

"Okay," Priest said, "we—"

"One moment," Dulles interrupted. He pulled out his tobacco pouch and began stuffing his pipe. Brown bits stuck to his thumb and he flicked them to the carpet. "This isn't done yet, Wood."

"It is for Marlene and me. For Katrin too. I've delivered so many pages to you. I'm Kappa. I'm the best you have. But it's done now."

"Just hear me out, please. We're right in the most decisive phase of the war. Hundreds of thousands of American boys are now fighting Hitler's armies, ten thousand miles from home. I need you where you are, Wood. I need you inside your foreign ministry while it's coming apart, a state that can only make things that much easier for you."

"Easier? Did you listen to what I just said? My Marlene was questioned by the Gestapo. More people than ever are disappearing in Berlin. Get me and my woman out of there!"

"Hold out a little longer. Keep the faith. Every piece of intelligence you can provide us makes our advance easier. With the war in the Pacific as well. You can save lives."

"Other people's lives."

"Allen, there has to be some way to accommodate him," Priest said.

"Wait, Will. One second." Dulles leaned over the desk and met Fritz's eyes. "None of us has ever been as deep inside as you are now. You cannot walk away from there. Not now. I promise you I will personally take care of you—after the war. But you cannot walk away from there. You don't simply abandon your post."

"What goddamn post? Listen to me. Put a plan into motion, using whatever means are at your disposal, to get Marlene and me out of there."

"Not now, Wood. Not yet. You have to hold out a little longer."

"Why didn't you have the Wolf's Lair bombed?"

Dulles looked at Priest, who spread his palms as if to say that Dulles should be the one to tell him. Dulles furrowed his gray brows. His left eye twitched.

"A few more weeks. A few more deliveries by courier mail. I know you can't get much through by mail, so make sure what you send is crucial intelligence. I swear to you, Mr. Wood! You must hold out. Stay just a little longer."

"How about this, Fritz . . ." Priest went into Greta Stone's former office and came back seconds later holding a bundle of dollars. "Here's twenty thousand, as a small compensation. I'll hold the money for you and Marlene. At least let me do that much. Will you take it?"

"Every last cent, Will."

"I must be off," Dulles said. He rose and looked down on Fritz, exhaling through his mustache. He left without saying good-bye.

"Asshole," Fritz said.

"Some whisky, Fritz? A lot of whisky?"

As if there were peace, as if there were calm and time for leisure, the two men sank into armchairs, sipped their whisky, and chatted about sports and literature. They were stealing time they did not have. The time flew by yet also stood still as the men laughed and shared anecdotes from their lives, lowering their voices when speaking of absent loved ones, and then Priest explained why Dulles had learned not to refuse anyone seeking to meet with him. Before the First World War—or during, he wasn't sure exactly—a young man had come to Bern and insisted upon talking with Dulles. But Dulles got the opportunity to play tennis with a charming young lady and so he cancelled. Later, he learned that this man was Vladimir Lenin. Since then, he's always agreed to even the oddest sounding request to meet.

"So I have Lenin to thank? Maybe he wasn't so evil after all."

"The guy was a bastard."

"Will, you incurable cowboy." Fritz paused a moment. "Could I keep doing work for you after the war? Provided you see to it that Marlene gets out of Berlin. I've learned how to pretend to be someone I'm not. I've been doing it for years. I can lie and deceive. Sometimes, I didn't even know who I was anymore."

"There's a lot that needs to play out before we can think about what comes next."

"Were you able to get anything done about Katrin?"

"Not yet. But I'm looking into it. I promise. Think you can pull it off, Fritz?"

Fritz clenched his teeth and pictured those Gestapo faces bearing down on Marlene, so close she had to smell their breath.

As Fritz arrived at the diplomatic mission the next morning, Weygand was just getting into a car. He saw Fritz and pointed at him, his finger twitching.

In the hallway he ran into the woman he'd chatted with about flowers the day before. She asked him in a whisper what was to become of them. Fritz said it would work out somehow. She placed a hand on his shoulder and pulled him close. "I've been spitting in Weygand's coffee for years," she said.

Fritz laughed and told her she was a treasure. He asked for her take on von Lützow. Hard to say, she whispered. A decent man, actually. The type of man who could've been a manager in a savings bank somewhere. Or a German teacher. She asked Fritz what he had always wanted to be.

"Fritz Kolbe," he said.

◆ ◆ ◆

Von Lützow was sitting rigid at his desk. He stared at Fritz as if searching for something in his face, perhaps searching for something inside of himself. Fritz greeted him cordially. For several minutes they sat across from one another in silence. There was not one document on the polished desktop, no pages, no envelopes. The photo of his wife was gone. Fritz didn't much like being stared at for so long. He wouldn't have thought von Lützow capable of the stamina such an act required. Sometimes Fritz returned the stare for a while, only to look back at the desktop, made to gleam by the green-shaded lamp.

"Yesterday I tried to reach von Ribbentrop," von Lützow said. "Impossible. Then I called Berlin and asked to speak to von Günther. He was not there, or more specifically, no one seemed to know where he'd gone. I eventually reached a department head in Salzburg. He was drunk."

Fritz lit a cigarette. Had von Lützow really tried to blow the whistle on him? Had he in fact betrayed him, and were Gestapo officers now creeping up to the office door? Fritz didn't want von Lützow to see what he was thinking. He forced himself to stay calm, feeling grateful for the camouflage the cigarette provided.

"I wanted to ask the gentlemen about your assessment of the situation. I wanted to say: aside from the banking sector, one might think we've been forgotten here. In fact, it turns out there is a bit more happening in that sector than I knew. Yet as you so aptly put it, I am the boss here."

Von Lützow opened a desk drawer and took out a large unmarked envelope. He placed it before him on the desk and laid both hands on it.

"My wife, Herr Kolbe, is a committed National Socialist."

"I understand."

"In Berlin, you say, they're talking about Weygand and not me?"

"If you make the right decision now, they'll be talking about you."

"You think so?"

Fritz wished he understood better what motivated people. If von Lützow ended up cooperating with him, it wouldn't be because of one clear reason. So many factors entered into the decision: his wife, children, Weygand, the ignored phone calls, service to Hitler, the peace and calm of Switzerland, and countless other matters Fritz could only guess at. Who really knew what doubts and conflicts raged within people? The dangerous ones were those who felt no conflicts at all. They were not living beings—they were nothing but ticking clocks.

Fritz took out the business card Dulles had given him and pushed it across the table. "A safe contact. Someone who knows the score and has certain powers, most importantly access. He's completely reliable."

Von Lützow didn't touch the card. He reached into his jacket and placed a little key atop the envelope.

"To my safe. There's only one other key, which I have."

He pushed the envelope across the table with both hands. The key twinkled in the lamp's light. Fritz took the key, then folded the envelope and slid it in his inside pocket.

"I am the boss here," von Lützow said.

"That you are."

At the door, Fritz turned back one last time. Von Lützow sat at the desk looking like he'd been poured from lead.

"We did everything wrong," von Lützow said.

Fritz wasn't sure, but he thought he saw tears glistening in the man's eyes.

"Not everything," Fritz said. He patted the envelope inside his jacket.

"I hope I never see you again, Kolbe."

Despite Fritz's hopes, the journey back to Berlin was just as disastrous as the trip out had been. The train finally neared the capital after almost two days but halted well before any buildings could be seen. Fritz guessed why instantly. He jumped out of the stinking car, climbed up the iron rungs, and stood up on the roof, which was sticky from soot.

There had to be a thousand bombers overhead. Bright-yellow blasts flashed throughout the city, the earth trembling with them. Billows of smoke from glowing fires rose into the evening sky, darkening and fading into the clouds and black fumes caused by antiaircraft shells bursting. Spotlights cast their monstrous smoggy fingers into the sky, as if feeling a way through the chaos. As Fritz watched, sporadic explosions sent more flames surging into the smoke-clogged air. A fiery ball fell from the sky, wildfires blazed away around the city, and airplanes flickered and vanished as the waves of explosions raged on and on. Before him was the black silhouette of a city that kept shaking, shaking. Somewhere inside this inferno Marlene was huddled, her hands pressed to her ears or a cloth over her mouth.

Fritz climbed down and ran along the locomotive shouting, "Keep going!"

The engine driver leaned out the window and looked at Fritz. "Are you crazy?"

Fritz yanked out his diplomatic ID. "I'm traveling with documents crucial to the war effort. I must reach the Foreign Office. Get us there."

"Please, don't push me. Anyway, you look pretty athletic. You can't miss the way—just follow the light."

"Just get the train moving, for God's sake."

"We won't be traveling into Berlin today, not now. Then once all that business is over, we'll start chugging toward the outskirts of the city, all nice and easy. And when we get there, Mr. Big ID, it's quitting time for me."

"Then just drive to the outskirts now. Go, drive on."

Fritz climbed up into the cab and pulled out his revolver. His hand stayed calm and steady. *That's how quickly this happens,* he thought, *how the instinct kicks right in.* The locomotive driver looked down at the gun, then into Fritz's eyes.

"So you're one of those types," he said.

"To the outskirts. Now."

"You can't just charge in there any way you want to, man."

"Drive on."

The engine driver began to work the heavy, squeaking iron levers, and the locomotive rolled forward, slow and lurching. Fritz stuck the gun back into his pocket.

"I'm sorry," he said. "But my wife is in there."

My wife, he thought. *She's my wife. Marlene.*

"Nothing happened to me," Fritz says. "Unbelievably, I didn't receive so much as a scratch throughout the whole war. Physically, that is."

"You really ran right into all that?" Veronika asks.

"It was over by the time we got there. The city was so hot I could hardly breathe. I was stumbling over corpses. I don't know how I ever got through. I don't know how long it took me either. I had to take massive detours because of the fires. That raid was a particularly bad one for the city center. I started in the place where I best knew my way around: the Foreign Office, on Wilhelmstrasse. I climbed through a melted window and took one of those tunnels I told you about that ran from the Office to the air-raid shelter under the Adlon.

"And then? My God. There she stood. Marlene. We were reunited down there. We laughed and we cried. You know what else? My apartment was still standing. The neighboring building was badly hit. But my place, our wartime love nest, was left unscathed. We were able to go back there, around four in the morning. The dead were everywhere. Everything was burning. It was an indescribable scene. Ghastly. But Marlene and I? We were hand in hand, in love, beside ourselves with excitement—all because we'd soon be alone together again."

Berlin burned and collapsed, her streets blotted with smoldering corpses, the sirens wailing, heavy smoke stinging people's eyes and clogging their lungs. A scorched person leaned against a black streetlight, its lipless mouth with stumps for teeth open wide for one last scream at the foul skies above.

In the apartment, Marlene and Fritz clawed at each other, their kisses like bites, their bare bodies on the floor those of mere creatures wringing out a savage love. They joined together more deeply and fervidly than ever before, writhing around together before at last becoming one sweating body stammering out their love.

Over the next few chaotic days at the Office, Fritz tried to locate von Günther but couldn't reach him anywhere. No one seemed to know where he'd gone. Work slowed to a trickle in those few offices that were still operating, and some departments had moved out completely, their phone lines disconnected, communication now impossible. Only two receptionists remained, and they sat in neglected rooms, knitting. The rasping sound of People's Receivers still blasted from some rooms, Goebbels screaming about retribution and bombs upon bombs, and about the German Volk's fanatical will to persevere in this great hour.

Some mail did still come for von Günther, as did messages delivered by bewildered men from the telegraph and radio desks. Fritz sifted through it all immediately, determined what information would have relevance for the Americans, and then summarized it.

Motorcycle couriers covered in grime brought communiqués from Foreign Minister von Ribbentrop informing them of internal decrees. Fritz could hardly believe the topics—mundane matters like carpools, new letterheads, shortened vacations, washrooms closing on account of Berlin's diminishing water supply. He would thank the courier, sign for the document, and chuckle.

Whenever he got the chance, he navigated his way through the debris-constricted streets and paths to Charité Hospital, hoping to at least put his arms around Marlene. The Charité was now little more than a frontline hospital tent. He didn't know how Marlene could stand it. The constant screaming, groaning, and crying disturbed him so deeply, he left feeling as though he himself had been wounded. The Marlene he held tight in his arms wore a gown damp with blood and had no words left to speak.

"As soon as I track down von Günther, we're getting out of here," he whispered. Marlene shook her head. She smelled of sweat, cigarettes, and disinfectant. She pointed at the back of a tall doctor farther down the hallway who was passing between the wounded into an operating area shielded by a tattered tarp. "The professor," she murmured. "He's staying until the very end."

"We're not," Fritz said. He placed his hands on Marlene's cheeks, but she avoided his eyes. She was caught up completely in the world of the screaming wounded, and Fritz admired her work ethic and her dedication. *Soon*, he thought, *soon*. He watched as a soldier passed, carrying a rifle on his shoulder and a machine gun in his hands. The man was covered in the same gray grit that coated the concrete floor, where trails of dried blood were marked by shoe prints.

Out in the courtyard of the Charité, a sea of stretchers held the wounded, their bloody bandages oozing red or dried brown, interrupting the drabness of war with their color. Fritz was picking a path through the chaos to the street when he heard a long-forgotten sound from his past.

"Uncle Fritz!"

The voice sounded exhausted. Fritz looked into the grimy faces beneath the bandages and the shot-up helmets. He saw a hand waving and stepped over the corpses, making his way through the wispy cigarette smoke and dull moans.

"Horst!"

The man on the stretcher propped himself up on his elbows. His face had aged, and his hair was graying. Fritz crouched down. Horst smelled like stale urine and earth. "This sure is something," Horst said.

"Horst. My God . . ." Fritz wanted to put a hand on his friend's son's shoulder or cradle his head against his chest, but he restrained himself. "How are you doing?"

"Got it twice in the upper thigh. I'll be all right. So you're still in Berlin?"

"The Office hasn't fallen down completely yet. God. Imagine us seeing each other like this."

"Cape Town sounds pretty good now, doesn't it?"

Horst lowered himself back down, rested his head on his bent arm, and patted at his uniform pockets. Fritz said he still had cigarettes and lit him one.

"Did my mother really kill herself, Uncle Fritz?"

"You don't have to call me uncle anymore."

"Did she?"

Fritz sat on the cold ground next to Horst's stretcher, pulled up one leg, and found room among the misery around them to stretch out the other.

"She wasn't well, Horst."

"No one is well here."

"You must get out of Berlin."

Horst gazed at him with eyes much too old for his face. Fritz was just grateful not to hear the boy raving about heroism or one last battle.

"You know how it looks to me? Like my father was betrayed by someone," Horst said.

The boy's words stung Fritz and turned his stomach.

Horst shook a fist. "Can you imagine, Fritz? Someone betraying the fact that Papa went to Ireland?"

"Who could have done it?"

Orderlies and nurses were lifting several stretchers and hauling them through the splintered double doors, into the hospital's maws. Why had he run into the boy here? Fritz couldn't look him in the face.

"He was a good man, my father. A good man."

Something was surging up inside Fritz, fluid and watery. His fingers cramped around his bent knee.

"When I catch this traitor I'm going to take him out, Fritz."

"Horst, just make sure that you can get to the West."

"Do you know something? About Dublin?"

Fritz laid a hand over his eyes. "He always wanted . . . to live with you and Käthe in Ireland."

"Are you crying?"

"Don't be ridiculous."

Horst flicked his cigarette stub carelessly toward the gray expanse of bodies. He waved Fritz closer to him. Fritz could smell his stale breath.

"The war has brought out the very worst in us."

"I'll try and get you out of here, Horst."

Horst grabbed on to Fritz's forearm, his grip weak. "Don't worry about it, truly. I didn't get it so bad. I'll be fine. What are you going to do next?"

"Whatever I'm assigned. I'm not quite sure yet."

"Maybe we'll see each other again sometime. Good luck."

"Same to you."

As Fritz tried to stand, his muscles nearly gave out. He fought to straighten up, buckled a moment, and caught himself.

"Someday, after the war, it'll come out who it was," Horst said. "I've killed so many people. One more won't matter."

Fritz looked back around at Horst. On the beach at Camps Bay, the sea washed in bright blue and turquoise. The boy had been a towhead then.

"Every goddamn corpse is one too many," Fritz said.

"You're not serious?"

"I am, Horst. Completely."

"Would it have changed anything if I had been here? With my mother?"

"Don't blame yourself."

"You have another cigarette?"

"Sure I do." Fritz drew the pack from his jacket with trembling fingers. As he lit Horst's cigarette, their hands brushed each other.

"I'm going to put a bullet in that bastard's head," Horst said without taking the wagging cigarette from his mouth.

Fritz bent down and grabbed him by the collar. "The fucking Nazis are to blame for all this. The fucking Nazis. Filthy depraved vermin. If anyone betrayed your father, it's them."

"You might want to be more careful, Fritz Kolbe."

He pushed Horst down and walked away. Once Fritz got to the battered front gate, he heard Horst's voice cut through the moaning that blanketed the ground like fog.

"It didn't really matter," Horst said.

Fritz turned. Horst was up on his elbows, his face white.

"That we didn't catch any fish. It didn't matter."

Fritz left, and among the countless people wandering the city, so desperate and worn out, those who happened to see him all saw a man crying. But there was nothing special about that.

A man in a leather jacket stood at the window in Fritz's office. Another in a stained suit sat at his desk, flipping through documents.

"Fritz Kolbe? Gestapo."

Why was he not scared? He'd nearly wet himself at that first border crossing in Basel, and when the Russians had kidnapped him, he'd gone completely weak from fright. Now, he felt nothing. Perhaps the war and his document smuggling had used up all his apprehension or buried it so deep that it couldn't find a way back out. He wondered if it was the same guy who questioned Marlene. Had he laid a hand on her?

"Where were you during the attempt on the Führer's life?" the man at his desk said.

"Paris," he said.

"You oversee top-secret material here."

"Nothing ever goes missing."

"You were recently in Switzerland."

"That's right. Let me get to my desk," Fritz said.

The man sucked in his cheeks and scrunched up his forehead, trying to look dangerous. He slowly pushed the chair back to give Fritz room. Fritz handed him a memo about Paris, tapping on von Günther's signature. He then pulled his travel papers from the drawer and added his diplomatic ID with its visa stamps.

"You are not a member of the Nazi Party."

"What the Führer requires now above all are those who can maintain order, absolute order. Take a look around this place. I'm the one keeping this office running."

"We're going to your apartment now."

"I can't leave yet. I'm one of the few who remain that Ambassador von Günther can still rely on."

"Shut your mouth and get moving," the man at the window said.

"And you'll take responsibility? What if the Herr Ambassador—"

"Get going!"

Fritz stood still. He silently counted . . . *Twenty-one, twenty-two, twenty-three.*

"Fine," he said, "I'll take you to my apartment."

At the apartment, they heaved his furniture away from the walls, broke dishes, ripped the mattress from the bed, and busted open picture frames. The safari photo sailed onto the kitchen floor.

"What's with all the blank paper lying around here?"

"I write."

"You what?"

Fritz showed them a pencil.

"Heil Hitler," they said. And then they were gone. Their malice hung in the air like the stench of spoiled food.

It took three more days for Fritz to reach von Günther by phone, in Salzburg. He told Fritz he was traveling to naval headquarters next and then would be returning to Berlin. Fritz should attempt to keep things running as well as he could. The connection was poor, but Fritz sensed von Günther's nervousness.

Back at home, Fritz spun the globe Marlene had repaired and drank cognac. Despite the water shortage, he'd scrubbed the sheets after the Gestapo men touched them. They were not yet dry, so he and Marlene placed an old wool blanket beneath the covers.

From the West, the Allied armies under Eisenhower, Montgomery, and Patton were advancing ever closer to the heart of Germany; in the East, there was no stopping the oncoming storm of the Russian army. The Luftwaffe barely existed anymore, and Hitler had become a ghost for good. Many were whispering that he wasn't even alive anymore.

The closer combat operations got, the more Fritz began to grasp the truth of Will Priest's and Musorksky's words: the war would continue. Differently, maybe, yet it would continue, especially for Fritz. He hadn't been able to see it before, but now he was beginning to realize what they'd meant. The obscure, inexplicable espionage campaign he'd waged with such resolve would not end simply because Hitler was dead and the weapons were cooling off. He tried to think of ways to safeguard Marlene and himself and to secure a future for Katrin. But what could he do without help? People like Dulles, Will, and Greta Stone knew tricks a man like Fritz knew nothing about. And how many people had he made enemies of along the way?

When Marlene came home to him late that night, he told her everything he'd been thinking. He said nothing about running into Braunwein's son.

"People will understand in the end, won't they, Marlene?"

"Who could understand any of what's happened here?" She kissed him. "You're always quoting your father's adage about doing what is right and so on. But in this place and time? Even the right thing comes out looking dirty, degenerate. There's no way around it. In the end, though, we will go on living. Understand? We will live."

The next day, von Günther quietly showed up at the Foreign Office. He looked agitated, his broad face covered with red splotches. He was on the phone for over an hour, and then he packed up a bunch of files, took them to the bombed-out rear courtyard, and dumped them into the burn barrels, now distended from all the heat. When he came back he shut the door to Fritz's office and stood before him at the desk. He drummed his fingers on the desktop. "Still no chair?"

"I haven't had time, Herr Ambassador."

"I'm arranging a car for you, Kolbe. A full tank, with two more gas cans in the trunk. Yes? Ration coupons, travel permits, all of it. I need you to drive to Bavaria and, and . . ."

Fritz waited. "And what?" he said finally.

"Have you heard what's happened in Bern?"

Fritz lit a cigarette and pushed the pack across to von Günther. What could have happened in Bern? At this point, there wasn't anything left that could go wrong.

"It's von Lützow. All these characters are losing their nerve, looking for a way out. And there he sits in Switzerland, with no idea of the challenges we face here. Disgusting."

He talked, Fritz thought. *Von Lützow couldn't take the pressure and he talked.* He felt at the revolver in his jacket pocket, then paused.

Think it through, he told himself. If von Lützow had spilled anything, von Günther wouldn't be speaking like this with him right now. Fritz's name could not have come up, not yet. Maybe von Lützow hadn't turned himself in, but rather Weygand had had him arrested because he'd aroused suspicion. Fritz clenched his teeth.

"It's that same question of greatness," von Günther said. "Not everyone can achieve it. Imagine if the Führer had surrounded himself only with people who possessed greatness. You get my meaning? Not his degree of greatness, no, that is a rare thing. But a certain caliber of greatness, yes? My point being that greatness cannot be transferred, nor can it be predicted."

What was the man talking about? It seemed to Fritz that Nazis just spat out a bunch of nouns, clumsily strung together. Fritz felt certain that verbs were important too. They conveyed movement and life. This was precisely the reason why those Nazi speeches always sounded so dull to him—nothing moved in them. The words were all just stones.

"So what's happened, Herr von Günther?"

"The man put a bullet through his head. At home. The children were in the house. Can you even imagine such a thing? What an asshole."

◆ ◆ ◆

"Von Lützow couldn't do it," Fritz says. "Another one dead."

"And the gold transfers?" Wegner asks.

"After examining the documents I gave them, the Americans were able to poke their noses into even more matters—and after the war too. Von Lützow had met with the man whose card I'd given him. Later on, I kept hearing how von Lützow had been so well liked. Among the diplomats abroad he was considered serious and not fanatical, an agreeable sort one could easily talk to. Almost a tragic figure, torn between his loyalty to the Fatherland and his scruples."

"Do you know what became of Weygand?" Wegner asks.

"I have no idea, as usual," Fritz says.

Wegner flips through his notes. He scratches his head, not sure whether he should laugh or curse. "Living well in Austria. He married von Lützow's widow."

"Oh God," Fritz says. "So, let's sum up the results of my last wartime trip to Bern . . . A man, likely German, was shadowing me and then disappears without a trace, and no one speaks of him again. There is a failed attempt to recruit me that surely ends badly for Musorksky. Von Lützow puts a bullet in his head while his daughters are playing. And me, I go turn my pistol on some harmless, fed-up engine driver."

Fritz smooths out the papers, sliding them around on the table.

"Musorksky was right about Gehlen," he says. "He was a vicious Nazi, through and through. And the Americans? They hand him a brand-new life on a silver platter. I ran into him one more time. He asked me if I wanted to work for him. For him, any hostility he felt toward me was beside the point. And no one would have stood up against his decision if I'd agreed. One snap of his fingers and my reputation would have been permanently rehabilitated. It's insane."

"Goodness, Herr Kolbe," Veronika says. "You must be, I don't know . . . you must be ready to explode. Did you ever see Horst Braunwein again?"

"Never. I have no idea what became of him."

"Then there's von Günther," Wegner says. "His reason for providing you with a car was rather scandalous, wasn't it?"

Fritz grins and pours schnapps. He puts some logs on the fire, leaves the stove hatch open, and looks around the table. He grabs his old Berlin map, crumples it up, and throws it into the flames. The dry paper ignites in seconds.

"Here's von Ribbentrop," Veronika says.

Fritz throws him into the fire.

"Gehlen?" Veronika asks.

"Not Gehlen. He's still alive."

"Von Günther? And the photos from the Foreign Office receptions?"

"Those too, yes." Fritz takes the photos from her and tosses them into the fire.

"Von Günther's motive was scandalous, yes," he says, "and also surprisingly normal."

Fritz cursed when von Günther told him about von Lützow's death. He hadn't wanted that. Those poor girls. That poor man. Yet another dead body in the wake of Fritz Kolbe alias George Wood, Kappa spy.

"Does anyone know why?"

Von Günther shook his head.

"He didn't need to shoot himself over that."

"What is *that*, Kolbe?"

"How should I know? The enemy getting near, or whatever."

"Be that as it may," von Günther said. "You know that I know about your relationship with Marlene Wiese, and you know that I know she's married. You are also aware that I have always trusted you and appreciate the work you've done, and I think I can rightly say that things haven't gone too badly for you with me as your superior. And about that little act I put on back then, in front of von Ribbentrop, well, let's wipe the slate clean, all right?"

So von Günther remembered the moment too. Could it have been embarrassing for him after all?

"Say it, Kolbe. It wasn't—isn't—so bad being my personal aide, am I right?"

"If you say so, Herr Ambassador."

"How is the lady?"

"She's working in Charité Hospital. So, not exactly well."

"You do know that my wife has left the city with the children. Well, there is a . . ." Von Günther scratched at one of the splotches on his face. "There is someone else still here, whom I wish to get out of Berlin, yes? A . . . a person, Herr Kolbe. A person I'm intimately involved with."

Von Günther's cheeks were turning red. He'd placed himself at Fritz's mercy, revealing a part of his personal life to his aide, to his outer office man, something he'd never done before. Most likely, he had no choice. He probably couldn't fly the coop himself, the pressures being too great, surveillance too tight.

"It's a work trip, yes? I'm about to hand you some documents which you'll then deliver, once you've dropped off the lady, to Lindau on Lake Constance. The Office has a little branch there. You'll drop the lady off near Lake Niedersonthofen—I have friends there—and drive on from there. All the paperwork is in order. Officially, you'll be working for me in Lindau."

Von Günther didn't once look at Fritz. He sucked on his cigarette greedily and pointed at the office walls. "Just why is there no portrait of the Führer hanging in here? Goddamn it. I've let you get away with quite a lot, Kolbe. Don't forget that."

Von Günther went into his office and slammed the door.

Fritz rushed over to the Charité. Most of the buildings still standing were just façades riddled with holes. Many had been baked by fire so often, he wouldn't dare lean against them. Burned-out and looted cars rotted along the shattered streets; the contents of households lay covered in gray dust atop piles of debris. Many of the ruins had been hung with signs: "We're all still alive. Headed south," or "Open for business down in the cellar." Some of the streets were clogged with glassy-eyed refugees, and foreign forced laborers were clearing paths, their backs crooked as they shoveled. At the temporary bridge over the Spree an antiaircraft gun was positioned with its scratched-up barrel aiming into the skies.

All the prosthetics had vanished from Marlene's office. Two filthy bandaged soldiers lay on the floor smoking bent cigarettes. Fritz asked them about Marlene, but the men said they hadn't seen a woman and they'd been lying here for an eternity already and no one was caring for them. After fifteen minutes of searching for her, he asked several nurses where she was. No one knew. He grabbed a doctor by the arm. "Marlene Wiese? Where's Marlene?"

"Who?"

"The professor's assistant."

"Don't know her, man. Now leave me alone."

He wandered up and down the stairs checking makeshift rooms that were separated only by blood-spattered tarps, but he couldn't find Marlene in the stinking, groaning chaos. He returned to his office in distress, packed up a few things, and pedaled home. In his apartment he threw a suitcase onto the bed and stowed his mended editions of *Antigone* and *Michael Kohlhaas* inside along with the tins of earth samples for Katrin. He wrapped his globe in layers of newspaper.

Marlene came home early that evening. Fritz ran up to her and hugged her so tight she nearly fell to the floor. "Where were you?"

"Operating, Fritz."

"The whole day?"

"The whole year. Maybe longer. I have no idea."

She sat in the kitchen and lit up a cigarette. "It's all shit now, Fritz. Truly. Just shit."

"I know. Shall I make you some tea?"

"Do we have any coffee?"

"Enough for one cup."

Marlene took out the clips in her hair and tossed them onto the table. She let her head hang. She told him she'd spoken with the professor. He supported her decision, had nothing against her leaving—on the contrary, he even advised her to. The time for contemplating and for making complicated decisions had passed. And Marlene was simply getting too tired, too distraught, to stay.

"I'm coming with you, Fritz. Let's head south. No bombs are falling out in the country. And nurses are needed everywhere."

"What about your husband?"

"I haven't thought about him for weeks, not for a minute. Not one time. That's the way life goes sometimes. Yesterday, I got a letter from him. He's fine. I do know that he's hoping to find some way of giving himself up to the Americans real soon."

"For a moment, I was hoping—"

"Stop, Fritz. Let it go. This fucking war. Do we have anything left to eat?"

"A loaf of bread and a few slices of sausage. Even a few tablespoons of butter."

"He knows."

"What?"

"My husband. Gerhard. He said in his letter that he could tell that time you came into my office in the Charité. He knows. He's taking it hard." Marlene buried her face in her hands and sobbed. She stammered the name of her husband. *Gerhard.* "We spent so much of our lives together. He's such a good man. He cried so hard when our boy died." The stretch of kitchen floor between Fritz and Marlene seemed to grow ever longer. Fritz held out a hand to Marlene, but he didn't touch her. She was crying about another man and for her dead son.

"You know what else he wrote? To us?"

Fritz crossed his arms, then let them drop again. He reached out to touch Marlene's wet face.

"He wishes us well. He says things all would've been different without this war. But my God, Fritz, he wishes us well." Sobs shook Marlene's body. Fritz had never felt so distant from her. He fought an urge to leave the apartment.

"Marlene?"

He slowly moved over to her. He opened his arms, stood before her, and placed his arms around her body, first gently and then ever tighter. He knew that this moment would determine, finally, if she were his or not. Marlene removed her hands from her face, pressed her cheek to his, and embraced him.

Fritz could smell the blood and despair of the Charité in her hair and on her clothes. With water being rationed and most water lines destroyed, a bath was out of the question. But he could still heat up a big pot of water and add a little soap so that she could wash herself. He fixed her the bread and cup of coffee he'd promised.

She would be his wife. His Marlene. They would travel south and, from there, relocate someplace outside Germany, through some connection Will would establish without the great Allen Dulles ever knowing about it. He remembered that blue sky over Africa. Perhaps Katrin was gazing up into the sky of his dreams at this very moment.

"Will you be mine, Marlene?"

She looked at him and nodded.

Two days later a Mercedes was dropped off in front of the Office. The driver came into Fritz's office, threw the keys on the desk, and left.

Fritz drove the car to the Kurfürstendamm. How many hundreds of times had he ridden his old bicycle along this same route? Now the bike was nothing but a twisted pile of metal, the chain come off, the bell gone. After the last air raid he'd gone over to the destroyed U-Bahn entrance, where his bike had been chained, and found what remained of it. He had been sad for a moment, strangely and incomprehensibly so, since he hadn't realized this bike meant something to him. *How absurd*, he'd thought. Along the edge of the cratered square, corpses were being dumped onto a truck like sandbags, and here he was feeling shaken up over a bike.

Once he had loaded up the car with his things from the apartment, he drove back to the Office. Marlene was sitting on the steps out front, smiling at him. She was wearing a blue overcoat and a hat, and the way she sat there among those crumbling walls and slopes of stone and debris was to him the picture of life itself. He took her into his office, where he stashed his notes inside his jacket and overcoat, shoved all necessary papers into his briefcase, and then looked at the clock. The woman was supposed to meet them there at eleven and she knew the score, von Günther had said. The ambassador was traveling to Salzburg again, but he also promised to meet with Admiral Dönitz to, as he put it, "get everything ready."

Frau Meiner was of medium height, modestly dressed, and friendly. The three of them introduced themselves anxiously, shaking hands but not looking at one another.

"Well, then," Marlene said, "let's go for a little joyride."

Frau Meiner smiled. "I won't be a burden on you two," she said. "And luggage, well . . ." She held up her tiny suitcase.

"That'll get better again too," Fritz said. He looked around his office one last time. So many years. He would never come back, not to this office, not to this Berlin. He went over to von Günther's office, opened the desk cabinet, and pulled out an unopened bottle of Napoléon Cognac.

"Your . . . uh, Herr von Günther won't object," he said.

The corners of Frau Meiner's mouth curled up timidly. "Go ahead and call him my boyfriend, Herr Kolbe. That's what he is. Whether he comes personally to take me south or not."

Marlene placed a hand on her arm.

Fritz carried the woman's suitcase out and loaded it into the car. Then he went back in again. At his typewriter, he depressed the *SS* key so that its hammer was sticking upright. Then he bent it with all his strength, the metal turning white where it almost snapped. He took down his Allgäu picture, laid it on the desk, and added the scribbled figure of a man to the landscape, a dark square figure holding out an arm to his side. He tried making the second figure more rounded, but didn't succeed. This second tiny figure had an arm out too; the two were holding hands. As he stepped out into the corridor, he found Müller standing there, hands on his hips. He looked even thinner now, quite fragile, his shoulders as bony as ever.

Fritz held up his papers. "Official trip, Müller."

"I'll need to verify that, Herr Kolbe."

"Then call von Günther. And hold down the fort."

"Heil Hitler."

Fritz began to leave, then turned to the man one last time. "Were you there, Müller? On the *Louisiana?*"

"I don't know what you're talking about."

Fritz laughed. "Even now, you still won't answer?"

"Hail victory, Herr Kolbe."

"Exactly, Müller. To victory."

As Fritz came out onto the street, he saw Gisela standing with Marlene at the car. She wore a wool cap over her curls. Frau Meiner was standing to the side, giving the two friends room to talk.

"Can we take her with us?" Marlene asked.

Before Fritz could reply Gisela said she knew it wasn't possible. "It's not so bad. I'll stay here. Things are coming to an end, but there will be a new beginning. I'll be fine, Marlene."

"Watch out for yourself, Gisela," Fritz said.

"And you watch after this lady here. She's something real special."

"I know."

Marlene and Gisela hugged while Frau Meiner sobbed. She wished Gisela the best of luck.

14

On Toward the Sun

"Then we left Berlin," Fritz says. "Or what was left of it. It must have been horrible when the Russians marched in after that and the senseless house-by-house fighting began." He spears a piece of cheese and a little radish. "Still time for another beer," he says.

Wegner nods. He's down to the last few pages in his notepad, and he's circling things again.

"To me it felt like we were driving toward the sun. All the terrible things really seemed to be finally coming to an end. It would have been so nice too if they had."

He goes outside. It's dark and stars hang in the sky, and the mountain peaks glow as if painted a bright white. Below, a few dots of light move along the stream like grains of salt. The bottles he pulls from the well are cooler than the ones he took in the daytime, and he goes back into the cabin. He feels quite good; he feels freer now. He knows that there's still one big hurdle left to clear, yet he senses that he's finally prepared for it.

"I think I'm getting a little tipsy," Veronika says.

"And I still have to drive after this," Wegner says.

"The roof loft has two little sleeping areas," Fritz says. "So, drink one more beer with me. I'd like it if you stayed."

"Marlene's been gone a long time," Veronika says.

"She likes being in the city," Fritz says.

He starts organizing his papers, folding them, stacking them according to subjects.

"I found that whole situation with Frau Meiner pretty amusing," he says. "A person gets a certain idea in their head. When you hear about someone's having an affair, you always think it's this amazing woman, say someone highly attractive or noticeably younger than the man, or alternately, some dolled-up old cow. But Frau Meiner was von Günther's age and quite inconspicuous actually, a very pleasant person. I tried to learn how and where she met von Günther, but I didn't want to be indiscreet. We came through the journey just fine. The Gestapo stopped us once. My papers didn't mean so much to men like that. We argued. Then I managed to get one of them to call naval headquarters. He actually got von Günther on the line. We were allowed to drive on after that. We dropped off Frau Meiner at Lake Niedersonthofen. She wished Marlene and me all the best. She said we were a nice couple."

Now comes another hard part, Fritz thinks and rubs at his eyes. He can hear Frau Meiner's words as if they were spoken just yesterday. He sees her waving at them as they drive away. Even though people come out of the house to greet her, she looks lonely and deserted.

"Marlene and I drove on. When we reached the Allgäu region, I remember stopping in a meadow at one point. We looked all around us. We could hardly believe it. Not one single bomb crater, no antiaircraft guns, no military columns anywhere. Marlene laughed. She was happy. She got out and skipped across the meadow, waving at a cow. I was so overcome with joy, I thought the cow might wave back any second. We found shelter for the night on a farm. Nice people. They set out bowls of fresh milk for us, fried eggs, apples from their stocks. We hardly knew such things existed anymore. It was glorious. *Life,* Marlene called it. We got our own tiny room. It smelled like dung heaps and mountain air. We clung to each other the whole night."

He drinks a gulp of beer.

"Why do people barely notice those brief moments of happiness?" he asks. "If we hadn't remembered happiness existed, we would've perished in that war. Marlene was always thinking of happiness somehow. It was the framework for her life. I love that so much about her."

"How come I never hear men talking about women like this?" Veronika asks.

"The man you let kiss you one day will talk about you like this," Fritz says.

"It's true," Wegner says. He stares at his beer bottle.

Veronika gives him a sidelong glance. "That would be nice," she says.

"We arrived in Lindau the next day. I went directly to our field office there. It was a joke. There were two people working in one room—under that stern gaze of Adolf Hitler. One was completely intimidated; the other acted the big Nazi. He was a real loudmouth, an honorary SS man, just the kind von Ribbentrop liked. I didn't stick around long. Marlene was waiting for me at the harbor, sitting under the stone lion statue there and looking out over Lake Constance. A boat was patrolling the lake using a spotlight, and soldiers were watching the banks. I hadn't told her about Will's plans. That evening we set off from Lindau. My papers helped—we were only stopped once . . .

"I notice I'm telling this faster and faster, that I'm trying to reach the ending—a supposed ending that turned out to be nothing of the sort . . .

"Marlene and I were granted some time together before the war struck once again. At the arranged location, a rowboat was waiting out on the water. I didn't see him at first, but I heard his voice. It was so familiar to me, so closely bound to the life I'd been leading in the Nazi Reich.

"*Hello, Fritz,* he said."

◆ ◆ ◆

"Hello, Fritz."

Fritz hadn't imagined hearing the man's voice would affect him so. The sound of it brought freedom and the final unmasking he'd long desired. Holding Marlene's hand, he felt through the darkness and pushed aside branches that stretched out like the strings of bows.

"Will? Will, is that you?"

"It's me. It's about time you got here."

Fritz could now make out Priest's silhouette and the side of a boat landed on the beach, its wet hull gleaming. "Nice and cloudy tonight," Priest said. "Good for us." He climbed out of the boat, a cool wind wafting along the bank, and shook Marlene's hand. "Nice to meet you, Frau Wiese. This man here talks of nothing but you."

"As he should," Marlene said. "You're my first real American."

Fritz laughed. He could tell that Priest was genuinely happy to see him. He handed Priest both suitcases and Priest loaded them into the boat. Then he helped Marlene in, and Fritz after her, the boat wobbling under his feet. Priest pushed off and water rushed along the boat's hull. Then Priest swung himself over the side and into the boat, his legs dripping wet. He sat in the middle and reached for a box at his feet. In the dark Fritz could just make out the subtle shine of two machine guns. Priest handed him one. The metal felt cool. "Safari," he said. Priest's inexplicable silliness was contagious. Deliverance rode in this boat, and so did a feeling of elation. The danger still ahead of them barely registered. Fritz said, "You drink up Dulles's secret whisky stash or what, Will? He's not always like this, Marlene."

Marlene laughed quietly. "I think it's nice," she whispered.

"You hear that, Fritz?"

"Shut up, Will."

Priest started rowing, slowly and gently. He was careful to dip the blades into the water silently, and the more water that rushed past the boat, the more euphoric Fritz grew. Marlene sat at the bow. Fritz gazed at the contours of her cheeks. He would have liked to go over to her and kiss her. He breathed in the nice cool air and looked back at the lights on the shore. A patrol boat was casting its spotlight far in the distance. Things would all go well from this point on. There was only this one stretch of lake left, only Will's oar strokes, and then they'd go underground at some secure hideout in Switzerland.

Fritz sat in the stern of the boat while Priest quietly, evenly dragged the oars through the water. Up in the bow, Marlene was dipping her fingertips into the lake. Suddenly, the memories came back to Fritz again. He ran after Katrin on the beach at Camps Bay, felt those strange men grip his shoulders on board the *Louisiana*, and saw von Günther in the Foreign Office for the first time and his own contorted face.

Walter and Käthe were laughing with him, and then Käthe was shrinking away, gone gray, her eyes robbed of all life. He saw the documents with swastikas and Reich eagles, and he heard Marlene laughing in Frau Hansen's tiny office. Then William Priest beckoned him down a hallway, he met Allen Dulles and Greta Stone, and he noticed the secret glances exchanged between Weygand and von Lützow's wife.

He heard that young boy in Berlin screaming, *Papa! Papa!* and he saw Marlene naked and vulnerable before him. He felt the cobblestones of Bern's narrow lanes under his feet. Next von Ribbentrop was glaring at him, and Hitler walked through the shadows of trees at the Wolf's Lair. Marlene was sitting out in front of the Foreign Office in her blue overcoat, waiting for him, quite un-German behavior for a German lady, though she couldn't care less. In the corridors of the White House, they were talking about one George Wood, and then there was Marlene's straight, slim nose, the loveliest nose he'd ever seen.

It all had to be written down. His name didn't need to be mentioned, but this story of revolt against tyranny had to be told, and an accounting must be given of the ones who must pay for that tyranny.

As the boat skidded onto the sand of the opposite bank and Priest pulled in the oars, Fritz closed his eyes a moment. He heard Marlene's voice. "Is this really Switzerland?"

"Welcome, Madame," Priest said. He climbed past her and out of the boat and held out a hand to her. Fritz sat there a moment longer, looking back over his shoulder. The lights of Lindau glowed timidly in the black night. They might as well have originated from another planet, they seemed so far away. As he stepped onto dry ground, he felt like an explorer discovering some unknown island.

Priest took the machine gun from him and shouldered it. Marlene was standing over by a car talking with a gray-haired man who was smoking a pipe.

"Mr. Wood."

"Mr. Dulles."

"I can't believe you never told me your real name." Marlene smiled.

"George Wood," he said and kissed her hand. "Will she be safe, Mr. Dulles?"

"That she will. Did you bring us any new intelligence?"

Even at a time like this, Fritz thought. He pulled thin papers from his pockets and socks and handed them over to Dulles.

"That's all of it," he said.

"Hold on," Dulles muttered. "You should know I never agreed to all this. Mr. Priest seems to be taking a bit too much upon himself."

"I told him about my mission to Lindau," Fritz said. "He merely lent me a hand. Marlene and I were going to get away one way or another. Would've tried to, in any case. And without any help from you, Mr. Dulles."

They drove through the darkness, Marlene and Fritz sitting in the back of the car, holding hands. Priest was at the wheel and Dulles turned to them every so often, telling Marlene about Washington and New York and explaining that in the States there was only a very small, select circle of top-ranking individuals who knew of George Wood.

"I personally told the president that Wood is the most important spy of this whole war."

"The president?" Marlene looked at Fritz. It felt awkward for him to be portrayed as a hero—he'd never wanted that. He felt a tingle in his chest nevertheless and straightened his shoulders. Marlene squeezed his hand and looked out the window at the gray woods rushing by.

"The president?" she repeated. "Of America? Fritz! Just where am I anyway?"

"With me," Fritz said. He turned to Will. "Where are you putting us up?"

"The last place anyone would expect you to go," Priest said.

"Smack dab in the middle of Bern," Dulles said. "A little apartment, nothing special, but adequate. You won't be able to leave the apartment, but we'll see to it that you'll have everything you need. It's just for a few weeks more."

"Thanks, Will. That's very good of you."

"We've done it, Fritz," Marlene said. "We've done it. My God, we're going to live."

The apartment was in a building built in the Middle Ages, on Langmauer Lane not far from the rush of the Aare. From their window they could see Kornhaus Bridge off to the right. Time ceased to exist in those two rooms with a fireplace and a small kitchen. And though each of them needed to be alone now and then, the doors always stayed open and they never suffered a moment of boredom or monotony. They chatted, they read, or they read to each other; they cooked and lay in bed—a lot. Fritz put out his globe. "Now you can spin in peace again, dear world," he said. He was glad Marlene was happy. She seemed to have gotten over leaving Charité Hospital and appeared resolved not to let her conscience torment her anymore. And so she began, cautiously at first and then with increasing determination, to talk about their future together.

William Priest came by twice a week, bringing supplies and the international papers. He said little about the OSS's espionage activities. He mentioned Greta Stone once to say she sent her regards. "Our good Greta is on her way back to Europe. She's been assigned directly to Eisenhower on the Western Front. She has the highest security rating."

"How's she doing?"

"Better than ever. She's where the action is."

"Where the action is, isn't always the best place to be. Not in the long run."

"In America it is."

"Will, come on."

"That's just how it is."

"Do you know what's happened to Weygand?"

"He was ordered back to the Reich but he took off. He's a little fish."

"What about Gehlen?"

Priest lit a cigarette.

"Will? General Gehlen?"

"That's classified, Fritz. All right? Now, make sure you keep the radio on nice and loud for the next few days. It can't last much longer now."

Books lay open around them in bed. Sausage, cheese, and radishes wobbled on a plate balanced atop their bunched-up sheets. Fritz kissed the curve of Marlene's breast as she licked mustard off her fingers.

"The merry month of May begins today," Fritz said.

"Merry is good," Marlene said. Fritz started kissing her nipples, but Marlene pushed him away after only a few seconds. She had never done that before, not in a private moment like this. What was wrong now?

She was holding him back with her arms stiff, staring at him. "Listen. Listen to what they're saying on the radio."

"This afternoon our Führer, Adolf Hitler, has fallen at his command post in the Reich Chancellery, fighting to the last breath against Bolshevism, and for Germany . . ."

It took a while for them to comprehend it. They fell completely silent, then they felt for each other's hands and squeezed firmly for a long time.

Hitler was dead.

"It's over, Fritz."

Fritz slowly climbed out of bed. *Rising from the dead.* That was his first thought. The words loomed large in his mind. He flexed his muscles until they quivered.

He screamed one long *"Yeessss . . ."* out into the apartment.

"She's turning to look at me, Marlene. She's turning my way. She's waving."

"Who is, Fritz?"

"Katrin. My daughter."

"Oh my God, and we're alive."

She got out of bed naked and they embraced, and Fritz closed his eyes as he held his woman tight.

A week later, the document of unconditional surrender was signed. The war in Europe was over.

Fritz and Marlene pushed open the door onto the street. They laughed and hugged each other out in the sunshine. They could not comprehend that it was over, and yet the end was all they could think about. They left their hideaway and strolled through Bern together, just as Fritz always wanted them to. The springtime sun seemed to be shining just for them, Fritz said, and he showed Marlene the building on Herrengasse where the OSS kept their clandestine office. He walked with her past the German diplomatic mission on Willading Lane. The doors stood open, crates were piling up in the front yard which smelled of blossoms, and someone had taken down all the curtains. He considered showing Marlene Weygand's and von Lützow's offices, but decided to let it be and showed her his hotel on Bubenbergplatz instead.

"So that's where you always stayed?" she said.

He pointed at the window of his room. "Right there," he said, and it felt like it had been decades ago. "Those were the good old days," he said.

Marlene yanked him close to her. "You can't be serious."

"Not for one second," he said. But was that entirely true? He felt keenly the weight of the war ending, of Hitler dying, and of his reclaimed freedom. But there was something else there too: an intuition, a hint of a feeling, connected to the room behind that window. Did George Wood—Kappa—still exist? Or had he died along with Adolf Hitler?

Fritz called Eugen Sacher and the three of them met for dinner in a restaurant on Herrengasse. He and Eugen hugged, unable to care less about the other tables staring at them.

"Nice restaurant," Eugen said. He placed a hand on Fritz's forearm. "Man, was I ever scared back when this all started."

He said that he was now getting plenty of business from over in Central Europe. "So many deals coming in, it's crazy. You two can't imagine all the goods going back and forth these days."

"Doing business with former Nazis?" Fritz asked.

"Come on, Fritz."

"Our lives were in real danger, Eugen. Walter and Käthe are dead, and so are millions of others."

"I know that. But life goes on. It always does. That's a good thing."

"A story can only move on once a chapter is completely finished."

Marlene reached for his hand. He was convinced that she shared his opinions on the subject, but she didn't want to argue now and he understood that. It wasn't a topic that should be avoided in the future, but they were still recovering from the war, and Fritz didn't want to disturb her peaceful meal. He kissed her cheek and waved at the waiter to bring more white wine to go with the fish. Eugen, seeming to sense their shared understanding, said only that, naturally, he would not be doing business with ex-Nazis.

"You have to be able to recognize them first," Fritz said, "before you can avoid them."

"Something a certain friend of mine hasn't worried nearly enough about."

"Gentlemen, please," Marlene said. "That's enough."

The next day William Priest called and summoned Fritz to the OSS office on Herrengasse. Fritz asked if he could bring Marlene.

"Don't say crap like that, Fritz. Of course you can't," Priest said and hung up.

Gone were the days of discreet meetings with just Greta, Priest, and Dulles. Now, about a dozen extra telephones were ringing, and carpets and runners were lying over countless cables. Twenty men, many of them in uniform, were talking over one another, handing phone receivers back and forth and paging through documents.

Dulles told Fritz he was looking forward to a secluded and secure new office in Berlin and to one in the States after that. He sat at his desk, frowning at all the men and sucking on his extinguished pipe.

"Between you and me, Mr. Wood—"

"Kolbe."

"Huh?"

"Kolbe, Fritz Kolbe."

"Now, between you and me, this here"—Dulles pointed with his pipe—"is not my preference. Proper focus demands that a small group of people tell a larger group what they should be doing."

Priest pulled Fritz aside.

"We have some more assignments for you. You're being officially recruited. From now on, you'll be getting paid dollars for your work. You'll get more details in the next few days. But listen, Fritz, you have to keep a low profile. Wooldridge from MI6—you know, the Brit—came to us again. He's still obsessed with the idea that there's a massive leak right in London. The British have long known that a certain George Wood was a prime source and still is. But they're also convinced any new enemy will soon be putting out even more feelers, trying to find you. Such an ungodly mess. Our work goes on everywhere. Berlin, Bern, London, Washington, Moscow—and now Vienna, brand new on the market. No one has any perspective."

"But I can finally contact Katrin, right?"

Priest shook his head. "It was smart of you to keep her out of all this. But you'll have to wait a little longer. Things are too chaotic now. Once some sort of structure is in place, once we've determined what position we're taking . . . then, Fritz, then. You've endured it this long. Keep Katrin out of it a little longer."

"Did you get a message to her?"

"Of course." Priest placed a hand on his shoulder. "Look, you've made yourself plenty of enemies. And at least some of them now find themselves in new territory. They're reacting differently, thinking differently. I know that this all sounds pretty muddled, but muddled is the way things are at the moment. I want you to keep your head down."

"I've had it up to here with keeping my head down, Will."

"That doesn't matter."

"What about Marlene?"

"Having a woman at your side just gives them one more way to put pressure on you."

Fritz cursed.

"Here in Bern, you should be fine. Just don't go dancing at too many parties." Priest shook Fritz's hand. "By the way," he said, "she's a wonderful woman."

"Without Marlene, I couldn't have done it."

Fritz squeezed between two of Dulles's men into Greta's former office on his way to the exit.

A young lieutenant said quietly, "Pardon me, please, sir, are you George Wood?"

Fritz looked around. Another man glanced at him. Priest was standing in the doorway. Sensing Fritz's hesitation, Priest shook his head at him as if to say, *Not a word.*

The lieutenant's smile was almost bashful. Something about him reminded Fritz of Horst Braunwein.

"Pleasure to meet you," Fritz said.

Priest groaned.

"The pleasure's all mine, Mr. Wood." The lieutenant shook his hand. "Terrific job. Really fantastic."

As Fritz turned to leave the room with all its shrillness and chatter, he heard the other man mutter something.

"You know, he's a traitor . . ."

Fritz turned back, advanced on the man, and cocked his arm.

No more shadowboxing, no imagined Nazi henchmen. This time, a young, baby-faced American in uniform got a swift fist to the mouth.

As he walked out, Fritz shut the door on the remark, on the men who stood staring at him like dolls, on the moaning man with his bloody split lip. He went down the stairs but did not exit the front door to Herrengasse; he used the hallway to the garden gate instead. This was the very spot where William Priest had met him on his first trip to Bern, where he had stood in the darkness, waving Fritz toward him and another world.

"From there I went straight to a newspaper's offices and talked my way in to see the editor-in-chief. I told him I had a first-rate espionage story to tell, only my name couldn't get mentioned."

"That wasn't too smart," Veronika says.

Fritz looks out at the night, the window reflecting the glow of the lamp and the fiery oranges flickering behind the woodstove's hatch.

"I know," he says.

"I spoke with the reporter," Wegner says. "He served in a volunteer brigade during the war. He fought against the Nazis and lost his left arm. He was still filled with blind rage over it. He's the one you told your story to, Herr Kolbe?"

"When I was leaving the Americans' office and heard someone call me a traitor . . . I already told you earlier that I thought my story needed to be written down. Anyway, this reporter had agreed to sit on the story and keep my name a secret. It felt good to finally tell someone. Not everything, of course—never all of it. Nothing personal, nothing about the Braunweins or von Lützow, nothing about Marlene. I gave him a broad outline of my espionage activities, though. I needed to get it out, goddamn it."

"I can understand, Herr Kolbe," Veronika says.

"Where is Marlene?" Wegner asks. Fritz looks at him. In the lamp's glow the young man's face looks sallow, his eyes like dark marbles.

"Eugen Sacher did tell you about it, am I right? He told you what happened. He's still worried about me, isn't he?"

Veronika and Wegner light cigarettes at the same time and fog themselves in. Fritz sorts the papers, intending to put them all back in the cabinet. Then he pauses, snaps the cabinet door shut again, and opens the woodstove's blazing mouth wide.

"Did you get everything you need?" he asks.

"Did you, Herr Kolbe?" Veronika asks.

Fritz does not understand why these two are so fond of him. But they are, each in their own way. He can see that they like him and have sympathy for him, for whatever reason.

"Not yet. But I'll keep trying," Fritz says.

"Why did she leave you?" Veronika asks.

Fritz sits, the papers on his lap, the memories deep inside him. There is silence.

"General Gehlen," he says at last, "turned himself in to the Americans in Southern Germany. He demanded to speak to a top-ranking officer. When Dulles got word of it, he left Bern at once. Gehlen was brought to the States, along with several others. He claimed he'd stashed in the Alps hundreds of crates full of secret files about the Russians. He was interrogated for months. Dulles told me about it later. He said Gehlen was actually a good man and no Nazi. In fact, Dulles said, he was rather surprisingly apolitical, if you didn't count seeing communism as an enemy. The rest of it didn't really matter to him. Gehlen was a man of service and great intelligence, highly professional, clever, virtually indispensable.

"It was just as Musorksky predicted. I told Dulles that Gehlen was a committed Nazi. No, Dulles said, he was committed only to his work, and from now on the Americans would be the ones to set his agenda.

"After that, I worked awhile for the OSS in Berlin, gathering material against Nazis, even running a small department. But they got rid of me before long. Priest figured Berlin was too dangerous for me because of the Russians. Marlene and I took a ship to America, where we were supposedly Dulles's guests. Mind you, he barely had time for me. Marlene and I had too much time on our hands, and she wasn't sure what we were supposed to be doing in the States. I ended up taking her back to Germany, of my own initiative. Around that time, that reporter's article was published. As you can imagine, it wasn't too hard for some people to figure out just who had been smuggling documents out of the Foreign Office. The name Fritz Kolbe became notorious.

Priest was in Berlin at the time. All he said was *Goddamn it, Fritz, what have you done? Have you lost your mind?"*

"And Marlene?" Veronika asks. "What did Marlene have to say about it?"

◆ ◆ ◆

Marlene threw the newspaper onto the table. The paper struck an open pack of American cigarettes, causing the individual white sticks to roll across the tabletop. Through a glued-shut window, the sun shone onto the mismatched furniture, paper-thin carpet, and their few surviving books. Marlene planted her hands on her hips. She stammered, unable to find the right words. She picked the paper back up and threw it into Fritz's lap.

"Page three," she said.

Fritz skimmed the article. Two more installments were promised to follow. "The Spy Who Betrayed Hitler." A black-and-white drawing showed a bald man with a hook nose bent over a dimly lit desk. An older man in a suit sat at the desk, and another man stood in a corner behind him. The bald man was pressing a finger on a map rolled out to its edges. *"Bomb this,"* the caption read.

"I'm not bald," Fritz said.

Marlene stamped her foot and screamed at him. Fritz had never seen her do that before. He tried to make eye contact with her from his shabby armchair.

"I thought you didn't want to play the hero!" She slapped at the paper. "What are you doing with your life, Fritz? What?" She yanked her nurse smock from its hook. "I'm finally working again. I have been for a few months now."

"No one's giving me work. Certainly not the Germans."

She lit a cigarette and pointed at his face with the hand holding it. "We found this apartment. Here in Berlin, in broken-down Charlottenburg, all because I'm a nurse. Two rooms, even if the dividing wall's just a curtain. When we want, we can stroll through the palace gardens, even though they're just as bad. We finally have a little peace and quiet, some small prospects for the future. And what do you go and do?" She cursed and slammed the door shut behind her.

Fritz stared at the newspaper. He hadn't wanted to upset Marlene; that was the last thing in the world he'd wanted to do. "I want justice," he said, as if the goddess herself were standing right before him.

He called William Priest at the OSS office near Memorial Church. Priest turned surly upon hearing his voice. "Greta was here," he informed Fritz. "You know what she said?"

"I'm sure you're going to tell me."

"That stupid Fritz Kolbe."

"I thought Fritz Kolbe was dead."

"He's alive again now."

"You can all kiss my ass," Fritz said and slammed down the phone.

◆ ◆ ◆

"I testified at the Nuremberg Trials. Whenever Priest came near me he'd make a face and say that something just didn't smell right. I tried to get work—I reached out to the newly formed government agencies and to what would become the new Foreign Office, but I kept coming up empty.

"Since then, von Lützow has been portrayed as an anti-Nazi who was driven to suicide by peculiar circumstances in Bern. Former members of the Foreign Office have had their pretrial detention credited to their sentences and are now finding new positions. They're all taking a stand against me. It didn't take long for me to get labeled a traitor to the Fatherland and a murderer. Meanwhile, hostility between the Russians on one side and the Western Allies on the other was growing by the day, and Berlin was becoming more dangerous for me."

"Do you know what von Günther said, Herr Kolbe?" Wegner says. "Get this: von Günther was one of the few to admit to a degree of guilt, but he got a very mild sentence since it couldn't be proved he took part in any crimes. Then when the topic of Fritz Kolbe came up, he made you out to be a hero. He said that he wouldn't have dared try taking action the way you did. However . . . Hold on, I have the quote here somewhere. Ah yes, here it is:

I knew very early on what Herr Kolbe was doing. He must have known he couldn't take top-secret files from the Office and hand them over to the Americans without me knowing about it. I would never claim that what I did was on the same level as Herr Kolbe's actions—I didn't have the strength this man had to resist Hitler. However, I must mention that it was I who watched Herr Kolbe's back for him. He didn't know I was doing it; I never told him everything that I did so that he could carry on. So if you'll permit me to say it, and I hope I won't be misunderstood: you could say that I was Fritz Kolbe's right-hand man—his unseen helper.

The tragedy of his story comes down to the fact that from where he sat in the Foreign Office, he lacked the greater perspective I had. So what happened in Bern, when Herr Kolbe pressured Consul von Lützow, can be attributed to Fritz Kolbe gravely misjudging the situation. He is a great man, but he drew the wrong conclusions in the wrong game. Now, regarding Herr Kolbe's recent efforts to find a position in the newly formed German government . . . It's a sensitive subject, upon which, in all modesty, I wouldn't wish to pass judgment. I've made amends for my deeds. I assure you, we men in the Foreign Office were the very ones who served as a bulwark against the spread of National Socialism. I can't help but wonder whether Fritz Kolbe had sought out the right friends within this system.

Fritz stares at Wegner. His heart thumps in his chest. He leaps from the chair, looking for something to smash. "Von Günther said that?"

Wegner holds up the page containing the statement. Fritz rips it from his hand and tears it up. He kicks the stove's hatch open and tosses the shreds into the blaze. "That cowardly fucking pig!" he screams.

"He's a lawyer in Mannheim now. His wife and daughters still live with him."

Fritz slaps his hands to his face. From out of the past he hears that voice calling, *Kolbe? Kolbe!*

"So he was watching my back, was he?" Fritz stammers. "Watching mine? That goddamn bastard." He sits down again, shaking his head.

"Is it true that no one ever found out who was behind the attack?" Veronika asks.

"Will Priest tried everything," Fritz says, hanging his head. "He's convinced that the Germans had a hand in it, but he never found any proof. You know, he did play a part in setting up Gehlen in his new role working for the Americans. By 1946 the US was already fully funding the Gehlen Organization, an intelligence agency run by Gehlen and his Nazi comrades for the purpose of delivering valuable information on the Russians.

"Was it someone who was afraid of what I knew—Gehlen's people, the Russians, the old-boy network? Priest said I should get out of Berlin for a few weeks, told me there were elements in play that were making him real uneasy. Marlene and I had just gotten our apartment looking nice, there in the rubble of Berlin, probably the largest and most unlikely construction site the world's ever seen. We were getting used to a life in which there were no bombs falling, no corpses in the street. It felt strange, the way life was returning to that devastated city: people sitting out in front of cafés, surrounded by mountains of rubble and watching carts on rails get loaded up all around them. We couldn't quite believe it, but we were living. Hitler was dead, none of us had ever been a Nazi— and we were living. We were loving one another in peace for the first time. The hoped-for end to the war had become a reality. Marlene was so happy. We lived modestly, but that didn't matter to us. I remember that my globe, the one Marlene glued together, was standing in the middle of our little living-room table. This same one, here in the cabin.

"Good old Will Priest urged me to leave Berlin for a while, along with Marlene. She didn't want to go. She was extremely angry with me about that article. And my God, was she right. We should have stayed. But I convinced her. If I hadn't, she would have stayed in Berlin and everything would have turned out differently."

Fritz goes in the kitchen, runs water into the kettle, and sets it on the gas flame. He gets the teapot ready and leans on the table for support.

After it happened, he distanced himself from it all. He hadn't known about the quote Wegner read him. So, von Günther says he watched Fritz's back for him? The kitchen utensils clank as he pulls open the silverware drawer and looks at the revolver.

It had all gone so wrong. It had taken him a long time to grasp that all the lies and the masquerading had created a split personality. His espionage work had developed in him an ability to bury things more deeply than he might want to admit, or was capable of seeing. When he told Veronika and Wegner that Marlene had gone shopping in Bern, he had in that moment believed the words, and he'd put his faith in the truth of them. They had come out so clear, with such an utter lack of hesitation, he might simply have been saying the sky is blue. An irrefutable claim. Everything flowed together now: von Günther's statement, the incident in Southern Germany, his memories of the prosthetics in Marlene's hospital office.

Steam shoots from the kettle. Fritz pours the tea and then grabs cups from the cabinet and an antique porcelain sugar bowl. He was such a wreck, for heaven's sake. He probably couldn't blame Eugen Sacher for wanting to send him to a psychiatrist.

He carries the tray back into the main room, now warm from the fire fed by paper documents from his past.

"Will Priest had me temporarily assigned to a unit in Kempten that was identifying Nazis and assessing less crucial intelligence provided by Gehlen before sending it on to Dulles in Berlin. Will figured two or three weeks would be enough for the dust to settle."

Fritz remembers things more clearly now, the walls within him having crumbled like the buildings of Berlin. He remembers Kempten, Southern Germany, the Allgäu.

"Marlene and I were forced off the road by another car," he says. "We tumbled down a hillside, over and over, everything spinning. I heard Marlene screaming. It went on and on, everything twisting and bending around me. There was light and then darkness; sky above, then down below. Glass like diamonds showered all over us. The car crashed against a boulder, tottered some, and then lay still, something hissing as if someone were letting out a long sigh. I was wedged in one spot and couldn't turn to Marlene. But I kept hearing her, you know? I felt her misery, her pain. She was whispering my name, but I couldn't turn her way. I heard shots. Soon I heard someone approaching. It was a voice that was familiar to me. Will. I screamed at him to first get Marlene out, Marlene first."

Fritz screams, "Marlene! Marlene!" He leaps up, knocking over the chair. "It's all right there. All of it."

Fritz stares at the images and writings he'd pinned to the lime-washed beam of the cabin, at his life—at his two lives, maybe more than that. Time both stands still and overlaps, chaos and calm fighting for the upper hand within him.

"I must apologize. This whole time, I've been talking about someone I never wanted to be," he says.

"That you *mostly* didn't want to be," Veronika says.

"Sure, mostly, perhaps—but that's bad enough. I thought I was doing something unforgettable. But it turns out the only one who hasn't forgotten is me."

"No, Herr Kolbe. You're not the only one," Veronika says.

Wegner lifts a pen. "This?" he says. "It never forgets a thing."

"I don't know what happened after that," Fritz tells them. "I lost consciousness when Will was pulling me from the car. I only woke up later, in the hospital."

◆　◆　◆

After the accident, Fritz wore a turban-like bandage around his head; his left leg was in splints, and his hands were wrapped in thick bandages. It was hard to hold a cup with both hands. Yet every morning Fritz walked down the hospital corridor to the other ward and brought Marlene that cup of coffee.

He looked out the windows at Southern Germany—at the rolling meadows of the Allgäu, green waves under a blue sky. His heart was racing the way it had during his most dangerous moments in Bern and Berlin. Marlene's bed was positioned so she could see outside. Whenever he entered her room she would turn her head to the window and the morning sun would find her face. He would put her coffee down and try talking to her. She never said a word. Those times when she did try turning to him after a few minutes, her eyes welled with tears. Fritz had known about her condition for days but felt stuck in his feelings of complete bewilderment.

"I'm so sorry, Marlene," he said.

She turned her head back to the window and looked out, her skin stretched over her cheekbones. Fritz could see she longed for peace.

"Speak to me, darling. Please. Say something. Anything. Scream at me. Curse me. But please just say something."

She was wearing gray hospital pajamas, buttoned to the top. The blanket was white. There in the place where Marlene's left leg should have been, the blanket lay flat.

"Marlene, it was . . . it was just a stupid impulse. When that American officer called me a traitor, I . . ." His bandaged hands trembled. "I didn't mean to do it, Marlene. You know I love you."

She wiped at her eyes.

"I love you," he said, "I love you."

"I know, Fritz."

"It was just that split second," he cried. "I was only thinking of myself that one time, just that once." He tried wiping his eyes with his bound hands. "Katrin will be so fond of you, Marlene."

She gazed at him and smiled. He knelt before her bed and she stroked his sparse hair. "I love you too, Fritz."

"Really?"

"Yes. I love you." She withdrew her hand from his head and pointed at him. "I want to live, Fritz. *Live*." She reached for the back of his neck, pulled him to her, and kissed him. "You betrayed us."

The next day, she was gone. A nurse gave Fritz the letter that had been left for him—by a very amusing lady:

Dear Fritz,

I'm not one to go around assigning blame. I don't believe in it, at least not when it comes to people like you, or Marlene, or me—or even Jimmy, the American GI I've been hitting the town with in this funny old Berlin of ours. He's adorable. Anyway, after all that's happened, I wanted you to know: I'm looking after your Marlene, and if you tell me how and where I can reach you, I'll keep writing you to tell you how she's doing. And of course, I'll write you if I think the moment's arrived when you can try things with Marlene again. She really does love you, believe me. It was just all too much. That's not too hard to understand, is it? Man, Fritz. Marlene and you—it's so amazing what you two dared to do!

Try not to worry too much, my dear Fritz.

Best wishes,

Gisela

◆ ◆ ◆

"This is what happens when people get close to me."

"Herr Kolbe, don't say that," Veronika says.

Wegner has written everything down. He looks at Fritz and sips from his teacup. It's clear that he wants to say something but can't find a way. Fritz drinks his tea. "Better than beer actually," he says of it.

Then he tells them, "Will Priest had been following us for a few days. An informant in Berlin had tipped him off that certain people were getting restless about Fritz Kolbe. There were no details, as usual. He couldn't tell who was in the other car. He fired at them. The car was found a day later, completely burned, with no trace of the occupants.

"For a long time Will tried to find out who had been behind the attempt. The Gehlen Organization suggested it could have been an accident, a hit-and-run. In any case, no one attempted any investigation whatsoever. All they said was that they were glad no one was killed. My God: to this day, I still don't know who tried to kill Marlene and me. I have no idea. Somewhere out there are people who do know; there are people out there who tried to do it.

"Soon after that, the pressure on me increased in Germany yet again. I didn't stand a chance anymore in my homeland. Then Eugen Sacher came along, and he—"

"Helped pick you back up?" Veronika asks.

"That's a tough thing for a man to admit," Fritz says.

"You're forgetting one thing, Herr Kolbe: you can do it. You *are* doing it."

A great wave of fatigue was hitting Fritz, making his arms and chest feel weak and his vision turn poor.

"Stay here tonight," he says. "I have to go to bed now. Take the two beds upstairs."

His bedroom is so small there's only a narrow path around the bed. Fritz stares into the darkness, listening to the wind and the sound of trees moving outside the open window. As he breathes in the fresh air, he thinks of his love for his Marlene Wiese with her silver leg and of Katrin, who at some point received the obscure and anonymous message that she should not believe certain things she might hear about her father, delivered with a package full of tins that held samples of dirt from Berlin, Paris, Bern—and the Wolf's Lair.

He's up long before his young guests and makes breakfast, then drinks a cup of coffee outside. The sun is shining; the green of the valley stretches out and rises high up the hillsides.

When Wegner and Veronika come to sit with him, Fritz holds back a grin. He is almost certain he heard the two of them in the night—not completely certain, but close.

"The sun's shining," he says.

"Can I take a photo? Of you here, out in front of the cabin?"

"Sure."

After Veronika fetches her camera Wegner stands beside her, their shoulders touching: a young couple watching Fritz. They whisper to one another and laugh. Fritz can feel the cabin's timbers at his back and the sun's warmth on his face. He smells the coffee and the land. He hears the camera clicking. Wegner sits down with him while Veronika gazes at the countryside.

"I will take my time, Herr Kolbe. I'm going to write a first-class article—you can be sure of it. And before I publish it, I'll send it to you. Agreed? I have big hopes for this article, but I want to get your approval first."

"Fine, Herr Wegner. I'm not sure where I'll be, but Eugen Sacher will always know how to get in contact with me."

A half hour later, Eugen Sacher's car rolls to a stop before the dilapidated gate. Eugen climbs out, removes his hat, and laughs. He and Fritz look at each other. Eugen opens his arms and stands there, giving a look that both begs pardon and demands to know.

"All finished?" he asks.

"All finished," Fritz says, blinking at Eugen because of the sun. "These two here"—he nods at Veronika and Wegner—"they knew a bit more than they were supposed to."

Eugen holds up his hands. "I only gave them hints, Fritz. So what now?"

"I'm climbing up that mountain there," Fritz says. "You stay here and cook something decent, something good and hearty. When I come back this evening, I'll be hungry, Eugen. Very hungry. Tomorrow you can take me with you to Bern. Then I'm taking the train to Berlin. I'm going to go get Marlene. I love that woman so much that there's enough love for the both of us. I'm going to get Marlene out of Germany. We have to be together."

"Germany needs time to heal," Veronika says.

"Yes, it does," Fritz says. "After all that."

He slaps at his thighs and looks at the three of them, one after the other.

"One more thing: I'm finally going to call Katrin in Africa. She's going to get along so well with Marlene. What was it that Marlene always said? *Live. We will live.*"

AFTERWORD

Fritz Kolbe died in 1971 in Bern. Three Americans attended his funeral and laid down a wreath. The inscription on the ribbon did not mention that the wreath was sent by the CIA.

Fritz Kolbe married a woman he met in Charité Hospital during the war. She could have been named Marlene.

He never again settled in Germany after the war. He didn't appear on any of the lists of German resistance fighters.

In the mid-1960s the President of the German Bundestag, Eugen Gerstenmaier, "exonerated" Fritz Kolbe from all accusations of treason—partially at the prompting of Allen Dulles. Nevertheless, Gerstenmaier did not inform Fritz Kolbe directly but instead sent word to a friend of Kolbe's who lived in Switzerland, possibly the man named Eugen Sacher in this novel.

In 2005, after French journalist Lucas Delattre published his biography of Kolbe, then German Foreign Minister Joschka Fischer gave a speech about Kolbe and named a hall at the Foreign Office after him.

Allen Dulles stated that he would never have become head of the CIA if it were not for Fritz Kolbe, and said furthermore that a truly great espionage novel needed to be written about Kolbe. I don't know if I've done that. This novel is likely not written in the way Allen Dulles would have wanted it.

The double agent that the head of British MI6 in Bern thought he had in his sights was the most famous double agent in the history of espionage: Kim Philby. He was the one who knew of Fritz Kolbe's activities while the war was still on.

General Gehlen became the undisputed head of the BND (*Bundesnachrichtendienst*), Germany's Federal Intelligence Service, the successor to the Gehlen Organization. He ran the BND until 1968 and helped countless men with questionable Nazi pasts find posts in West German intelligence.

This novel would never have been possible without information from the aforementioned Kolbe biography by Lucas Delattre, *A Spy at the Heart of the Third Reich: The Extraordinary Story of Fritz Kolbe, America's Most Important Spy in World War II* (2005). Nor would it exist without the help and support of friends, confidants, colleagues, and strangers: Lily, Ben, Heidi, Matthias Fieber, Rainer Christiansen, Alexander Häusser, Angelika Wollermann, Timon Schlichenmaier, Julia Kaufhold, the staff of the political archive at the Federal Foreign Office in Berlin, my agent Lars Schultze-Kossack, his assistant Lisbeth Körbelin, and the team at my German publisher, Pendragon Verlag. For the English translation: Kathrin Scheel of This Book Travels foreign-rights agency, and my translator Steve Anderson.

ABOUT THE AUTHOR

Photo © 2016 Friedrun Reinhold

Andreas Kollender was born in Duisburg, Germany, and studied German literature and philosophy. He has worked as a builder, a salesman, and a bartender, and now lives in Hamburg as an author and teacher of creative writing.

ABOUT THE TRANSLATOR

Photo © René Chambers

Steve Anderson is a translator, an editor, and a novelist. His latest novel is *Lost Kin* (2016). Anderson was a Fulbright Fellow in Munich, Germany. He lives in Portland, Oregon.